THE WOMAN IN SUITE 11

ALSO BY RUTH WARE

In a Dark, Dark Wood

The Woman in Cabin 10

The Lying Game

The Death of Mrs. Westaway

The Turn of the Key

One by One

The It Girl

Zero Days

One Perfect Couple

THE WOMAN IN SUITE 11

RUTH WARE

SIMON & SCHUSTER

London · New York · Amsterdam/Antwerp · Sydney/Melbourne · Toronto · New Delhi

First published in the United States by Simon & Schuster, LLC, 2025

First published in Great Britain by Simon & Schuster UK Ltd, 2025

Copyright © Ruth Ware, 2025

The right of Ruth Ware to be identified as author of this work has been asserted in accordance with the Copyright, Designs and Patents Act, 1988.

1 3 5 7 9 10 8 6 4 2

Simon & Schuster UK Ltd, 1st Floor
222 Gray's Inn Road, London WC1X 8HB

For more than 100 years, Simon & Schuster has championed authors and the stories they create. By respecting the copyright of an author's intellectual property, you enable Simon & Schuster and the author to continue publishing exceptional books for years to come. We thank you for supporting the author's copyright by purchasing an authorised edition of this book.

No amount of this book may be reproduced or stored in any format, nor may it be uploaded to any website, database, language-learning model, or other repository, retrieval, or artificial intelligence system without express permission. All rights reserved. Inquiries may be directed to Simon & Schuster, 222 Gray's Inn Road, London WC1X 8HB or RightsMailbox@simonandschuster.co.uk

Simon & Schuster Australia, Sydney

Simon & Schuster India, New Delhi

www.simonandschuster.co.uk
www.simonandschuster.com.au
www.simonandschuster.co.in

The authorised representative in the EEA is Simon & Schuster Netherlands BV, Herculesplein 96, 3584 AA Utrecht, Netherlands. info@simonandschuster.nl

Simon & Schuster strongly believes in freedom of expression and stands against censorship in all its forms. For more information, visit BooksBelong.com

A CIP catalogue record for this book is available from the British Library

Hardback ISBN: 978-1-3985-2672-3
Trade Paperback ISBN: 978-1-3985-2673-0
eBook ISBN: 978-1-3985-2675-4
Audio ISBN: 978-1-3985-2676-1

This book is a work of fiction. Names, characters, places and incidents are either a product of the author's imagination or are used fictitiously. Any resemblance to actual people living or dead, events or locales is entirely coincidental.

Typeset in the UK by Palimpsest Book Production Limited, Falkirk, Stirlingshire
Printed and Bound in the UK using 100% Renewable Electricity at CPI Group (UK) Ltd

MIX
Paper | Supporting responsible forestry
FSC® C013604
www.fsc.org

To everyone who wanted more

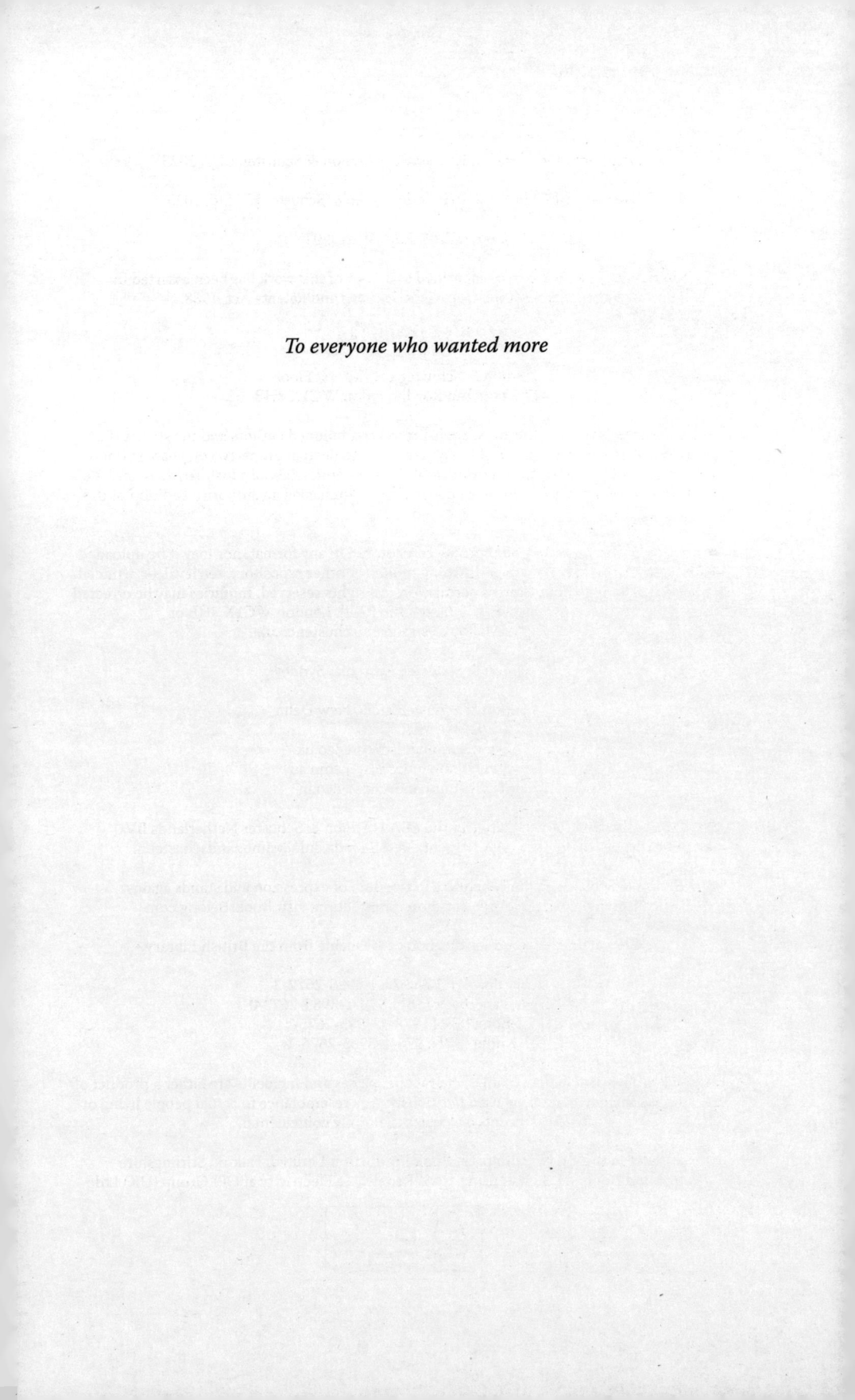

THE
WOMAN
IN
SUITE 11

In my dream, I was trapped. Locked in a cell, deep underwater, where no one could hear my cries.

There was no way to escape; I could only run from side to side of the little room, scrabbling at the locked door with my nails, tearing back the orange nylon curtains to find no window behind – just a blank plastic panel, cruelly mocking.

Desperately, I cast around for something, anything to help me break out of my prison – a piece of wood to pry open the door, something heavy to batter the lock. But there was nothing – only a metal bunk bolted to the wall and a rubber tray on the floor.

The door was fitted and flush with no helpful crack I could get my fingers into, no gap at the bottom I could peer beneath or shout into.

And as I scratched at the unforgiving plastic with broken, bloody nails, I realized: there was no way out. I was utterly and completely trapped. And the knowledge threatened to overwhelm me.

When I woke up, it was with a huge wash of relief. I lay there, my eyes closed, feeling my heart pounding and the blood singing in my ears. It was just a dream – the bad old dream I'd had more times than I could count. Just a stupid, recurring nightmare – a memory of a horror I had long since escaped. I was safe at home, where no one could hurt me.

Except . . . was I? Even before I opened my eyes, I could tell something was wrong. I wasn't in my comfortable bed at home, my husband lying beside me, a pair of little toddler feet jammed into my stomach. I was alone, lying on a thin, hard mattress with pain in my back and hips. And the sounds were wrong too – there was no friendly rattle from our old air-conditioning unit, no honking of horns or wail of sirens in the New York night.

No, here there was only the clang of doors, the sound of footsteps, the shout of male voices raised in anger.

'If you don't calm down –' I heard, and then something I couldn't make out.

My heartbeat began to quicken again, and I sat up, opening my eyes with a feeling of dread as the events of the day before came flooding back. There was no fake window, no beige panel behind nylon curtains. And the door wasn't plastic. But there was a door. It was metal and barred. And it was very much locked.

My dream hadn't been just a dream. I *was* trapped. I *was* locked in a cell. And I had no idea how I was going to get out.

PART ONE

PART ONE

1

When I walked into the bedroom, I sucked in my breath. The room looked like a bomb had hit it. Overturned drawers, duvet and pillows tumbled on the floor, a little side table upside down on the bed, and chairs strewn around like someone had been bowling with them, knocking them over like ninepins. There were clothes everywhere – on the carpet, on the bedside table, hanging off the window blind – I could barely even see the rug for the mess. In the middle of all of it was Delilah, my elderly tabby cat, washing herself placidly on top of a tumbled pile of what *had* been clean and folded laundry a couple of hours ago.

There were only two possible explanations. One, I'd been burgled in the night by someone searching for something with a frightening level of determination. Or two, Judah had let the boys dress themselves for school and this was the result. And I was pretty sure I knew which one it was.

Sighing, I picked up the chairs, retrieved Teddy's sippy cup from under his toddler bed, and shooed Delilah off the crumpled pile of washing. Then I began stuffing Eli's clothes back in his chest of drawers. *You're Rawrsome!* said a little hoodie lying across the rug, complete with an appliqué dinosaur roaring. Why didn't adult clothes have affirmations like that? There were days when I felt like I needed the boost of a smiley T. rex saying he believed in me – and today was one.

'HOW WAS THE interview?' Judah pulled off his headphones and looked up from his laptop as I set the sippy cup down on the kitchen counter. I never fail to get a lift walking into the main room of our apartment – it was what sold it to us in the first place. It's long, almost the whole length of the old tenement, with a dark polished wood floor and tall windows overlooking the neighbours' rooftops, and today it was full of low autumn sunshine and sparkling dust motes.

When we bought the place, it had two bedrooms, and we'd used one for ourselves and kept the other for an office/guest room. But then I got pregnant, and the office had become first a nursery and then the bedroom of two little boys. Now we worked – well, Judah worked – mostly from the kitchen table in a little alcove off the side of the main living space.

He'd been deep in a Zoom call when I got back, but now he had the air of someone very willing to be distracted. I shook my head.

'Okay, but I don't think I'll get it. The girl who interviewed me was really nice, but she told me I was overqualified. Twice.'

'Translation: they don't think they can afford you,' Judah said with a shrug. He pushed his reading glasses up on his forehead. 'I told you – you should be aiming higher.'

'It's all very well to say that, but I've been out of the game a long time.' I was trying not to let the irritation spill over into my voice, but I wasn't sure I was succeeding. It was easy for Judah to talk – he'd walked into a cushy staff post at the *New York Times*, of all places, right before the pandemic hit. He'd won the journalist equivalent of the lottery – and the fact that he knew it didn't make it any easier for me to stop comparing our career trajectories. 'Staff jobs aren't easy to come by, Jude, especially not for someone with a five-year gap on their CV.'

'I know,' Judah said. He stood up and came across to me, took me into his arms. 'I know, I'm sorry, I'm not trying to make out like the jobs are there just waiting for you to pull them off the tree, I just think . . . you don't value yourself high enough sometimes.'

'I value myself fine, trust me. But I've barely worked since Eli was born – and that's a big red flag for a lot of people.'

Eli had been, not a pandemic baby exactly, but born right before it hit. I'd been riding high on the success of my one and only book, *Dark Waters*, about my nightmare experience on board a cruise ship called the *Aurora* in the Norwegian fjords. Judah had just been hired as permanent staff at the *New York Times*. We'd bought an apartment in the trendy Manhattan neighbourhood of Tribeca on the strength of my book advance and his newly minted salary. The next step – surely it had to be trying for a baby?

For some reason, maybe the uncertainty of that word *trying*, I had assumed the process would take months, if not a couple of years. In reality, Eli had come along faster than either of us had expected and parenting a newborn had hit both of us like the proverbial ton of bricks. It seemed impossible that such a tiny person could wreak such devastation on two orderly lives and for me, three and a half thousand miles away from my home country and my mum, it had hit particularly hard. For a while things had got a little rocky – I had felt my mental health sliding back into a very dark place, my old medications no longer really working, the new ones fraught with unexpected side effects and dosage complications. But between us, we'd got things back on track. The hormonal tsunami retreated. Eli fell into a routine. Judah and I made things work, and I found a cocktail of antidepressants that put me back on an even keel. And then, just as I'd been thinking about hiring a childminder (or a sitter, as they called them here) and going back to work, the pandemic hit.

In a way, a way I'd never admit out loud, I'd been glad. Of course it had been tough – the isolation, the worry about my mother, far away in what the *Guardian* was calling 'Plague Island'. But it had also let me off the hook – the school and nursery closures had given me two glorious years at home with Eli with no real possibility of looking for full-time work, and then, when Teddy came along, the clock had reset and I'd been back in babyland again, albeit with tweaked medication and a better handle on how everything worked.

But now, somehow, we were six years on. Eli was in kindergarten. Teddy had just started pre-K. The book advance had disappeared into everyday living expenses. And both Judah and I agreed it was time for me to get back on the horse.

Only the horse was proving hard to catch.

I'd done a fair amount of freelancing – some here in the States, some for old bosses and contacts back in the UK. But what I wanted was a staff job with a pension and health insurance. At least I was a US citizen now, which gave me some measure of security. One of the things I had dreamed about obsessively, sweaty nightmares, back in the dark days of postnatal anxiety, had been my green card expiring and ICE coming to batter down the door. The idea had haunted me no matter how many times Judah told me it wasn't going to happen – that as the wife of a US citizen and the mother of two, I wasn't going to get deported. But even with that precious US passport, I was still aware that if anything happened to Judah, I would be pretty screwed. Our life here, our health insurance, our mortgage payments, they all rested on his job. And I didn't want that. And not just for me – I didn't want it for Judah either. I didn't want the whole burden of keeping our little family afloat to rest on his shoulders.

I tightened my arms around him, resting my forehead for a moment on his broad chest, then straightened up and smiled.

'You know what, it'll be fine. Something will turn up – it's just a matter of knocking on enough doors, right?'

'Absolutely.' Judah smoothed the hair back from my face and smiled down at me. 'I mean, the *Times* position seemed like pie in the sky for me until it wasn't. You're an amazing writer with some seriously impressive credits on your CV. Something will come along for you. And in the meantime, keep your hand in, keep writing freelance stuff. And the right door will open, I know it.'

'I love you, Judah Lewis,' I said. And I meant it. With my whole being.

'I love you, Laura Blacklock,' he said back, smiling his lopsided smile that always tugged at my heart. We gazed into each other's eyes for a long minute, and I thought again, as I had a thousand times before, how lucky I was to have ended up here – with this man I loved, who still quickened my pulse after ten years and two kids, in this beautiful apartment that neither of us could have dreamed of affording a decade ago. My life could have ended in a watery grave in Norway. It very nearly had. Every day since was a gift – and one I never stopped being grateful for.

The ping of Judah's work computer made us break apart, still smiling at each other.

'Sorry,' he said. 'That's my calendar reminder. I've got a team call at half past.'

'Gotta earn that crust,' I said. And then, seeing the pile of mail on the table, 'Oh, by the way, I brought the mail up. There's a couple of parcels for you. I think one's those shirts you ordered.'

Judah nodded and began sorting through the mix of junk mail, packages and bills, before stopping with a groan at a thick embossed envelope. He tossed it to me.

'Yet another wedding, I assume. I'm amazed you've got any single friends left. Who is it this time?'

I looked down at the envelope, frowning. It did look a lot like a wedding invitation – stiff card, expensive cream paper. And it had a European stamp, but not UK. I wasn't sure what country, in fact. The text on the stamp said *Helvetia,* which sounded vaguely Scandinavian but wasn't any country or currency I could put my finger on. It was hand addressed to *Mme. Laura Blacklock* in thick black ink and beautiful calligraphy.

Only one way to find out.

I ripped open the top, wincing a little as I cut myself on the stiff edge of the envelope, and then pulled out the card and sucked the blood off my finger as I read it.

> **Marcus Leidmann and the Leidmann Group**
> **cordially invites**
> *Mme. Laura Blacklock*
> **to attend the press opening of**
> **Le Grand Hotel du Lac**
> **Saint-Cergue les Bains**
> **Lake Geneva**
> **Switzerland**
> **Monday 4th – Thursday 7th November**
> **RSVP press@theleidmanngroup.ch**

On the reverse was the same text in French, and below both sets of text was a discreet QR code labeled *more information / plus d'informations.*

Judah must have seen something, I don't know what, in my face, because as I finished reading he looked up, curiously.

'Not a wedding invitation?'

'No. A press thing actually.' I handed him the card and he read it over, then tapped the name at the top.

'I've heard of him. Marcus Leidmann. He's the CEO of the Leidmann Group. Do you know it?'

I took the card back and shook my head. 'Are they a travel firm?'

'They're kind of everything – they're a bit like a smaller version of Tata Steel, you know, started off with heavy manufacturing, then diversified into everything from railways to communications – but I didn't know they were into hotels. That must be new.'

I shrugged. 'Probably a good time to move into travel. I mean, a lot of places went bust in the pandemic, so I guess a canny investor gets in at the bottom. Well, nice opportunity for someone to get wined and dined at this Marcus guy's expense.'

I plucked the card from his fingers and was about to toss it in the bin when Judah stopped me.

'What d'you mean? Nice opportunity for you, if you want it.'

I laughed.

'I can't go to Switzerland, Judah! Who'd take the boys to school? Who'd pick them up?'

'Uh . . . me?' Judah said. He looked a little offended. 'Like I did this morning when you were at your interview, *if* you remember. We all survived.'

I opened my mouth to retort that the boys' bedroom had looked like a war zone and that was just *one* morning, but then shut it again. I didn't want to be one of those women who nitpicked every time their husbands did something slightly differently to the way they would have done it. And it probably was good for the boys to be asked to take a bit more responsibility for getting themselves ready in the morning – it was just a shame they'd destroyed their room in the process.

'But what's the point?' I said instead, changing tack. 'I don't have a commission to write about it. I mean a free holiday is nice, but I'm not even sure if it *is* free. I'd probably have to pay for my own flights.'

'One,' Judah said, ticking the items off on his fingers, 'you've been saying you want to see your mom for, like, two years. Even if you have to self-fund your flights, this'd be a tax-deductible trip to Europe, which isn't nothing. Two, the place'll probably be lousy with travel writers and editors, so great chance to do a bit of networking. You might even catch up with some old faces. Three, Lo, you've been stuck at home with the kids for *six fuckin' years*. If anyone deserves a free holiday, it's you. This is the universe telling you to get back on the horse. And hey, it's pretty flattering they thought of you, isn't it?'

I looked down at the card I was holding, now slightly smeared with blood from the paper cut on my finger. The thought of catching up with old acquaintances wasn't exactly enticing in some cases, but Judah's other points were valid. There was the lure of seeing my mum, which I'd been putting off for far too long, and that last remark . . . I couldn't deny that one had hit home. It *was* pretty flattering someone had thought of me. For a while after the publication of *Dark Waters*, I'd been a minor celebrity on the travel-writing circuit with a steady flow of invitations to attend the openings of everything from new resorts to luxury train routes. During the pandemic, that flow had slowed to a trickle and then dried up completely, and somehow it had never resumed. But it was nice to think that my name was still out there, still on people's Rolodexes – if anyone still used Rolodexes anymore.

Yes, it *was* pretty flattering that someone had thought of me. And it was a reminder that however I'd felt walking home after the interview, I wasn't a nobody. Maybe I was a bit more rawrsome than I realized. And maybe . . . maybe Judah was right. Maybe this was the universe telling me so.

2

'Mummy!' Eli barrelled out of the door at kindergarten like a little brown-haired firework, slammed his head into my middle, and hugged me with a fierceness that suggested that I'd been away for a week. 'I missed you soooo much.'

'You saw me last night at bedtime!'

'But you were gone this morning. Before I woke up!' His tone was reproachful. Teddy, hanging off my other arm, nodded vigorously.

'You left us!'

'I did, but Daddy took care of you, didn't he?'

'We had to get dressed *by ourselves*.' Eli's expression was tragic, as if Judah had left him home alone overnight rather than just asking him to choose his own T-shirt. 'I told him that you always pick my pants out for me, but he said I was a big boy and could do it myself.'

Pants. By which he meant *trousers*, of course, not *underwear*. I would never get used to those words coming out of the mouths of my own children – but they *were* half Judah's, I supposed, and getting more American by the day. When Eli had started at nursery, his accent was pretty similar to mine, a product of the amount of time he spent with me and the fact that I'd raised him on a steady diet of *Peppa Pig* and *Octonauts*. But within about five minutes of walking through the door at pre-K, or so it seemed, he'd picked up a flawless little New York accent, almost as broad as Judah's Brooklyn one. Now he switched back and forth – American with his friends, a little more English with me and on Zoom calls with his English grandparents. At least I'd managed to hang on to 'Mummy'. Other people were moms. Not me.

'Can we goooo,' Teddy demanded now. He was jumping around excitedly. 'I want to go to the park. Can we go to the park?'

'Well . . .' I looked at the time on my phone, then at the weather, which was predicting rain, then gave a mental shrug. What did it matter. It would give Judah another hour to get his work done, and if it rained, we all had coats. 'Okay, then. But only for half an hour.'

AT THE LITTLE play park, the boys scrambled on the climbing frame, hung from the monkey bars, splashed in the puddles, and generally wore themselves out while I dithered between supervising them and crafting persuasive emails on my phone to a few of my remaining travel contacts, pitching a piece on the Grand Hotel du Lac. One problem was the *plus d'informations* on the QR code hadn't actually turned up a great deal of specificity. What would have been useful was some kind of hook or unique selling point – the first carbon-neutral hotel in the Swiss Alps or something. The only hotel in Europe with a swimming pool made of solid gold. Okay, that one seemed unlikely, but looking at the photos on the website, I thought it was maybe just fractionally less unlikely than being carbon-neutral. The hotel did look beautiful – and it was absolutely clear that no expense had been spared on either the building itself, which was a stunning eighteenth-century château on the shores of Lake Geneva, or on the renovations, which positively oozed money, from the hand-painted Delft tiles in the bathrooms to the enormous glass-sided infinity pool overlooking the lake. I didn't imagine I'd be doing much swimming in November, but I could very easily imagine snuggling up next to one of the antique ceramic woodstoves that dotted the lounges and parlours of the hotel or settling down to a martini in the 1920s wood-panelled cocktail bar. The website promised everything from winter sleigh rides to heli-skiing in nearby Morzine, so it was clear this was going to be a year-round destination for the super-rich. I just wasn't sure how newsworthy that was.

The other problem was that so many print magazines had gone out of business since I'd last been seriously pitching, and the ones that remained were mostly glorified blogs, with budgets to match. When the third reply came back to the same effect – yes to the piece, but 'we can't offer much in the way of a fee' – I sighed and shut down my email. Judah had said this was the universe telling me to get back on the horse, and maybe it was, but I wished it had offered me a fat pay cheque to shore up its hints. The fees I was being offered wouldn't even cover the flights.

Still, this *was* a pretty sweet opportunity, and it was also an excuse to see my mum, who'd lost her husband a couple of years before the pandemic and had been looking increasingly frail since a hip operation last year. Maybe I should just say fuck it and get as many puff pieces out of it as I could? It wasn't exactly the hard-hitting investigative stuff I'd once dreamed of doing, but it would be a byline, and maybe that was all that mattered at this point in the game.

Across the play park, Teddy fell off the swings and began to wail, interrupting my introspection. They were both tired, ready to head home for hot chocolate, *Bluey* and dinner. As I picked up the sobbing Teddy, brushed off the worst of the puddle water, and fished in my tote bag for a Dino Bar to comfort him, I made up my mind: it was time. I was going to say yes.

We were almost out of the park when my phone pinged with an incoming message. I pulled it out of my bag, thinking it might be Judah asking when we'd be home for supper. But it wasn't. It was a reply from an old contact, now working on the features desk at the *Financial Times*, according to LinkedIn. She'd been my boss at *Velocity*, the travel magazine where I'd cut my teeth a decade ago, but I had no idea if she was still in travel. I'd shot off an email more out of hope than any real expectation of a response. Now I clicked, assuming it would be the usual polite brush-off. Only it wasn't. Not quite.

Lo, great to hear from you and glad you're back on the beat. Sorry to say, I don't think we'd be in the market for a piece on the hotel. Sounds nice, but without some kind of hook, I don't think it's got the angle we'd need. But if you could get an interview with Marcus Leidmann, THAT I could definitely place. We'd be talking full-profile, 2000 words plus, depending on what he came out with. He's famously private, though, so that might not be on the cards. But just putting it out there. You don't ask, you don't get, right?

Rowan

It had started to rain again, the raindrops trickling down my forehead and splashing onto the phone screen as I stood there reading and then rereading Rowan's message.

'Muuuumm,' Eli said impatiently, hopping from foot to foot. 'Can we *go*, I need to pee really bad!'

'Sorry, honey,' I said. I shut down the phone and shoved it back into my pocket. 'Just a work thing. Let's get you both home.'

But as we began the wet walk back to our apartment, the rain dripping off the end of my nose and Teddy griping about how his pants were wet and his butt hurt, I couldn't stop a smile from spreading across my face. I was back. Back on the horse. And it felt good.

3

'What time is the cab?' Judah was sitting on the bed, but I could feel him mentally hovering over me while I packed my case like an anxious parent sending his firstborn away to camp.

'Three. I don't have to be at the airport until half four, but I thought with the traffic . . . '

'Yeah, good call. And you've got all your documents in your carry-on luggage? Travel insurance? Passports? Medication?'

'Yes, yes and yes.' My passports were in my handbag, and now I held them up – my old travel-worn British passport and my brand-new stiff US one. 'It'll be kind of exciting to christen my American one. I've never travelled as an American citizen before!'

'You know you *have* to use that one at US customs, yes? If you're a dual citizen, you have to use your US one to enter and leave the country.'

'Yes, I know. I can use Google just like you, Judah.'

'And you've got all the details of where you're staying and who's picking you up at the airport?'

'*Yes*, Judah, love, stop fussing! I know it's been a while, but I *did* do this for a living, you know.'

'I know, I know, I'm sorry.' Judah had the grace to look a little sheepish. Truth be told, I wasn't that bothered about my passports.

I was more concerned about what the dress code would be for this place and whether any of my pre-pregnancy dresses would still fit. It was a long time since I'd been away for work and almost as long since I'd gone anywhere fancy. I honestly wasn't sure if any of my extremely limited stock of evening dresses would still zip up. Judging by the photos on the website, the Hotel du Lac daytime vibe for this season was skinny jeans, fur-lined boots, and Scandinavian knits, which I could just about manage. The knits and the jeans, anyway. I didn't have any fur-lined boots. Regular ones would have to do. But the evening photos were all willowy European women clad in monochrome designer dresses and . . . that might be a problem.

I was holding up what had been my favourite little black dress in the mirror and trying to gauge whether it was smart enough for a Michelin-starred restaurant when Teddy came trailing disconsolately through the bedroom door, his dinosaur plushie in tow.

'Whyyyy do you have to go?' he said for maybe the twentieth time.

'Because I have to work, honey.' I shrugged out of my top and pulled the black dress over my head. Only one way to find out if it still fit.

'Mommies don't *have* to work,' Teddy argued. 'Daddies have to work but mommies only work if they want to.'

'What?' I gave a snort as my head appeared out of the top of the dress. 'Where did you get that?'

Teddy didn't answer, but when I thought about it, I guessed it made sense in toddler logic. After all, I hadn't worked for most of his childhood, and while there were several working mothers in his friend group, there were half a dozen more who worked part-time or not at all. It probably did look from Teddy's perspective like the dads always worked full-time but the mums did it only when they wanted to.

I zipped up the dress – noting with satisfaction that yes, it still did go all the way up – and then knelt in front of him.

'Listen, love, sometimes mummies stop working when their babies are little, like I did, and sometimes daddies do too. But I used to work before you were born, and now you're a big boy, I need to start doing it again.'

Need. Need was the right word. Not *have to*, because the truth was, I didn't totally have to. We could have rumbled on for a while longer on Judah's salary if we cut out some luxuries. But I needed to do this for me – and maybe I needed to do it for Teddy and Eli too.

'I will miss you and Eli so much while I'm away, but it's only a week—'

'A *whole week!*' Teddy broke in tragically as if this were brand-new information, though we'd discussed it several times already.

'Yes, a week,' I said patiently. 'Remember? I'm spending three days in Switzerland working, and then I'm going to see Granny Pam in England for a couple of days to make sure she's okay. And then I'm coming home. And I will miss you a ton, but you and Daddy and Eli will have a great time taking care of each other. Daddy will probably let you do all sorts of things I don't' – Judah, in the background, grinning and nodding his head emphatically – 'and Granny Gail is going to come and give Daddy a hand, and you love it when she comes to stay, don't you?'

'Granny Gail is coming?' Teddy looked a little mollified. He loved Judah's mum, who was a doting and extremely indulgent grandmother with absolutely no boundaries as far as her grandchildren were concerned. I nodded.

'Yes. For three days. So, you see? You're going to have a brilliant time. And when I get back I'll bring you a present—'

'A present?' Teddy's face lit up. 'What will it be?'

I shrugged.

'It's going to be a surprise. Something special from Switzerland.'

'But what will it be?'

'Well, if I told you, it wouldn't be a surprise, would it?' Fuck. What on earth did Switzerland have that the US didn't? Toblerone? You could buy that here. Cuckoo clocks? Well, I'd figure it out. And Teddy was barely four – what did he know? I could bring him back Lego, for all he'd care – he just wanted something to unwrap. 'Something very exciting.'

'But I want it *noooow*!' Teddy wailed, back full circle to the disconsolate toddler he'd been when he walked in. Behind Teddy, Judah was laughing, and I rolled my eyes, knowing that this was what the saying *making a rod for your own back* had been invented for. 'Why can't I have it now?'

I pulled the dress off my head, wriggled back into my T-shirt, picked him up, and kissed his chubby little cheek, still smelling faintly of milk and Cheerios from breakfast.

'You can't have it now, but you can have this now.' I blew a raspberry on his cheek and he giggled, and then I pulled up his T-shirt and blew another on his tummy. 'And this.' Teddy gave a shriek of pretended outrage that was actually delight, and I swung him over and blew a third just above his waistband. 'And that. And any more whinging and you'll get Mrs Tickle Monster!'

'Not Mrs Tickle Monster!' Teddy shouted in pretend distress, and he wriggled to the ground and ran away, giggling helplessly.

'Yes, Mrs Tickle Monster!' I shouted, following him. 'In fact, she might be here already and she's ready to *tickle*.'

'Eli!' Teddy shouted, laughing hysterically. 'Eli, help me, Mrs Tickle Monster is here! Heeeelp!'

'Oh, man,' Judah said from across the room, his face creased with laughter. 'What have you done? You're never going to get your packing finished before the cab comes. He's going to be wanting Mrs Tickle Monster from now until bedtime.'

'Ah, screw the cab,' I said, going across to him. I threw my arms around his rib cage, ran my fingers up under his sweatshirt, and dug them into the soft skin above his hips. 'I'll have you know Mrs Tickle Monster is a very fast packer.'

'Is she, now?' Judah said, grinning. 'Well, can she pack like this?' And he pulled me up into his arms and stomped out of the bedroom, holding me like a caveman in a cartoon carrying his wife. 'Boys! I've captured Mrs Tickle Monster. Do your worst!'

SOME FOUR HOURS later, as the cab drew away from the curb into the bustling New York traffic, I turned and watched the faces of Judah, Eli and Teddy getting smaller and smaller. Judah was standing at the side of the road wearing a huge encouraging grin. Eli was holding Judah's hand and waving but with an extremely uncertain expression on his face. Teddy hadn't even waited for the cab door to close before he burst into sobs, leaning out of Judah's arms to stretch his hands out towards my departing car, the tears rolling unchecked down his little round cheeks.

I could feel the tightening in my own throat in sympathy and a prickling behind my eyes as Teddy flung himself into Judah's neck, and then the cab turned a corner and the little figures disappeared from sight. More to distract myself from the thought of everything I was leaving behind than because I really wanted to work, I pulled out my phone and began scrolling through the press pack the Leidmann Group PR department had sent over – itinerary, information on the hotel, stats on the Swiss tourist industry . . .

Only two pieces of information were missing, and naturally they were the two I'd been most hoping to receive. The first was a list of the other guests. Long ago, a colleague had told me that he always phoned in advance of any press event to request a copy of the guest list so he could google the other attendees ahead of time. The colleague, I had mixed feelings about. Truth be told, he was actually more of an ex, and we hadn't parted on great terms. But as far as advice went, it was sound, and it was something I'd done routinely ever since he'd told me his hack. It didn't always bear fruit – some places were justifiably cagey. If the guest list was starry, they worried about the security and privacy of their celebrity invitees. Others withheld the information for the exact opposite reason: a poor turnout and a total lack of any interesting RSVPs, which they didn't want to admit to a journalist. But surprisingly often, organizations were happy to oblige, and being furnished with the names of interesting guests in advance enabled you to look much better informed and connected than you really were.

Unfortunately, the Leidmann Group's press office had told me that the guest list was confidential but 'comprised high-profile figures in finance, journalism, and the travel industry', which probably meant the same half dozen bloggers and influencers that you always met at these dos.

The second unknown, however, was even more frustrating. I'd been hoping for an email agreeing to my request to interview Marcus Leidmann while I was over there, but the decision was still pending. The press officer I'd spoken to hadn't exactly said no, but she hadn't exactly said yes either, even when I'd waved the lure of the *Financial Times* under her nose. It would have been extremely comforting to have a firm 'Yes, he'll talk to you' with a date and time in writing, but one thing I had winkled out of her was a clear confirmation that Marcus Leidmann would definitely be attending the hotel opening in person. Even if I couldn't get a formal interview, it wasn't impossible that I might be able to wrangle enough conversation out of him at dinner to spin into some kind of piece.

The problem was, the more I googled, the more I realized Rowan had been understating it when she'd said he was extremely private. He had never given an interview, or at least not one that I could find, and all the quotes from him seemed to be bland-as-oatmeal PR guff pulled from corporate press releases. He was 'delighted' at the acquisition of yet another company. 'Sorrowed' at the passing of some titan of industry. 'Pleased' at the quarterly results of some fund or other. Nothing that gave you any insight into the man himself or any hint of his personality.

The profiles that did exist seemed to have been done without his cooperation and were short and strictly factual, focusing on publicly available information like his business dealings and investments. So far, I had managed to find out his approximate age (somewhere around seventy, if my maths was right), his marital status (widowed, many years ago), and the number of children he had (one son, Pieter, age thirty-five, heir apparent to the Leidmann Group). He was not a self-made man; Leidmann and Leidmann had been founded by his grandfather and great-uncle, both Belgian industrialists from the Flemish part of the country, early in the twentieth century and had been greatly expanded by his father during the seventies, eighties and nineties. Leidmann Senior had taken a flourishing metalwork company and turned it into a major international player, a corporation with a finger in everything from car manufacturing to shipping and much else besides. Judah's comparison to the Tata Group wasn't far off – by the late nineties the Leidmann Group had become almost as sprawling as the Indian behemoth.

But it was since Marcus had taken over as CEO in the early 2000s, that the company had really become the global phenomenon it was today. He had trimmed, consolidated and branched out into the hitherto untapped markets of investment and international finance, without, as far as I could tell, ever putting a foot wrong, and the consensus of the business world seemed to be a grudging acknowledgment that, silver spoon or not, Marcus Leidmann was an extremely slick operator who would probably have made a success of himself no matter what his start in life.

Because the majority of the Leidmann Group was privately owned and not listed on any stock exchange, there was little information available about the net value of its dozens of nested companies, funds and investments, so guesses at Marcus Leidmann's personal wealth were just that – guesses. But both *Forbes* and the *Sunday Times* Rich List put his personal net worth at somewhere north of two billion dollars, and some places gave much higher estimates. Either way, it seemed safe to say that this was a man of considerable means.

If I didn't get at least *some* time alone and on the record with Marcus Leidmann, it was going to be very hard to come up with something substantial enough for Rowan to give me a piece, let alone a full-profile slot. But if I did, if I managed to get even a short one-to-one, enough to spin into something I could present as an exclusive interview, well, the payoff would be pretty high. It wasn't just the fee – though the *Financial Times* was one of the few places which still paid reliably and well. It was the lure of the byline on my CV. The *FT* was up there with the best of them, ranked alongside the *Wall Street Journal* and the *New York Times*: solid, prestigious, a name recognized on both sides of the Atlantic for serious journalism. A recent publication credit with them would open doors for me, there was no two ways about it. And if that meant crossing continents on the strength of a maybe – well, that was what I'd have to do. Worst-case scenario, I got a free stay in a fancy hotel. Best, I got an audience with one of the most powerful and elusive men in Europe – and a stamp on my CV that could revitalize my career. And that was a gamble I was prepared to take.

4

'Just one moment, ma'am.' The woman at the Swiss Air check-in desk holding my US passport was frowning at the screen and I felt my heart sink a little. Fuck. Was there some box I'd forgotten to tick? Was it my passport? Or . . . oh God, had I made a mistake in the booking? Even after nearly ten years in the US, I still wasn't above getting tripped up by the American convention of putting the month before the day. If I'd accidentally booked for 11 April instead of 4 November, Judah would never let me forget it, but no matter how often he tried to persuade me that month, day, year was the logical sequence, I would never get used to it. Who the hell went middle, small, large? It made no sense.

'Is there a problem?' I managed, but the woman had left her seat and walked over to speak to one of her colleagues, someone who looked ominously like a senior manager. I felt acid stress rise in my throat. Had I been bumped off the flight? Could they do that for transatlantic crossings?

'My apologies, Ms Blacklock.' The check-in clerk was smiling as she sat back down, but that didn't mean much – Americans were always smiling. Even when it was terrible news, they smiled sympathetically. 'I was just a little bit puzzled because you'd already checked in online under your original seat allocation, but it's no problem at all. I'll just need to reissue your boarding pass to take account of the upgrade. Make sure you scan the new one when you go through security.'

'I'm sorry?' I thought I'd misheard for a moment. 'Did you say the *upgrade*?' I looked down at myself, wondering if I'd worn some magically alluring outfit, but it was just the same-old, same-old, what I believed the kids were calling *athleisure* these days. I had heard of spontaneous upgrades, but they usually involved a long shaggy-dog story about someone's honeymoon or a terrible bereavement. I'd never heard of it happening to someone completely ordinary just out of the goodwill of the airline.

'Yes, it seems that your employer upgraded your booking to first class.'

'To *first class*?' I'd never traveled first class in my life. Business class was cushy enough and a considerable bump up from what I'd actually booked, which was premium economy, and that only as a concession to the fact that it was an overnight flight, and I wanted to be able to recline my seat without feeling hideously guilty about the person behind. 'I'm really sorry, there must be some mistake. I'm a freelancer, I don't have an employer. And I certainly didn't upgrade myself.'

'Hmm... well, I'm looking at the booking and it was all paid for earlier today, upgrade to first class, JFK to Geneva International. I have the booking confirmation here. Possibly a gift from a friend?'

I felt my heart sink. Was this Judah's idea of a romantic gesture? Surely not. A last-minute upgrade to first class would cost... well, I didn't want to think about it. Certainly thousands of dollars. Maybe even more. Even business would have been an extravagance we couldn't really afford. First class was insane.

But the only other people who had my flight details were the Leidmann Group press office, so they could arrange the collection from the airport, and it wasn't likely they'd be shelling out tens of thousands of dollars on some journalist they'd never met. And the idea of a mistake seemed equally far-fetched. Airlines didn't make mistakes like this, surely?

No, the only explanation I could think of was that Judah had put in a last-minute Hail Mary upgrade bid at the lowest possible amount that had somehow scraped over the bar. There was no way he would have paid to upgrade me outright – we just couldn't afford it – but he might have chucked a couple of hundred dollars at it, figuring it would be a nice surprise if it went through.

'And the first-class lounge is just at the top of the stairs after you go through security,' the check-in clerk finished, handing over my boarding pass. 'Will there be anything else, Ms Blacklock?'

'Um . . . no.' I felt slightly punch-drunk, and as I walked towards security, a part of me was still expecting someone to come running after me to inform me of the airline's mistake, but there were no footsteps, no call of *Ms Blacklock! Sorry, there was a misunderstanding* . . .

When I got to security, I was about to head automatically through the channel marked ALL PASSENGERS when I noticed a separate one marked PREMIUM. Underneath, in smaller letters, the sign read FIRST-CLASS AND PRIORITY-PASS MEMBERS. Well, this would be a good opportunity to test the reissued boarding pass and probably less embarrassing to get turned away here than at the gate. I felt like an impostor as I headed towards the cordoned-off area, and when I showed my boarding pass to the uniformed woman standing by the entrance, I was more than half anticipating she'd direct me back the way I'd come, but she only nodded and waved me past the snaking queues of economy passengers to a much shorter line featuring people with far more expensive coats. Standing in front of me at the scanner was a tall woman with long silky black hair and dark glasses and the highest heels I'd ever seen in an airport. She was pulling chunky gold rings off her fingers one by one and complaining to her husband in a language that I couldn't identify, but sounded like Arabic. Her husband, obviously used to his wife's grumbling, was standing tapping at his iPhone, clearly not really listening while making soothing remarks. Then he threw his phone in the plastic tray and they walked through the gate together.

I was just putting my own items in the tray when my plastic bag of liquids and gels suddenly split, and travel-size toiletries and tubes of make-up went skittering down the conveyor belt and onto the floor. Red-faced and flustered, I began to scrabble for my items, expecting the security guard on the other side of the belt to start barking admonishments at me about overfilling my liquids bag and probably send me back to the start of the line to get a new one and maybe dump some items but . . . to my surprise, he didn't. Instead, he simply handed me a new plastic bag along with a bottle of eye make-up remover that had fallen down his side of the belt and smiled at my stammered apologies.

'You're good. No hurry.'

'Thank you so much, I'm *so* sorry. Should I . . . ' I looked doubtfully at the lipstick in my hand. It wasn't going to fit. 'Should I throw this?'

'No, you're all good, that's not a liquid, ma'am.'

'Really?' I thought back to the last time I'd flown. I was sure the guard had told me that lipsticks counted as a gel – that was why I'd had it in there in the first place. 'God, thank you so much!'

'No problem,' he said, then waved me through the metal-detector gate.

A couple of minutes later, I was all done and on my way – throwing a guilty look over my shoulder at the endless queues on the economy side. However it had happened, clearly the boarding pass was real, this wasn't a mistake, and I owed Judah the most appreciative text message of our entire relationship. The whole thing had taken so little time that I now had almost three hours to kill – but that was okay, because I had the luxury of a first-class lounge waiting for me. If only I could find it.

IT TOOK ME two false starts, and in the end, I resorted to asking an airport official for directions, but some twenty minutes later, I was past the rather snooty lady on the check-in desk and relaxing in a plush armchair with a glass of free champagne in my hand. I had flown business class only a handful of times, mostly when I was promoting *Dark Waters* and my publisher had arranged my travel, and I had never got over the thrill of walking into a room filled with drinks and snacks and being invited to help myself. I was going to be professional on this trip – for all it was a jolly, and a pretty rare one at that, I had told myself sternly that I wouldn't fall for the lure of free booze and make a fool out of myself, not least because I rarely drank now, and I was pretty sure that two glasses would have me under the table, with a head-splitting hangover the following day.

But this was different. We weren't even in Switzerland yet, and I didn't have anyone to impress. One glass couldn't hurt – and besides, I owed it to Judah to make the most of his gift, didn't I?

Thinking of Judah made me realize that I hadn't said thank you for the surprise. I pulled out my phone, took a snap of the beaded flute against the backdrop of the big plate-glass windows overlooking the runway, and sent it to Judah with the caption *Thank you so much! Hope it wasn't too $$$*. It stayed unread, which wasn't surprising. It was five o'clock, which was peak cooking-supper, kids-melting-down, everyone-tired-and-demanding-attention time, and Judah probably had his hands full.

It wasn't until my flight was called, and I was standing up, draining my second cup of complimentary tea (not as good as the champagne, if I were being honest, but I was trying to be professional), and looking about for my coat and bag that my phone buzzed with Judah's reply.

??? Sorry, not sure what this means! xo

I frowned – but there was no time to reply now. The flight board had gone from GO TO GATE to BOARDING in the five minutes I'd been scrabbling about for my belongings. Explanations would have to wait.

FIRST CLASS WAS... well, first class was first class. That was the only way I could think of to describe it. It was just... beyond.

To begin with, I was ushered past the surging crowd of business-class passengers slowly scanning their boarding passes and pointed down a separate corridor. At the plane's door, a cabin attendant greeted each of us by name – there were only three other first-class passengers – and showed us to what she described as our 'suites', which were more like little cubicles, each equipped with a huge wide-screen TV, flat bed, and ottoman, and a sliding door for extra privacy.

'May I offer you some complimentary pyjamas?' the attendant asked as she stowed my bag for me and hung my coat – not that I needed the help, as the acres of storage space were total overkill for my modest little carry-on.

'I'm sorry?' I thought she'd said *pyjamas*, but that couldn't be right. Maybe it was some snack I'd not heard of.

'Complimentary pyjamas,' the attendant repeated. 'We offer them to all our first-class guests on overnight flights.'

'I – I mean... sure,' I said, bewildered, and she disappeared behind a curtain and came back with a wash bag and a neatly tied package of the softest brushed-cotton pyjamas I'd ever encountered. I don't know what I'd been expecting – something faintly disposable, perhaps, like the paper knickers you get when you have a spray tan. But these were just honest-to-God regular pj's, size small, and a pair of cozy slippers.

'They're yours to keep,' she said with a smile. 'Now, may I offer you a drink? We have champagne, white wine, red wine, mimosas, cocktails...'

'I – I guess I'll have a glass of champagne,' I said. I could hear the business-class passengers filling up the cabin next door and turned to look, but the air hostess twitched the curtain across the divide, as if people in my position couldn't possibly be expected to have to see lowly business-class travellers.

'Perfect. It's Laurent-Perrier Grand Siècle Brut, Ms Blacklock, is that okay?'

I simply nodded – and the next fifteen or twenty minutes were spent playing around with my seat settings, sipping champagne, studying the menu, and scrolling through the extensive film collection on offer on my wide-screen TV. It was only when the captain's voice came over the speakers to announce takeoff and to instruct passengers to pay attention to the safety briefing that I realized I hadn't replied to Judah.

For a moment I thought about phoning him – it would be quicker to thrash out this mystery over the phone, and a big part of me wanted to hear his voice and get his reassurance that the kids were okay, that Teddy had cheered up after I'd left, that Eli wasn't feeling under pressure to be the brave big boy. But it was seven thirty. He'd be right in the middle of baths and bedtime, and the attendants were already going around the cabin asking people to switch off phones and stow laptops.

I read his text again, frowning this time, trying to make sure it meant what I thought it did. But it was as unequivocally baffled as before:

??? Sorry, not sure what this means! xo

Okay, I hadn't specifically mentioned the upgrade, but a photo of champagne in a first-class lounge was self-explanatory . . . wasn't it? If Judah had upgraded me, surely he'd have known what I meant. But if it wasn't Judah, then . . . who? Were we back to some kind of paperwork fuck-up? Was some furious passenger with a confirmation code one digit removed from mine about to turn up and demand their first-class seat? The thought wasn't comforting, but there was no point in worrying about it now. I'd done my best – I'd queried it and been brushed off. They couldn't *make* me pay for an upgrade I hadn't asked for, and if I got bumped back to premium economy, well, it was only what I'd paid for in the first place – and I'd had two free glasses of champagne out of it. It wasn't a bad bargain, even if I didn't relish the thought of giving up my lie-flat bed, unlimited champagne, and the miso-marinated perch with port wine sauce I had my eye on from the menu.

Either way, it was too complicated to explain to Judah right now, with the engines revving as we began to taxi.

Don't worry, I tapped out hastily. *Slight mystery this end, but I'll explain when I get there. Taking off now. Love you.*

I pressed send, watched the WhatsApp disappear into the ether, and switched my phone to airplane mode. Then I lay back and prepared to enjoy my brief taste of luxury for however long it lasted.

5

My first glimpse of the Grand Hotel du Lac was as we rounded the corner of the road that circumnavigated Lake Geneva, and I didn't immediately recognize it. I thought, *Wow, what a stunning place – like a fairy-tale castle*. It wasn't until the car slowed and then turned in between two imposing gate pillars that I began to put two and two together and realized that the fairy-tale castle was actually *the* fairy-tale castle, the hotel I had been picturing in delicious anticipation for the past few weeks, just seen from a slightly different angle to the photos in the press pack.

As we pulled out from the darkness of the tree-lined drive, however, I knew where I was instantly. That view – the picture-perfect miniature château framed by the astonishingly blue waters of Lake Geneva and, behind that, the towering Alps – was unmistakable. It was the view I'd drooled over as I booked my flights and sorted out all the myriad admin of travel.

The castle itself was supposed to date back to the twelfth century, but very little of the original structure remained. Perhaps a turret or two in the far corner, if that. In the eighteenth century it had been heavily remodelled in the classical style and now it was a white stucco U-shaped building with a tall central section and two symmetrical side wings enclosing the cobbled courtyard where my chauffeur-driven car was sweeping to a halt.

As we swung round the urn in the centre of the courtyard, I had a confused impression of a graceful flight of wide limestone steps leading down from huge double doors flanked on either side by a line of what were presumably hotel staff, each standing to attention on a step and smiling, all with crisp, almost military uniforms and shining buttons. The effect was somewhere between *The Sound of Music* and *Downton Abbey*.

We had barely ground to a halt when two . . . I wanted to say *footmen*, but *bellhops* was probably the correct term, really – ran forwards. One opened the car door and held out a white-gloved hand to help me out – not that I needed it; I've been successfully exiting cars without assistance since I was a small child.

The other disappeared around the rear, presumably to do something with my luggage.

'Oh, don't worry,' I said, looking over my shoulder. 'I can manage my own—'

'Please, allow me, Ms Blacklock,' the man said with a bow. 'I will ensure everything is carried up to your suite.'

I watched my case disappear with mixed feelings. I was already slightly unsettled by being addressed by name before I'd even introduced myself, and the sight of my case being carried away didn't help. For some reason, a combination of anxiety over tipping expectations and general concerns over stuff getting lost, I never like having people take my luggage for me. I prefer to carry my own cases to my room and know where they are at all times. But clearly that wasn't an option here. My case had already been whisked away before I reached the shallow stone steps up to the gleaming front door, and now the other footman – I might as well give in to the term – showed me up the short flight and into the lobby.

Inside, the effect was not so much that of a hotel as of a super-luxurious and extremely comfortable home. There were embroidered armchairs, wooden floors, a baby grand piano, Turkish rugs, and a crackling log fire in a huge, beautifully painted enamelled stove. The wintry sun was sparkling through the tall windows overlooking the lake, and the only clue that this wasn't a private residence was a small desk in one corner which held an iPad and a bell to summon assistance. There was a feeling of . . . well, no point in beating around the bush. It was a feeling of money. Of enormous amounts of money invested in everything from the art on the walls to the exquisitely restored parquet flooring, right down to the exquisite view of the lake framed by trees that had not a single branch out of place. I had interviewed enough millionaires to recognize it. This kind of luxury didn't come cheap – and there was no faking it.

The footman showed me to an armchair in front of the fire, and as I sank into its feather-stuffed cushions, a female staff member wearing a crisp white apron materialized.

'May I offer you a welcome drink, Ms Blacklock?' She spoke with a slightly stilted German accent that for some reason made me feel like I was in a Wes Anderson movie. Something to do with the gently off-kilter rhythm of her speech. 'Champagne? Mimosa? Or a tea or coffee?'

I looked at the ornate ormolu clock on the bookcase across the room. The dial said ten past twelve, which meant it must be something like 6 a.m. in New York. Either way, champagne didn't seem like a great idea.

'Coffee, thank you.'

'Wonderful. Would you like regular, French press, cappuccino, espresso, ristretto, Americano, macchiato, Viennois . . .'

She was still reeling off the possibilities as I tried to cudgel my brain into a decision. I'd already forgotten half the options she'd listed, so I plumped for a cappuccino.

The woman smiled, nodded, and disappeared, and her place was taken by another woman, slightly older and in a different uniform, with an iPad in her hand.

'Ms Blacklock, so wonderful to meet you.' Her English was immaculate, just the smallest hint of a French accent. 'My name is Cecile Lacombe. Did you have a good flight?'

'It was great, thank you.' As she said it, something struck me. 'Listen, sorry if this sounds mad but . . . you didn't upgrade me, did you?'

'Upgrade you?' Cecile looked puzzled. 'You are in suite two, Monte Rosa, which is one of my favourite rooms in the château, but—'

'Oh, no, I'm sorry,' I interrupted, mentally wincing at the fact that she clearly thought I was an obnoxious journalist trying to score an extra freebie on top of all the ones I'd already had. 'I didn't mean here, I'm sure the room is wonderful! No, someone upgraded my flight, and I was a little puzzled about who. I thought perhaps it was someone at the Leidmann Group?'

'I don't think so.' Cecile looked as confused as me now. 'I believe all the journalists are paying for their own flights, but I can check with the press office if you would like?'

'Don't worry,' I said. 'I only wanted to thank whoever it was, but it . . . it was probably a friend.' Though if not Judah, I couldn't think who. 'Or maybe I just got lucky with the check-in desk!'

'Well, I am glad the gods of travel have smiled on you,' Cecile said, clearly relieved to have the puzzle off her desk. 'Now, I have all your information pre-filled, but if you could just check the form and sign at the bottom . . .'

I did so and then, as I handed the iPad back, I screwed up my courage to ask the question that I'd already asked half a dozen times before, with no result.

'Um . . . Cecile, talking of the press office, I'm not sure if this is your remit, but I've been speaking to your colleagues there about organizing an interview with Mr Leidmann. We, um, we left the details a bit up in the air' – that was an understatement, but you didn't get anywhere in journalism without being a little pushy – 'and I wondered, do you think he might be available to speak to me any time today?'

'I don't know, I'm afraid, Ms Blacklock,' Cecile said with what looked like real regret in her face. 'Was it Mr Marcus Leidmann or Mr Pieter Leidmann you were hoping to speak with?'

'Oh, Marcus,' I said hastily. Pieter might be a possible last resort, but I had to start by shooting for the bull's-eye. 'Are they both here?'

'Yes, they are both here, and Mr Pieter Leidmann will be attending the dinner tonight, but I am not sure about his father. If you can leave it with me, I will pass the request on to his secretary. And now . . . oh, here is Johanna with your coffee.'

I turned to see the member of staff I had spoken to before standing at Cecile's elbow with a silver tray bearing an alarming number of cups, jugs, dishes, and spoons.

'Johanna, I was just about to show Ms Blacklock to her room. Could you follow us with the coffee? It's Monte Rosa.'

'Oh, I can carry my own—' I began, but then subsided. Johanna was already hurrying towards the elevator. Evidently nobody trusted me to walk in a straight line with a full cup of coffee. And perhaps they were right.

NOW, THIS *IS A SUITE*. That was my first thought as Cecile handed over the beautiful wrought-iron room key, closed the door softly behind her, and withdrew, leaving me contemplating the exquisite eighteenth-century bedroom I had been allocated, overlooking the lake. It was . . . well, it was unbelievable. Long elegant windows with what appeared to be the original glass rippling gently in the sunshine, high walls in palest Eau de Nil, a ceiling frosted and embellished like an aristocratic wedding cake, a four-poster bed, a deep indigo chaise longue, a polished rolltop desk, and, just visible through a half-open door, a fully fledged dressing room, complete with chairs, tables, and freestanding bath.

As far as suites went, it put the Swiss Air one to shame – and then some.

Johanna had set the tray of coffee and tiny featherlight patisseries gently down on the little polished card table by the window. I sank into the soft sea-green armchair and as I raised the delicate china cup to my lips, I felt a sense of . . . I'm not sure what it was exactly. Peace, maybe, or just a kind of incredulous gratitude for my luck in snagging this trip of a lifetime.

The coffee was nutty and aromatic with velvet-soft foam and just the tiniest grating of nutmeg on the top – how had they guessed that I preferred that to chocolate? Maybe if you paid enough, you got telepathy on top of everything else. I wasn't sure what this place cost – the website hadn't included room tariffs – but going by Google, a suite as large and luxurious as this one had to be pushing two thousand dollars a night. Maybe more. The antiques dotted around the room were real, not imitation, and views like this didn't come cheap.

And talking of views . . . I took a long sip of nutmeg-scented foam and turned to look out across the still waters of Lake Geneva towards the Alps, already glistening with the first snow of the impending winter. There was Mont Blanc, a peak that I thought might be the Matterhorn, as well as many others whose names I didn't know. It was . . . it was . . . oh, I didn't have the words to do it justice – the serene blue of the lake, the greens and golds of the Swiss autumn foliage, and, rising from it all, the awe-inspiring peaks and ridges of the mountain ranges and the pale cloud-streaked sky.

I remembered the pictures on the hotel website of families splashing in the lake in summer, the cerulean blue of the sky and the vivid green of the hills, but I couldn't imagine anything more beautiful than this. How lucky I was to be here. I just wished Judah and the boys were here to share it. Though as I bit into a miniature chocolate parfait, the rich dark taste exploding in my mouth, a part of me was more than a little relieved that I didn't have to worry about chocolaty handprints on those immaculate Eau de Nil walls.

But imagining Teddy and Eli was making my heart clench with

homesickness, and now I pulled out my phone and looked at it, trying to calculate what time it would be there. Quarter to seven in the morning was the answer, if my maths was right. And today was . . . here I had to glance at the date stamp on my phone. Flying overnight had messed up my internal clock. Today was Monday. Which meant Judah was probably scrabbling around for schoolbags and clean socks and yelling at Teddy that he could wipe his own butt, he was a big boy.

No. Phoning now would be a mistake. Judah would be stressed and irritable; the boys would get upset and want to FaceTime me, which would make getting them out of the door to school harder . . . it would end with Judah annoyed, the boys crying, and me a puddle of maternal guilt on the floor.

Instead, I took a snap out of the window and sent it to Judah with the caption *Arrived safely in Geneva and now installed at the hotel. SO glad you made me come, this place is unreal. It's a pretty far cry from Cheerios for breakfast and trying to find Teddy's shoes, ha-ha. Hope the boys are behaving. Imagine now isn't a good time, but will you phone me later? xx*

Then I took another sip of my coffee. I had only three more days to make the most of paradise. I might as well enjoy it.

THE OTHER JOURNALISTS and 'high-profile figures' were arriving over the course of the day, so there was nothing in the schedule until a drinks reception at 6 p.m. I spent the day wandering the extensive grounds of the château, swimming in the pool (contrary to my expectations, it was heated and very pleasant, even in November, though getting out was a bit of an ordeal), then undoing all the exercise by eating an unbelievably good afternoon tea in the Petit Salon.

I was just finishing the last pastry when a voice from the main reception hall made me stop in my tracks.

'Great, thanks, very comfortable. And the Rolls from Bourg-Saint-Maurice was a nice touch. Listen, can you tell me anything more about the guest list for tonight's dinner? The girl in the press office wasn't very forthcoming when I asked.'

I frowned. It couldn't be. Could it?

I wasn't honestly sure if I wanted to find out, but if it *was* him, there was no way of putting off the encounter forever. And it was better to know for sure than spend all afternoon uneasily wondering. But it was with a distinct sense of trepidation that I stood up, brushed the crumbs off my lap, and ventured back to the foyer.

My initial impression was that I'd made a mistake – the only guest in the foyer was a man in his . . . maybe sixties, perhaps seventies, standing by the window and leafing through a big coffee-table book titled *Les 100 Plus Beaux Chateaux de France* that did indeed look very beautiful. He had thick glasses and a neat little goatee.

But then I turned the corner and there, standing by the desk with the iPad, was . . . Ben Howard. He'd shaved off his beard since I'd last encountered him, and his tousled black hair was now closer to salt-and-pepper, but there was no mistaking that grin or the way he was standing, leaning nonchalantly up against the wood panelling.

I felt my heart speed up – and not in a good way. The last time I'd seen him had been during the worst period of my life, and the time before *that* had been him dumping me during probably the second-worst period of my life and definitely my worst mental-health crisis.

But he had tried to be a good friend to me in between, even if he hadn't always succeeded. And the fact that I associated his face with some of the most terrifying events that had ever happened to me, an episode of my life so strange that it had fuelled my one and only book, *Dark Waters*, and so nightmarish that it literally still haunted my dreams . . . none of that was his fault.

I was still standing there, frozen, debating whether to go and say something when Ben picked up his bag, turned and saw me. For a second, he looked as shocked as I felt. And then his face split into a huge grin and he bounded forwards and put both arms around me in a crushing bear hug. He let me go before going back in for a one, two, one Continental kiss on each cheek.

'Lo fucking Blacklock,' he breathed, holding me at arm's length as he looked me up and down appreciatively in a way that I didn't entirely like but also didn't entirely hate. I was aware that my smile in no way matched his and didn't really reach my eyes . . . and also that I wasn't completely sorry about that. Ben Howard had some ground to make up as far as any friendship between us was concerned. 'You look . . . I mean, bloody hell, Blacklock, you look amazing. Have you even aged?'

I rolled my eyes. Ten years, two kids, all the usual stresses and strains – yes, I'd aged. I was past forty and looked it, so his words strained credulity at best.

'Thanks, Ben, but you don't need to roll out the cheese.'

'I'm serious! I mean, jeez, look at me.' He gestured at his greying temples. 'I'm an old fucking man! And you're . . . well, hell, there's no point in beating around the bush. You're still hot, Blacklock.' His eyes went to my hands, and I saw one eyebrow go up; I realized too late what he was looking for. 'Still married to the Yank?'

'Yes, very happily.' I was cursing myself for not wearing my rings. Since having Teddy and Eli, I no longer wore them every day – the engagement ring had a stone that was a little too large for practicality, and the wedding band was a slender antique that had belonged to Judah's great-grandmother and felt a little fragile for chasing two boisterous toddlers across the monkey bars. Now I kept them in my jewellery case for date nights and special occasions, but I made a mental note to put them both on for dinner. 'With two kids. You?'

'A girlfriend,' Ben said with a shrug. 'No kids. I mean, we've only been together six months, so it's a bit early for that. Plus she's only twenty-six.'

'Twenty-*six*?' I tried to keep my expression neutral, but I knew that it probably wasn't. Twenty-six was... well, I was trying to do the maths in my head, and it was a hell of an age gap. Ben was a year older than me, so... seventeen years? Did they have anything in common? 'Is she...' I tried to think what to say that wasn't hopelessly loaded. *Is she potty-trained? Does her mama know that she's out?* 'Is it serious?'

Ben shrugged again. 'Who knows. Just taking things one day at a time. But, man, this is a coincidence, isn't it? Are you still in travel? I'm guessing so if you're here.'

I opened my mouth to answer and then shut it again, not completely sure what to say. *Still* kind of implied I'd been hammering away at the coalface all these years instead of the reality – that I'd checked out for half a decade.

'Um, well, I guess I took kind of a career break,' I said at last. 'After the boys were born. But... yeah, I suppose I'm sort of getting back in the game. You?'

'Still serving my time,' Ben said with a twisted grin. 'Got made redundant from the *Independent* a few years back. Now I'm doing a mix of work for *Condé Nast*, *Forbes*, and a bit of corporate stuff, scouting for this new flight-free-holiday app. They want curated picks, so scraping data off Tripadvisor isn't going to cut it. The whole USP is supposed to be that a real human being has visited the place and given it their personal seal of approval.'

'Sounds fun,' I said, and I meant it. It did sound like a pretty sweet gig, but I knew that it wasn't really what Ben had dreamed of back when we'd been together. He'd seen himself more in the Paul Theroux / Bruce Chatwin mould, a serious man of letters, travelling the world to distil its essence in a series of piercing pen portraits. The trouble was the world had changed a lot since Bruce Chatwin's day. No one wanted to hear middle-aged white men wanging on about their spiritual voyages in developing nations, and in any case Ben wasn't a quarter of the writer Chatwin had been. He was a competent wordsmith who could string a nice sentence together but no more.

He completely lacked Chatwin's human insight – into both others and himself.

But now wasn't the time to start interrogating that, and Ben wasn't the only one who'd parked his dreams somewhere along the way. I'd made pragmatic choices too, abandoning my journalism-school ambitions of being a modern-day Martha Gellhorn or a second Kate Adie in favour of paying the mortgage and looking after my kids. And that was fine. We were in our forties now. Well past time to grow up and settle down. Even if some of us had only done the second part of that. God, I had to stop being such a judgy bitch.

'Well,' I said, more warmly than I really meant but guiltily conscious of my own uncharitable thoughts, 'great to run into you, Ben.'

'Yeah,' Ben said. He was looking at me with an intensity I didn't fully like. 'Yeah, really great to see you too. Listen, Lo, I . . . I read your book.'

Oh. I felt something shift uneasily inside me. Normally I enjoyed meeting readers – but when those readers were not just people from your own life, but people who featured in the book . . . was Ben about to chew me out for my portrayal of him? I tried to remember exactly what I had said about him. From memory, it wasn't super-flattering.

'Yes?' I said, keeping my tone as bright as I could. 'What did you think?'

'I mean . . . it was great,' Ben said. 'Really, really great. I don't know what kind of advance you got, but you deserved every single penny of it. But look, I never realized—' He swallowed, took a breath, and started again. 'I never realized how everything affected you. Your mental health and all that, the way no one listened to you about what happened on that boat. And I know . . . ' He took another breath. I had the sense that he was working up to saying something difficult and half of me wanted him to spit it out, to admit how he'd treated me, how they'd *all* treated me, when all I had done was tell the truth. But the other half didn't want him to say it, didn't want to have to deal with assuaging Ben Howard's guilt. 'I know I was probably part of that. I mean, I *know* I was part of that. You make that pretty clear in the book. So I wanted to say . . . I wanted to say I'm sorry.'

Sorry. One word. It was a pretty thin apology weighed against everything that had happened to me. But ultimately Ben had been a pretty small cog in a much larger wheel – and a part of me just wanted to move on. I couldn't spend all week rehashing past grievances.

'Thanks.' I made my smile as sincere as I could. 'Really. But, look, it's water under the bridge, we're both older, wiser . . . ' There was an awkward silence, and then, casting round for an excuse to get us both out of this conversation, my eyes fell on the ormolu clock, now reading five minutes past five. 'Well, I guess I should probably go and dress for the drinks reception. It's at six, isn't it?'

'Yeah, six.' Ben consulted his watch and did a slightly stagy double take, as if he too was eager for an out from this encounter. 'Blimey, I hadn't realized it was so late. I need a shower after eight hours sitting on trains. Do you think it's black-tie tonight? I brought my DJ but I don't want to wear it if I'm going to be the only person there in a bow tie.'

I shrugged.

'I don't know – one of the few advantages of being a woman is there's not such a gulf between smart and black-tie. The press schedule said *cocktail attire*, which, I agree, is a bit ambiguous. I'm going to be wearing a dress, if that helps.'

'Not really,' Ben said with a slightly wry grin. 'But good to know you're not going starkers. Well, see you there, Blacklock.'

'See you there,' I echoed, and then with a feeling that was something close to relief, I turned my back on Ben Howard and walked in the opposite direction as fast as I reasonably could and without looking back.

6

When I let myself back into my room, I saw that the bed had been neatly made, the clothes I'd left strewn around had magically disappeared, there were fresh flowers in the vase by the window, and a saucer of little pieces of something I thought might be stollen was sitting under a small glass dome on the coffee table.

I walked across to the espresso maker, turned it on, and waited while the dark, creamy coffee slowly filled the bone-china cup. Then I sat down by the window, popped a piece of stollen in my mouth, and looked out across the lake.

My room faced west, and the November sun was just setting behind the Alps, turning the snow-covered peaks rose gold. As my weight sank into the softly plump cushions, I felt the tension from my encounter with Ben drain away. None of it mattered. Ben didn't matter. Just because the last time I'd seen him had bad memories attached . . . that was ten years in the past. Water under the bridge. This week was supposed to be about new opportunities, new contacts – a new era of my life. And starting it with a view like the one facing me now . . . well, I wasn't going to complain.

I closed my eyes, let the featherlight stollen melt on my tongue, and exhaled a long breath.

Then I picked up my phone and dialled Judah's number.

'Y'ello?' His clipped, absent tone told me that he hadn't looked at the caller ID and had probably just automatically tapped the Answer button on his Bluetooth headphones.

'Judah,' I said. 'It's me.'

I felt rather than heard him sit up.

'Lo! Honey, it's so great to hear your voice. How's things?'

'Great. I mean, God, more than great. This place is stunning. I'm sitting here . . . wait, hang on, I'm going to put you on FaceTime.'

I changed the call to a video and showed Judah my room, the rose-tinted sunset peaks, the glittering reflections in the calm lake, the four-poster bed, the stollen . . . going by his expression, he seemed to be most jealous of the stollen, though to be fair, that might just have been because the tiny phone camera made the view hard to take in.

'That looks delicious. I had Teddy's leftover toast for breakfast and I'm already thinking about lunch.'

'Whereas I'm about to start getting ready for dinner. I wish you were here.' I couldn't keep the wistfulness out of my voice. 'I'm really out of practice with these things. The idea of sitting down with a table of complete strangers is kind of daunting. Although I met—' I paused for a beat, wondering whether to tell Judah about meeting Ben, then realized I'd kind of committed myself. 'I met Ben Howard earlier, in reception.'

'Huh,' Judah said. His voice was noncommittal. He'd never been jealous of my exes. He knew there wasn't anything to be jealous *of*, but he also knew that my time with Ben hadn't been completely happy and that Ben himself was bound up with a lot of my most painful memories. 'That that must have been weird.'

'It was. It gave me a pretty big jolt, to tell the truth. I thought . . .' I swallowed, then took a sip of coffee to try to hide how much this was affecting me. 'I kind of thought I was over what happened on board the *Aurora*. I'm realizing . . . I'm not. Not really.'

'It's not too late for that therapy we talked about,' Judah said mildly, and I made a face, then remembered we were on a video call and rearranged my expression to something more neutral, hoping Judah hadn't clocked it. The truth is, I've never been a fan of talking therapies. Too many softly-spoken guys with thinning hair trying to get me to talk about my childhood when what I really need is to stop having a panic attack every time I leave the house.

'Maybe I'll look into it when I get home,' I said, and Judah laughed. Evidently, he *had* seen my *Yeah, right,* expression.

'Sure you will, babe.'

'Ugh, I'd far rather stay here and talk to you, but I have to go,' I said reluctantly. 'We've got a drinks reception in half an hour, and I need to get changed.'

'It's okay, I have to go too,' Judah said. 'I've got a meeting in fifteen. I love you.'

'I love you too. Shall I call you later, when the boys are home?'

'We could try,' Judah said. 'If you're done before seven our time, give it a go. After that, I think it might just upset them before bed.'

'Okay. I love you.'

'You already said that,' Judah said, but his voice was soft, gentle. I shut my eyes, wishing, wishing I was back at home in New York, could bury my face in his neck, breathe in his comforting smell of coffee and cologne and laundry liquid and something that was indefinably just *him*.

'I don't care,' I said. 'Once isn't enough for how much I love you.'

'I love you too, hon.'

'If I don't manage to speak to the boys, give them a kiss from me, okay?'

'Sure. And did I mention I love you?'

I gave a laugh, a slightly shaky one.

'Love you too.'

And then there was a click, and he was gone.

For a long moment I just sat, staring out at the fast-darkening mountains. The sun had slipped below the horizon now, and only faintest red streaks still stained the shadowy snow.

Then I stood up and forced myself towards the bathroom for the fastest possible shower and change.

THE SHOWER WAS huge, gleaming, and scaldingly hot in the most delicious way, and I spent longer in there than I meant to. Fortunately, the hair dryer in the bathroom appeared to have been designed using rocket engines, and my hair was sleek and dry in about half the time my battered old Braun usually took.

I pulled it into an updo that miraculously came together on the first try, wriggled into my dress, then picked out my favourite earrings and necklace. Plus, of course, my wedding and engagement rings – there was no way I was risking any more 'misunderstandings' over dinner.

I was beginning to make myself up in the enormous looking glass – trying my best to ignore the pull-out mirror, which had a blinding ring light that was, frankly, a hate crime at that level of magnification – when I reached into my make-up bag for my mascara and came out with . . . one that was not mine.

For a long moment, I just stood there, the little pink and green tube lying innocently in the palm of my hand, my heart pounding sickeningly in my chest as I looked down at it, wondering how on earth it had got into my bag.

Because it wasn't just not mine, it was a brand I never bought now, never even looked at if I could possibly help it. The last time I had worn that particular type of mascara had been on board the *Aurora* cruise ship, and now the little pink and green tube brought back memories that I really didn't want to relive – and certainly not before a night out.

The question was, where had it come from?

The first thing I did was dump the whole contents of the bag out onto the dressing table – but there was nothing else amiss, or not that I could see. My own tube of MAC mascara was there along with the rest of my make-up. And there was nothing else that I didn't recognize. But then a different memory came back to me: my liquids bag exploding at JFK, me scrabbling around for my toiletries and cleansers. Had I accidentally scooped up someone else's mascara while stuffing my own belongings back in the bag?

That must be the explanation. But . . . still. Seeing it there, so unexpected and unexplained . . . it gave me a jolt I didn't like, and it brought back memories of another press trip, one where I'd had a little too much to drink and seen something no one else had believed. Something that had almost cost me my life.

Well, whatever the answer, this tube wasn't mine, and I wasn't about to lose any sleep over the mystery.

I pressed down on the pedal bin, and when it opened, I dropped the pink and green mascara in. It landed with a satisfyingly final *clang*. And then I let the lid drop – and resolved to put the whole thing out of my mind.

'BLACKLOCK!' THE FIRST person I saw when I entered the Grand Salon was Ben, waving at me from the far side of the room. I suppressed a sigh – I didn't really want to spend this whole trip reliving old times with him, but it probably *was* better than going cold into a room where I knew no one at all – and crossed the wide expanse of Persian carpet to where he was standing, looking a little uncomfortable in a dark suit and tie.

He was talking to someone who had his back to me, a big man with slicked-back thinning hair, wearing a tuxedo that fitted his imposing frame like a glove. As I walked up to the two of them, the other man turned, and I realized with a shock that I knew him too. He smiled with a look rather like a cat that has got at the butter and is *very* pleased with itself.

It was the food critic and travel writer Alexander Belhomme. And the last time I had seen him was when we had been sailing towards Norway aboard the *Aurora*.

'Well, well, *well*. If it isn't the heroine of the North Sea, intrepid reporter Miss Laura Blacklock.' He picked up my right hand, hanging limply at my side, and kissed it, his lips warm against my knuckles and unpleasantly moist, as if he'd just licked them. 'And none the worse for your ordeal, I see. How *very* delightful to see you again – and Mr. Howard too! "When shall we three meet again, in thunder, lightning, or in rain? When the hurly-burly's done – when the battle's lost and won!"'

'Um—' I swallowed. I was so taken aback that I honestly couldn't think of anything to say. Seeing Ben had been shock enough, but seeing Alexander was unsettling in a way I couldn't articulate. And yet . . . travel writing was a small world, particularly the kind of elite food-oriented travel that Alexander specialized in – all Michelin stars and high-end tasting menus. Was it any wonder that he'd been invited along to a hotel that was quite clearly gunning for that market? 'Alexander – I – gosh, I'm sorry. I wasn't expecting to see you here. I'm a little lost for words.'

'And I too!' Alexander said, though he didn't seem it in the least. 'If our mutual friend Mr Howard had not had the courtesy to give me a few minutes' grace, I would have thought you were a ghost! I confess, I thought you'd more or less retired from the circuit to raise your adorable moppets?'

'I mean, I sort of had,' I said carefully, ignoring the *adorable moppets* reference, which sounded suspiciously close to a jibe. 'But it wasn't completely intentional. I took a few years out while I was writing and promoting *Dark Waters* – that was my book about what happened on the *Aurora*. And then, you know, COVID hit. Bad time for travel writers.'

'Oh, my dear!' Alexander fanned himself theatrically. 'You do *not* need to tell *me*. It was very slim pickings at chez Belhomme for a while there. Thank goodness I have my recipe blog now, or I think I would honestly have lost the will to continue.'

'You have a recipe blog?' I don't know why I was surprised. Perhaps because Alexander had always struck me as so resolutely old-school and more than a little elitist, and a blog seemed neither.

He gave a little shrug.

'I do what I can to bring the religion of food to the masses. And since the restaurants were closed over lockdown, it turned out Mrs Belhomme was not the only person googling the correct way to prepare *foie gras à la strasbourgeoise*.'

'Of course,' I said. There was no way I was going to reveal I had no idea what that was, though I could tell Alexander was dying for me to ask. 'And how is your wife?'

I'd never found anyone who'd actually met Alexander's wife, but apparently, she did exist.

'Oh, sadly, out of sorts,' Alexander said, shaking his head. 'She's never been fond of this world—' He waved his hand at the room, encompassing the beautiful ornate plasterwork, the sparkling chandeliers, the tuxedo-clad waiters, and the guests in their suits, ties and cocktail dresses. 'She has always been a homebody, but since COVID she's become even more of a recluse. Still, she is touchingly eager not to hold *moi* back. Very much the wind beneath my wings, urging me on to greater heights.'

Since Alexander bore more than a passing resemblance to a penguin in his current garb – black and white and sleekly rotund – this phrase struck me as funny, and I had to suppress a smile as Ben earnestly replied with something about the value of a supportive partner.

'Champagne, madam?' came a voice from behind me and I turned to see a handsome young waiter holding a tray of frosted glasses. I was about to take one, then changed my mind.

'Actually, do you have anything soft? Non-alcoholic?' I added in case English wasn't his first language, but the waiter was already nodding.

'My colleague is following with a tray of elderflower cordial and quince *pressé*.'

'Thank you.'

The colleague proved to be on the other side of the room, so I occupied myself with the canapés instead. I had just popped a tiny square of melba toast topped with meltingly delicious chicken-liver parfait and a scrap of shaved truffle into my mouth when Alexander turned away from where Ben was talking about his new flight-free-travel gig and said, a little confidentially, 'I read it, you know, my dear.'

'Read what?' I tried to swallow the canapé faster than was wise and coughed as a melba toast crumb caught in my throat. Where *was* that elderflower cordial? 'Ben's new flightless travel thing?'

'Oh, tush. Wrangling train reservations is something I leave for itinerant students and the likes of our mutual friend Mr Howard. No, I was meaning your book. *Deep Water*, isn't that right?'

'*Dark Waters*,' I said a little curtly. The uneasy feeling I'd had earlier with Ben was back. I hadn't said anything awful in the book about Alexander, but I was also uncomfortably aware that I hadn't been particularly kind. He'd appeared as a figure of almost comic relief between the more serious sections, and now I was wondering how he felt about that.

'*Some* people might have taken your characterization of *moi* amiss, you know, my dear,' Alexander said. He was studying me over his glass of champagne, a slightly austere expression on his plump face, but then a smile tweaked at the corner of mouth. 'Fortunately, *I* have a sense of humour.'

'I'm sorry,' I said. I felt my face going a little red. 'You know, you're so much in the hands of editors with these things. My publisher – they wanted broad-brush characterizations, really. Big characters readers could remember. I had to do a certain amount of exaggeration . . . there really wasn't space to do justice to everyone on board. I hope you don't mind.'

'Mind? No. "The play's the thing," as the Bard would say,' Alexander said. 'Your only duty is to your art, I quite understand *that*. But I commend your bravery all the same.'

'I'm not sure I really *was* brave.' The statement wasn't false modesty. I'd had time to think about my actions on board the *Aurora* over the years, and more and more I'd come to the conclusion that I hadn't been brave – instead I'd been compelled by some impulse I didn't fully understand even now, a kind of saviour complex, an inability to walk away from an injustice or someone in danger. It was an aspect of my character I didn't particularly like – and one that had got me into trouble more than once over the years. 'I didn't really have a choice at the time. Or at least, it felt that way.'

'Oh, I didn't mean your actions on the boat,' Alexander said unexpectedly.

I frowned. 'Sorry, what do you mean, then?'

'I meant your actions in writing the book. You destroyed some very powerful people, my dear, exposed the secrets of some very wealthy individuals. There are those who would not thank you for that.'

'Well, they're dead,' I said shortly – more shortly than I had intended, but his words had unsettled me. 'Most of them, anyway.'

'Oh, no, no.' Alexander wagged his finger at me. 'The wealthy are never really dead; you of all people should know that.'

'I'm pretty sure they die just like everyone else, actually,' I retorted. Alexander had always loved the sound of his own voice, but seriously, what was he on about?

But Alexander was shaking his head, leaning in towards me as if imparting a secret. His breath smelled of wine and goat cheese parfait.

'*They* die, of course. *Sans doute.* But their wealth, their fortune, lives on, and with it their influence. Money does not die, Laura. And nor do secrets. There are plenty of people who might wish that book unwritten.'

There was a long pause. I found I was staring at Alexander Belhomme, unsure what he was trying to tell me. Was this a threat? A warning?

I was still trying to make up my mind as he gave a little bow and moved off to talk to another guest. At the same time, a waiter appeared in front of me holding a tray of the promised elderflower cordial in brimming, cut-glass coupes. I took one and was just raising it to my lips when I heard the click of a lens at my elbow and turned. My glass almost fell from my fingers. I caught it just in time, slopping elderflower cordial onto the polished boards, and managed to stammer out, '*Cole?* Cole Lederer?'

'Wait . . . ' He put his camera down, staring at me. 'It's not – Lo Blacklock?'

'Yes. Jesus Christ, is there anyone here who wasn't on the *Aurora*?' Okay, that was hyperbole. There was an entire roomful of people I didn't recognize or knew only by reputation from other travel outlets. But how many people had there been on that voyage? Ten? Twelve? To find four of them here in Switzerland seemed . . . well, it seemed like something more than an accident, and that thought was making me more than a little uneasy.

'What do you mean? Who else is here?' Cole said, frowning, and I realized that I was standing between him and Ben and Alexander. I stepped back, waving a hand in their direction, and Cole raised an eyebrow.

'Well, I never. Talk about coincidence. I've seen Ben on the circuit, but I haven't run into what's-his-name . . . Alexander, right?

Well, not since I last saw you, I guess. How are you, Lo? You look—' He eyed me up and down in an appraising but slightly clinical way that somehow didn't feel as intrusive as it had when Ben had done it. Ben's gaze had felt . . . personal. But Cole's glance felt professional, more like a doctor sizing up a patient or a farmer assessing a cow. 'You look damn good,' he said at last, and I laughed.

'Coming from someone who photographs the world's top models, I'll take that as politeness, but thanks.'

Cole shook his head. 'It's true. You know I've never been interested in any of that bullshit. Yes, those women are beautiful, but I don't care about that. It's people with interesting minds and interesting stories that make for a good photo. You've got both. But it doesn't hurt that you're a good-looking woman as well.'

'You look good too,' I said, returning the compliment mainly to save my own blushes, but it was true. He'd been in his forties when I'd met him on board the *Aurora*, and ten years hadn't really changed him. His dark hair was a little greyer, perhaps, but he had the same saturnine good looks, the same hint of contained strength beneath the dinner jacket, and the same wolfish smile that showed his incisors, giving him a slightly predatory air. 'What have you been up to since . . . you know.' *Since we last met, when I was kidnapped and nearly murdered on board the boat we were both staying on*, was what I meant, but *you know* seemed to cover it better.

Cole shrugged. 'The usual, I guess. Got divorced, got remarried. Had a kid.'

'Oh, wow, that's a lot to fit into ten years. Congratulations! Anyone I'd know?'

I meant the wife, of course, not the kid. I was expecting the answer to be some model whose name I vaguely recognized but couldn't place, but to my surprise Cole looked a little uncomfortable, a hint of a flush appearing high on his cheekbones.

'Well... actually, yes. Chloe – you remember Chloe Jenssen?'

'Chloe? Of course I remember Chloe!' I said, then realized why the blush. When we met, Chloe had been married to Lars Jenssen, an investment banker and another guest on board the cruise. They'd struck me as a pretty good couple but presumably their marriage had not survived Chloe's meeting with Cole. 'That's so great! Is she here?'

'Well, the kid is great – he's a real cutie – the marriage, not so much. We got divorced last year. I'm, um... well, let's just say, I don't think I ever fitted into the income bracket Chloe wished to become accustomed to.'

'Oh, Cole, I'm sure that's not true,' I said. I meant it less as a boost to his masculinity than as a defence of Chloe, who I'd always liked a lot, but Cole took it as the first.

'Trust me, photography can be glamorous, but even at my level, it doesn't pay. So anyway, to answer your original question, no, she's not here, and neither is Lars, thank fuck. So as far as the other *Aurora* alumni go, I think you're safe. I imagine you're not in any hurry to relive those days.'

I cracked a smile at that. It was a relief, in a way, to talk to someone who recognized that meeting up like this might be triggering some unwanted memories. For that matter, Cole probably had some unwanted memories of his own from that trip, though I doubted they were in the same league as mine.

'You heard about Tina, I suppose?' Cole said.

'Tina?' I frowned. Tina was the editor of the *Vernean*, an upscale travel magazine that had, as far as I was aware, weathered the digital revolution quite successfully. It now existed in both an online version, listing top-ten luxury hotels in high-end resorts as Google fodder for the affiliate links, and an exceedingly sleek paper edition, the kind of thing you'd find in the waiting rooms of plastic surgery clinics and private investment firms. 'No, is she here too?'

'I'm afraid . . . well, she died,' Cole said. 'Maybe three, four years ago? Lung cancer.'

'Fuck.' I was surprised how gutted I felt. Tina had been one of those iron-spined women who'd clawed their way up the corporate ladder in the eighties, high heels, shoulder pads, and all, and had refused to cede an inch ever since. 'Really? Shit, poor Tina. Not surprising, though, I guess. I never saw her without a cigarette in her hand. But ugh. What a way to go.'

'Right? And Archer . . . well, he's, um, persona non grata, I guess you knew that?'

I nodded at that. I hadn't kept fully up with the story, which had broken around the time I was knee-deep in nappies and new parenthood with Eli, but Archer, a well-known extreme-travel TV presenter, had been one of the early casualties of the MeToo reckoning, with various increasingly unpleasant stories of his behaviour on set with young production assistants coming out of the woodwork. The studio had attempted to ignore it for a while, but in the end the tide of allegations was too much and Archer had sunk beneath them. He resurfaced occasionally at various low-budget events, switching on the Christmas lights in some seaside town that thought political correctness had gone too far, a comment slot on GB News, that kind of thing. But nothing reputable. Nothing compared to where he had been when we'd met. And certainly nothing Marcus Leidmann would want to be associated with.

'I heard. I can't say I was particularly surprised, unfortunately. But, wow, even four out of the ten of us is a lot, don't you think?'

Cole shrugged. 'I don't know. I mean, high-end travel is a niche game.'

'Do you think?' I was dubious. 'It feels like with so many blogs and podcasts cropping up every second . . . I mean, every influencer thinks they're a travel journalist now.'

'But that's exactly what I mean, citizen journalism has taken over. The pool of actual professionals you could call on for this kind of thing, people like Ben and Alexander and Tina, God rest her soul, it's small, and it's getting smaller. It's hardly surprising you see the same faces.'

I shrugged. He had a point.

'Well, you may be right. Talking of influencers, I should probably go and circulate a bit. Who should I meet, do you think? I'm so out of touch.'

'Good question . . . who indeed.' Cole scanned the room, his face thoughtful. 'Well, I'd say definitely Pieter Leidmann. Do you know him?'

'Marcus's son, tipped to be the next CEO of the Leidmann Group, right?' I said, and Cole nodded. 'But no, I don't *know him*, know him. Which one is he?'

'He's that guy over there, talking to the woman in red.' Cole pointed with his glass at a small group of people, and I squinted, trying to make out who he was indicating.

'That short Italian-looking guy?'

Cole shook his head.

'No, the one opposite in the grey suit.'

I don't know why, but his answer surprised me, perhaps because the Italian man seemed to be the one holding forth, the person all the others in the group were looking at, laughing at his jokes. The man in grey . . . there was no way I would have put him down for the heir to one of Europe's largest fortunes. He was tall and rather gangly-looking with a pleasant face but a weak chin and the rounded shoulders of someone used to stooping to talk. As I watched, the Italian guy said something directly to him and clapped his shoulder, and the group burst into admiring, rather sycophantic laughter. One of the women put her hand on Pieter's arm, leaning in towards him with a confidential air that showed a cleavage dripping with diamonds. Well, that part tracked. Even if Pieter didn't have the aura of command, the rest of the group were certainly treating him as if he was someone important.

'He doesn't quite fit the type, does he?' Cole said, a little dryly, and I shook my head.

'No. I don't know what I expected him to look like but . . . not that.'

'The impression I get is that he's far too nice for a billionaire. His dad, on the other hand . . . well, you'll see if you meet him. He's charming, but you don't make that kind of money by being a pushover. Or if you do, you certainly don't hang on to it.'

I nodded, thinking about the truth of Cole's words, then realized I had been staring just a little too long and dragged my attention back.

'Is Marcus here?'

Cole shook his head.

'Not seen him, but I imagine he'll be giving a speech at some point. He's definitely supposed to be in attendance this weekend. Who else . . . Francois Beaufort is quite an interesting chap. Editor in chief of a suite of French magazines. He's quite a good customer of mine. Commissioned a big gallery piece on climate travel last year – you know, posh people going to the Arctic to wave goodbye to the vanishing icecaps. Treks in the Gobi Desert to see the dried-up waterholes. I got this great shot of a couple staring mournfully at a dead goat in Kenya, and in the background you could just see their helicopter. Kind of says it all. Anyway, he's a good payer, and he's always open to pitches for that kind of stuff – you know, aspirational with a slightly sharp edge. Am I right in thinking you're freelance now?'

'I am,' I said, 'but unfortunately, we writers don't have the luxury of transcending language barriers. I imagine he's looking for Francophone writers and, um, I'm not.'

'Oh, good point.' Cole gave a laugh and was about to add something else when there was a tinging sound from the far side of the room and a little expectant ripple as it became clear someone was going to give a speech.

'Good evening.' The speaker was a woman, rather petite compared to the sea of businessmen, so I couldn't see very much apart from the top of her blonde head. She had a strong French accent but spoke slowly enough that her words were clear. She seemed to be looking down, and I had the impression she was reading from a script. 'My name is Adeline LeBlanc, head of international relations at the Leidmann Group. Although the roots of TLG are in manufacturing, our longstanding role in the railway and aeronautical industries means that travel has been in our blood from the very beginning, and so Journeys by Leidmann, our new boutique travel collection, feels like a natural extension of our brand portfolio. The Grand Hotel du Lac is the flagship property of Journeys and a benchmark for the extraordinary quality and flair we aspire to achieve in every destination. Watching this dream become a reality has been one of the most exciting projects I have been privileged to be part of and an extraordinary first step on our very first Journey. And now, if you will allow me to introduce Pieter Leidmann, president of the Journeys division and the person at the heart of its success. Pieter!'

She moved to one side, clapping vigorously, and the crowd followed her lead, applauding as best they could. I was holding the glass of cordial in one hand and a tiny plate in the other, so I could only tap the heels of my hands together awkwardly, making a faint flapping sound that didn't really contribute much. The tall man Cole had pointed out a few minutes ago smiled and took her place.

'Ladies and gentlemen, journalists, writers, photographers, social media gurus – we have, all of us here tonight, one thing in common: We are travellers.' Pieter Leidmann was much easier to make out. For starters, his height meant that I could see him, even from the far side of the room. He had a nice face, and now that he was standing up to address the audience, the slight impression of weakness was lessened. If I'd been casting someone to play him in a film, I'd have picked Jeremy Strong. Or maybe Adam Scott; there was a hint of humour in his face. And second, he did not seem to be reading from notes, and his English was impeccable, just a slight Germanic quality to the word *have*, a hint of an *f* creeping in where it shouldn't have been. 'And, fellow travellers, I would like to invite you on a journey. Journeys by Leidmann is just that. It is an invitation from my family to yours to experience something magical. For travel is a magic like no other. It brings us together. It creates memories.'

As he spoke, I saw Ben get out his phone and begin recording, and I wondered if I should do the same, but the truth was, Pieter's words, as he moved on to talk about the Leidmann Group and the legacy of his grandfather and great-grandfather, were pretty generic. Nothing I couldn't have cribbed together from Wikipedia and the TLG website with a strong helping of corporate cliché. *Natural blossoming... hope for the future... sustainable...* blah-blah-blah. I could see the attention of the people in the room beginning to wander, Francois Beaufort looking surreptitiously at his phone, the woman in red turning to gaze out of the window.

But I didn't really care about the dryness of the speech. I was more interested in studying Pieter himself. There was the understated grey suit, one that could have belonged to a middle manager in a leisure centre in Croydon. The sweep of sandy hair covering what looked like an incipient bald patch. A bolder man might have shaved his head, owned his age. Pieter seemed to be trying to deny it. He wasn't, as far as I could make out, wearing a wedding ring, though it was hard to be sure. But when he reached up to adjust his glasses, I saw no telltale flash of gold.

'... And to sum up, I hope that this moment now, in this room,' Pieter said, and I dragged my attention back to his words, realizing that he must be coming to a conclusion, 'overlooking the extraordinary beauty of Lake Geneva, will be just that: the beginning of a journey of discovery and the creation of something remarkable.'

There was another smattering of applause and Alexander Belhomme leaned across to speak under cover of the sound.

'What will be remarkable is if I survive five more minutes of speeches without any further sustenance. I hope dinner is worth it.'

FORTUNATELY, DINNER WAS. I was seated opposite Cole and next to a nice editor from Croatian *Vogue* who spoke excellent English and entertained me with celebrity gossip all night. Alexander was at the same table and kept up a steady stream of amusingly acidic remarks about the temperature of the hazelnut and artichoke soup we had as an amuse-bouche and the suitability, or not, of the wine matches, but I could tell that it was just professional carping. He cleaned his plate at every course, and as the waitress moved in to clear the table for dessert, I saw him swiping surreptitiously with his finger at the last remaining slick of cheese.

The only fly in the ointment was that I had my back to a beautiful enamel wood-burning stove that was throwing out an incredible amount of heat, and as the evening wore on, I found my cheeks getting hotter and redder and knew the wine was going to my head. When I refused the dessert-wine pairing and instead asked for another bottle of Badoit, Alexander made a moue of disapproval.

'The Miss Blacklock I remember from days of yore would have scorned to turn down a wine as juicy and seductive as Château d'Yquem 2005.'

That was probably true, unfortunately. It was also exactly what had got me into trouble the last time I had seen Alexander, and I didn't intend to make the same mistakes this trip.

'Well, this Miss Blacklock is now a Mrs,' I said, holding up my left hand and trying to make the whole thing into a joke. 'And these days, a hard night's drinking is two glasses of sauvignon blanc, so I'm already well over my usual limit.'

'You are old friends?' The Croatian editor looked from Alexander to me as if trying to match us up.

'Laura and I shared a truly once-in-a-lifetime trip to the Norwegian fjords almost exactly ten years ago,' Alexander said with a little sidelong glance at me, as if daring me to dispute his description. I laughed.

'Once-in-a-lifetime is right. You couldn't pay me to go through that experience again.'

'Really?' The Croatian editor looked suitably intrigued, and Alexander leaned across the table.

'Here is when I prove my worth as a friend and recommend you read Miss Blacklock's *extremely* frank memoir-slash-exposé on the subject, *Dark Waters*. Utterly shocking and *well* worth the cover price, let me assure you.'

'You have written a memoir?' The editor turned to me, her eyebrows raised, looking flatteringly impressed. 'But you are so young! And I thought you were a travel journalist?'

'I was. Am.' I felt a little put on the spot. 'It's not really a memoir. It's more . . . well, I was involved in uncovering a disappearance on board a boat called the *Aurora*. Basically—' I stopped, knowing how improbable this would all sound in the context of our current plush surroundings but unable to think of a better way of summing up what had happened to me. 'Basically, I witnessed a woman being thrown overboard in the middle of the night, but there was no record of her ever having been on board, so no one believed me. Not until I managed to uncover concrete evidence of a conspiracy.'

And nearly got myself killed in the process, I thought but didn't add.

'But what had happened?' The *Vogue* editor looked justifiably thrilled, even without details of my near-death experience. 'Did you catch the murderer? Who was it?'

It was Alexander who answered for me, tapping the side of his nose with his finger.

'Ah, my dear madam, you cannot ask an author to give away the denouement! You will, as the saying goes, have to buy the book to find out.'

'I have to admit, I haven't read it either,' Cole said. His expression was intrigued. 'It sounds like I should pick up a copy. Do I feature?'

I nodded, my cheeks flaming hotter than ever and not just from the heat of the fire behind me – but I was saved from explaining further by the appearance of Pieter Leidmann.

While the rest of the table paid him a suitable number of compliments about the delicious meal and the magical setting of the hotel, I tried to figure out how I could tactfully ask what I really wanted to know – which was where his father was. An exclusive with Pieter would be fine, but he wasn't one of the world's most influential business tycoons. What the *FT* wanted was the real McCoy – but I couldn't figure out how to say *And where's your dad?* without it coming across as borderline rude.

In the end, by great good luck, I didn't have to, because the Croatian *Vogue* editor asked the question for me.

'And will we see your father?' She looked up at him, batting what surely had to be false eyelashes. 'I must tell you that the rumour of his presence is part of what has brought us all here!'

'Of course. And yes, he will be here soon,' Pieter said a little shortly. His lips had thinned, and I was thankful I hadn't been the one to ask. It plainly wasn't the first time the question had come up, and I guessed he must be thoroughly sick of everyone doing the conversational equivalent of looking over his shoulder at a party, searching for his more famous parent. 'Unfortunately, he's had to attend to some calls tonight, but he'll be joining us for the shooting tomorrow.'

'I'm sorry, did you say *shooting*?' The words came out before I could stop them, and I knew my voice sounded shocked and probably a little prim, but Pieter seemed less annoyed by that question than the one about his father and only smiled.

'Yes, hunting and shooting is a very popular autumn pastime in France and Switzerland. In fact, it's an important control measure for some of the more invasive types of animals. Of course, participation will be strictly optional. We have a foraging walk planned for those who wish for a more peaceful day.' He gave a short, slightly self-deprecating laugh. 'I must admit, I rather wish I could join that myself. I actually don't love killing animals, although as a meat-eater, that seems a little hypocritical to admit. But hunting, and specifically shooting, is my father's great joy – he was quite a high-ranked competitive shooter as a young man. So it's important to him that I take a part in his interests.'

'What will we be foraging?' the Croatian editor asked. 'Mushrooms?'

'Mushrooms, yes. Also nuts. Truffles. That kind of thing.'

'Truffles?' Alexander said with the air of someone whose ears have just pricked up. 'Oh, my dear, count me in. I'm an absolute sucker for truffles – well, mushrooms of any kind, really, cèpes, chanterelles – and truth be told, nature made me a lover, not a fighter. I can't bear the sight of blood – unless it's in a *boudin noir*, of course!' He gave a hearty laugh. 'I've never pretended to be anything other than a raging hypocrite.'

'Of course,' Pieter said with a smile. 'I believe we may be a little too late for cèpes, but chanterelles are plentiful in this region, and there are some famous spots for winter truffles as well as . . . ' He stopped. 'Hmm, I am not sure of the English name. In Flemish they are *bosbessen*.'

'Blueberries?' suggested another woman at the table, but Pieter shook his head a little doubtfully.

'I am not sure. They are not exactly the same as American blueberries. They are smaller and the flavour is more intense.'

'Bilberries,' Alexander said knowledgeably. 'Also known as blaeberries in Scotland. Like blueberries but incomparably more delicious and, as you say, Pieter, the flavour is far more intense.'

'Quite so,' Pieter said with a little bow. 'Well, I will leave you to finish your meal in peace, but I hope to see you at one of the two activities tomorrow. It will be my pleasure to show you the beauty of the Alpine countryside.'

Then he turned and moved on with the practised ease of someone who was well used to socializing and mingling.

As we watched him go, I found myself stifling a yawn.

'Are we that boring?' Cole said with a grin, and I shook my head.

'I'm sorry, I'm so jet-lagged. I shouldn't be, really – it's only . . .' I glanced at my phone, trying to do the calculation in my head. 'It must be five p.m. in the States, but I flew overnight and my body clock is screwed.'

'I'm not surprised.' Cole pushed back his chair and stretched, the joints in his shoulders clicking audibly. 'I mean, I'm pretty whacked and I don't even have jet lag as an excuse. I might call it a night.'

'I think I will too,' I said. Alexander put his hand over his right lapel, feigning a painful blow to the heart.

'So soon? It is the nightingale and not the lark!'

'Well, this nightingale needs her beauty sleep if she's going to sing tomorrow.' I wasn't sure that the metaphor quite stood up, but I was too tired to care. 'Good night, Alexander. It was lovely to catch up. And thank you for the kind words about the book.'

Alexander rose as I did, the automatic action of someone brought up to stand when a woman did.

'Enchanting to see you again, my dear. And delightful to see you looking so very *well*. You don't look a day older than when we parted company in Norway, truly.'

'You don't need to rub it in,' Cole said with a laugh. 'Not all of us have aged so well. Well, good night, folks. Can I walk you up, Lo?'

'I—' I was a little taken aback by the request. It felt chivalrous, but in a slightly odd way. I was in a hotel. I didn't need to be walked back to my room for safety reasons and I didn't really know Cole well enough to parse his motives. It felt . . . as I stood there, trying to think what to say, the realization crystallized. It felt like an excuse to find out where my room was. And I wasn't sure if I was totally comfortable with that. Still, we were spending several days together in a hotel that was best described as boutique. He'd find out eventually. 'Um . . . okay, sure,' I said at last. 'Thanks.'

I gathered up my things and we left the room together. The conversation at our table didn't falter – Alexander had simply moved his chair around to the *Vogue* editor and was prodding her for clues about which celebrity she'd refused to name in an earlier, particularly scurrilous anecdote about a bratwurst and a stapler. But I could feel Ben Howard's eyes following Cole and me as we left the room, and his gaze was appraising. I could tell that he was drawing conclusions that I didn't particularly like.

'I'm really sorry it didn't work out with Chloe,' I said to Cole as we made our way up the gracefully curving flight of stairs in the main hallway. It was true, but it was also a calculated move, just in case Ben was right about Cole's agenda. Bring it back to our relationships – a subtle reminder that even if Cole was single, I wasn't. Cole shrugged philosophically.

'Me too. I thought she might be the one, but I guess not. Maybe third time lucky?'

'Is there a candidate for number three?' I asked with a smile, making it clear that I was teasing rather than goading. Cole shook his head.

'Not really. If I'm being totally honest, I'm starting to think . . . ' He stopped, looking out of the window at the lights from the hotel glittering in the still, black waters of the lake, then gave a little sigh. 'I'm starting to think that maybe I'm just not the marrying kind. The kid is great, though – I don't regret that part of it. I love him to bits.'

'What's his name?'

'Eddie. He's two.'

'Oh, I have an Edward! We call him Teddy, though. And an Eli.'

'And you're still married to that American, right?'

I nodded. 'Yes. He's a journalist.'

'I know,' Cole said, slightly unexpectedly. 'Judah Lewis, yes? I met him once.'

'You *met* him?' I knew I sounded shocked, but Cole just nodded.

'Yeah, I was doing some work for the *New York Times*. Only realized the connection afterwards, but he seemed like a good guy.'

'Huh.' We were almost at my door. 'Yeah, he is a good guy. I'm . . . I'm really lucky.'

'You are,' Cole said. I stopped outside my door and took a breath to say *Well, good night, then,* but before I could get the words out, Cole spoke again in a slight rush, with the air of someone who's got something to get off their chest. 'Listen, Lo – I haven't read your book but Alexander bringing it up tonight made me realize . . . maybe I should have.'

'Oh, honestly—' I began, ready to give my usual brush-off when people admitted they hadn't read my work, but Cole was barrelling on as if determined to say whatever was troubling him.

'Because what you said, about not going through that again, it made me realize – what happened to you on the *Aurora*, it was fucked up. And I honestly can't remember, but if I played a part in that, if I let you down by sweeping stuff under the carpet, refusing to listen when you raised concerns—'

'You didn't,' I said, although that wasn't completely true. I had tried to tell so many people what I'd seen on that boat. And none of them had taken me seriously. I honestly couldn't remember if Cole was one of them, but if he was, he certainly wasn't the main culprit. The person I had tried hardest to persuade, the person with the greatest responsibility to get to the bottom of what had happened, had been the head of security on the ship, and he had basically accused me of being too drunk or too drugged up to know what I'd seen.

That had stung, still stung if I was being honest, but what had stung even worse was the reaction of Ben Howard, my ex, but still, I'd thought, my friend. Ben had said to my face that he believed me but behind my back he'd questioned my reliability. In a way, a way I was fully realizing only now, I had never really forgiven him for the betrayal.

'Honestly, Cole,' I said, 'it wasn't you — it was . . . well, it was mostly other people. In fact, I think you were pretty sympathetic, from what I can remember. You gave me one of the most important leads — one of the pieces of evidence that enabled me to put it all together. Do you remember showing me the photos on your camera? That was the moment I realized I wasn't imagining things.'

'And then someone knocked my camera into the Jacuzzi,' Cole said. He shook his head, his mouth twisted. 'I didn't realize who at the time; it was only afterwards, when it all came out, that I figured it out. Back then I thought . . . well, to be honest, I thought it might have been you.'

'And I thought it might have been you,' I said. 'I just — I had no idea who knew what on that boat. And so many people refusing to believe you or claiming not to — it messes with your head, you know?'

'I can only imagine,' Cole said ruefully. 'I'm really sorry, Lo. Sorry you went through that, I mean. I'd like to think . . . ' He stopped, then rubbed his hand over his face. He looked suddenly weary and every inch his age. 'Well, I was going to say, I'd like to think I'd react very differently if someone came to me today with allegations like that, but . . . I don't know. I don't honestly know if I would. I just hope I'm a better person these days.'

There was a moment's silence. I wasn't sure what to say. I didn't feel it was my place to give Cole absolution for his part in what had happened all those years ago. The only person who could was dead, and even if Cole *had* read my book, he wouldn't know the full story of what had happened on that boat. No one did. Not even me.

The only person still alive who knew the truth was Carrie.

Carrie.

I hadn't spoken her name aloud for the longest time. I hadn't seen or heard from her for almost ten years – she might be dead too, for all I knew.

'Look, it was terrible,' I said at last. 'Really terrible. It took me a long time to get over it – and I'm not sure I'm okay even now. But it's in the past, and I have a wonderful husband and two amazing kids and a really good life. On the whole, I've been bloody lucky. And if anyone's to blame for what happened on that boat, it's certainly not you. Or Alexander.' Or even Ben fucking Howard, though I was damned if I was going to say that out loud. 'So . . . give yourself a break, okay, Cole?'

'Okay,' Cole said. Then he leaned forward and gently, very gently, giving me plenty of time to pull back or lean away, he kissed me on the cheek. I stood there, still and quiet, and let him. It felt . . . strange. I'd been kissed by men other than Judah before, of course. Dozens of times. Our friends in New York were the kind of huggy-kissy media types who went in for an air kiss the first time they met you. But this . . . the feel of Cole's warm lips on my cheek in the silent corridor, his hand on my shoulder . . . it felt intimate in a way that I wasn't quite ready for. It didn't help that Cole was still pretty darned hot. And I was married, not dead.

As he pulled away, my heart was thumping at a rate that I devoutly hoped he couldn't hear, but if he could, he gave no sign of it, only gave that rueful smile, much less cocky and wolfish than the grin I'd got to know on board the *Aurora*.

'Good night, Lo, you're a good person.'

'Good night, Cole,' I said. I stood, my hand on the key of my door, and watched as he made his way along the landing, then rounded the corner. Then I let out a trembling exhalation that seemed to come from every cell in my body. 'You too.'

7

When I unlocked the door to my room, I had only two things in mind: one, phoning Judah and trying to get a few minutes with the boys between supper and baths, and two, falling into bed. I was *so* tired. I'd expected that the jet lag would make it hard to sleep, but apparently even a lie-flat airplane seat couldn't make five hours of noisy, interrupted sleep equal to eight hours in a proper bed. What with that and meeting Ben, Cole and Alexander, at my first professional encounter in months, I was shattered.

In my absence, someone had come and turned down the bed, switched the lights to soft evening lamps, removed the counterpane and throw pillows, and placed a little box of macarons on the bedside table in case I was still peckish after the evening meal.

I wasn't, but that didn't stop me going across to check out the potential middle-of-the-night snack options in case my jet lag woke me up at 5 a.m. There was a note underneath the box written on thick hotel stationery, and I opened it up.

Please come to suite 11 as <u>soon</u> as possible.

I frowned. As soon as possible? What did that mean? Whoever had written this note couldn't possibly want to see me at — I checked my phone — half past eleven. But they'd put it here while I was at the dinner, so they must have known I wouldn't receive it until I went up to bed. And they had also underlined *soon*. Twice. Maybe they did mean literally now.

In which case, was someone making it some kind of pass? The equivalent of slipping someone your hotel-room key at the bar? That was possible, but the more I thought about it, the more unlikely it seemed. I wasn't unrealistic about my own charms — I'd had enough men hitting on me to know that, in actual fact, charm didn't really come into it. If a certain kind of guy thought he had a chance, he'd give it a try. No, it was more the tone of the note, which was . . . brusque. And fairly businesslike. And also the fact that whoever had left that note must have gone through the hotel reception to do it.

I picked up the receiver of the phone beside the bed and dialled zero There was a short pause and then a young woman came on the line and said something in French.

'Um, hi,' I said, feeling that awkwardness I always do when confronted with my own British tendency to assume everyone speaks my language. 'I'm sorry, I don't speak much French, do you speak English?'

'But of course,' said the woman on the other end. 'I'm so sorry, Ms Blacklock, I failed to notice your room number. How may I help you?'

'I have a slightly odd problem. Someone has left a message on my bedside table and the signature is unclear.' A white lie, but I felt she might be more likely to answer my question if it seemed like the person had actually tried to tell me their identity. 'Do you know who sent it? I assume it must have come via reception.'

'I'm sorry,' the woman said, and she did sound genuinely regretful. 'I have only just come on shift tonight. My colleague Luisa was the person on reception all evening, and she has gone home.'

'Ah. Okay.' I looked down at the note in my hand and had another thought. 'It does have a room number, suite eleven. Can you tell me who's staying in that room?'

'Of course,' the woman said again with a lack of hesitation that surprised me, given data protection laws. I'd more than half expected a polite brush-off. 'Please give me one moment . . .' There was a short pause and I heard the sound of rattling computer keys. 'That would be one of the suites reserved for Mr Leidmann.'

'Mr Leidmann?' I felt my heart begin to speed up. 'Marcus Leidmann?'

'Correct. May I help you with anything else, Ms Blacklock?'

'No, no, that's absolutely fine. Thank you so much.'

I put the phone down and sat on the bed, trying to make sense of what I'd just been told. Was the note really from Marcus Leidmann? It was true that I'd been trying to get hold of him for days now. But did he really want to be interviewed at half past eleven at night?

Or maybe it was from his secretary, trying to schedule an interview tomorrow?

There was only one way to find out.

I stood up, feeling my tiredness beginning to melt away with the shot of nerves, and appraised myself in the mirror: neat black off-the-shoulder cocktail dress, dark hair still piled high in a makeshift chignon. All things considered, other than a shadowy smear of mascara beneath my eyes, my evening look had held up remarkably well. I licked my finger and wiped away the dark smudges, then tucked a few stray strands of hair back in place. I looked respectable. Professional. In fact, as Cole's words from earlier came back to me, I straightened my spine and admitted it: I looked damn good.

Well, if it was now or never, I was bloody well going to make sure it was now. And if it was an offer of an interview first thing tomorrow, I'd get that pinned down before Mr Leidmann could change his mind.

I picked up my phone, notepad and pen, gripped my room key firmly in my hand, and set off down the corridor.

IT TOOK ME a good ten minutes to track down suite 11, and by the time I found it, I was out of breath from going up and down staircases and doubling back on myself. The château wasn't large, but it had clearly been extended and modernized over the years, not always in a way that made sense with the original architecture, and getting from one wing to another wasn't as straightforward as it looked.

When I was finally standing outside a door that read MONT BLANC 11, it was quarter to midnight, and I was having serious second thoughts. But I'd come this far. And the note *had* said as soon as possible. Maybe he was one of those eccentric insomniacs like Jack Dorsey. Didn't he famously survive on four hours' sleep? Or was I mixing him up with Steve Jobs?

Either way, this might be my only chance. Steeling my nerve, I knocked on the door of suite 11. And waited.

And waited.

I had just turned away when I caught sight of something out of the corner of my eye — something that made me stop. It was a flash of light from the fish-eye lens in the centre of the door. Someone had opened the peephole and was peering through.

I took an involuntary step back. And then, just as suddenly, the door sprang open.

I don't know who I'd been expecting — Marcus Leidmann himself was my fantasy, though that seemed optimistic. More likely a secretary or an assistant. Perhaps a grumpy fellow guest in pyjamas, victim of some weird misunderstanding. But the person who was actually facing me — the person standing *right there* in the doorway of suite 11, macaron in hand — was a figure that had haunted my dreams, my nightmares, and my waking hours for ten long years, ever since I'd said goodbye to her on the shores of a Norwegian fjord.

It was Carrie. And she was standing right in front of me.

reddit.com

r/investing

fatboysimp
Time to sell stock in Leidmans Group?

Hey guys, is anyone else hearing the news that the CEO of Leidmans Group has died in his hotel room? Predictions? Time to sell my stock?

> **diamondhamz**
> Okay first of all dude its the Leidmann Group – two ns, no s. Second, it's a private listed company so even if your correct about Marcus Leidmann, I highly doubt you have any stock to sell. Usual BS from fatboy smh
>
> > **LayLadyLay**
> > *it's
> >
> > *you're
> >
> > Diamondhamz, if you're going to correct people about their spelling, maybe check your own first. Actually TLG *do* have a controlling interest in several publicly traded entities so it's not impossible that if this is true (big if) it might affect the value of those stocks. And TLG is probably big enough to affect the wider European stock market. They're a pretty major player with a finger in a lot of pies, so if this is true, it could cause a lot of interesting ripples.

OP, do you have a link to where you got this information? I've googled and can't find anything credible.

LayLadyLay

Hello? OP, I'll repeat in case you didn't see my reply to diamondhamz, do you have a link to this? It's a pretty serious statement to make without any evidence.

diamondhamz

No reply from fatboy as usual. Like I said – full of bs. Downvote and ignore, sigh

PART
TWO

8

Carrie.

Carrie.

The woman who had hit me, and locked me up, and almost left me to die.

But she was also the woman who had fought for me, lied for me, and ultimately saved my life at great cost to her own.

I hadn't seen her for ten years, but I had never forgotten her face – that laughing, vivacious face, full of a life and vigour that no amount of tragedy and terror could stamp out.

And now she was here, standing in front of me, as vivid as one of my recurring nightmares but this time flesh-and-blood real.

'Carrie?' I gasped. The word seemed to stick in my throat. I felt like I might be about to throw up.

'Ta-da!' She popped the macaron she was holding into her mouth and gave a little twirl. 'Glad you recognized me. Have I changed?'

Yes was the honest answer. She had aged – a lot. When we'd met I would have said she was a few years younger than me. Now she looked easily five years older, maybe more. To start with, she was extremely thin, thinner even than she'd been on board the *Aurora*. You could see her collarbones sticking up through the fabric of her dress, and the hand that had been holding the macaron was almost skeletal, with long, beautifully manicured nails. The thinness didn't entirely suit her.

But it wasn't just that. She looked like she had seen a lot. Been through a lot. Her face was not just thin, but also drawn, with fine lines around the mouth and eyes that no amount of Botox and filler could entirely erase.

The strange thing was that she also looked . . . wealthy. Wealthy in a way that Carrie had not been when I knew her. And wealthy in a way that didn't entirely make sense for someone who was supposed to be on the run from the police. When I first met her, she'd been wearing an old Pink Floyd T-shirt and not much else, her nails had been bitten, her long dark hair had been mussed and tangled down her back, and she'd looked like what she was: a young woman with not much cash but a boatload of determination and ambition.

Now I could still see the determination and maybe the ambition, but I could see money too. Not just in the manicure but in the expensively dyed hair, the Botox around her eyes and the expert boob job, and the floating dress that screamed *designer*. I'd lived in Manhattan long enough that I could spot haute couture a mile off these days, even if I couldn't afford it. And the rings on her fingers and the earrings dripping from her ears, unless I was very much mistaken, those were real. Real gold, and real gems too.

'Lo fucking Blacklock,' Carrie said, and whatever else was different, her voice hadn't changed a bit. It was low and full of amusement. And it jerked me back ten years and straight into a nightmare.

All of a sudden, I found myself stumbling past Carrie to the en suite bathroom, which fortunately was in the same place as the one in my room. I didn't have time to shut the door – I barely had time to rake my hair off my face – and as I heaved the beautifully prepared and lovingly served tasting menu into the porcelain bowl, I could see, out of the corner of my eye, Carrie standing in the doorway, laughing.

'Well, I didn't expect you to fall into my arms, but I didn't think you'd puke at the sight of me. Drank too much already?'

'Actually' – I stood up, wiped my streaming eyes, and blew my nose into a piece of toilet paper – 'no. I don't really drink these days.' My voice was croaky and shaking, and when I straightened, I could feel my trembling fingers curling around the tissue in my fist as if preparing to punch someone. Maybe I would. 'Carrie, what the *fuck* are you doing here?'

I don't know what I meant – in Switzerland, in the hotel, in Marcus Leidmann's *room*. All of them, probably, but Carrie only shrugged.

'I could ask the same thing of you. Oh, did you like my little calling card?'

'Calling card?' I was bewildered now and not trying to hide it. 'What calling card?'

'Duh. The mascara! Remember? My little joke. I assumed with the note, you'd put two and two together and guess who sent it. You took your fucking time, by the way.'

I felt anger prickle the back of my neck.

'*I* took my time? I came as soon as I got your note. And by the way, the note wasn't *with* the mascara. I found that earlier today inside my wash bag. I only got the note just now, when I came back from dinner. Someone had put it on the nightstand.'

'Ugh.' Carrie made an irritated face. 'Fucking maids, always tidying stuff up. I left the note hours ago, on your bed, with the mascara on top, but I guess the girl didn't realize they belonged together. Oh, well, it doesn't matter, you're here now.'

But something else had occurred to me.

'Wait, *you* left it on my bed? How the hell did you get into my room?'

Carrie gave a little conspiratorial smile.

'Ah. Well, that would be telling. But . . . since we're old friends, Marcus has a master key to all the rooms. I mean, it *is* his hotel.'

'*Marcus*?' I blinked. 'Do you mean Marcus Leidmann? Do you know him? Are you working here?'

'Oh, Lo.' Carrie sat on the end of the bed. 'That is a story and a half. And no, I'm not working here – at least, not in the way you're probably thinking.'

'What do you mean, a story and a half? Where have you been?'

'I've *been* on the fucking run.' Carrie's expression hardly changed – too much Botox, I suspected – but her eyes narrowed slightly, her lip curled, and her voice was bitter.

'Then what are you doing here?'

'Hiding,' Carrie spat. 'Thanks to Marcus fucking Leidmann.'

'Carrie . . . ' I stopped, holding on to the edge of the sink like a life raft. I had so many questions crowding to the tip of my tongue that I honestly wasn't sure where to start. All I knew was that my head was hurting from throwing up, and the huge adrenaline shock of finding Carrie here, in the Hotel du Lac, was wearing off, leaving me wired and trembling. I needed to sit down. I *wanted* to call Judah, but that had just gone out the window, at least for tonight.

Instead, I cupped some water in my hands to rinse out my mouth, then walked shakily back into the bedroom and across to the pair of tapestry armchairs in front of the window. I sank into the nearer one, gripping the carved arms as though they could anchor me to reality. 'Carrie, you've lost me. Can you just start from the beginning? That money I found in my account years ago, that was you, yes?'

'The Swiss francs?' Carrie came across and sat opposite me. There was a box of macarons on the table, similar to the one the maids had left on my nightstand. She put a coffee one in her mouth and spoke around it. 'God, I'd nearly forgotten about that. Yes, that was me. Obviously, the money wasn't mine, but I sent it to you. My way of . . . well, apologizing, I guess. I hope you did something fun with it.'

'How on earth did you get hold of it?' I asked.

'I stole some ID. You can probably guess whose.' She gave a little shrug. 'It wasn't like she'd be using it anymore.'

I felt a kind of sickness in my stomach. Yes, I could guess whose. The woman who'd disappeared from the *Aurora* without a trace – and whose death I'd tried so hard to prove and then avenge. I had got justice for her in the end – a kind of justice, anyway – but hearing Carrie talk about her so casually was horribly jarring.

'It was good enough to get me out of Norway, and from there I made my way to Switzerland. And it turns out Swiss banks aren't very picky.'

'What do you mean?'

Carrie sighed, as if how she'd got hold of forty thousand Swiss francs was a mere detail and being asked to explain a tiresome formality.

'So, when I ran, I just took anything I thought looked promising from the boat. Passports, credit cards, that kind of thing. And the credit cards mostly turned out to be a bust – I had no idea what the PINs were for most of them, and they wouldn't work without. I think there was one American Express card that let me sign, but I was scared to use it too often in case the police were tracking it. But there was all this other paperwork – numbered accounts for these weird banks I'd never heard of in Geneva and Zurich. And I remembered reading ages ago about Swiss numbered accounts and how they were famously super-discreet.'

I nodded. I'd heard the same things, though I had no idea how much was urban legend.

'Was it true?'

'Well, it was and it wasn't. I knew I was taking a risk, just rocking up to a dead woman's bank and hoping that they hadn't heard that she'd karked it. But I thought maybe *numbered* meant no name attached. I had this idea that I'd just show them some magic code and they'd let me into a vault, but it turned out that wasn't quite how it worked. They did know who owned the account, and they wanted to see ID for any withdrawals. But when I handed over the passport . . . well, they didn't ask too many questions after that. They just gave me the money. And they kept giving it. At first, I didn't think that was too weird, but later, after the news about what happened went public . . . I kept expecting them to stop me accessing the account, and no one did. At least, not right away.'

'What do you mean?'

'I got away with it for about a year. Just kept withdrawing a few thousand francs here, a few thousand francs there. I used different branches in case I turned up and found the police waiting, but honestly, the bank staff didn't seem to give much of a shit. But then one day, I walked into a branch in Basel, went through the usual routine of asking for twenty thousand francs, and the manager said, "This account is closed." Just like that. And he gave me this . . . ' She swallowed; I could see the muscles in her throat working beneath the fine skin. I could imagine the horrible shock it must have been, the realization that her lifeline had been cut off. 'He gave me this *look*. Like he *knew*. I don't know what was on his screen, but I think it must have been very clear from the file that the account holder was dead. I didn't say anything, and nor did he. I got the impression that they weren't the kind of organization to get their hands dirty or make a scene. But I knew that the jig was up, and when I tried the other accounts, I found the same thing. They were closed. All closed.'

'What did you do?' A part of me was horrified at Carrie's casual telling of this – leeching off a dead woman without so much as a qualm. But another part of me was fascinated. It was so simple. And it answered a question I'd always wondered about but never quite found the courage to ask – where *had* that forty thousand francs come from? I hadn't known what to do with it. I didn't want to tell the police about it; Carrie had, after all, risked her life to save mine, and it seemed like a pretty poor repayment to deliberately flag her whereabouts to the police. But equally, I hadn't wanted to spend it. Drop in the ocean or not, I suspected this was money that belonged to a dead woman, money I had no right to.

In the end, I'd donated it to charity. However it had ended up in my account, it felt like blood money – and the only way to cleanse it was to try to make it do some good in the world.

Now Carrie shrugged.

'What could I do? Nothing. I'd stockpiled enough to get by – I mean, I wasn't stupid, I knew this day was coming. So I just walked out, went to a coffee shop – Swiss pastries are fucking amazing, FYI – and sat there and tried to figure out what I was going to do now the money was cut off. I knew if I could get back to England, I could come up with something, maybe work under a different name. But I couldn't figure out how to get there. I could travel okay within Europe, obviously, but crossing the Channel meant having a passport, and I was pretty sure that my fake ID would be useless now. I drank, like, three cups of coffee, still hadn't made up my mind what to do, but when I got up to pay, this man at the table next to me leaned over and said, "Allow me." He looked rich. And he was good-looking. So I let him pay – I mean, twelve francs is twelve francs, right?'

The question was so clearly rhetorical that I didn't bother answering, but I didn't need to – she was still speaking, her expression sour.

'Big fucking mistake. Of course he wanted to talk. What was a beautiful English girl like me doing in Basel, et cetera, et cetera. I lied, naturally, said my name was Olivia Langdale, that I worked for a big hotel chain. He said I looked sad and that it was a crime for someone as pretty as me to be alone in a city like this; could he take me to dinner? I said yes, another big fucking mistake. We went to the Cheval Blanc. Like, the most expensive place in Basel,' she added in response to my blank look. 'Michelin stars coming out the wazoo. Très fancy. And of course, I'm sitting there eating smoked eel with fermented beetroot or something equally up its own arse thinking I've lucked out. We have this amazing evening, and I'm bullshitting my tits off, talking about my imaginary job in the imaginary hotel chain I work for. And, on the other hand, he is being honest. Or at least, fairly honest. He tells me his name is Marcus Leidmann, he's a Belgian businessman, in Basel to oversee some operations. It's lonely work. He's a widower. Hint, hint. And I'm like, *ka-ching*! Money worries over, at least for the moment. Gravy train a-go-go!'

She stopped, looking out the window at the sliver of darkness showing between the heavy silk curtains.

'So the evening turned into evenings. And then into nights. And then, eventually, into days and weeks. I met his son; we took a trip back to Belgium to see his country house. And all the time I'm thinking, *Okay, this is pretty sweet and it's an answer to my fucking prayers about the money and the place to stay, but I'm going to have to extricate myself at some point because (a) he's bloody ancient, he must be sixty-five, seventy if he's a day, and I'm not really into that older guy thing, and (b) at some point he's going to want to do something that requires ID – like get on a plane. And then the jig will be up.*'

'But . . . ' I frowned. Carrie was talking as if this was years ago – maybe a year or two at most after we'd parted ways. But she was still here. 'But you didn't? You didn't get out?'

Carrie gave a laugh, but there was not a shred of amusement in her voice.

'I did not. It's not that I didn't try. I kept talking about needing to get back to the UK, and he kept begging – well, not really begging, more like *telling* me to stay – but it was all getting a bit weird, a bit oppressive. He was getting more . . . demanding.' She swallowed, and I had a sudden unpleasant rush of images of the kind of demands a powerful man might make of his much younger, much more vulnerable mistress. 'It all came to a head one day about a year in, and do you know, I can't even remember what triggered it. I do remember where we were – we were staying at his country estate in Flanders. He'd had guests over, and I got a little drunk, and then later, when most of them had gone home, we had an argument. I think I was flirting with someone, just one of his security guards. More to make a point than because I was actually going to do anything. And he kind of . . . snapped. He dragged me up to my room by my hair, not seeming to care that his friends were watching, and when I started threatening him, saying that was it, that was the last straw, I would leave him, and this time I meant it – that's when he comes out with it: he knows who I am. He was there in the bank the day I met him. He saw me pretending to be a dead woman, heard the name on the account, and somehow, some-fucking-how, and I still have no idea how, he has it all figured out – or at least enough to know that I'm in huge fucking trouble. He knows about the *Aurora*, knows I'm wanted by Interpol for my part in what happened, and he makes it crystal fucking clear that if I ever, *ever* threaten him again or refuse him again or generally give him the slightest reason at all, I will be in handcuffs so fast, I won't be able to blink.'

I put my hands to my mouth, feeling sick again but in a very different way this time.

'Carrie, shit, I – when *was* this?'

'Maybe . . . seven, seven and a half years ago?' Her face was twisted, as if she was trying to give a rueful, self-deprecating smile but couldn't quite make herself do it. I thought that if she'd been a different kind of woman, she would have cried, but Carrie, the Carrie I knew, would never do that.

'You've been living with this for seven years? Living under his thumb?'

'Lo, you don't even want to know the things he's made me do. Him and his . . . friends.' She gave a shudder, and I felt the nausea and horror rise inside me again. I shut my eyes, pressed my fingers to the sockets. Whatever Carrie deserved for the crimes of her past, it surely wasn't this.

'God, Carrie—' I didn't know what to say. 'Carrie, I'm so – I'm so sorry. But, listen, this can't be right. Wouldn't it be better to turn yourself in than live like this?'

'Are you joking?' Her voice was filled with frank horror. 'Listen to me, Lo, people *died* on that boat, you made that pretty fucking clear, and as far as the police are concerned, *I'm* the one who got away. I'm the last person left they can pin this on.'

'You weren't—' I started, but Carrie was shaking her head, her heavy jewelled earrings swinging.

'They've given people life in prison for a lot less, and you know it. Hell, depending on where they try me, I could end up with the death penalty.'

I bit my lip. She was right – and there was no getting away from it. But at the same time, could it really be worse than the living nightmare she was describing with Marcus?

Carrie must have seen the thoughts running through my head, because her expression softened.

'Look, I don't want to pretend it's all been bad. I'm not going to say it's been easy, but . . . well, he's given me a good life. He's kept me safe, more than safe. I've been able to travel all over Europe on Marcus's private jet, eat at the best restaurants, stay at the best hotels. All under the eyes of the authorities – because how could Olivia Langdale, girlfriend of a respected billionaire businessman, possibly be a wanted criminal? I think he loves me in his own way. But, well, I'm getting worried. Worried about him, about his . . . boundaries. A few weeks ago, I stood up to him. I refused to do what he . . . well, never mind that. But I said I wanted out. And he said—' She stopped, swallowed, her throat working convulsively. 'He said he'd see me dead first. He said if I left him, he'd have me killed.'

There was a long silence. I didn't completely trust Carrie – I never had – and now I found myself staring at her as if trying to see into her soul, see if she were fucking with me. She stared back, her eyes wide and full of fear – and to my surprise, I found myself believing her. But when I answered, I tried to do it as a reporter, with all the scepticism I could muster.

'Carrie, that's just what men like him say. You can't possibly think he really meant it? He's a well-known businessman, for goodness' sake. He can't go around murdering people.'

Carrie shrugged a little tremulously.

'A few weeks ago? I'd probably have agreed with you. I was frightened, sure, I mean, it's never nice being threatened, but at the time I kind of laughed it off. But maybe that's what made him do it.' She swallowed again. I could see that her teeth were clenched, the muscles in her jaw working as she fought to keep control of her fear. 'Prove that he's serious, I mean. Because that's what all this is about.' She waved a hand in an expansive gesture that encompassed most of the room. I frowned, puzzled.

'What do you mean? The hotel?'

'Not the hotel. *This.* You. Alexander. Cole Lederer. Ben What's-his-face. You think you're all here by coincidence?'

'*What?*' I was truly puzzled now. 'What do you mean? Marcus invited us here deliberately?'

'Yes. He picked four people guaranteed to put the fear of God into me. He's showing me that I'm not free at all, that I'll never be free. That if I thought I was going to pass the weekend swanning around the hotel, eating and drinking, I could think again. I've had to spend the last twenty-four hours cowering in my room in case anyone saw me. You think I like eating room-service schnitzel when everyone downstairs is pigging out on foie gras and canapés? This is *him*, Lo. This is Marcus spelling out loud and clear that he has the power of life and death over me, and I had better not piss him off.' There were tears in her eyes, I saw, and when she spoke again, her voice was strangled, as if she were holding back a sob of fear. 'I never felt like a prisoner before, not really. I didn't always like what he was doing, but I never felt afraid. But when I walked down into the foyer yesterday and saw Cole Lederer standing there in the corner, I knew. This whole weekend, this is Marcus telling me in terms even a four-year-old could understand that I'm his prisoner, and he can do whatever the fuck he wants to me, because I'm trapped. And there's nothing I can do about it.'

'Jesus.' Suddenly it all made sense. I *hadn't* been wrong. Four people, all from the *Aurora*, it *wasn't* coincidence. It was very fucking deliberate. And my heart sank as I realized why I'd been asked. Not because my name was still on people's Rolodexes or because of my reputation as a writer. I was here not because of who I was, but because of who I was to Carrie. A reminder. A threat. A living, breathing blackmail note.

The realization should have been the least of my problems, and it was, but the kick in the stomach still felt real.

Marcus Leidmann had never wanted to meet me. Of course he hadn't. Why would he? I was just some nobody hack writer – with a past he could exploit.

'Fuck,' I said softly. It was weird being able to swear aloud without thinking about Eli and Teddy. 'Fuck. *Fuck*.'

'Right?' Carrie said bitterly. 'But *fuck* is a verb, Lo, and I'm going to fuck him right back.'

There was something in her face, some expression beneath the Botoxed stillness, that made a sudden chill run down my spine.

'What do you mean?'

'He made a big mistake inviting you all here. Especially you, Lo. Because you're my passport to freedom. You're going to help me escape.'

9

'I'm . . . what?' I blinked. It was almost midnight and I'd had five hours of sleep in the past forty-eight. It was no wonder I felt like I was hearing things. It sounded like Carrie had said I was part of some grand plan to help her escape the clutches of one of the most powerful men in Europe, all while presumably evading the attention of the police. But that was insane. I wasn't James Bond or Jason Bourne. What did she imagine I was about to do – stuff her in my hold luggage when I went back to the US?

'Listen to me.' Carrie leaned forward, her expression deadly earnest. 'Lo, listen to me. Marcus didn't realize this when he sent for you, but you're the answer to my prayers. We look alike, we're close enough in age – and you're a dual citizen. Right?'

'Carrie.' I felt a sense of foreboding begin to build in the pit of my stomach. 'Carrie, what are you on about?'

'You have a US passport, don't you? I read an interview with you after your book came out where you said something about applying for US citizenship. Nice author photo, by the way.'

'Okay.' I ignored what sounded suspiciously like a jibe about the photo and the disquieting realization that Carrie had been keeping tabs on me all this time. 'But I don't see what that has to do—'

'If you have two passports,' Carrie spelled it out for me, 'you can get me back to the UK on the spare one.'

I felt the colour drain from my face. Carrie must have seen my expression because she began to speak very fast, as if she knew if she lost me now, her last chance would be gone.

'Lo, listen to me – I've thought it all out. We can go on the Eurostar – there won't be any checks until we get to Paris, and even then, they don't have biometric scanners, and the queues are always terrible. They barely look at you. And, Lo, you *owe* me, you know you do. I saved your life.'

'You were the one who put me in danger in the first place!' I exploded. 'I wouldn't have needed saving if it hadn't been for you!'

'But I did do it,' Carrie insisted. Her thin hands were twisted together, her knuckles showing white, like bones, in the low bedtime lighting. 'I did save you. And you're the reason I'm in this mess, Lo. I risked everything to save you.'

'You were saving yourself,' I snapped back. 'And you know it.'

'Bullshit. I could have left you to rot in that cabin and walked away, and no one would ever have known I was there. I *saved your life* and I don't think it's too much to ask you to do something that's basically risk-free—'

'Okay.' I stood up, unable to take this any longer. 'Okay, look, Carrie, I'm prepared to accept some of what you said, but *risk-free* – that's just delusional. Of course there's a risk in it for me. If I let you use my fucking passport, that's a crime. And that's without the whole aiding-and-abetting-a-wanted-person stuff. Plus, this is post-Brexit, you know. They don't just wave you through anymore – there are stamps, there's a paper trail. They *check*.'

'If I'm caught, you can just say it's stolen!' Carrie said. Her Botoxed eyes were open very wide with an innocence that made me want to scoff. 'Seriously, Lo, think about it. What's the worst that could happen to you? *I'm* the one committing a crime. You're just going home. If I get hauled off in handcuffs, you have the easiest alibi in the world – you just say, "I have no idea who this woman is, my passport was stolen at the hotel, she must have followed me from there." End of story. And if we get caught, then I'll back you up, of course I will. But we *won't* get caught – why would we? When was the last time anyone looked at you twice at passport control?'

'Ugh.' I sank back into the armchair and put my head in my hands, trying to figure this out. Carrie's words were persuasive – if I stuck to the story that my passport had gone missing at the hotel, and Carrie said she'd stolen it, I didn't see how anyone could prove otherwise. But could I really trust Carrie to stick her neck out for me again?

She did it once, whispered my subconscious. *She saved your life. This is pretty small change in comparison.*

Carrie said nothing; she simply watched me, as if she knew that there was nothing to be gained from pushing me now.

'Look,' I said at last, 'I take your point that it's fairly low risk for me, but you have to understand, I don't just have myself to think about anymore. I have kids. I can't afford to end up in some French jail. Can't you . . . ' I had been about to say *report Marcus to the police* but she'd just finished explaining why that wasn't possible. She was wanted for murder. She would end up in jail, and very likely nothing would happen to Marcus Leidmann at all. Maybe she was right. Maybe this *was* the only option.

'Lo, listen to me,' Carrie said. She had both hands flat on the table, her face pleading, as though she'd sensed that I was weakening and knew to press her advantage. 'I've worked it all out. We travel on the same day, on the same train. Chances are, no one will notice that both of your passports were swiped. If it's saved on some system, they'll think it was just an admin error – you gave the wrong one at the desk and then had to give the other.'

'And the two seat bookings?'

'It's not exactly unheard of to book two seats – they actually tell you to do it if you're travelling with a musical instrument. And having two people with the same name on board must happen all the time – how many dads give their sons the same name as themselves? Honestly, I don't think two seats with the same name will raise any flags.'

'Jesus.' I felt sick. Was there really no third option between saying yes and leaving Carrie to Marcus Leidmann's tender mercies? 'Fuck. *Fuck*. Carrie . . . this is a big ask. Huge, in fact.'

'Huger than saving your life?' Carrie asked. 'Huger than leaving me to whatever Marcus wants to do to me?' She was leaning over the table, her expression intent, and suddenly I couldn't meet her eyes any longer.

Instead of answering, I stood up, running my hands through my hair. My reflection stared back at me from the dark glass panes in the tall windows. My carefully coiffed updo was in tatters, coiled strands hanging around my face. My eyes looked haunted. I felt ten years older than the hopeful competent journalist who had tapped confidently on the door of suite 11. I did not want to say yes to this. But to say no . . . to say no might be leaving Carrie to die. Or to a fate worse than death, if everything she'd said about Marcus was true.

'I'll think about it,' I said. 'Okay? Let me sleep on it. I'll come and find you tomorrow, tell you my decision.'

I'd been expecting Carrie to be disappointed, but she wasn't. Instead she broke into a smile as wide as if I'd said yes.

'Thank you, Lo.' She stood up and put her arms around me. 'I know what a big ask this is, I truly do. But I promise, it's all going to go swimmingly. And when we get to the UK . . . fuck, you know what? I'll treat you to the best hotel I can think of. I've got one last hit of cash. May as well go out with a bang, right?'

'You don't need to do that,' I said with a weak smile. 'I haven't even said yes yet.' Plus, if we got as far as the UK, I was going to cut and run as quickly as possible. But Carrie was shaking her head.

'No, I do. I need that money gone. It's brought me nothing but bad luck – I should never have taken it. And once I'm in the UK, I can start again. I'll figure out a way to get a fake ID; it can't be *that* hard. Or I'll just work under the table – plenty of people do it, and I'm not proud, I don't mind scrubbing dishes or waiting tables. Hell, I used to be a bloody good waitress before I met Marcus! And besides' – she squeezed the arm that was still resting around my waist – 'you deserve a bit of luxury. You enjoyed the upgrade, right?'

'Upgrade?' I stared at her. There was a sudden cold feeling around my heart. 'What upgrade?'

'On the flight, silly! I told the press office you were a VIP and they should pull some strings. I thought if Marcus was dragging you out here to embarrass me, it was the least I could do.'

'Wait – that was *you*?' I felt stupefied. 'But – Carrie, are you nuts? We should be putting as much distance between us as possible so Marcus doesn't suspect anything. If he realizes I'm helping you, we're both fucked. And you just drew a big arrow from you to me.'

For a moment Carrie looked put out, as if realizing I had a point. Then she seemed to shake it off.

'You're being ridiculous. The press office book travel all the time. They're never going to remember one upgrade, let alone tell Marcus.'

'Still, it's a paper trail, Carrie. One Marcus might find when we both disappear.'

'First, *you're* not going to disappear,' Carrie pointed out with a touch of irritation. 'You're going to travel to the UK just as planned. There's nothing suspicious in that. Second, he already knows I know you, so what difference does it make? And third—'

'He may know I know you,' I snapped, 'but he doesn't know we're in touch. *That's* the difference, Carrie. As far as he knows, I'm your worst nightmare. Why would you be upgrading me?'

'And third,' Carrie said, barrelling on as if I hadn't spoken, 'it's already *done*, so there's no point in stressing. It is what it is, Lo. I can't undo it so let's move on.'

For a long moment, we both stood there staring at each other like two bristling cats. Carrie's arms were folded defiantly. I felt like wringing her neck. It was all coming flooding back – the same old impulsive act-first, question-later Carrie. The Carrie who had wired me forty thousand francs, blowing her own cover story. The Carrie who had hit me and locked me up and nearly left me for dead. The Carrie who had got dragged into the whole sorry mess in the first place – the mess that had landed her here, now, on the run from the law and at the mercy of a man like Marcus Leidmann.

Fuck. *Fuck.*

She was a loose cannon; she always had been. Was I really considering travelling halfway across Europe with this woman, putting my own safety in her hands? Could I trust her not to panic and do something stupid at customs?

I was about to open my mouth and tell her I'd changed my mind, I didn't need to think about this overnight because I wasn't going to do it, when there was a sudden noise – the sound of a key turning in the door. Carrie heard it at the same moment I did – and all the colour drained from her face.

'Shit. He's back.'

'Who's back?'

'Marcus, of course!' She began pushing me almost violently across the room, so hard that I nearly tripped. For a minute I wasn't sure what she was trying to do – shove me into a cupboard? Then I realized there was a door concealed in the panelling beside the bed, one which must lead into the next room.

'Go!' Carrie hissed as she yanked open the door and propelled me through into the darkened room beyond. 'Let yourself out into the corridor. But be quick, that's his room. He'll come through in—'

She broke off as the door behind her swung open, and then, without another word, she pulled the communicating door between the two rooms shut. As the panelling clicked back into place, I was plunged into complete and utter darkness.

For a long moment I just stood, frozen, trying to let my eyes adjust. My heart was beating in my throat and I could hear a man's voice – presumably Marcus's – coming through the panelling. I knew that I needed to hurry, that he could be coming through the adjoining door any second, but I was also painfully aware that tripping over a chair in the dark would be the worst possible thing I could do.

After what felt like an agonizingly long time, my eyes adjusted enough for me to see a dark shape to my right, probably a bed, and, what was more promising, a faint golden glimmer coming from across the room. It was a thin bar of light down at floor level – and it must be filtering under the door from the corridor.

I took a step forward, towards the light, and then another, and then, to my horror, I felt my foot catch on something in the dark – a tall teetering something shaped like a floor lamp or a hat stand that tipped precariously away from me as its centre of balance shifted.

Time seemed to slow down as I leaped forwards, hands outstretched to the darkness, my scrabbling fingers reaching out for whatever I'd knocked. I was horribly aware that at any moment it could crash to the ground and expose Carrie before her escape had even started.

But then my fingers closed over a metal tube, and I pulled it back towards me, steadying it on what felt like three legs. Only when it was firmly upright again did I carefully, oh so painfully carefully, let go of the tube. Then I continued creeping slowly and cautiously towards the thin crack of light – all the time holding my breath and listening for the noise of the communicating door opening behind me.

'What you're talking about . . . ' I heard faintly through the wood in a man's irritable voice, followed the sound of Carrie speaking, her tone placating and cheerful.

'Have a macaron, darling? . . . very good . . . tomorrow?'

At last, after what felt like an interminable age, I was there at the door, my hand on the latch, and quietly, quietly, I turned it – letting the blindingly bright light from the corridor come flooding into the room.

I was about to close the door behind me and scurry thankfully back to my suite when something, maybe that stupid reporter's instinct that I could never quite quell, made me stop. I opened the door again, a little wider this time, and stared back into the darkness of the room I had just left, illuminated by a single shaft of light from the open door. What *was* it I had stumbled over in the darkness? A lamp? It was a strange place to put one, if so.

I saw it almost immediately – a tall, thin black pole halfway between the communicating door and the bed – but it took me a beat to realize what I was seeing and still longer to understand why it was there.

It was a tripod, one made to hold a camera, though it was currently empty.

And it was facing the bed.

For a long moment I just looked at it, standing silently in the empty room, feeling a little sick. I was thinking of Carrie, of the note in her voice when she had said *I'm getting worried. Worried about him, about his . . . boundaries.* I was thinking of the thing that she had refused to do, the act she had refused to name, and thinking about why a wealthy man like Marcus might need a mistress who could not say no to him, a mistress who could never expose his secrets because she would be exposing herself in the process.

I was thinking about what those secrets might be – things Carrie couldn't bring herself to say aloud, even to me.

Then quietly, very quietly, I shut the door and made my way back to my room.

10

When I got back to my room I undressed and lay down in bed – but sleep wouldn't come. It wasn't just that the jet lag had well and truly kicked in – it was my own nerves, strung to the breaking point.

As I lay there in the dark, periodically tapping my phone to show me the hours cycling through midnight, 1 a.m., 2 a.m. . . . I couldn't stop thinking about Carrie, about the fear and disgust in her voice as she'd described Marcus and his friends, and about that tripod standing silently in the darkness, waiting for who knew what. But also about what she'd said. About the notion that I *owed* her. Was it true?

It was certainly true that she had saved my life. It was also true that I wouldn't have been in that predicament in the first place if not for her.

No, I didn't think I did owe Carrie – at least, not for the tit-for-tat reasons that she thought I did.

But my experiences on the *Aurora* had taught me one thing – the lengths that powerful men would go to to get what they wanted. To get what they felt they *deserved*. From what Carrie had said, Marcus Leidmann clearly felt that he deserved Carrie mind, body and soul, whether she consented or not. And I couldn't leave her in that situation. I just couldn't. But breaking the law – making myself an accessory to the escape of a wanted person – was there really no other option?

By the time a faint, predawn light was glimmering over the snowy mountains, I was no closer to making a decision. I didn't trust Carrie – I never had. She was fickle and impulsive and perfectly capable of betraying others to suit herself. But I also knew that there was no way I could walk away from another woman in trouble, and certainly not the kind of trouble she had described. It was that impulse, that inability to walk away, that had got me into danger on the *Aurora*, and ten years on, I knew myself better and knew the weaknesses of my own character, but that part of me had not changed, and I knew that if I walked away from this and let something happen to Carrie, I could never live with my decision.

No, if I did this – and I was still not certain I would – but if I did act to save Carrie from the situation she had found herself in, it would be for one reason and one reason only: not because I owed her, but because it was the right thing to do.

I DON'T KNOW when I fell asleep, but when I did, I dreamed. It was the old, bad dream – the one I'd had more times than I could count in the days and weeks after I returned from Norway, waking up trembling and sweating with Judah shaking my shoulder and whispering, *Lo, Lo, honey, you're okay. I've got you. You're okay.*

This time . . . this time, though, it was different. It started out the same, with me waking up trapped in a cabin far below sea level, surrounded by the pressure of innumerable tons of water and the knowledge that if anything happened, I would drown without anyone knowing I had even been on board.

But in this version of the dream, I had woken up because there was someone banging at the cabin door. I lay there on the thin bunk listening to the hammering, my heart thumping with fear at who might be outside. Was it Carrie? And if so, had she come to save me or kill me?

The blankets over me felt unbearably heavy, and when I tried to turn over, they tangled in my legs, trapping me, pinning me down, crushing me with their weight.

The thumping came again, and with it, this time, a voice. *Lo! Lo, are you in there?*

Was it Carrie? But that wasn't Carrie's voice – it was a man's voice. And one that was intimately familiar in a way that I couldn't identify but which made my stomach curdle. If only I could get up, if only I could free myself of these blankets . . .

The hammering came again.

'Lo! Jesus Christ, are you even awake?'

The grey, claustrophobic little cabin shimmered and shifted, and with a huge effort, I dragged my eyes open, for real this time, squinting at the sudden brightness, and then sat up, pushing my hair out of my face and trying to remember where I was and figure out who was yelling at the door.

I found the where first. Geneva. The Hotel du Lac. And the person shouting through the door was . . . oh God. I nearly groaned and put my face back into the pillow. It was Ben fucking Howard, my least favourite ex.

'Coming!' I yelled hoarsely, and stumbled out of bed, wrapping a robe around myself. I checked myself in the mirror for decency – I wasn't showing any excess skin, but I could have done without the bird's-nest hair and panda eyes – and then I opened the door, peering out into the blindingly bright corridor.

'What?'

'Sorry.' Ben looked penitent. 'Did I wake you?'

'Yes.' I didn't try to hide my irritation. 'I couldn't get to sleep last night. What is it?'

'Well, it's just that everyone's getting ready to leave for the press trip. I thought you wanted to come?'

'What?' I dived for the bedside table and snatched up my phone, then groaned. It was 10.30 a.m. Swiss time. I had slept right through my alarm – and breakfast. 'Fuck. *Fuck*. Fucking jet lag.'

'So you do want to come?'

'Yes! Yes, I want to come. Shit. Can you tell them to wait?'

'I can try.' Ben looked doubtful. 'I think the shooting party have already left, but I can tell the foraging lot you're coming.'

'Yes, I'm coming. I'll be—' Shit, how fast could I shower? 'Five minutes. Less.' That was a lie, but maybe it would keep them on the drive.

'Okay,' Ben said. 'I'll do my—' but I had slammed the door in his face and run to the shower.

TEN MINUTES LATER I ran panting through the foyer, ignoring the cheery greetings from the staff in reception, and skidded to a halt beside the Land Rover idling in the driveway.

'I'm sorry.' I gasped as the driver got out of his seat and came around to open the rear door for me. 'I'm so sorry . . . I overslept. Thank you so much for waiting.'

'It is no problem,' the driver said. He had an Italian accent and was extremely handsome and he gestured towards the open passenger door with a rather formal flourish that would have been slightly ridiculous in a Brit but which he managed to make look suave as hell. 'I pray you.'

I slid into the back seat and then looked around to find Ben Howard, Cole Lederer, and a woman whose name I didn't know grinning at me from the other passenger seats.

'Hi, everyone,' I said weakly. 'Sorry to keep you waiting. I'm Lo,' I said to the strange woman, who nodded.

'Hiya! Kelly.' She was extremely pretty with long tangled blonde hair that I strongly suspected were extensions. 'I'm a food Instagrammer! A foodstagrammer? I always think there should be a better name.'

'Nice to meet you,' I said, but I was too distracted to ask any proper questions. The seat belt was jamming every time I tried to pull it out.

'Do you—' Ben began, but I shook my head.

'No, I'm—'

But before I finished, Cole had twisted around from the front seat and taken the belt out of my hand. Whether it was his angle or just the fact that he wasn't angrily yanking it, in his hands it unrolled meekly, and I shoved the latch crossly into the socket.

'You're welcome,' Cole said with that wolfish smile. He looked as if he knew exactly how flustered I was and how irritated it had made me that he'd been able to fix the belt when I hadn't. I made a face at him, and he laughed.

'Right,' Ben said. He looked a little annoyed himself, but I wasn't sure why. Was it because I'd let Cole fix the belt and refused him? It seemed unlikely. Now he looked around at the others, his smile bright but a little strained. 'Right, are we ready?'

The rest of the car nodded, and with a scrunch of wheels on gravel, we were off.

AFTER THE SWEATY, panicked start, the rest of the morning was actually quite pleasant. As Kelly and Ben flirted companionably next to me, the driver took us through a maze of country roads, past farmhouses, stone cottages, and half-timbered inns, all backdropped by the astonishing beauty of the snow-tipped mountains.

The villages themselves were almost absurdly cute, in that Swiss cuckoo-clock style of ornate wooden fretwork and sparkling paint, but when we turned into a lane between two grassy meadows filled with solemn Alpine cattle wearing bells around their necks, I actually laughed. It was too much – from the babbling brook running alongside the track to the mellow chiming of the cowbells, the entire scene could have been lifted from *The Sound of Music*. I half expected a nun to come running out from the trees and break into song.

The car turned through an open gate and began bumping along a rutted dirt track that led deep into the forest. PROPRIÉTÉ PRIVÉE read an ancient sign. I turned my head as we drove past it, trying to read the rest of the message. *défense d'entrer*, I made out. *chasse interdite*.

No trespassing. Hunting forbidden. As we splashed through a shallow ford, I heard the sound of gunshots filtering through the trees and gave a mental shrug. Presumably the signs didn't apply if you were a guest of Marcus Leidmann. Hell, maybe this was his forest.

We got out of the car in a clearing at the end of the track where our guide was waiting – a husky blond man with a huge beard who introduced himself as Gottfried.

Gottfried led us even deeper into the forest, down old cart tracks, boar paths, across streams – Kelly almost fell in with a shriek and had to grab hold of Ben to save herself – all the while showing us what felt like dozens of different types of fungi, some edible, some apparently fairly poisonous. He rattled on about the differences between chanterelles, girolles, false chanterelles, winter chanterelles, and various other types of mushrooms, differences that I didn't ever completely get to the bottom of. By the time I'd been told about gills and pores, teeth and ridges, warts, scales, fleece, rings, double rings, caps and bulbs, I was more confused than ever. It didn't help that they all seemed to have several different names – apparently what the English called chanterelles, the French called girolles, and what the French called chanterelles, the English called winter chanterelles. Both had completely different names in Gottfried's native German, and by the end of it we had a basket of fungi but I wasn't much wiser about which of them were safe to eat, which was perhaps the point of the exercise; presumably Gottfried didn't want to put himself out of business too soon. Still, the woods were beautiful, and the fresh cool air was just what I needed to reset my jet lag. The only thing that spoiled the tranquility was the continuing sound of gunshots – and the fact that we seemed to be walking towards it.

By one o'clock I was famished, not helped by the lack of breakfast, and when Gottfried announced that we were going to meet the hunting party for a 'delicious lunch', it was all I could do to stop my stomach growling.

The lunch stop proved to be the most upmarket rustic picnic I had ever encountered. It was a beautifully spread table in a clearing in the centre of the forest, surrounded by sheepskin-topped logs to serve as stools and laid with soft, unbleached linen and antique silverware. An array of crusty breads and crisp salads were already prepared, and across the clearing were three blazing wood fires, clearly destined to cook our lunch. One had a spit full of dead animals already turning above the flames. I wasn't sure what types of creatures; it was hard to make out, but the bodies looked small, so perhaps pheasants or rabbits. The second fire was surmounted by a Dutch oven containing some kind of bubbling stew, maybe a cassoulet. And the third had a frying pan balanced over a grill. Gottfried handed our foraged mushrooms to an attendant, who tipped the whole basketful into the pan, along with a generous measure of butter, with what seemed to me to be a worrying level of trust in our competence. I was *fairly* sure that Gottfried would have filtered out anything dodgy, but I'd noticed Ben popping what he claimed were winter chanterelles and oyster mushrooms into the basket with a confidence that seemed at best misplaced and at worst foolhardy.

I was eyeing the fires and trying to decide whether I preferred risking my life with the mushrooms or spitting out birdshot with the pheasants when I heard a deep, slightly accented voice over my shoulder.

'Miss Blacklock? Allow me to introduce myself.'

I turned around – and came face to face with Marcus Leidmann.

For a moment I had no idea what to say. My heart was hammering with a mix of stage fright and something else. This was it – this was my chance to pin him down for an interview for Rowan, but I was no longer sure that I could disentangle the business entrepreneur Rowan wanted to hear about from the account I'd had from Carrie the previous evening.

My first thought was that he was very old, older even than I'd imagined from Carrie's description. I should have expected it – Pieter was thirty-five, according to his Wikipedia page, so it was unlikely Marcus would be under sixty, but he looked older than that, closer to seventy-five, maybe.

But my second, and somewhat surprised, thought was that he was handsome – much more handsome than his son, in fact. He had a kind of Donald Sutherland quality: a neatly clipped beard, side-swept white hair, and a beaked nose that sat well with his slightly hawkish expression. He looked like someone accustomed to leading and unaccustomed to being told no – and I could understand what it was that had made Carrie accept his first invitation. But it was hard to match up the austere, patrician countenance of the person standing in front of me with the man she'd described to me last night.

I was still staring at him, mesmerized, trying to think what to say when I realized that he had finished introducing himself and was holding out his hand. When I took it, his fingers were cold and his grip was very, very firm – the grip of someone used to working in an alpha-male environment, where the strength of your handshake was supposed to say something about your character. When he let go, I resisted the urge to massage my knuckles and forced my face into a smile that I hoped didn't betray my unease. Two weeks ago, I would have given my right arm for this opportunity, but now – well, now, everything had changed. To begin with, Marcus Leidmann knew who I was. And not just in the sense of *Lo Blacklock, travel writer, author, journalist*. He knew who I was because he knew Carrie – there was a good chance that he knew things about me that I hadn't admitted to anyone else.

The problem was, I wasn't sure if I knew who *he* was. I had been given three very different versions of Marcus Leidmann: the business mogul, the monster Carrie had described to me, and the man standing in front of me. Which one was the real Marcus Leidmann? And how could I tell?

'Mr Leidmann,' I managed. 'It's, well, it's so good to finally meet you. Did your press office tell you I've been asking about an interview?'

'My assistant mentioned it, yes. For the *Financial Times*, is that correct? I'm sorry I haven't been easier to pin down.' His English was excellent, quite as good as his son's, with an easy, idiomatic turn of phrase that could only have come from early exposure. 'My schedule tends to the unpredictable. But I have half an hour now, if that's any good to you?'

I opened my mouth – then closed it again. Half an hour would have been great, but I didn't have my pen, my Dictaphone, or my notebook – Reporting 101, and something I was now kicking myself about. I hadn't even prepped any questions. I'd thought about what I'd cover, but I'd been waiting to find out how much time I was allocated. Now that seemed unbelievably stupid. Of course it was more likely I'd get a snatched half hour. Why hadn't I scribbled out some basic points in my notebook? Why hadn't I brought it with me?

Well, I hadn't, and there was no use crying over spilled milk. What I did have was my phone, and given I was unlikely to get a second chance, it would have to do.

'Half an hour would be great, though if I'm able to follow up later, that would be even better.' I smiled, trying for charming, and wondering if I had twigs in my hair from foraging. If I did, Marcus Leidmann wasn't rude enough to point it out.

'Great. Shall we sit?' He indicated the sheepskin-topped log and I nodded and sat, fumbling out my phone, and frantically trying to find the recording app I used as a back-up for interviews. When I was sure it was running, I cleared my throat and began.

'Mr Leidmann—'

'Please, call me Marcus.'

For some reason, the words, routine as they were, caught me off guard.

'Oh. Well, um, of course. Thank you, Marcus. And please, call me Lo.'

'Lo? Short for Laura, correct?'

'Yes.' The fact that he knew my name shouldn't have been surprising – I was certain his staff would have briefed him comprehensively before we met – but there was somehow still a strangeness to it. A faux intimacy that didn't sit quite right with our relative statuses. We weren't just Lo and Marcus, shooting the breeze – he was one of the wealthiest men in Europe, if not the world, and I was a reporter who went overdrawn every time I had to pay the sitter and who hadn't had a byline for five years. I was trying to think what to say, how to lead into the questions I wanted to ask, when he spoke again, and this time his remark was even more unexpected.

'I very much enjoyed your book, by the way. *Dark Waters*, isn't that right?'

'You've read my book?' I didn't mean for my tone to come out quite as incredulous as it sounded. After all, *Dark Waters* had been a bestseller both in the US and the UK, and I'd been a minor celebrity on the talk-show circuit for a few months. It wasn't *that* unlikely that Marcus Leidmann would have bothered to get hold of a copy before agreeing to an interview. But the actual words still gave me a frisson of unease – not unlike the jolt I'd experienced on hearing the same thing from Ben, but for completely different reasons. With Ben and, to a lesser extent, Alexander and Cole, I'd been worried about their reactions, about how they'd take seeing their flaws and faults laid out in black and white. With Marcus Leidmann, it was my own portrayal I was concerned about. I had been honest in that book – more than honest. I'd written about my mental health, my fears, my own fragility. Knowing that Marcus had read all that, had spent time in my head . . . well, it was a strange and not entirely pleasant feeling.

'I did,' he said gravely. 'It was excellent. *Unputdownable*, I think is the word, much as I detest such an unwieldy term. You are an extremely good writer, Laura. Almost forensically observant, but you have the gift of making what you describe both vivid and compelling.'

'I – um, thank you,' I said, trying not to show how flustered his compliments were making me. 'That's really kind of you to say.'

'I am not being kind.' He said it matter-of-factly. 'If I make a statement, you may rest assured it is because it is a simple truth. And the truth is, you are a very good writer and an excellent observer of human nature.'

There was no denying that receiving compliments from one of the most powerful men in the world was . . . well, it was intoxicating. Hearing the words from his lips, feeling the intensity of his blue eyes locked onto mine, I could suddenly see what had made Carrie fall for him, if only initially.

In spite of that, I didn't buy his *simple truth* line. It was flattering, and maybe he genuinely did think I was a good writer, but he was saying all this for a reason. What I couldn't work out was exactly what that reason was. Was he trying to charm me? Or knock me off balance? Because mixed with the flush of pride was an uneasy feeling that we were starting out this interview on the wrong foot, with him knowing more about me than I did about him. I was supposed to be the one asking the questions, and instead we were talking about me. Maybe that was deliberate on his part; maybe it wasn't. But either way, I had to get us back on track.

'Well, you know the way to a writer's heart is buying their book,' I said, trying for a jocular tone. 'So thank you for that, and thank you for this.' I waved a hand to encompass the forest, the clearing, the food – and him. 'For agreeing to talk to me today. I know you don't give many interviews.'

'I don't,' he conceded equably. His blue eyes were still fixed on my face in a way that made it hard to concentrate.

'And . . . um . . . if you don't mind me asking, why is that? I mean, well, I feel like increasingly part of the role of a, uh, a modern CEO is to be the face of the company.' Fuck. Was that true? I was making this up as I went along, and from Marcus Leidmann's expression, I thought he knew it. This was why I wasn't a business reporter. I had absolutely no idea what the hell a modern CEO did – and I cared less. What I wanted to know was what made him tick. What I *really* wanted to know was what had made him pursue a woman like Carrie and exert his power over her so brutally. But that was a subject I absolutely couldn't broach. Not without betraying her trust.

'You're probably right. I suspect I am not a very modern CEO,' Marcus Leidmann said. There was a smile twitching at the corner of his mouth, and to my own irritation, I found myself echoing it back. I had to keep reminding myself what Carrie had told me – what kind of a man he was behind closed doors. But it was hard to reconcile the two pictures. The slightly sardonic elderly man sitting opposite me didn't look like someone capable of kidnap and blackmail. Had Carrie been stringing me along? But then the image of that darkened bedroom came back to me, of the tripod standing sentry in the dark, and I shivered.

'I tend to the old-fashioned view that business is business and private life is private,' Marcus was continuing, 'and I prefer to keep the two separate.'

'But is that hard in a family business?' I countered. 'I mean, the Leidmann Group is very much a family affair, isn't it? It was founded by your grandfather and great-uncle, and you intend, I assume, to pass the reins to your son one of these days. When family and work are so intertwined, doesn't that necessarily make business personal, and personal matters business?'

'Well, as to the succession, that's undecided,' Marcus Leidmann said. His words were casual, but I tried to hide my surprise. Was he really going to pass over his own son? That was the first I'd heard of it, if so; all the articles I'd read seemed to taken for granted that Pieter would be picking up the reins from his father, and probably sooner rather than later. My own assumption had been that giving Pieter his own division in the shape of Journeys by Leidmann had been a way to prep him for the leadership of the company as a whole in the not-too-distant future. Now Marcus seemed to be saying that was very much not a done deal – and the hiving off of Journeys took on a different complexion. A consolation prize, perhaps? His own little fiefdom so he'd be too tied up to interfere in the running of the rest of the Leidmann Group? But Marcus was still speaking. 'However, it's true that it's difficult to keep entirely out of the spotlight when it's your name above the door. That exposure . . . well, it's something I've had to get used to, but it's not something I have to enjoy. I imagine *you* would understand that, Laura.'

'What do you mean?' I felt puzzled and a little nettled. The way he kept trying to bat the ball back into my court every time I asked him a question was putting me on edge, and it wasn't hard to remember that this was a man who was used to tough negotiation, to unsettling his opponents quite deliberately. *Was that what he was doing?*

Marcus shrugged at the question.

'Just that *Dark Waters* . . . well, it was a deeply personal book. And yet you come across as someone to whom confessional journalism doesn't come naturally. I imagine that must be a strange experience.'

I opened my mouth – then shut it again. It was so close to what I had been thinking just moments before when he first brought up the subject of my book that I didn't know whether to be impressed or unnerved. Was I really that easy to read? I had the disquieting impression that Marcus was manipulating me like a puppet, and it was suddenly less difficult to believe than it had been a few moments ago that this was someone who was used to being in control and not in an entirely pleasant way.

I *had* to get this interview back on track. I needed a question that would stroke his ego, draw him out of the slightly combative back-and-forth we seemed to have fallen into, yet get to the heart of who he was as a person.

'What drives you?' I asked at last. It felt like a question he might enjoy answering. 'I mean, by most measures you're someone who's already at the top of the tree. You're one of the richest men in the world. You don't have shareholders to answer to, your family are more than provided for.' I was laying it on thick, and I knew it, but there was no harm in a little flattery. That was something I'd learned over years of interviewing people. It didn't work on everyone – some people it just made uncomfortable – but I didn't think compliments would unnerve Marcus. On the contrary, it might lull him into opening up a little. 'You must have achieved pretty much everything you set out to do – you've transformed the Leidmann Group from a successful family firm into a truly global player. You could retire today, and yet I don't get the impression that's on your radar. What – well,

I mean to boil it down to the simplest question, what makes you get out of bed every day?'

'What drives me . . .' Marcus said thoughtfully. 'It is a good question. When I was a younger man, I would have said it was ambition and a wish to honour my family, preserve the name, but I think that was largely hypocrisy on my own part. A desire not to admit the basic driving force underlying business.'

'Money?'

Marcus shook his head. 'Money is largely meaningless to me. I'm not a man of expensive tastes. In truth, I'm happiest with a gun over my shoulder traipsing the forests of Wallonia, where I grew up. No, money is valuable only in terms of what it represents, which is an ability to get what I want.'

'And what's that?' I found I was leaning forward, curious. Marcus gave a little smile, crinkling the skin at the corners of his mouth, but there was nothing warm about the expression. I had the impression of someone far older than his actual years staring out through his eyes.

'Power, Laura.' He held my gaze, his bright blue irises locked to mine. You could have heard a leaf drop. 'Power is the only thing worth having. It is the reason I have kept the Leidmann Group private all these years. I have never been a drug user, but the exercise of power . . . that is a very heady drug indeed, and one that is very hard to give up.'

There was total and complete silence between us. From far across the clearing, I could hear the rest of the group talking, the crackle of the fire someone had started, but between Marcus and me, there was absolute stillness. I could feel my own pulse throbbing softly in my jaw, and for a moment had the wild idea that Marcus could hear it, and knew exactly how unsettled he was making me. I thought of Carrie, of what she'd said in suite 11 as she pleaded with me to help her: *This is him, Lo. This is Marcus illustrating loud and clear that he has the power of life and death over me.*

At the time, I hadn't believed her, or not completely. Now . . . now I thought that perhaps I did.

'Tell me about your wife.' The question was impulsive – I hadn't known I was going to ask it until the words left my mouth – but the fact was, I wasn't just here for the *FT*. Not anymore. This might be my only chance to get to the truth of what Carrie had told me, and this question, sideways as it was, was as close as I could come to that subject. If it had the benefit of knocking Marcus off balance just a little, well, so much the better. But when Marcus raised one eyebrow in a distinctly chilly way, I realized that I might have overstepped the mark. Making him walk out of the interview wouldn't help anyone, least of all Carrie. 'I'm sorry,' I added hastily. 'I hope that didn't come across as tactless. I know you're a widower, but I suppose what I'm asking is, what was her role in building up the company? You must miss her very much. Most of the CEOs I've interviewed' – number, up until now, precisely zero, but I was planning to gloss over that in the actual article – 'tend to stress the importance of a supportive spouse to act as a sounding board and take on the emotional admin of family life, to free up their husband – and, let's be honest, it is normally the husbands – to concentrate on their careers. Would you say that was her role? Or was she more directly involved in the company's success? I suppose I just feel as if she's a rather invisible player in the Leidmann Group story and I'd love to know a bit more about her.'

I was talking too much and I knew it. But I had misstepped, and talking seemed like the best way to defuse the sudden chill I had felt when I mentioned Marcus's late wife. Unfortunately, the coldly austere silence did not abate, and I found myself casting about for something else to say, some way to explain my sudden interest in Pieter's mother.

'As a mum myself, I mean.'

As soon as the words had left my mouth, I regretted them. It was a cast-iron rule I had made for myself when talking about *Dark*

Waters: don't bring the kids into this. Not just because of the weirdos who had floated to the surface in my brief five minutes of fame but because I didn't want my professional accomplishments to be overshadowed by my childbearing status. And now here I was doing it to myself.

At least my words seemed to have had the desired effect. Marcus looked up, frowning a little.

'Oh, yes, your children. Two boys, is that right? And, remind me, what are their names? Eli and . . . Edward? Teddy?'

I felt a cold shock run through me. It was as violent and physical as the moment I had plunged into the cold waters of a Norwegian fjord ten long years ago – and almost as unpleasant.

'*What* did you say?'

'Your children.' Marcus's austere expression had vanished and he looked, if anything, slightly amused. 'Isn't that their names? I do my research, Laura. Just as you do, I'm sure.' He paused, his blue eyes fixed on mine, almost as if he was savouring my discomfort.

I had already drawn breath, ready to snap back a retort. I'm not sure what I was going to say: *What the hell? How dare you poke into my private life?* But I couldn't say that. Not when it was exactly what I was doing to him.

There was a long, uncomfortable pause. Uncomfortable for me, at least. Marcus looked as if he was rather enjoying turning the tables. But at last, taking pity on my nonplussed state, he smiled and broke the silence.

'To answer your question, Laura, Elke wasn't really involved. She was what I suppose the Germans would call a good hausfrau – very Kinder und Küche. Not so much Kirche; we've never been a religious family, and Elke was no exception. But I wouldn't say she had any interest in my business. Her sole concern was Pieter. She had little notion of any wider concerns than keeping her child happy. She was a rather limited person in many ways.'

He stopped as if expecting me to respond, but I had no idea what to say, particularly regarding the last remark. *A rather limited person?* It seemed like an extraordinarily dismissive summary of a woman who had presumably meant a lot to him at some point. Most people – certainly most CEOs, I thought – would have at least pretended to value their spouses' contributions a little more highly, particularly if that spouse was dead. But maybe I was being hard on him – maybe there was something refreshing about Marcus's honesty? Was a hypocritical show of false warmth really preferable?

'Now it's my turn to apologize for my tactlessness,' Marcus said, clearly correctly interpreting my silence. 'I'm sorry; that probably came over as a little unappreciative. But you have to remember, Elke died many years ago – times were different then. And the truth is, she wasn't involved in my business, and I don't think she would have wanted to be. That didn't mean that she wasn't a good wife and mother.'

I opened my mouth to say – I wasn't sure what. Perhaps that *good* seemed like the most milquetoast adjective he could possibly have picked, given that he was talking about the mother of his child. Perhaps that he was speaking as if his marriage had taken place in the 1950s, but Pieter had been born in 1989. Times were different, yes. Back then people still thought George Michael was straight and that shoulder pads were essential office wear. But they weren't *that* different. Not Kinder, Küche, Kirche different.

'How did she die?' The words came out before I could think better of them, and I saw an expression of shock and something else – could it be anger? – flit across Marcus's face.

Ha, I thought, a little vindictively, remembering my own shock of a few minutes ago – but then puzzlement overtook the momentary satisfaction. Why was that such a dangerous question?

He opened his mouth, and I braced myself, but before he could speak, a female voice came from behind us.

'I am sorry, Mr Leidmann, but may I interrupt for one moment?'

Turning, I saw the blonde woman from the night before, Adeline LeBlanc. Her hands were gripping each other so tightly I could see the tendons, and she looked extremely tense.

Marcus nodded, a little stiffly.

'Of course. What is it, Adeline?'

'I do apologize, Mr Leidmann, but an urgent issue has arisen. There is *un problème*—' She slipped into rapid French, words I didn't understand but which seemed to have to do with something financial, perhaps legal. I heard *notaire* and *contrat*. Marcus Leidmann listened attentively, then turned back to me, his expression apparently regretful.

'Miss Blacklock, I am so sorry, but we will have to postpone this delightful discussion. A rather important deal has run into some issues, and I am required back in the hotel. Heinrich.' He looked across the clearing at a very tall, very broad man in a suit. One huge hand was resting lightly over a bulge at his hip that could have been a holstered radio but looked very much like something else. Perhaps that was the point. 'Would you please summon the car?'

Heinrich, who had cold grey eyes, the build of a bodyguard, and the haircut of a US Marine, gave a short nod and strode away into the trees, presumably towards wherever they had left the SUV.

'I am so sorry, Miss Blacklock,' Adeline LeBlanc said tightly. Up close, she looked much younger than I had thought last night, perhaps barely thirty. Certainly very young to be . . . what was it she had said? Head of international relations? Perhaps that was why her manner was so stressed and brittle – I knew, after all, what it felt like to be a young woman out of your professional depth. 'My deepest apologies for having to cut this meeting short.'

'Adeline, please ask Mathilde to make sure that we diarize another interview slot for Miss Blacklock,' Marcus said. He had already stood up and was brushing sheep's wool strands from his dark trousers. I switched off the recording app and followed suit. I wasn't at all sure this office emergency existed. Could it really be a coincidence that Adeline had stepped in the moment I asked about Marcus Leidmann's dead wife? I wondered if she understood the impression his last remark had made better than he did and was pulling him out of a sticky situation before I could press my advantage.

'Miss Blacklock,' Marcus was saying, with what sounded like genuine regret in his voice. 'It has been a pleasure.' He took my hand and bent over it in a way that was both like and yet startlingly unlike Alexander Belhomme's gesture from the night before. But where Alexander's lips had brushed my knuckles in a moist kiss I could almost still feel, Marcus Leidmann's did not touch me – the gesture was more of a formal obeisance, but one that somehow came over without a shred of subservience. It had the air almost of a military salute. And then he straightened and moved in the direction Adeline was pointing, towards the car already idling at the edge of the clearing.

He was almost there when there was a rustling in the bushes at one side of the clearing, and a group of men emerged, carrying shotguns broken over their arms and what looked to me like a rather sad collection of dead birds over their shoulders. Marcus paused with his hand on the car door, scanning the group, and then his eyes alighted on Pieter, hovering somewhere at the back, and he crooked his finger, beckoning his son towards the car.

Pieter hesitated for a moment, a flash of something – could it be reluctance? Resignation? – passing over his expression, and then he broke away from the group and walked towards his father, a smile plastered over his face.

'Papa,' he said, followed by something in what I guessed was Flemish, but Marcus spoke quickly, cutting through his son's remarks. I couldn't understand what he was saying, but his tone was unmistakably disapproving, and he gestured towards the single bird Pieter was carrying, then across the clearing to where the other men were unloading two, three, five birds apiece in some cases. Flemish or not, the message was pretty clear: *Is that all you managed?*

Pieter flushed, and I saw him glance at me as if embarrassed all this was playing out in public, and then he said something that sounded to my ear defensive. An excuse, perhaps. *I was looking after our guests. I didn't have much luck.* I remembered his words from the night before. *I actually don't love killing animals... But it's important to him that I take a part in his interests.* It seemed unlikely that he was admitting that to his father.

Whatever he had said, the words didn't mollify Marcus. Without dignifying his son's remarks with an answer, he climbed into the car.

The door slammed, and I was turning away, ready to rejoin the others, when there was a soft whir, and I saw out of the corner of my eye the darkened window winding slowly down. I assumed Marcus had a last retort for his son, who was still standing there looking a little deflated, but instead he called out, 'Miss Blacklock?'

I turned back. Marcus's previous irritation seemed to have dissipated, and there was a slight smile tugging at the corners of his lips. It was almost as if crushing his son had put him in a better mood.

'Yes, Mr Leidmann?'

'Thank you for your time. And do give my regards to your children – and your husband. Judah Lewis of the *New York Times*, I believe? A very talented reporter. They must miss you very much.'

And then the car pulled away, bumping over the ruts and mud of the clearing. I watched it go, a faint sense of unease churning in my stomach at the mention of Judah and the children. Was it a threat? I didn't see how it could be, but there was something a little calculated in the way he had brought the conversation back to them, back to that moment when I realized how much digging he had done on me, and back to everything I had to lose.

As the car disappeared from view I wondered . . . wondered which of the three versions of Marcus Leidmann I had just met: the monster Carrie had described, the power-hungry business mogul I had expected, or the kindly, cultured man he had tried to present. I had no idea – and I felt no closer to finding out which was the real Marcus.

11

When we got back to the hotel, I ran myself a bath and then lay in the suds and listened to the section of interview I had managed to record. There was nowhere near enough material for a full profile, but the line about Pieter was intriguing, and if Rowan agreed, there was a chance I could spin it into a sidebar piece, which would at least give me a byline.

Everything I'd read in the newspapers before coming here had strongly implied, if not outright stated, that Pieter was the heir apparent to the Leidmann fortune and the CEO position when his father stepped down. But the more I listened to Marcus's casual *That's undecided*, the less sure I was that he intended for Pieter to take over. At the very least, if he was planning to hand over to his son at some point in the near future, it was a bizarre thing to say when silence would have been just as good an option.

Most of all, though, I found myself listening to Marcus Leidmann, to the rise and fall of his voice, trying to fit the person I'd encountered with the portrait of the man Carrie had painted for me last night.

The more I listened, the more confused I felt. This was clearly a man who exercised ruthless control over himself and everyone around him. I had felt it in the nervous energy emanating from

Adeline LeBlanc. And I had felt it too in the way that Marcus had pulled himself back from the brink of his reaction to my question about his wife. Even his presence here – Journeys was supposed to be Pieter's project, Pieter's baby. And yet here was his father still looming over everything. One way to read Marcus's behaviour was as a supportive father, pitching in to help his son's endeavour succeed. The other way was as a man unable to let even a single iota of power out of his grip.

And yet, in spite of everything, in spite of what Carrie had said, I could see why she had fallen for him. It wasn't just the compliments he'd paid my work; I was a good enough reporter not to let my head be turned by that. It was something about *him*, some indefinable dominance and charisma that was hard to pin down but was very real. There was a moment there when I had wanted him to like me – *wanted* to do as he said.

In a way, it shouldn't have been a surprise. You didn't get to his position in life without being able to lead and inspire, even charm. And it explained how Carrie had got herself into this position in the first place, something I'd found hard to understand when we spoke, *why* she'd ended up under the thumb of a man almost twice her age.

But now . . . now I understood, or I thought I did. That combination of power and magnetism, it was a seductive mix, even when tinged with the darkness I thought I had seen. And I also understood why Marcus was hesitating about handing the company over to Pieter. Because Pieter, pleasant though he seemed to be, had absolutely none of that magnetism.

The question was, why on earth had Marcus admitted those doubts, even tacitly, to me? He was clearly an intensely private man – what could he possibly gain by talking to a reporter about the matter of the succession? And yet he didn't strike me as someone who would let his mouth run away with him, someone who would say things without thinking, in spite of that odd remark about his wife.

The more I thought about it, the more I thought I knew. The request I'd put in to the Leidmann Group press office was for an interview in the *Financial Times*, one of the most important business newspapers in the world. I had heard of politicians hinting at a controversial policy in an interview purely to see how the columnists reacted – with plausible deniability if the reception was bad. Was Marcus doing something similar? Was he putting out an idea, hinting that he might pass over Pieter, just to see how the financial markets reacted?

The idea made sense, except for one thing: the Leidmann Group was not a publicly traded entity; it was a private family firm not listed on the stock exchange, so how the market reacted wasn't really Marcus's concern. Unless . . . and here I stopped, chewing my fingernail, listening to the soft hiss of water in the heated towel rail and the sound of the wind outside the bathroom window. Unless he *was* planning to float on the stock exchange and dump his son and heir in the bargain. Was that possible?

I pressed play again, and shut my eyes, listening to Marcus's casual, throwaway tone. *Well, as to the succession, that's undecided.* It was a strange way to speak about something so momentous, so potentially *cruel* to his son if the news leaked out, and as I replayed it, it struck me that it was the same slightly dismissive tone he had used about his wife. *She was a rather limited person in many ways.* Rewind. Play. *A rather limited person.*

Was that a normal way to talk about your dead wife?

As the question occurred to me, I realized something else: I still had no idea how she had died.

I shut off the recording app, fired up Google, and typed *Elke Leidmann death* into the search bar.

The results were sparse and not particularly interesting; just a Wikipedia entry with her date of death, shockingly young – she had been only twenty-eight – and below that a short factual piece on the

Leidmann Group website. But when I clicked on the reference in the Wikipedia piece, it took me to something I hadn't expected – a cached article from a defunct student newspaper featuring an interview with a very young Pieter Leidmann.

The interview itself was nothing remarkable. The occasion seemed to be Pieter's role as the Fool in a student production of *King Lear*, and most of the piece was about his dreams of being an actor or perhaps a filmmaker. So much, so banal. But towards the end, he spoke about his mother, and how her death had affected him.

> 'Of course I don't really remember my own mother,' Pieter Leidmann admits with a wry expression. 'She died when I was very young. She had a very difficult pregnancy with me, and my father was advised in the strongest possible terms that having another child would probably kill her. Unfortunately, it did.' He shakes his head sadly.

Taking out the rather stilted journalistic clichés about wry expressions – I wasn't sure what that even meant – it was a heart-stoppingly sad paragraph. A woman, forbidden from having more children, killed by her desire for just one more baby. And presumably, given Pieter seemed to be an only child, the baby had died too. A double tragedy.

The question was, *was* it her desire? Or was it Marcus's desire for a back-up heir? The mention of *my father*, fleeting as it was, somehow made it sound like Pieter held his father at least partially responsible. Was that true? Had Marcus persuaded his wife into the pregnancy that killed her? If so, that could explain the flash of anger in his eyes when I'd asked about her death.

The problem was, the opposite could be true as well. If Elke had put her desire for a second child over her love for Pieter and Marcus, well, it would be understandable if her husband was still angry about that decision, even decades later. But if Marcus *had* pushed her into a second pregnancy, or even just gone along with it in spite of knowing it could kill her, then it made his dismissive remark about her more than a little cold. It made it psychotic.

I had just pressed play on the recording, about to listen to his words for perhaps the hundredth time, when something stopped me. It was a sound – an unmistakable sound – from my room.

I shot up, my head and shoulders popping out of the foam like an anxious meerkat's, and pressed pause on the app, my heart thumping.

'Hello?' I called. Was it housekeeping? Had I forgotten to put out the Do Not Disturb sign? 'Hello? I'm in the bath, could you come back later?'

But no one replied. I was just beginning to think I'd misheard, led astray by noises from the room above or in the corridor, when I heard another sound, this one quite unmistakable, and I swished round in the bath to see the handle of the bathroom door turning, turning . . .

'I'm in here!' I called out, my voice annoyingly squeaky and panicked. 'I'm in the bath!'

But the door didn't stop opening. I heard a gurgling, throaty laugh, a laugh that sent my pulse racing faster; the door opened even wider, and Carrie slid through the gap and into the bathroom.

'Jesus!' I sat up straight, then realized I was completely naked and slunk down in the foam. 'Carrie, seriously, what the fuck? I've got no clothes on!'

'Oh, relax.' Carrie shut the door behind her and then put the toilet lid down and made herself comfortable. 'It's not like I haven't seen tits before. We've both got a pair.'

I was about to demand how the hell she'd got into my room, but then I remembered the master key. Dammit. Instead I said, rather haughtily, 'Maybe next time knock, okay?'

'Oh, sure,' Carrie said as if pacifying an angry child. 'Because standing in the corridor banging on the door of a woman I'm supposed to be hiding from would in no way give *the entire fucking game away*. I'm here to check in, like we agreed – have you made your mind up? I don't want to pressure you, but, well, there's not much time.'

Shit. I felt my stomach shift uneasily. Carrie was right – I was supposed to be leaving the day after tomorrow. It was now or never. And I still wasn't completely sure what to do.

'Please, Lo,' Carrie said, and suddenly all the boisterousness and bluster was gone, and her voice was very low with a tremble in it that seemed to twist at my heart. 'I promised myself I wouldn't beg, but ... please.'

I closed my eyes and pressed my fingertips to the sockets, wishing, wishing I could discuss this with Judah – but I knew what he would say. *Are you crazy? Risking your reputation for a woman who nearly got you killed?*

And he'd be right. But Carrie was right too – she *had* saved my life, and, more to the point, if she was telling the truth about her situation, and I was beginning to think that she might be, I just couldn't bring myself to walk away and abandon her to this cage of her own making, plaything of a man like Marcus Leidmann. I had no real idea whether he would kill her, but it no longer seemed impossible.

I thought of the cold voice on the recording, dismissing the woman who'd died giving birth to his child. I thought of the camera in the darkness of the bedroom, pointed at the bed. I thought of the tremble in Carrie's voice, the fear in her eyes. And I thought of the number of women who tried to leave their lovers every day and were killed for it. This wasn't exactly pie in the sky, after all. It wasn't even particularly unusual. I knew from pieces I'd written and researched that the most dangerous point in an abusive relationship was the moment someone tried to leave. And that was just ordinary, everyday people – let alone someone with the power and reach of a reclusive billionaire, someone who had been accustomed to getting exactly what he wanted for decade after decade.

No. Whether or not she was right about how far Marcus would go, the fear I'd heard in Carrie's voice, that fear wasn't fake. Carrie, at least, was certain that she was in danger. And if I refused to believe that, if I refused to help her and something happened – well, I'd never be able to live with myself.

'Okay,' I said. My voice in the echoing silence of the bathroom sounded strange and hollow. 'Okay, I'll do it.'

'Wait, you'll do it?' Carrie leaned forward on the toilet as though she couldn't completely believe what she'd just heard. 'You'll really do it?'

'Yes, I'll do it.' As I said the words, I wondered if I was making a huge mistake – but I also knew I had no other option. However much I wanted to wash my hands of this, there was no way my conscience would let me walk away and leave Carrie to her fate.

'Oh my God, Lo Blacklock, I fucking love you!' Her eyes were shining. 'Seriously – I will make this up to you, I swear. Never mind an interview – I can give you the biggest exclusive of your life, a story the papers will be queuing up to cover. Just wait until I'm out of his clutches, and I'll tell you everything – all his dirty schemes, where all the bodies are buried. You can *make* him talk to you.'

'You don't need to repay me,' I said a little wearily. If I was going to break the law for Carrie, I'd do it for the right reasons, not as some slightly grubby quid pro quo in exchange for a scoop. That felt a little too close to blackmail for my taste. 'Just – just don't get us caught.'

'We won't get caught,' Carrie said jubilantly. I wished I had half her certainty. 'Okay, first' – she began ticking the items off on her fingers – 'the tickets. Obviously, I can't go by plane – the security is too tight, and the risk of being caught by the biometric scanners is too high. So, like we discussed, you'll need to cancel your flight and rebook on the Eurostar.'

'You want both of us to go on the same train? Isn't that a risk?'

Carrie shook her head.

'No, it's the opposite. You *have* to be seen boarding the train for this to work. I need your tracks to cover mine. There's a TGV from Geneva to Paris – we can catch that, and then get the Eurostar from the Gare du Nord. I don't need a reservation for the TGV; I can buy a ticket with cash at the gate.'

I nodded slowly. 'Okay. What about the Eurostar tickets? Do I reserve both at the same time? In the same carriage?'

Carrie nodded.

'I've been thinking about that, and I think you should. If they realize on the computer that you've booked twice, it'll look less suspicious if the seats are side by side – they'll just assume you needed the extra room for some reason. But here's the thing. You're not going to like this, but I think we should leave tomorrow.'

'Tomorrow?' The unease shifted again in my stomach. 'But I'm not meant to be leaving until—'

'Until Thursday,' Carrie said. She leaned forward, her long dark hair framing her face, her huge gemstone earrings dangling by sharp collarbones. 'I know. But hear me out, Lo. The press office know you're flying on to the UK on Thursday; you told them your flight times so they could book your transfers. If you make up some emergency – your mum fell, I don't know, any old BS – it's the perfect explanation for why you've changed plans. You tell them you have to leave Wednesday, and the cost of changing your flights was too expensive so you're taking the train.'

'Ugh.' I ran my hands through wet hair. The irritating thing was that Carrie was right – it was a good explanation. But I hated the feeling that she was calling the shots, the way events seemed to be spiraling out of control. 'I don't like this, Carrie – why can't you go on ahead on Wednesday by Eurostar, and I'll follow on the plane?'

'Two reasons,' Carrie said. Her expression was impatient. 'One, because, like I said, I need you with me to create a paper trail. When Marcus discovers I'm gone, he's going to turn heaven and earth upside down to figure out where I went – and if he realizes that one of his guests supposedly left twice, once on Wednesday and once on Thursday, that's going to create a giant red flag. Two, because the UK isn't part of Europe anymore. I googled and, apparently, they keep records now of how long people stay in the Schengen zone. If you turn up at the airport the day after someone with your name supposedly left the country, I think there's a good chance a big klaxon will go off. Whereas two people of the same name leaving on the same train at the same time . . . I think there's more chance they'll think that's an admin error.'

I didn't say anything. I had no idea if she was right – did they computerize those records? I had seen them scanning passports at the border, and there was a stamp in my UK passport showing my entry to Switzerland. The realization gave me another thought.

'My US passport doesn't have a stamp.'

'What?' Carrie frowned at me.

'My passport. I entered Switzerland on my British passport. But that means my US passport doesn't have an entry stamp in it. One of us is going to have to explain that at the border.'

'Fuck.' Carrie looked piqued at that. 'I had no idea they did that – I haven't travelled outside the EU since Brexit. Well, I guess . . .' She looked at me as if gauging how annoyed I was going to be. 'I guess . . . I mean, you are really you. So maybe . . .'

I sighed. The uneasy feeling was getting stronger.

'Yes, you're right, I am really me – so I should take the passport without the stamp. Bollocks. What do I say? My other passport was lost or stolen?'

'You'll be able to talk your way through,' Carrie said confidently. 'I know it. You're charming, Lo, people want to help you. And those guys on the desk – they don't give a shit. They'll just want to clear the queue.'

'I hope so. Carrie, I have a really bad feeling about this.'

'Don't. It's all going to be fine – and when we get to the UK, I'm going to treat you to the night of your life somewhere really special. I mean, it's not like your mum expects you until the next day, is it?'

I sighed again, and this time Carrie got up, dusting down her expensive silk trousers.

'Right. I'd better be getting back before Marcus notices I'm gone. Book the half-eight TGV for tomorrow. Tell Aimee in the press office that you're changing your plans and will need a different transfer.'

'What about you?'

'I'll meet you at the station. I'm not sure how, but I'll make it work. I'll hitch if I have to.' She leaned over the sink basin, peering at herself in the steamed-up mirror as if checking her immaculate hair and make-up. 'Oh, and Lo?'

'Yes?'

'Don't eat the mushrooms at dinner.' And with that remark and her wicked curving smile, she turned and left.

It was only after she'd gone that I saw what she'd really been doing at the sink. Not admiring her make-up at all – or not just that.

No. Written across the steamy mirror, in small dripping capitals, were the words STOP WORRYING.

AT DINNER THAT night, Carrie's remark about the mushrooms came back to me when the first course arrived – a thimbleful of creamy beige soup in a clear glass cup.

'*Un velouté de champignons,*' said the white-aproned waiter, setting the last one down with a little flourish. 'Velouté of mushrooms with crouton of *pain de campagne*. Made with the mushrooms foraged by your party today.' He gave a bow to Ben and me, and we exchanged a glance. Ben lifted the cup to his lips.

'Hope everyone paid attention in class or we might be about to suffer the consequences,' he said a little dryly.

'Kind of the definition of *fuck about and find out*,' said Kelly, the food influencer, with a slightly hysterical giggle. She poked Ben playfully in the arm in a way that would have had me grinding my teeth but which Ben didn't seem to mind. 'Hopefully that Gottfried bloke knows his business, right?'

'Right,' Ben said. He sipped a little nervously, then gave a shrug. 'Well, if nothing else, it tastes good. So even if we end up poisoned, we die happy.'

Kelly gave another laugh, tossed back her blonde hair, and then gulped down the little glassful like she was taking a shot of tequila.

I dipped a spoon in and tasted the creamy liquid, just a dot on the tip of my tongue. Ben was right. It was good – very good, actually. Rich, creamy, with the earthy umami punch of wild mushrooms. I had no idea if that was a good sign or not – what did false chanterelles taste like? What did real chanterelles taste like, for that matter? I couldn't remember ever having had them. And why had Carrie told me not to eat them? Was she just fucking with me? It seemed more than likely; she'd always had a strange sense of humour.

For a long moment I looked down at the soup, wondering what to do. Should I leave it? That seemed unforgivably rude, and everyone else around the room was sipping with apparent enjoyment. Gottfried's voice listing the side effects of false chanterelles came back to me: *hallucinations, paranoia, upset digestion*. Well, if the worst that could happen was a few bad dreams to add to the ones I was already having . . . I made up my mind and downed the soup, then sat back trying to act like I was unconcerned.

For the rest of the night, the table teased each other – Kelly pretending hallucinations, Ben clutching his stomach in fake digestive distress. But I was thinking more about Carrie. About why she'd dropped that last goading remark. If she'd been honestly trying to protect me, wouldn't she have said something more specific? But why deliberately mess around with me like that? She needed me on her side, for God's sake – she couldn't afford to antagonize me right now, let alone get me struck down with diarrhea on the very day I was supposed to be facilitating her escape.

But as I watched Ben dramatically clutching his stomach and moaning while Kelly laughed, I knew one thing: at the bottom of it all, in spite of my unease, in spite of everything Carrie had done to me, I didn't think she would hurt me, and not just for her own selfish reasons. Yes, she had a twisted sense of humour – and morality – but on some very basic level, I was convinced that when push came to shove, she would have my back. She always had done. Somewhere along the line, we had become a team. Reluctant. Unlikely. Often ill-tempered. But a team nonetheless. And ultimately, that was what had made me drink that soup: because I didn't think, in the end, Carrie would let me go down to dinner and poison myself. Not after all we'd been through.

WHEN THE LAST delicious course had passed my lips – a *tête de moine* cheese shaved into flowerlike petals and sprinkled with morsels of candied apple and pain d'épices, a kind of crispy gingerbread – I pretended to glance at my phone, then stood and walked over to the corner of the room as if I wanted to give whatever I was reading my full attention.

I felt Ben's eyes follow me, and I knew that I had to get this part right. It was essential that the story of my early departure made sense, and my performance had to be convincing.

For what felt like a long time but could only have been a minute or less, I stood there, my back half turned, scrolling down my phone with an anxious expression. Then I pretended to tap out a response and returned to the table.

'Everything all right?' Ben said, his voice casual. I bit my lip, trying for an expression halfway between concern and uncertainty.

'I'm not sure. My mum had a fall a few days ago and she's been kind of brushing it off, but it sounds like . . . well, it sounds like it could be more serious than she's letting on.'

'What does your stepdad say?'

'Oh.' This time the emotion was real, not feigned. I'd forgotten Ben wouldn't know about my stepdad. 'He, well, he died. A few years ago now. Heart trouble.'

'Oh, man.' Ben's face was full of contrition. 'Hey, I'm so sorry. I had no idea. I know you were close.'

'Yeah, it was pretty awful. I'm just grateful it happened before lockdown, otherwise it would have been even worse. But anyway, Mum's all alone now pretty much and I just . . . yeah, I'm a bit worried. She's not been right since her hip operation last year.'

'But you're seeing her Thursday, aren't you?'

'I'm supposed to be. But now I'm wondering whether I shouldn't fly out a day early.'

'Is everything all right?' The voice came from over my shoulder and I turned to see Pieter standing behind me. 'I'm sorry,' he said with a smile. 'I didn't mean to eavesdrop.' He pronounced it with that soft *f* sound I had noticed before: '*eefs*-drop'. 'I hope nothing is wrong?'

'It's my mum,' I said a little awkwardly. 'She's not been well and I've had a few concerning messages from her. Something's obviously happened, and she's trying to make light of it, but I'm worried. She says she's in hospital but also that it's nothing serious, which sounds like a contradiction in terms to me.'

'Pam's not what you'd call a drama queen,' Ben said. He had met my mum several times back when we were dating, and they'd always been fond of each other. 'If she broke her leg, she'd be telling you it's just a scratch, she'll be fine in the morning.'

'I think I have to go check it out,' I said as if making up my mind. 'I'm so sorry, Pieter. I was really looking forward to the pony trekking tomorrow, but I just – I'd hate myself if it turns out something bad has happened, and I spent the day taking pictures of mountains while my mum was unwell.'

'Of course,' Pieter said. He looked truly worried for me, and I felt a painful twinge of conscience that I pushed away. 'Is there anything we can do? Would you like me to see if the travel department can reroute your flights?'

Fuck. I had to shut that one down, and quick.

'No, no, honestly. I need to figure out the logistics depending on . . . um . . . ' Think. Think! A flash of inspiration came to me. 'Um, which hospital she's in and so on. It might be better for me to take the Eurostar if she's gone into UCH. The terminal is really close to the inpatient department. But I might need help rearranging my transfer. I'm so sorry for ducking out of the activities tomorrow, though – I know you were keen to show everyone the mountains.'

'Please, no apologies are needed,' Pieter said, his brow furrowed as he gazed at me with what looked like real concern. 'We only have one mother, after all. I imagine you would never be able to forgive yourself if something happened and you didn't do what you could to help.'

The emotion in his voice made me do a double take – it was almost a little too much, even for someone deliberately projecting corporate sympathy. But then I remembered the article I'd read about his own mother's death, and guilt twisted in my gut. The guilt and fear that I was faking, Pieter must have lived for real, wondering if there was anything he could have done. If he'd been enough for both his parents, would they have chosen to risk another child? And here was I playing the exact same part.

But Pieter was speaking and I dragged my attention back to him.

'Mother must come first, that's not even a question, so please put all of us at the hotel out of your mind. Perhaps you can come back another time.'

'I would love that,' I said with real gratitude. From everything Carrie had said, I didn't think Pieter knew anything about his father's ulterior motive in inviting me along. Which meant that as far as he knew, I was here on his dime, at his invitation, to help launch his new hotel brand. He'd given me a very valuable and extremely limited press place at his flagship launch, and I was pulling out halfway through. He could have been an asshole about that but was choosing not to be. 'Thank you, Pieter. Honestly, I'm so grateful for everything you and your staff have done, it's been the most magical experience.'

'And as for the transfer, please just say the word. The hotel staff can sort that, so just call reception anytime, day or night, and they can reschedule.'

'Thank you, Pieter,' I said again. I stood up, phone in hand. 'I'm honoured you invited me, and I'm so sad to be cutting out early, but I think it's the right decision. If you don't mind, I'm going to go up and try to rebook now.'

'Of course,' Pieter said. He took my hand in his, the grip soft and pliant, and I couldn't help remembering the deliberate alpha-male vice of his father's handshake the day before and contrasting the two. 'And, please, Laura, give my best wishes to your mother. I truly hope she is okay.'

'I will,' I said, pushing down that pang of guilt even further. I had to believe this. I had to make my concern for my mother real. 'Thank you, Pieter. Good night, everyone.'

'Au revoir, ma chère Laura,' Alexander said. 'Parting is such sweet sorrow, but I trust we shall meet again.'

'Good night,' Ben said. He had half risen from the table. 'But, listen, do you want me to come up with you – help you sort out the logistics?'

In an instant, I felt my expression shift from worried to irritated and strove to smooth it over, shaking my head with a gratitude I really didn't feel.

'Thanks, Ben, but honestly, no. I'm fine.' *And I do know how to cancel a flight, so stop being a creep.*

'Okay, well, anything I can do. Good night, Lo.' And then, before I could react, he bent forward and kissed my cheek, close to my mouth, his lips soft and warm and still a little damp from the coffee he had been sipping moments before.

It was all I could do not to recoil.

I knew on some level that I was being unfair. It was so close to the kiss Cole had given me the night before, a kiss I hadn't exactly welcomed but hadn't tried to prevent either, that to judge Ben by different standards felt hypocritical. But at the same time, Ben and I had a history that Cole and I didn't. And yes, if I was being brutally honest, Cole was hot and Ben . . . well, objectively I could tell that he was fairly easy on the eye, but that ship had sailed long ago as far as I was concerned. I felt no attraction to him whatsoever now.

I stood, rigid, trying not to flinch as he pressed me closer and whispered, 'Take care, okay, Blacklock? And anything you need tonight, I'm here for you. Just call.'

'Thanks,' I said thinly as he released me. 'But I'll be fine. You take care too, okay?'

Ben nodded, and I walked unsteadily across the dining room to the reception area.

I hadn't even made it to the stairs when I heard another male voice calling my name.

'Lo?'

Fuck. I couldn't take any more. Not tonight.

With a sigh that was audible to me and possibly to the other person, I turned, then softened when I saw Cole standing there.

'Hey, everything okay?' He came across to me. He had his coat on and his camera around his neck, and I guessed he'd been outside taking pictures of the lake and the stars. 'You look a bit pissed off. Did something happen?'

'Sorry,' I said wearily. 'I just . . . look, you might as well know, I've decided to leave tomorrow. My mum's not well.'

'Shit.' Cole's forehead furrowed with what seemed like real concern, and I felt the same twinge of conscience I had with Pieter and pushed it back down, this time with an irritation that made my pulse spike. Fuck this. It was a white lie to do something I needed to do. Why did I feel so bad? None of them knew Mum apart from Ben, and I certainly didn't owe *him* anything.

'It's nothing serious,' I said. 'But I wouldn't feel right about staying. I'm going to change my flights. So . . . this is probably goodbye.'

'Well, I'm sorry you're going, obviously, but you have to do what's right for your mum. Listen, though, Lo, are *you* okay?'

His question stopped me in my tracks. It was, I realized, the first time someone had asked me that in a long time, and the realization gave me a strange pain in my heart. I couldn't even remember the last time Judah had asked me that – not explicitly, though I felt his care in everything he did. But to hear those words aloud . . .

'I'm fine,' I said at last. 'But . . . thanks for asking, Cole. It means a lot.'

'Okay,' Cole said. His expression was serious. 'I'm glad you're all right. Just . . . you know. I get the impression you're one of those people who spends more time thinking about other people and I just wanted to say . . . it's great you're taking care of your mum, but don't forget to take care of yourself.'

I don't know why, but the words, or maybe the gentleness of his voice, brought a sudden tightening to my throat. I had spent so long, so many years, being the person who looked after everyone else – the boys, Judah, worrying about my mum from afar. Now Carrie. When *did* I have time to take care of myself?

I wasn't sure that I trusted myself to speak, so instead, I gave a shaky smile, trying not to let him see how his words had affected me, then made my way over to the stairs.

'Good night, Lo,' he said as I turned the corner at the landing, and I swallowed against the tightness in my throat, looking down at him, at his salt-and-pepper hair, his handsome face.

'Good night, Cole. And goodbye.'

12

As I climbed aboard my carriage on the 8:30 a.m. TGV from Geneva to Paris and walked slowly down the aisle, searching for my reserved seat, I couldn't stop glancing anxiously out of the window at the platform. I hadn't seen Carrie since she left me sitting in the bath, and now I found myself wishing we'd discussed her plan in more detail.

There was no way she could have got on the train before me – I'd been waiting on the platform before the doors opened. But now there was only a couple of minutes left until departure, and still no sign of her. Was she late? Or had something happened?

My seat was a window one, fortunately on the side next to the platform, and I slid apologetically past the Swiss businessman sitting next to me, and raised the blind and peered out, searching for anyone who might be her.

A hard frost had set in overnight, and the passengers hurrying along the windswept concrete were bundled up in coats and scarves. Their faces were difficult to make out, but I couldn't see anyone who resembled Carrie, with her designer clothes and long, immaculately cut dark hair swinging in the chilly air. An old woman hobbled past, her gait slow, and then a pair of students in their late teens or early twenties. Two men, deep in conversation. A pregnant blonde too far along for her coat to button properly. A stressed-looking mum with a little boy who kept dropping his mittens. No one who could fit Carrie's description in terms of age or sex. Fuck, where was she?

At last, the whistle blew and the doors up and down the platform began to close. I sank back into the leather seat with a feeling in my stomach that was mingled relief and dread. Relief because, well, if Carrie hadn't made the train, I'd done my part. I'd done everything I'd agreed to do, and it wasn't my fault if it hadn't worked out. But dread because if Carrie had failed, that meant she was trapped with Marcus Leidmann. Maybe forever.

Slowly, slowly, then gradually picking up speed, the train drew away from the platform, and the die was cast. There was nothing I could do except sit back and hope that somehow, wherever she was, Carrie would be okay.

For the next half hour, I tried to distract myself. I scrolled my phone, did Wordle and the *New York Times* Spelling Bee, and looked wistfully at the WhatsApp photos of the boys that Judah had sent over. We'd had a hasty conversation last night, and I'd told him about my change of plans but not the real reason. It felt like a betrayal – and it probably was. But I knew what he'd say: *Are you nuts? Don't get involved. Carrie's made her bed, let her lie in it. Risking prosecution for a woman who nearly left you to die is insane.* And the problem was, in a lot of ways, he'd be right.

It wasn't like he was impartial. Judah hated Carrie, hated her as you can only hate someone who nearly killed the person you love. But the objections that imaginary Judah put forward in our imaginary argument were also my own; the worst-case scenarios he raised inside my head were the ones I'd run through myself. If he brought them up in real life, I didn't trust myself not to cave, abandon Carrie, look out for myself. And I couldn't do that. Not just because of what it would do to me to betray my conscience but because of what it might do to my marriage. If I listened to Judah and something terrible happened to Carrie, just as she'd predicted . . . well, I wouldn't be able to live with that.

So instead, I just said that I'd decided to leave a day early to spend more time with Mum, and Judah, in the middle of bath and bedtime with the boys, hadn't questioned it. He'd simply assumed that the hotel PR trip had turned out to be more boring than I'd anticipated. I hadn't told him about Cole or Alexander either – their presence at the hotel felt like a string of coincidences that might start Judah on an uncomfortable line of questioning.

Now, sitting on board the train and scrolling through photos of the boys in the bath, laughing in front of *Bluey*, running around the park with Judah's mum, Gail, I felt a huge wash of homesickness, and some of Judah's imaginary objections lodged themselves inside my head, mingling with my own doubts. What the hell was I doing here, risking everything for someone I hadn't seen for ten years?

'Excusez-moi,' said a female voice, and I looked up. The blonde woman from the platform was standing next to the table that separated my seat from the one opposite. She was holding an overstuffed tote bag with one hand, the other was cradling her bump. Her hair was scraped back in a messy bun, and her face was puffy in a way that I vividly remembered from late-stage pregnancy. She looked hot and sweaty and really much too pregnant to be standing in the swaying aisle of a moving train. 'Désolée de vous déranger, mais cette place, est-elle libre?'

She indicated the seat opposite me, and I realized she must be asking if she could sit there. I was just marshalling my limited French to figure out how to say *Sure, go ahead*, when the Swiss businessman to my left spoke, his expression austere.

'Oui, pour le moment. Mais c'est réservé depuis Bourg en Bresse.'

He pointed to the sign above the seat, showing that it was taken farther down the line.

'Pas de problème, je comprends,' said the woman a little wearily and turned to move down the carriage. As she did so, she glanced back over her shoulder and winked at me. It was the smallest, split-second movement, but in that instant her face changed completely and I realized, to my astonishment, who she was. It was Carrie. Carrie with cotton-wool padding in her cheeks and her face made up pinker and sweatier than she had ever appeared in real life, sporting a blonde wig, a cheap coat, and a fake bump sourced from God only knew where.

Then, before I could say anything, she passed on up the train, through the sliding doors at the carriage, and disappeared.

I felt a huge smile spreading across my face, though I almost could not have told you why. It wasn't just the relief that Carrie had made the train or the cheekiness of the deception. Perhaps it was the fact that in that moment, it had felt like the woman I'd met on board the *Aurora*, the laughing, defiant, fuck-the-world Carrie in her old Pink Floyd T-shirt, was back. And that felt good.

I SPENT THE next three hours alternating between anxiously flipping through apps on my phone and staring out of the window at the countryside as it changed from the towering cloud-wreathed Alps, to the vast wheat fields of middle France, dotted with slow-moving wind turbines, and finally to the grey concrete blocks and graffitied sidings of the Paris banlieues. By the time the train drew into the Gare de Lyon in central Paris, the temporary elation I'd felt at seeing Carrie had well and truly dissipated and my nerves were back. What if I got caught? What if *Carrie* got caught? I had to keep reminding myself of what Carrie had said when she first proposed the plan – that the stakes for me were low. In the worst-case scenario, I simply claimed I'd lost my passport, that someone at the hotel must have stolen it. There was no way anyone could prove I'd let Carrie take it willingly, and I didn't think the French authorities would care enough to try.

But the worst-case scenario for Carrie was much, much more serious, and as I heaved my roller bag along the cramped aisle and down the vertiginous steel steps to the platform, I found myself looking anxiously up and down the platform, hoping she was okay.

She should have been easy to spot with her bright blonde hair and huge belly, but I couldn't see her anywhere. Again, I cursed the fact that we hadn't made a proper plan; the folly of just assuming that we'd see each other in Paris was starting to sink in. Was Carrie intending to meet me here or at the Eurostar terminal in the Gare du Nord, on the other side of Paris?

I was just on the point of giving up and walking through the ticket barriers when I felt a tap on my shoulder and whirled around to find myself face to face with . . . myself. Or almost myself. It was uncanny, and for a second, I was completely speechless.

Somehow, presumably in the train toilets, Carrie had taken off the blonde wig and cut her flowing dark hair into a close match of my much shorter hairstyle. She'd taken out the pads in her cheeks and remade up her face, toning down her Alpine winter tan to my New York pallor and swapping out the dramatic eye make-up she'd worn at the hotel for something closer to my own neutral look. Her legs, in the dark skinny jeans I favoured, were thinner than mine had ever been – it had been a long time since I'd had anything approaching that kind of thigh gap – but she was wearing two sweaters and what I assumed must be a padded bra, and from the waist up, the effect was of someone more or less my height, my weight, wearing my style of clothes . . . in short, me. She'd even somehow found a way to round her jaw into a slightly softer shape that matched mine rather than her own snatched, angular look.

'Carrie!' I didn't try to keep the shock out of my voice. 'Bloody hell, you look . . . I mean, we could be twins.'

'Shh,' she hissed sternly. 'Keep your voice down, and don't call me Carrie.' She glanced over her shoulder, and I saw her face was etched in worried lines. 'Someone might overhear.'

'What?' Her paranoia was infectious, and I found myself looking back over my own shoulder at the fast-emptying platform. 'Who would know your name here? Did you see someone on the train?'

'I don't know.' She had turned up the collar of her coat, and now she hunched down inside it, pulling me into the shadow of a tall metal pillar. 'I thought I saw . . . I mean, it could just be my imagination.'

'What? Carrie, seriously, spit it out.' My nerves from earlier were back with a vengeance.

'I saw a guy on the train.' Her voice was reluctant, but I could see the tenseness in her jaw. 'Only from a distance, though, so I'm not sure. I was about to go into the next carriage, and I saw him through the glass, so I turned back. But I thought . . . I thought for a minute it was that bastard Heinrich.'

'Heinrich?' The name was familiar but I couldn't place it. Carrie made a face.

'One of Marcus's security guys. And not my favourite. He's a nasty piece of work – one of those people who definitely know where the bodies are buried, probably because he put them there.'

'Fuck.' I remembered now – the tall man in the forest clearing, his eyes the colour of flint chips. I remembered the way he had stood, watchful, one large hand resting on something holstered at his hip. I remembered the grim expression on his face and felt uneasiness coil in the pit of my stomach. 'Did he see you?'

'I don't think he could have. I didn't even open the door – just clocked him and did a one-eighty. But if it *was* him, it means Marcus is having you followed. And that's not good.'

'No shit,' I said irritably. I felt my pulse spike, my nerves jangling. Then something occurred to me. 'Wait . . . why would Marcus have *me* followed? Are you saying he knows what's going on?'

'I don't know,' Carrie hissed. She had a hunched, hunted look about her. 'Does he know about your part in this, do you mean? I doubt it. But he'll know I'm gone by now. I tried to take as little as possible in the hopes that he wouldn't realize I'd left completely.' She gestured to the tote bag in her hand, which was, now she mentioned it, a pretty modest size for someone running away from her entire life. 'But I can't hide the fact that my room's empty.' She glanced nervously over her shoulder and then leaned forward and whispered as if afraid of being overheard, 'I think he knows there's something wrong. I mean, I've tried to keep up appearances these past few weeks, but that's why he brought you all here in the first place – because he knew I was unhappy and wanted to make it very clear that leaving him wasn't an option. I just – I don't think you understand what it's like living with someone that controlling, Lo. He knows where I am and what I'm doing pretty much twenty-four hours a day. There's not a single moment I can call my own. Me disappearing, even for an hour or two – yes, that will have set off an alarm bell. And given I don't have a car, I imagine the station is the first place he'd look. You leaving at the exact same time . . . well, that might seem like something worth checking out, even if he's not sure the dots are connected.'

'So what are you saying?' I said at last. 'If that man – what did you say his name was? Heinrich? If it *was* him on the train, then are we screwed? Should we call this off before someone arrests you at passport control?'

Carrie stepped backwards, out of the shadow of the pillar, and looked up and down the platform. There was no one there, and she seemed to relax a little. She let out a shuddering breath.

'No. No, we can't call this off. If Marcus is already suspicious, then turning back now isn't going to help that – it'll only make things worse.'

'Are you sure?' I was having unpleasant mental images of being pulled aside at customs or of a man with cold grey eyes stepping out of the queue at the Eurostar terminal and bundling me into a car. But Carrie's fears seemed to have dissipated along with the crowd of people on the platform, and now she nodded firmly.

'Yes. Yes, I'm sure. I was probably wrong. Seeing ghosts. I'm out of practice being on the run.' She gave a shaky laugh and turned to look at herself in the train window, brushed a strand of hair away from her face. 'Anyway, I can't waste this haircut, it took me long enough. Not sure this length suits me, though.'

'Sorry I didn't think to get a haircut that was more flattering to you,' I snapped. 'For some reason, I didn't have *Let Carrie impersonate you* on my bingo card for this trip.'

Carrie gave another laugh, less shaky this time. It was closer to the gurgling, throaty laugh I remembered so well.

'Look, you're a MILF. Nothing wrong with that. It's just not my style. But that's fine. The less I look like me, the better.'

'Uh . . . thanks, I guess?' I decided to change the subject. The cleaning staff were moving down the platform, ready to service the train before it departed again, and Carrie and I were starting to look distinctly odd – two eerily identical women, huddled together behind the pillar. The last thing I wanted was to be questioned by an SNCF guard. 'Look, we should get moving. Do you think we ought to split up until we get to the Eurostar?'

Carrie nodded again, this time emphatically.

'Yeah, definitely. If Marcus did have a guy on the train and he sees one of us, hopefully that won't show up on his radar. But two of us would definitely register . . . plus, you know' – she gave a shrug, a hint of the old, insouciant Carrie breaking through – 'too many blokes with twin fantasies knocking around.'

I wasn't sure about the twin fantasies, but I saw her point. Separately, we were just two dark-haired women who looked a lot alike. Together, we were memorable – and that was the last thing we should risk.

'You should take the Métro,' Carrie was saying. She'd clearly worked all this out. 'And I'll take the RER. And we should go up to passport control at different times so we don't walk through too close together. And make sure we get different desks, in case someone remembers the name.'

'How are we going to do that?' I asked. 'If we go through at different times, how will we know which desk to pick?'

'Good point,' Carrie said. 'How about I aim as far left as I can, and you aim to the right?'

'Okay,' I said, but I felt uneasy. The last time I'd been to the Gare du Nord, passport control had been mayhem – a long single queue filtering through to multiple desks with little choice over which passport control officer you saw. 'And I guess you should go through first. If there's any issues, if they have to call someone to check my identity, it's better that it happens to me.'

If I'd been expecting Carrie to protest, I'd have been disappointed. She just nodded, like it was the obvious solution to leave me facing the music instead of her.

'Well, good luck,' I said. 'See you on the train?'

'See you on the train,' Carrie said. She looked as wired and strung out as I felt, but she also looked . . . I don't know. Exhilarated almost. Like someone who'd stepped on board a roller-coaster and was terrified but also excited.

At the ticket barrier we split up, Carrie walking in the direction marked RER, and me heading for the Métro, each of us disappearing into the crowd. I was almost at the escalator when I heard a voice calling my name.

'Lo. Oi, Lo, you silly bitch!'

I turned, my heart thumping, to see Carrie running across the concourse towards me, her coat flapping in the breeze. Shit. *Shit*. Had something gone wrong already?

'What is it?' I gasped as she came closer. She was panting, shaking her head, grinning all over her face.

'I'll give you three guesses.'

I felt a wash of anger flood over me, making my already stretched nerves tingle with a different kind of stress. I wanted, suddenly and piercingly, to slap her – and I think I might have done it if I hadn't been so afraid of the scene it would cause, the eyes that would be drawn to us. How could she act like this was all just a joke? It was this kind of attitude that had got her into her first scrape – and now this one. Didn't she realize this wasn't a game? Didn't she realize we could both end up in jail – her for murder, and me for aiding and abetting?

'Carrie, I have had it with your bullshit. If you don't tell me right now, I swear to God, I'm fucking off back to England on the next plane and letting you catch the shit that's imminently about to hit the fan.'

'All right, all right. Jesus, are you on the rag?' She saw that I was about to lose it and held up both hands. 'Passport, okay?'

For a second, I didn't understand what she was on about. Passport? This whole sodding dance was about the passports.

And then it clicked. The passport. *My* passport. My UK passport. I hadn't given it to her. She would have turned up at the gate, reached into her pocket, and come up with . . . nothing.

I felt a cold chill run over me, followed by a wash of relief . . . and embarrassment.

'Shit. Oh God, I'm so sorry. I'm such an idiot.' I scrambled in my bag, hunting through the travel documents, and pulled out a little red and gold booklet, still in its EU binding.

For a moment I looked at it, this travel-worn friend that had accompanied me on trips for almost ten years, seen me travel halfway around the world and back, taken me on that fateful trip to Norway where I'd met Carrie and almost lost my life, back to England where I'd married Judah, to Sri Lanka where we honeymooned, to New York where we'd made a home and I'd had my babies, and now back here – to Switzerland, to Paris, to this final moment.

Would I ever see it again? Maybe. Carrie had said she intended to give it back to me, but I didn't really know if I believed her.

And then Carrie plucked it out of my fingers and turned on her heel, her coat fanning out.

'See you on board!' she flung over her shoulder.

Then she ran back towards the entrance to the RER and disappeared.

13

Travel is always stressful, and the Eurostar terminal at the Gare du Nord hadn't got any more organized since I'd last used it – in fact, post-Brexit, it was, if anything, even more chaotic, with multiple long queues that moved with seemingly zero logic – agents shuffling people from line to line, opening ticket gates and then closing them, cordoning off areas apparently at random, and leaving the passengers fuming and grumbling with passive-aggressive quietness under their breath in a way that you didn't have to be fluent in three languages to understand. And it didn't help that every time I saw a tall man with a blond buzz cut, my mind went straight back to Carrie's panic on the train, my pulse spiking with secondhand anxiety.

At last, though, I was through the ticket gate – the barcode worked without a hitch – and standing in the snaking line waiting for passport control. I couldn't see Carrie, but I'd hung back long enough that I was certain she must be in front of me. How far, I didn't know. Had she made it through? Or had she been quietly taken into a side room for questioning before I'd arrived? Either way, I realized that I was cutting it pretty fine. The line for border control was long, and if I wasn't through security within the next twenty minutes or so, I might miss the train.

Apparently, I wasn't the only person worried about the time. As the queue inched along I could almost feel the irritation of the passengers around me rising, along with the stress levels of the staff walking up and down the line, trying to corral people waiting for the later train into a different area.

As I got closer to the front of the queue, I found I was clutching my US passport inside my pocket, the leather cover curving in my sweaty grip, as I contemplated how best to get myself to the right-hand side of the bank of desks. There seemed to be four largish family groups in front of me, and the right-most agent, the one I'd been hoping to use, had just opened up. Unless the family who stepped forward were really quick, there was no way that border agent was going to be free in time for me, but I might manage the second-to-the-right agent if I was lucky.

The next desk free was the one on the far left – good. But then the desk second to the right opened up. I balled my fist inside my sleeve and wiped a bead of sweat off the side of my nose. Fuck. *Fuck*. This was even more stressful than normal. I had to get it together before I faced the passport desk or they'd think I was some kind of drug smuggler.

The slot in the middle opened up and I was just starting to relax when, as the family in front of me was moving forward, the right-hand agent came free, and they switched direction, heading to the far right – the desk I had agreed with Carrie I would aim for.

No, *no*.

For a second, I thought about pushing past them, but that risked attention, and that was one thing I simply couldn't afford. And I also couldn't afford to linger, pretend to drop my phone or something, because the next slot to come up was probably going to be second from the left, and that would be even worse. We'd agreed that Carrie would head left, and I would head right. Now, exactly the scenario I had feared had come true: I didn't have a choice. I was going to have to take an agent in the middle. Which should be fine – as long as Carrie hadn't been in the same predicament.

'Excuse me,' said the woman behind me with great irritation, her heavy French accent barely masking her annoyance as I dithered. 'We do not wait for our health, you know?'

'Sorry,' I muttered, and then, realizing that I had no choice, I headed reluctantly for the middle desk.

When I handed over my passport, my heart was beating fast. This was the sticking point. The point where the agent was going to look for the dated entry stamp and make a corresponding exit stamp beside it. Only there wasn't going to be an entry stamp.

As he leafed through the stiff, brand-new pages, I felt my blood pressure rising and my palms getting even slippier.

'Um, are you looking for the entry stamp?' I managed. The guy didn't speak, but I hurried on. 'Because, here's the thing, I'm actually a dual national and I entered Switzerland on my UK passport, but, um, it actually got stolen. But if you need my entry date, I can show you my flight details. I flew into Geneva earlier this week. From JFK. Here's my flight confirmation.'

I was holding up my phone, but the guy wasn't looking at the screen; he was staring with great irritation down at the page and then looking over my shoulder at the huge snaking queue. I could almost see him calculating in his head. Stick to the letter of the law and pull me aside while he referred the problem up the chain . . . or chalk me up as a clueless tourist and send me on my way?

'I'm just so thankful I had my American passport,' I babbled, trying for a little laugh. 'I'd have been really stuck otherwise, you know!'

The agent looked again at the computer screen, reading something there, and I felt nausea rise in the back of my throat. Was he looking at the passenger list and seeing another Laura Blacklock had already passed through?

I shut my eyes. I felt the sweat slide down my back, and the acid churn in my gut.

And then the agent spoke. 'Allez-y.' He was holding out my US passport, the edge poking through the narrow slot at the bottom of the safety glass. For a second, I didn't compute what he was saying, and then he repeated it in English, his expression stern, as though he was pissed off at having done me a favour. 'Go. You can go.'

'Thank you,' I gasped. I almost snatched the passport from his grasp. 'Thank you so much.'

The British border guard behind him barely looked at me, just waved me through, and I was done. I hadn't been arrested. All I had to do now was get on the train and I was in the clear. The only question was: was the same true for Carrie?

'FUCKING *LEGEND*!'

I heard Carrie's voice ringing down the carriage before I'd even located my seat, and my head came up like a dog hearing a whistle.

'Carrie?'

'We did it!' She pushed her way out of her seat into the aisle, ignoring the elderly lady trying to get past, shoved through the flow of travellers, and gripped me in a fierce hug. 'How do you feel?'

'Sweaty,' I said with a shaky laugh. 'Stressed. Please don't ever make me do that again.'

'International life of crime not for you?' Carrie said with her gurgling laugh, and I shot her a look that said *Shut the hell up*. Carrie rolled her eyes, interpreting it correctly. 'Oh, relax, no one here gives a flying fuck.'

'What if that guy you saw on the TGV is here?'

'Well, if he is, he's not in this carriage, I just walked the length of it to check. But I'm starting to think I made a mistake about it being him I saw on the train, so calm your tits.'

'Do you mind?' A woman in front of us with a toddler sitting next to her turned around, her expression irritated. 'There's kiddies here. Mind your language. Your sister' – she pointed her finger at me – 'needs to mind her mouth.'

'You can take the stick out your arse and all,' Carrie said, and the woman gave a disgusted snort and turned back in her seat, leaving me mortified and Carrie giggling like a schoolkid. I could tell that she was buzzing with the success of getting out of France – and I was beginning to relax as well. There were no passport controls at the London end; you just walked straight out of the train, and customs was pretty much a formality. As long as Carrie could keep her mouth shut until we were safely through the gates at St Pancras, that was.

Luckily, after we settled into our seats and the train picked up pace, Carrie fell asleep. I don't know how she managed it – I was still too wired from the border security to even relax, let alone snooze. Instead, as Carrie slept, her head lolling against the window and occasionally jolting a little as we went over points or round bends in the track, I stared out past her profile, trying to fathom the series of events that had brought me here, to this moment. Was I really going to take Carrie up on her offer when we got to the UK – a night of luxury in a hotel? It seemed churlish not to, in a way – she clearly wanted to thank me for my part in getting her out of Switzerland, and I couldn't turn up at my mum's a day early, not without a lot of inconvenient explanations.

Maybe I should say yes. And then, after that, I could walk away, knowing that I'd done my part – that I'd repaid any possible debt to Carrie. Once, long ago, she had given me back my freedom. Now I had done the same for her – and after this, we'd be quits.

So yes, one last night to celebrate Carrie's freedom and all we'd overcome – and then that would be it. Forever. Done. The end.

BBC SUSSEX WEBSITE
Saturday 9 November

MAN KILLED AT SUSSEX HOTEL

Police were called yesterday to the Old Manor Hotel in West Tyning, Sussex, after the death of a guest.

A source said that the man, a Belgian national in his seventies, was found dead in the bathroom of the four-star luxury hotel just after 09.00 a.m. on Friday 8 November. It is understood that the death is being treated as suspicious.

A spokesperson for Sussex Police said the man's family has been contacted and that a British woman has been arrested and is being interviewed in connection with the inquiry.

Anyone with information regarding the crime is urged to contact Sussex Police on 101 or call Crimestoppers on 0800 555 111.

PART
THREE

PART THREE

14

'Wow.' We were walking down a long stone-flagged pathway between two lines of . . . I wasn't sure what kind of trees. Silver birches, maybe. Their slender trunks glimmered in the moonlight and in the golden glow coming from the house up ahead. At the base of each tree was a box-hedge topiary cut into severe perfection – cones, prisms, orbs, a few shapes I couldn't make out in the dim light. The effect was spare, ethereal, and stunningly beautiful.

Up ahead I could see the hotel – the Old Manor. It was a handsome stone building that had clearly been some kind of historic country house seat back in the day when people could afford servants and stables and sprawling lands. We were only an hour by train from London, outside a village I'd never heard of called West Tyning, but it felt like we were a million miles away. Somewhere in the trees above us, an owl hooted, and I let out a little gasp of delight.

'Pretty sweet, isn't it,' Carrie said, grinning. 'I stayed here once with Richard.'

Richard Bullmer. The owner of the *Aurora*. Even just hearing the name was like a splash of cold water on the back of my neck, and I was surprised Carrie could say it so casually. Perhaps she saw something in my face because she gave me one of her mocking grins.

'Oh, relax. He can't hurt either of us anymore.'

I didn't say anything. I hoped she was right, but the same couldn't be said of Marcus Leidmann.

We were halfway up the path when there was a slight noise, like someone stepping on a twig, but softer, and Carrie's tote bag fell to the ground, sending clothes and make-up scattering across the flagstones.

'Fuck,' Carrie said. She had dropped to her knees and was picking up her belongings. I saw a pink and green mascara roll to a stop in a flower bed and felt my stomach turn.

'What happened? Did the strap break?'

'I think so.' Carrie was examining the bag. 'No, it's the buckle. Fucking piece of designer shit. This cost almost three thousand euros; you'd think it'd last more than six months. Never mind, we're almost there.'

She heaved the bag back into her arms, holding it like a baby, and together we were about to ascend the worn stone steps that led up to a studded oak front door when she paused.

'Listen, I'll pay for everything, but you should check in alone. If they want my ID, it's going to get awkward. I'll just hang back, okay?'

'Okay,' I said. It did make sense, but I was still a little surprised that when we went inside, Carrie walked straight through and up the stairs as if she were already staying at the hotel. I, meanwhile, paused, getting my bearings.

The entrance hall was a luxurious lounge, complete with heavy oak beams and a massive inglenook fireplace with a carved surround. There were stone flags on the floor, Persian rugs, and a roaring log fire with tapestry armchairs dotted about the hearth in companionable little groups. In the corner by the fire, two elderly men were playing backgammon and sipping from matching brandy snifters. The whole atmosphere was completely different to the high ceilings and enormous light-filled windows of the Grand Hotel du

Lac, and yet I had the same impression I had noticed there: money. Money and a level of luxury that wasn't just about the staff and the surroundings but extended right down to the scent of woodsmoke and beeswax polish and the quiet contentment of the guests. The room was appointed with every luxury you could imagine, from the soft glow of candles on the mantelpiece to the tantalus of crystal decanters by the door – apparently free for guests to help themselves. The one thing I couldn't see was anything as crass and commercial as a reception desk.

I was just wondering where to go when a man's voice spoke from behind me.

'Are you checking in, madam?'

I swung around. A man in his sixties, wearing a tartan waistcoat and sporting an enormous white handlebar moustache, was standing there.

'Oh, hello, yes, I am. I have a reservation.'

'What name, may I ask?'

I opened my mouth to reply, then realized I didn't know. Fuck. What name would Carrie have put on the reservation? Surely not her own. Mine, maybe?

'Laura Blacklock?' I said, trying to sound more confident than I felt.

Apparently, that was the right answer, because the man opened a door in the panelling behind him and disappeared, then reappeared, smiling, with a paper form and a key card in a little envelope.

'Welcome to the Old Manor, Ms Blacklock. My name is Cavendish. We have you in Lark, a delightful junior suite on the second floor, one of our most charming and historic rooms. May I take your case?'

'Oh – um . . . sure.' I looked around for Carrie, but there was no sign of her. Was this guy going to show me up to the room? How would we find each other?

Since Cavendish had the key, I had no choice but to follow him up the creaking oak staircase, two flights that led to a long corridor punctuated by heavy doors of varying ages. The house seemed to have been extensively modified, a mix of Victorian, Georgian, and some much older features – probably Tudor – but it had been sympathetically done, and all the parts melded together into one luxurious whole.

Cavendish walked me down the long passage to a dark oak door that was plainly several centuries old, tapped the key card on an incongruously modern card-reader, and showed me into a room that was ... well, it was stunning – there was no other word for it. Huge oak four-poster in the centre, leaded windows that presumably overlooked the park, crackling fire in the fireplace ... even a small turret that seemed to house the bathroom.

Cavendish set my case on the luggage stand with a reverence it really didn't deserve and then sashayed about the room, showing me all the features that I, or rather Carrie, was paying for.

'Is there anything else I can assist you with, Ms Blacklock?' he asked as the tour came to an end.

I shook my head, realizing as I did that I had no cash and couldn't tip him – I could only hope that here in the UK, he wouldn't expect it.

'Thank you so much, but no, you've been super-kind.'

'Then I will leave you. Oh, may I ask, will you be dining with us?'

The question stopped me in my tracks. Would I? Could Carrie leave the room? I wasn't sure. 'I – I don't actually know. Do you have room service? I may be too tired.'

'We do; the menu is on the desk. If you would like to make a restaurant reservation, please call down to the front desk as soon as possible. I believe we do have space, but we always recommend reserving a table.'

'Of course,' I said, and Cavendish bowed and then disappeared, closing the door softly behind him.

When he'd gone, I strolled across to the enormous four-poster and clambered up, feeling like a child compared to its immense size. There, I stretched out on the embroidered counterpane, staring at the canopy above and wondering how much all this was costing Carrie.

I was still lying there, almost mesmerized by the tapestry pattern of the tester, when there was a knock at the door – an odd knock, almost like a signal, three sharp raps, a pause, and a final loud rap. I jumped up and ran over to open it. Outside was Carrie, holding her bag in her arms, and grinning like a cat that's got the cream.

'Ta-da! What do you reckon?'

'Pretty bloody lush.'

'I know, right? I asked for this room on the reservation form – it's one of the nicest. Did you try the cookies?'

'There are cookies?'

'Yes! And they're delicious.' She threw her bag on the floor next to the luggage stand, then stalked across to the cabinet that hid the coffee and tea paraphernalia, and dug inside what I hoped was a faux Ming vase but could have been real for all I knew. She drew out two crisp cookies, handed me one, and stuffed the other in her mouth. 'Mmm,' she said through a mouthful of crumbs. 'Stem ginger, fucking delicious. I'm starving.'

'Oh, that reminds me,' I said, remembering. 'The guy from the front desk, he said we'd need to reserve a table if we wanted to eat in the restaurant. I wasn't sure what you wanted to do – can you eat in public?'

'Well, I'm not planning to starve,' Carrie said. She flung herself down on the bed in a posture eerily similar to mine just a few minutes ago. 'But, yeah, we'd better pretend I'm not staying here. I'll put on the blonde wig and go out the fire escape, then come round to the front door. How's that?'

'Do you really think that will work?' I said doubtfully. Carrie rolled her eyes, and I remembered, suddenly, piercingly, that this was a woman who had spent almost a year pretending to be someone she wasn't, someone of an entirely different nationality to boot. Persuading a few hotel employees that she was no one in particular was probably neither here nor there.

Some two hours later, I was sitting alone at my reserved table in the restaurant nervously nibbling at the olives the waiter had left and sipping at an extremely strong martini when a deferential voice spoke over my shoulder.

'Ms Blacklock, your guest is here.'

I looked up to see a tall blonde woman standing behind him – and did a double take. It was Carrie, and she was wearing the wig she'd used for the pregnant woman on board the train, but she had styled it completely differently from earlier that day. Instead of a frazzled low bun scraped hastily back with a crocodile clip, the long tresses curled around her shoulders in shining golden waves, and her face had been made up to highlight her laughing dark eyes and sharp cheekbones. She was wearing a black wrap dress that was devastatingly simple but which even I could tell must have cost well north of a thousand dollars, a riviera of what I suspected were probably real sapphires, and a gigantic ring, and she looked like a movie star. If she was trying to be unmemorable, she was failing miserably.

'I'm so sorry I'm late, Lo, darling,' she said, and her voice was a flawless Californian drawl. 'The traffic was a bitch.'

'Um . . . ' I found myself wondering what to call her. *Carrie* would be monumentally stupid. 'No problem.'

'May I offer you a drink, Ms. . . .'

'Mrs Darnwell,' Carrie said to the waiter with a curving smile. 'But you can call me Angela. And the answer is yes, we'll have a bottle of champagne and two glasses.'

When the bottle arrived, she pushed my martini glass to one side and watched as the sommelier filled up both our flutes to the foaming brim. As the froth subsided, she picked hers up.

'Well, darling . . . here's to escape.'

'To escape,' I said. A laugh bubbled up inside me, an irrepressible, absurd, almost hysterical laugh that encompassed . . . I don't know. Relief? Maybe. But also a kind of joy at the sheer ridiculous daring of what Carrie and I had just accomplished. Against all the odds, she had done it – *we* had done it. Whisked her out from under the nose of one of the most powerful men in Europe and away to a new life. And now, my slate was clean, my debt was paid, and after one glorious celebratory night, I was going back to my real life, and I would never ever put myself through something like this again.

For this one night, though, I was going to enjoy myself.

I shook my hair over my shoulders, sat up straighter, and held out my glass to Carrie's. We locked eyes, and our glasses chinked.

Then Carrie put hers to her lips, and, her eyes on mine, chugged it back, one gulp after another, the muscles in her slim throat working as she swallowed.

When the glass was empty she slammed it down on the table, threw back her head, and laughed.

'Well, darling, here's to you. The best friend I ever had. The woman I quite literally died for. The absolutely fucking brilliant Lo Blacklock.'

The absolutely fucking brilliant Lo Blacklock. I liked the sound of that. I felt my lips curve in a smile I couldn't quite repress.

'To me,' I said. And I raised my glass to my own lips and drank. The champagne hit me as it always does, hard, with a kind of shivering exhilaration running down my back and up my spine, leaving me with the strange feeling of weightlessness. It was only as I put the glass down that I reflected on her words. Was I *really* the best friend she'd ever had? We'd spent maybe ten, at most twenty hours together – and that was counting the time Carrie had been asleep on the Eurostar. There was something a little sad in the idea that, even with such a flimsy foundation, I might still be the person she could rely on most in the world.

But Carrie didn't seem to be dwelling on her words. She had picked up her menu and was gazing down at the embossed pages with the expression of someone who intended to enjoy herself.

'Now, what are we going to *eat*?' she demanded. And I settled down to enjoy the meal.

15

When I woke the next day, the sun was streaming through the narrow crack between the thick William Morris curtains, and Carrie was flaked out beside me with her dark hair straggling over the pillow and her arms flung out like a small child.

My phone said the time was 9:35 a.m., which meant if I wanted to fit breakfast in before I left for the train station, I needed to get moving.

'Carrie,' I whispered. 'Carrie, are you awake?'

'I am now.' She spoke into the pillow, then sat up, raking the hair off her face. She hadn't taken off her make-up properly last night and those dramatic dark eyes were halfway down her cheeks. 'What time is it?'

'Nine thirty. I'm going to head down for breakfast. Are you coming?'

'God, no.' Carrie groaned. 'I'm still full from last night. I haven't eaten like that since . . . well, before I met Marcus. Actually, that fancy meal I was telling you about at the Cheval Blanc was probably the last time I ate as much as I wanted.'

'How come?' I asked curiously. I felt completely normal myself, even rather peckish, in spite of matching Carrie pretty much bite for bite, though not sip for sip. I was beginning to realize that my alcohol tolerance, never that high, had gone down the swanny since having kids.

'Oh, well.' Carrie stretched and yawned. 'You know. Marcus. He didn't like fat women.'

'I'm sorry, *what*?' I sat up properly. 'What kind of bullshit is that?'

Carrie shrugged. 'Yeah, I know. But there you go. Apparently, Pieter's mother had, quote-unquote, *let herself go* after Pieter was born. If I ever had the temerity to take a second piece of bread, I'd get the silent treatment and pointed remarks about unattractive women.'

'Wow.' I swung my legs over the edge of the bed and tried to process that. 'I mean, just . . . *wow*.'

'Right? It's not like he was such a picture with his clothes off.' She stretched again. 'But anyway, to answer your question, no, I don't want breakfast, but given we're supposed to be pretending I'm not here, it might look weird anyway. I think they'd smell a rat if your dinner guest turned up for a full English.'

I nodded. She had a point.

'I might have a bath instead,' Carrie said, yawning so wide I could see her back teeth. 'Do you mind?'

'Of course not. Do you want me to bring you anything? I could smuggle you up a croissant or something.'

Carrie shrugged. 'I mean, if there's some lying around, but I'll be quite happy with coffee.'

I nodded and then, as she disappeared into the bathroom, I began to get dressed, running thoughtfully over the plan for the day. Somehow – I still wasn't completely sure how – I had to get back to the train station, then catch a train to London and a connection to my mum's place near St Albans. I hadn't given her an ETA, but she thought I was coming from Switzerland, so she wouldn't be expecting me until mid-afternoon at the earliest.

My one regret was that I still hadn't managed to speak to the boys. I'd tried to call after dinner last night, but Judah's phone had gone to voicemail, which wasn't that surprising, given that when I checked the time, I realized the kids must be at their karate class. Instead, I'd sent a snap of the room and a message saying I was safe in the UK but off to bed and that I'd phone the next day. The problem was, it was currently nearly 4 a.m. there. Definitely not the moment for a chat. Maybe I could call from the train.

Sighing, I shoved my phone into my pocket and let myself out, along the thickly carpeted corridor and down the creaky oak stairs to the lounge I'd entered last night. From there I followed my nose towards the smell of bacon.

Breakfast was being served in a beautiful airy room overlooking the sprawling grounds – a glassed-in enclosure that managed to feel almost like it was part of the formal gardens but without the damp and cold that November in the UK inevitably entailed.

I was shown to my table, offered tea, coffee, and a newspaper of my choice, and then when my server had disappeared to fetch my flat white, I sidled up to the big trestle in the centre of the room and appraised what was available.

As far as hotel breakfasts went, this was no ordinary buffet of limp bacon and soggy tomatoes. Instead, there were bowls of thick Greek yogurt scattered with nuggets of homemade granola, little pots of macerated berries dripping with ruby juice, and a huge honeycomb propped in a frame with a little pearl-handled knife to cut off chunks. There were crumbling pastries, and jugs of freshly squeezed juices, a tureen of softly soaked Bircher muesli, and a huge pat of golden French butter studded with salt crystals. I felt my mouth watering at the sight of it. How could Carrie pass this up?

I returned to my table with a laden plate and the guilty knowledge that I'd taken far too much – and yet was almost certainly about to order something off the hot-food menu too. Probably the glistening, golden scrambled eggs I'd just seen go past.

I was just settling down to fork some mint-marinated strawberries into my mouth and do the *Guardian* crossword when my phone rang.

Frowning, my heart quickening a little, I put down my fork and dug in first the pocket of my jeans, then my cardigan, unable to remember where I'd put it. There were disapproving looks coming from all around the breakfast room, and I stood up, made an apologetic face to the other diners, and hastened out of the room – nearly careering into a waitress carrying a full English breakfast.

In the corridor outside the dining room, out of earshot of the other diners, I finally located the phone and then stood there, staring stupidly at the caller ID. I'd been hoping it was Judah – and fearing it was Carrie. She'd bought a cheap mobile phone from a little shop outside the Eurostar terminal. But it wasn't either. It was my mum. And she was calling from her mobile phone.

For a second, I just gaped at that one word – *Mum* – wondering what was important enough for her to make an international phone call on her mobile, something she didn't do in a hurry.

'Lo?' My mother's voice sounded . . . odd. A little quavery, and there was a lot of background noise. Was she out somewhere public? It would explain why she hadn't used the landline. 'Oh, Lo, love, thank goodness. I was just wondering whether to leave a message or call back.'

'Hey, Mum, is everything okay?'

'No, not really.' Her voice was . . . I don't know. Panicked almost? 'Oh Lord, where to start. This is probably costing me a fortune.'

'Mum, Mum, slow down. If you're worried about the money, I can call you back. Do you want me to do that?'

'No, no, I'll get on with it. Oh, Lo, it's terribly annoying, but I've had a fall.'

My blood seemed to run completely cold – it's a cliché, but that's the only way to describe it, the chilly prickle of shock that radiated out from my heart at her words. It wasn't just that I was upset about the fall – of course I was. But it was the fact that it was so close to the lie I'd made up as an excuse for changing my plans. Like it was almost *my* fault.

'Shit, Mum, when? What happened?'

'Just now. I was in the supermarket and I had a funny turn and ended up on my back somehow. I don't know if I slipped or what, but the manager insisted on calling an ambulance. I was phoning to let you know in case I'm not back home by this afternoon. You don't have a key, do you?'

Shit. Shit. *A funny turn.* What did that mean? Heart? Stroke?

'What do you mean, a funny turn?' I tried to keep the panic out of my voice, but I knew it was seeping in. 'And where are you?'

'I told you, I'm in the supermarket. I'm fine, but I wanted to let you know in case—'

'I'll come now. If I get a train—' I looked at the clock on my phone. It was gone ten. I had no idea whether there was a direct service from West Tyning to St Albans but I doubted it. Could I get a train to London and then change? And where would Mum end up? St Albans had an urgent care centre, but the nearest big hospital was probably Watford, or maybe Stevenage, depending on traffic. But Mum was squawking into the receiver, and I put the phone back to my ear.

'Goodness' sakes, no! That's why I was ringing.' She certainly didn't *sound* like she'd had a stroke. 'To say don't come for the moment. You won't be able to get into the house, so you might as well stay put until I know what's happening.'

'Mum, don't be silly.' I felt an impatient note in my voice rise and tried to push it back down, but honestly, my mum was impossible. Over the past few years her independent streak had turned into a stubborn refusal to admit that she was aging and might sometimes need help. 'Of course I'm coming, you need someone with you.'

'Laura Blacklock.' My mum's voice had taken on a stern, slightly indignant tone. 'I will not have you calling your mother silly.'

'I'm sorry, I didn't mean – but look, Mum, you've had a fall. It could be serious.'

'I know that, you wally! That's why I let them call an ambulance. If it ever turns up.' In a way, the fact that she had switched from disconsolate flapping to telling me off was a good sign. It was very much her comfort zone.

'*Wally*? Now who's hurling insults?' I retorted, then caught myself and forced a more conciliatory tone into my voice. 'Look, Mum, I'm sorry, I know it probably feels like I'm overreacting, but a fall at your age—'

'At my age!' my mother scoffed. 'I'm hardly in the grave yet, Lo. They'll probably just scan me and send me home. Now, look, I have to go, but I'll call you when I know more.'

'I just – okay.' I knew when I had lost an argument with my mother, and she certainly didn't sound like someone on her last legs. 'Just – please, keep me posted.'

'All right.' Her voice softened. 'I'm sorry this had to happen now, love. I know you were looking forward to coming home, and I didn't mean to spoil your visit.'

My throat was suddenly thick with tears and I swallowed, then spoke, my voice a little rougher than usual.

'Mum, don't be silly. It's fine. Now, go. Take care of yourself. And let me know what they say when you get to the hospital, okay?'

'Okay, love. Bye.'

And then she hung up and I was left staring down at the phone like it was the last link of a chain joining the two of us together – the last link of a chain that had just snapped.

The news seemed to have killed my appetite, and suddenly I didn't really fancy scrambled eggs anymore. Instead, I downed the last of my coffee, wrapped a miniature pain au chocolat and a tiny croissant in a napkin, slid them into my pocket, and walked slowly back up the stairs to our room.

Carrie was clearly just out of the bath when I entered, towelling her dark hair in front of the mirror. She looked up as I closed the door and raised one eyebrow.

'Everything okay? You look like the cat just got your canary. Don't tell me breakfast was shit, because I won't believe you.'

'No, breakfast was amazing.' I dug in my pocket and held out the croissants. 'I got these for you. No, it's just . . . well, I heard from my mum. She's had a fall. In the supermarket. She called it a *funny turn*.'

'Shit.' Carrie swung around from the mirror to look at me. 'You're kidding. What horrible luck!'

'I know. It feels almost like I made it happen, lying to everyone about her.'

'Don't be stupid!' Carrie said. She walked over to me and put her hand on my arm. 'You didn't make it happen. If you could make stuff happen by thinking about it, half the people I know would have been dead from cancer years ago.'

I let out a shocked laugh, but Carrie's words, though unsettlingly blunt, weren't untrue. And in my heart I knew it – I didn't really believe in karma, not the instant kind that would punish my mum because I'd told a fairly innocent fib. But it was still unnerving, and I couldn't shake a sense of guilt about it.

'She's being taken off to hospital, so I can't go anywhere until I know what's happening. I guess what I'm saying is, do you mind if I hang around for a bit? Or were you checking out too?'

'Oh.' Carrie turned back to the mirror. Her expression was . . . it was hard to say. She looked a little put out. Disconcerted, perhaps. 'Yeah, of course. No, actually I was going to stay another night until I figure out what I'm doing. Being back in the UK . . . well, it's screwing up my head more than I thought it would, if I'm being honest. I know I should check out, particularly at these prices, and go home, but I'm just – I'm not ready. Know what I mean? I feel like I need to decompress or something.'

'I get it,' I said. It had been strange for me too, walking through St Pancras, listening to all the English accents after so many years of American ones. Hearing people talk about *lifts* and *luggage trolleys* and *mobile phones*. And the constant, constant apologies, even when there was nothing to apologize for. I'd nearly laughed on the escalator when I'd accidentally whacked someone with my roller bag trying to get by him, and he'd said, reflexively, 'Sorry,' and moved to the right to let me pass. In New York he'd have been more likely to call me an asshole.

But Carrie had been abroad even longer than I had – and her homecoming would be far stranger and more bittersweet. Would she even be able to go home? I wasn't sure. She was still a wanted person, after all. Her parents' house might be under surveillance – if she had parents. Her family was a topic we'd never discussed. Did they even know she was alive?

'Well, look,' I said, a little awkwardly. 'I mean, hopefully she'll phone in the next few hours and let me know where they've sent her, but I don't want to get in your hair in the meantime, so I might go for a walk – blow away some cobwebs. There's no point sitting here waiting for the phone to ring. Do you want to come?'

Carrie smiled but shook her head. 'I'm fine. I'll stay here, if that's okay with you. I've got some stuff to work out. But you go.'

I nodded. Then I picked up my coat, shoved my feet into my sturdiest pair of shoes, and headed out.

THE COUNTRYSIDE AROUND the Old Manor was spectacular, and I walked farther than I'd meant. It was only when my stomach began to gripe with hunger that I looked at my phone and realized two things: one, it was getting on for three o'clock, and I'd completely forgotten to have any lunch. And two, my mum still hadn't phoned.

The route back to the hotel led through the village of West Tyning, and I could see, just a few metres farther down the high street, a tea shop with a sign that read HOMEMADE CAKES, SAUSAGE ROLLS, PASTIES.

Sausage rolls. There was something so extremely English about those two simple words side by side that I felt my heart clutch with a kind of homesickness. Not a pig in a blanket or a hot dog, but a true English sausage roll. Suddenly there was nothing I wanted more than crunchy, buttery pastry, salty sausage meat, a hint of pepper and spice . . . I hurried down the road and let myself into the tearoom.

As I waited for my order – a hot sausage roll and a cup of tea – I tried my mum's phone, but it went straight through to voicemail. I tapped out a WhatsApp.

Hey, Mum. How's it going? Have you been seen? What did the doctor say? Please let me know as soon as you know anything. I'm in London – not quite true, but close enough – *but I can be with you in a couple of hours if you tell me where you end up. Lo xx*

I pressed send and waited to see if the familiar *Mum is typing . . .* message popped up in response, but nothing happened, so I shut the app down and ate my sausage roll.

SHE HADN'T REPLIED by the time I got back to the hotel, and as I stepped under the stone porch, kicking the mud off my shoes on the grated doormat, I tried her again. Still no reply, and it was almost five – surely she'd have been seen by now. Had she let her phone run out of charge? I tried her landline on the off chance that she'd been sent home and hadn't bothered to tell me, but that just rang without answer.

I was about to send her a slightly terser chase when a noise from across the field in front of the hotel made me stop and turn. It was the sound of helicopter blades.

For a minute I stood there, shading my eyes as I looked up at the distant silhouette. I couldn't help thinking about how much Teddy and Eli would have enjoyed this – Teddy in particular was obsessed with anything that flew. *Cop-cop* had been his second word, after *Mumma* and before *Dada*, and both boys were fascinated by the private helicopters that ferried wealthy New Yorkers between Manhattan and their houses in the Hamptons. Seeing one here, though, in the English countryside was a little incongruous – and what was even stranger was that it was coming closer, hovering . . . Was it possible that it belonged to a guest at the hotel?

Staff were coming out from side entrances, and from over my shoulder I saw Cavendish appear in the main doorway.

'Is it landing?' I called, though the question was almost redundant, shouted as it was above the roar of the rotor blades. Cavendish nodded.

'I believe so. That field is officially a helipad, and we have the occasional guest who arrives by helicopter. I always enjoy the spectacle myself. They're rather majestic things, aren't they?'

I wasn't sure that *majestic* was the word I would have chosen, but it was undeniably impressive. I watched the huge machine lower itself into the field, the wind from the rotors stripping the last autumn leaves from the trees scattered around, and found myself wondering who would travel in such an ostentatious way. A celebrity, perhaps? It didn't feel impossible – the hotel had a calm understated luxury that I could imagine appealing to an A-lister.

As the blades finally touched down and the rotors slowed to a halt, I waited, telling myself that I wasn't just gawping – I was a reporter, and this was professional curiosity.

But the person who stepped out of helicopter and began walking slowly across the grass was not a celebrity.

It was, in fact, someone totally, heart-stoppingly unexpected.

For a long moment I stood, frozen, as the figure, with his little entourage, drew closer. My phone was hanging limp in my hand, and I stared stupidly as I willed myself to have made a mistake – for my eyes to be playing tricks on me.

It was only when the figure reached the gate to the car park that something inside me unlocked – releasing whatever had kept me rooted to the spot.

Ignoring the remaining mud on my shoes, ignoring Cavendish asking me if he could assist with anything, I turned and pushed past him into the entrance hall. And I ran. Across the lounge and up the first flight of oak stairs, praying all the time that he hadn't seen me.

There was no reason to think he had. I'd been far away, sheltered by the porch, and he had barely even looked in my direction. But I didn't feel safe, even after I'd run up both flights of stairs to the second floor, and down the long corridor to my room.

I didn't feel safe as I swiped the keycard shakily against the door lock, ignoring the Do Not Disturb sign, hissing Carrie's name as loudly as I dared.

And I didn't feel safe as the door opened then slammed shut behind me and I rested my back against it, my chest heaving and my heart hammering, as Carrie demanded to know what was going on.

The man getting out of the helicopter was the last person I'd expected to see, the last person I wanted to see.

It was Marcus Leidmann.

16

'Marcus?' Carrie stared at me blankly. '*Fuck*. But how? Are you sure it was him?'

'One thousand per cent. It was him, and two other people I couldn't make out, but I think they were Pieter and that LeBlanc woman.' My hands were shaking. 'You must have been right about it being Heinrich on the TGV. He *was* following us.'

'Ugh.' Carrie was pacing the room now, up and down, up and down. I'd expected her to be more jittery, but she was focused, her expression a kind of rigid calm. I could practically see her brain ticking, trying to work out what this meant. 'But I'm as certain as I can be that Heinrich *didn't* see me. Which means this is probably just a fishing expedition on Marcus's part – he can't possibly be sure I'm here.'

'Well, sure or not, he's downstairs. How the hell did he find us?'

'Oh, Lo.' Carrie gave me a world-weary look. 'When you've got the kind of money Marcus has, that kind of thing is child's play. He probably put two and two together about the fact that I disappeared around the same time you did, pulled some strings to find out where you were, and flew in to check the situation out. I mean, that was the whole point of this – that your tracks would cover mine. I always thought he'd find your paper trail. I just didn't expect him to do it quite so quickly.'

'So . . . what do we do? We should go, right?' I looked at my phone. It was gone five. 'Leave while we still can?'

'I don't know.' Carrie had reached the right-hand side of the room and turned on her heel to pace the other way. 'That's what I meant about him not being sure whether I'm here. I booked for two nights, so if we abandon the booking halfway through, I feel like that's basically telling Marcus that his suspicions are correct.'

'Are you saying you think we should *stay*?' I was taken aback. 'What about my mum?'

Carrie shrugged.

'You can go if you want – maybe he'll follow you. But, yeah . . . I think as far as I'm concerned, that's exactly what I'm saying. I'm not moving – I can't afford to, not while he's watching the exits.'

'Fuck.' I sat down on the bed. The more I thought about it, the more Carrie's logic made sense. Marcus *must* be following my tracks, not hers. Carrie had done nothing in her own name since leaving Switzerland. Which meant that bolting halfway through the reservation would be the worst thing the two of us could do. It would basically confirm his suspicions. On the other hand, staying put while Marcus prowled around downstairs and my mum languished in some hospital bed god only knew where . . .

'Look,' Carrie said as if making up her mind. 'You should go see your mum – of course you should. But I'm not going anywhere until he leaves. He doesn't own this place. He can't demand entry into any of the guest suites, and he won't call the police unless he's absolutely sure of himself. He wouldn't risk the scandal. Which means as long as I stay in this room and don't do anything to tip him off, I'm safe. But I'm not leaving. He could have someone stationed out front for all I know.'

'So you're going to hunker down until he gives up?' I asked. Carrie nodded, her expression bitter.

'I think I have to. He can't stay here forever. Maybe if you go to your mum's, he'll follow you.'

Setting aside the fact that I had no idea if she was home yet, the thought of using my frail, elderly mother as bait to draw Marcus away from Carrie was not an enticing one, but I didn't say that.

'If I check out, what happens to you? They'll clear the room.'

'I don't know,' Carrie said wearily. She sat down on the bench seat at the foot of the bed, her shoulders slumped. She looked worn out, and I couldn't blame her. She'd been so close, so tantalizingly close to freedom. And now this. 'Maybe just . . . don't check out? If you just walk out the front door with a swagger, I doubt anyone will stop you. But I dragged you into this – I realize that. So I'm not going to tell you what you should do. You have to do right by you and your mum. Stay, go – it's your decision. But I'm sticking here, at least for tonight. I can't afford to do anything else.'

'Okay,' I said slowly. 'Look . . . okay, just let me think about this—'

I knew my brain wasn't working at full speed. Everything was moving too fast. I had the sensation of being caught up in a current of someone else's machinations, the way I had on the *Aurora*. The idea of staying put wasn't attractive – but neither was the idea of a vengeful Marcus Leidmann rocking up at my mother's house, even supposing I could get in there tonight. She *still* hadn't replied to my texts, and the fact that I had no idea how she was doing or even which hospital she was in was starting to drive me more than a little crazy. One of the things I admired about my mum was that she was so independent – she had never pleaded with me to stay in the UK or made me feel guilty about raising her grandchildren so far from home. After my stepfather's death, Judah had tentatively floated the idea of bringing her out to live with us for a while, but she had firmly shot down the suggestion with a snappy remark about having a life of her own. But this refusal to admit that she needed any help at all was beginning to feel frustrating.

'Look,' I said at last. 'Let me phone my mum and see if she's got any news. We can take it from there.'

Carrie nodded, and I walked over to the window and dialled my mum's number again, looking out over the gardens, all muted blues and greys in the wintry twilight.

Her phone rang for a long time, and I was almost on the point of giving up when she picked it up and said in a hushed voice, 'What is it?'

'Mum, it's me, Lo.'

'I know who it is.' She was whispering. 'What is it?'

'Mum, why are you whispering?'

'You're not supposed to have mobile phones in hospital. Because of the heart monitors.'

'What? Mum, I don't think that's been a thing for, like, twenty years or something. Seriously, stop whispering. No one's going to mind you talking to your daughter. Where are you? Are you in A&E? Have you been seen?'

'I've been seen, but they're waiting on imaging. There's something wrong with my ankle but they're not sure if it's a fracture or just a sprain. The doctor said something about admitting me if it is a fracture, but it might not be here, they don't have a free orthopedic bed.'

'Shit.' I rubbed my face. 'Okay, where are they taking you? Which hospital?'

'I don't know yet, it might—' She stopped as if distracted by something at the other end of the phone, then said hurriedly, 'Sorry, love, I have to go, the doctor's coming.'

Before I could protest, there was a click, and the line went dead.

I sighed, feeling that familiar mix of love and irritation rising inside me, then I shut down my phone and put it away.

'Well, I have no idea what's going on with my mum, but it doesn't look like I can do anything for the moment. So I think the best thing is if I stay here and make myself as visible as possible – make it crystal clear that I'm not you, and he's barking up the wrong tree.'

'Okay,' Carrie said slowly. 'So, what, you go down to dinner by yourself and if you see him . . .'

'I guess I say hello?' The thought made my insides curdle with dread, but it would be too out of character to do anything else. There was no world in which I, a journalist who'd been chasing Marcus Leidmann for weeks for an interview, would ignore him when he turned up at the dinner table next to mine.

'I think you have to,' Carrie agreed, but her expression was worried. 'Just, Lo, be really, *really* careful. He's very intelligent. And he's very, very good at getting information out of people.'

'I'll be careful,' I said. I wished, though, even as I said the words, that I didn't have to be. I had thought we were home and dry. That was turning out to be very, very wrong.

17

'Is it . . . ' The voice that came from behind me was not the one I'd been dreading to hear all evening as I fought my way through five courses of food that was beautifully prepared and should have been totally delicious but which I was too sick with stress to enjoy. 'It is surely . . . Miss Blacklock, no?'

I turned around, already frowning with puzzlement – but even before my gaze had travelled up the long dark-suited body to the smiling face above me, I'd realized.

It was not Marcus Leidmann but his son, Pieter.

I felt my stomach crunch with nervous anticipation. Okay, this was it. Showtime.

'Mr Leidmann.' I stood, with some difficulty as my chair was caught on an edge of parquet and refused to budge at first, then screeched unappealingly across the wooden floor. 'Gosh, wow – what are you doing here? Scouting for Journeys?'

'Oh, please, call me Pieter,' he said, then made a funny finger-to-his-lips gesture, dipping his head, for all the world like a shy schoolboy. 'And as for the rest, yes, I suppose you could call this a spot of industrial espionage, so I am keeping my head down. But what a coincidence. Is this where your mother lives?'

'Well . . . ' I'd had time to think out this cover story in the bath, and now it reeled off my tongue fairly fluently. 'Actually, no, she lives in St Albans, but she's been transferred to a specialist unit near here. It wasn't very practical for me to keep shuttling back and forth from her house, so I thought I'd treat myself to a hotel.'

In point of fact, I'd googled, and the only hospital near the Old Manor was a burns unit – but I just had to hope that Pieter wouldn't know that or would be too tactful to ask why someone who had tripped and fallen needed skin grafts. It was just plausible that she could have been carrying a kettle, I supposed.

'I am so sorry,' Pieter said. He had pulled out a chair, and now he sat opposite me, his expression looking genuinely concerned. 'I have been thinking of you both. I hope she is doing okay?'

'Yeah, she's doing a lot better.' I pushed down the wave of guilt that came over me at the thought that I actually had no idea how she was doing or even where she was. I'd tried her again before dinner, and her phone had gone straight to voicemail, but that didn't mean much. My mother was of the generation that kept their mobiles switched off to save the battery. 'She's hoping to be transferred somewhere closer to home shortly. Then I'll be able to stay at her house.'

'Well, my sincere sympathies,' Pieter said, and he did look sympathetic. 'Can I ask, I hope it's not an intrusion, but . . . are you travelling alone?'

I felt myself stiffen. This was it – the question I'd been dreading.

I thought I'd covered my reaction fairly well, but perhaps Pieter had sensed some kind of recoil on my part because he hastened on.

'I only ask because I wondered whether you would like to join my father and me for dinner.' He indicated a table on the other side of the restaurant, and I turned to see Marcus, sitting quite alone, his back to the rest of the room. As I looked across at him, at his ramrod-straight spine and side-swept white hair, I found myself wondering what had happened to Adeline LeBlanc. And Heinrich, if it really had been him on the train. Perhaps, as members of staff, they didn't merit a seat in the restaurant. But Pieter was still speaking. 'I hate to think of you worrying about your mother alone. But perhaps . . . ' Was it my imagination or was there the smallest interrogative pause, dragging the question out with a sceptical intonation? 'Perhaps you're travelling with your family . . . or a friend?'

'No,' I said at last. My heart was thumping in my chest. I kept my voice very level, but to my ears least, it sounded pleasant and reasonably unruffled. 'No, I'm travelling alone. And thank you so much, that's an incredibly kind offer, but I'm actually just finishing up.' That part was true, thank God, and I could gesture to the coffee cup sitting on the table in front of me alongside an untouched plate of petits fours as proof. 'What about you, are you staying for long? It must be hard to tear yourself away from the Hotel du Lac.'

'Well, the grand press opening went very well.' Pieter had folded his arms, and I could feel him appraising me in turn. 'But now that is done and dusted, I think, to be honest, the staff would like me out of their hair so they can prepare the hotel for the first members of the public. As for how long I'm staying . . . it depends on a few factors.'

My heart was still beating uncomfortably hard, and I took a sip of coffee to cover it. I had to act at all costs like someone who had no idea why Pieter and his father were here. It was my only chance to protect Carrie. And I had a horrible feeling that I wasn't being very convincing. Instead of answering, I just kept gulping the coffee until the little cup was drained. Then I stood up. Pieter followed suit, and I realized for the first time how tall he was. Standing so close together, the top of my head was barely level with his chest, and I had to crick my head back uncomfortably to look at him as I picked up my bag.

'Well, it was lovely to see you again, Pieter. Perhaps we'll run across each other before I leave, but if not, I hope you have a great time in the UK, and, well, thanks again for the hospitality in Switzerland. It was a truly wonderful trip – and I'll send your PR teams copies of any pieces I'm able to place.'

'Thank you so much,' Pieter said. 'Though I must stress, this isn't a transactional thing for us – it is much more about building relationships that we hope will sustain Journeys into the future.'

'I think that's a great way to look at it.' I picked up my phone from where I'd left it, beside the petits fours. I had been going to take the plate up to Carrie, but I couldn't exactly do that now. 'Good night, Pieter.'

'Good night . . . Laura? If I may?' His smile as he asked the question seemed genuine this time – and it transformed his slightly weak face into something charming, much more charming in its own way than his father's chiselled determination. I wondered if he got that from his mother and realized, with a slight pang, that my earlier searches had thrown up not a single photograph of her.

'Please, call me Lo,' I said. Maybe I had been wronging him with my suspicion about his questions earlier. Maybe he knew nothing about any of this and had just come along for the ride with his father. Maybe he was just a nice guy asking nice questions to someone on her own who might want company. 'Take care, Pieter.'

And then I walked away, feeling his eyes on my back as I crossed the dining room and went up the stairs.

UP IN OUR room, Carrie pounced as soon as I opened the door.

'Was he there?'

'Marcus? Yes, he was there,' I said wearily. 'Along with Pieter.' I pulled a rolled-up napkin out of my clutch and unfurled it on the desk, revealing three slices of sourdough bread and a selection of cheeses. 'Are you hungry? I'm sorry I couldn't get you anything better. I asked for extra bread twice but after that I thought they'd smell a rat.'

'It's fine,' Carrie said impatiently. 'I had a big room-service lunch earlier. I'm not hungry.' She tightened the belt of the towelling bathrobe she was wearing. Her expression was a mix of anxiety and irritation, and I got the impression she had probably been pacing up here all evening, working herself up. 'Did you talk to him? Did he seem suspicious?'

'I talked to Pieter. As for being suspicious . . . ' I tried to think back, to that pause when Pieter had asked whether I was travelling alone. It had felt pointed at the time, pointed enough that my heart had started racing. Now I wasn't so sure. 'I don't know. He asked a few questions that seemed like they could be leading somewhere, questions about my mum and whether I was travelling alone. But he could have just been being nice.'

'He actually is pretty nice,' Carrie said, a little grudgingly. 'I've got to know him fairly well over the years, and aside from worshipping his piece-of-shit father in a frankly unhealthy way, he's a good bloke.'

'Pieter *worships* Marcus?' I don't know why, but her words surprised me. 'Really? I got the impression their relationship was a bit more lukewarm than that.' It was true I hadn't seen the two of them together very much, but I was thinking back to the newspaper article, the hint of blame, even disdain, I'd read between the lines. And I was thinking too of the way Marcus had talked about his son. It didn't feel like there was much warmth in either direction. Carrie shrugged.

'Look, it's tough growing up the son of one of Europe's richest men. I don't think Pieter would be human if he wasn't a bit starstruck by his dad. Does he want his dad's approval? Abso-fucking-lutely. Does he like him on a personal level?' She gave another shrug, this one slightly more dubious. 'I'd say the jury's out on that one. He certainly has no illusions about the fact that Marcus is capable of being entirely ruthless. Anyone who's seen him in action in the boardroom could tell you that.'

'And does he know about you?' I asked curiously. 'About you and Marcus, I mean. Do you think he knows that you're trying to get out?'

'Who knows. I mean, I think he knows that I've got something to hide. He must have realized it's pretty weird not to have a passport or bank cards in your own name. And I think he probably knows there's something not right between me and Marcus – you don't have to be Freud to tell that we're not happy. But I don't think he knows the extent of it. It's not the sort of thing you bring up over breakfast: *Hey, did I mention that I still have PTSD from some of the stuff your dad made me do?*' She threw herself backwards onto the bed, running her hands through her hair in exasperation. 'Fuuuuck. Why couldn't they just stay in Switzerland? Am I ever going to be free of that fucking coffin dodger?'

'Carrie.' I knew it wasn't my business, but I couldn't stop myself asking. 'Carrie, what *are* you going to do? I mean, assuming Marcus goes away tomorrow. You're never going to be able to resurface – you know that, right? You're condemning yourself to a life on the run, working under the table. Wouldn't it be better just to—'

'No,' Carrie said, her voice vehement. 'Lo, I know what you're going to say, and I'm not doing it. I'm not turning myself in. I've spent ten years imprisoned by that man. I'm not going to spend another ten in Belmarsh. I'll make this work – I have to.'

'I just—'

'Lo.' Carrie sat up in bed, glaring at me. 'Lo, will you just kindly shut the fuck up? You've done your bit getting me here and I'm very grateful, really, I am. But the rest is for me to solve so just—' She waved a hand, weary, impatient. 'Just let me fucking solve it, okay?'

'Okay,' I said.

'Okay,' Carrie said. She flopped back down, pulled the cover

over herself, then turned out her side light. 'Thank you. And good night.'

'Good night,' I said. 'Sleep well.'

But I knew I wouldn't.

18

I woke early the next day, my stomach heavy with dread, and it took me a moment to figure out where I was and the reason for the queasiness stirring in my gut. I was back in England, but not at home. My mum was presumably still in hospital – though, frankly, who knew – and I was staying in the Old Manor. Carrie was in bed beside me, and Marcus Leidmann was somewhere in the hotel and likely on both our trails.

I also felt bone-tired, probably because I had barely slept. I had confused memories of tossing and turning, unable to fall asleep, and, when I finally did drift off, of waking several times for water, stumbling to the loo, and tripping over one of Carrie's shoes. But maybe all that was a blessing. It hadn't given me time to dream, which was what I'd been dreading.

There was nothing on my phone from my mum, so I spent a few minutes updating Judah on the situation with my mum, then tapped out a text to her: *Mum, did you get my message yesterday? Where are you? Which hospital did you end up at? PLEASE CALL ME.*

I waited a few moments to see if the message status changed to *read* (it didn't), then sighed, shut down the app, and pulled myself up against the pillows.

As I did, I saw that Carrie was already awake. She had turned onto her back and was staring grimly up at the canopy of the four-poster.

'How long have you been awake?' I blurted out.

'About two hours.' Her voice was flat, with none of the thickness of someone who's just woken up. 'I didn't get much sleep. Listen, I've been thinking. We should split up.'

'Yeah?' I felt a rush of shame at the relief her words brought me. She was right, but that wasn't why I felt so thankful to hear her say it. 'Are you sure?'

'Yeah, I'm sure. If Marcus is tracking you, then we're safer apart than together.'

I nodded, hoping that my feelings didn't show on my face. I felt like a weasel for my eagerness to abandon Carrie, but the last thing I had ever wanted was to be caught up in this situation. Carrie had saved my life, but that didn't mean that I wanted any part of her chaotic, desperate existence, stumbling from one nightmare to another.

'You're probably right,' I said, trying to sound confident. 'With any luck, he'll follow me, see that we're not together, and give up the trail. So what do you think we should do?'

'I think you should check out, like a normal guest, and I'll . . . I don't know. I'll put my blonde wig on and dress up as a maid or something. I'll figure it out.'

'Okay . . . ' I said slowly. 'So . . . do you want to leave now? Or after breakfast?'

'After breakfast, I think, don't you?' She looked over at her burner phone, charging on the bedside table; it read 8:15 a.m. 'It'll look pretty weird to check out now.'

'Okay,' I said again. 'So I'll go down and show my face and you . . . you'll pack and whatever?'

'Yeah. Oh, and don't forget to put the Do Not Disturb out when you go, okay? Don't want the maid stumbling in.'

I nodded and swung my legs out of bed, feeling better by the moment.

Now that the plan was made, my instinct was to get on with it – get out of here and leave Carrie, and Marcus, and the Old Manor far behind. My mother still wasn't returning my calls, but if I had to, I'd get in a taxi and go round every hospital in Hertfordshire until I tracked her down.

I showered and dressed in record time, and ten minutes later, my hair still damp and dripping down my back, I was walking briskly down the corridor to breakfast.

The buffet spread was just as delicious as the morning before, but my appetite was well and truly shot, and it wasn't much of a sacrifice to wrap up some pastries in a napkin for Carrie instead of eating them myself. I got up, drained my cappuccino, and began to make my way back up the stairs with a lightness in my step that hadn't been there since I'd knocked on the door to suite 11 what felt like a lifetime ago. As I turned the corner of the first landing, I looked at my phone. It was 8:47. According to Trainline, there was a train for London that left at 9:45, and according to Google Maps, the station was a ten-minute taxi ride away. In an hour – maybe less – I would be out of this whole tangled web, and Carrie ... well, Carrie would just have to figure things out for herself. I had done all I could.

I was just turning off the second landing when one of the dark oak doors in front of me opened, and I heard someone speaking in what sounded to my uneducated ear like German but could have been Dutch. The speaker, a man, waited for a reply, then said something else in which I heard the words *room service* in accented English. Then he stepped out into the corridor, shutting the door behind him, and my heart leaped into my mouth.

It was Pieter Leidmann.

For a moment he just stood there, blocking the narrow corridor, and his face looked as surprised as mine. Then he gave a little laugh.

'Miss Blacklock! We must stop meeting like this. Are you going down to breakfast?'

'I'm just coming back, actually,' I said.

'And so we miss each other again. I am just going down. I was calling in on my father to ask if he wanted anything.'

'He isn't joining you?'

Pieter shook his head. 'He almost always takes breakfast in his room. First a bath, then coffee. Two eggs. Orange juice. Always the same thing. He's a man of habit – and not really a morning person. I was just asking him if he wanted it sent up, but he said he'd call down to room service himself.'

'Gotcha,' I said, and smiled. Then I looked covertly at my phone – the time was now 8:49 – and said a little awkwardly, 'Well, I should probably . . .'

'Oh, of course!' Pieter seemed suddenly to realize that he was blocking the corridor and stood aside. 'Good day, Lo. I hope to see you later?'

'I hope so too,' I said. But of course it was a lie. I hoped to be in a taxi to the train station before he'd finished breakfast – and never to see him again.

BACK IN OUR room, Carrie was in the bath, something I only realized when I barrelled in to brush my teeth and found her washing her hair, the handheld shower wand poised in her hand.

'Fuck! Sorry, sorry.' I shut the door and heard Carrie's laughter from the other side.

'Where did you think I'd gone?' Her voice was muffled by the closed door. 'Hiding under the bed?'

'I don't know! I didn't think. Next time, lock it!'

There was a snort from the other side of the door, and I heard the shower wand start running again and turned away to pack.

I was almost finished, searching around for my charging cables and wireless headphones, when a sound from the corridor outside made me pause. It had sounded like . . . I don't know. A scream. A woman's voice, high and panicked. I couldn't make out the words, but it sounded like someone calling for help.

Fuck. Surely nothing else could go wrong this trip? It was 9:17. It was getting quite tight for me to make my train, particularly as I still hadn't ordered a taxi. But the thought of some woman in another room being attacked or suffering a cardiac arrest while I packed my bags and ignored her cries for help . . .

Well, there was another train at 10:45 if worst came to worst.

Sighing, I put down the cable I'd been coiling up, picked up the key card, and stepped out into the hallway. I could hear a woman sobbing hysterically, but it was coming from further up the corridor, towards the landing. As I walked towards the sound, I could tell I wasn't the only person puzzled. A head stuck out of one door as I passed, a woman who'd apparently been in the middle of getting dressed, and went hastily back in when she saw I was handling the situation. An elderly man was peering out of another room.

But as I got closer, I began to feel more and more worried. It was fast becoming clear that the cries were coming from the room I had passed earlier that morning. Marcus Leidmann's room.

'Oh my God, somebody, please help!' I heard. I had a sudden extremely unpleasant flashback to the hotel room in Geneva – the tripod standing in the dark, angled at the bed, the sense of sinking dread I had felt at the realization of what it must mean. But this was broad daylight with people coming and going right outside – surely Marcus wouldn't be stupid enough to do anything like that here?

As I got closer, I saw that the door was just slightly ajar; the security latch had been flipped across, preventing it from closing.

'Hello?' I called. 'Who is this? Is everything okay?'

'No!' The suite was actually two separate rooms, a sitting room to the left and what must presumably be a bedroom to the right. The cry came from the direction of the bedroom, a woman's voice, shaking with what sounded like panic. 'No, it's not okay.'

I pushed open the bedroom door – but there was no one there. Just a large, beautifully appointed room, the bed freshly made. There was a door opposite me, open just a crack.

'Hello?' I called again, puzzled now. 'Hello?'

'I'm in the bathroom. There's a guest – he's had some kind of – oh God!'

She broke off, and I heard a slow splashing sound, as if something very large and heavy had fallen into water. In that instant, I realized two things. The first was that there was water oozing slowly out from beneath the bathroom door, soaking into the beige carpet and turning it a dark, soggy brown.

And the second was that I'd left my mobile phone back in my room.

For a moment I simply stood there, dithering. My instinct was to run away, back to the room, and dial 999. But something else – partly my own common sense telling me I needed to see what had happened in order to inform the emergency services, but partly another instinct, something darker, a kind of morbid curiosity – *something* was telling me to push open that door.

With a queasy dread churning in my stomach, I walked quickly across the expanse of beige carpet, past the four-poster bed, and pushed at the bathroom door. It swung inwards. And I saw.

In the centre of the bathroom was the maid's cart – and crouching over the still-running bath was one of the hotel cleaners. She was bending down, her arms outstretched, vainly trying to hold the naked body of Marcus Leidmann up out of the water.

She turned to me, her eyes wide, her expression desperate.

'Oh, thank God! I thought no one would come. I tried to get him out to give him CPR, but he keeps sliding under the water.'

I opened my mouth – and realized there was nothing I could say. Instead, I stumbled more than walked across the water-soaked bathroom floor, turned off the tap, and leaned past her to grab Marcus's other arm.

I had thought that getting him out of the bath would not be too difficult, but as I grabbed his arm and began to pull, I realized that had been extremely naive. He was immensely heavy, much heavier than he looked, and the tub was a huge, deep one with high sides. It was clear that we were not going to be able to get him out without help. More worryingly, he wasn't moving, not even twitching, as I might have expected if he'd had a heart attack or a seizure. His flesh was bluish, his lips were grey, his eyes were staring sightlessly, and there was pinkish foam and water flowing from his slackly open mouth.

'Try again,' I said to the cleaner. 'On three. One, two—'

'What the hell is going on?'

The voice came from behind us, and both the housekeeper I jumped convulsively. She swung round, letting her grip on Marcus go, and without her help to bear the weight, I couldn't hold my awkward grasp any longer. He slithered out of my hands, sliding back beneath the surface of the brimming tub – and I turned to see Pieter Leidmann standing in the open door of the bathroom. He was staring past me at the overflowing bath, his face as white as if he'd seen a ghost.

'My God, what is happening?'

He shoved past me, pushed the cleaner aside, and grabbed his father's arm.

'Papa? Papa?' Then, over his shoulder to the cleaner and me: 'For God's sake, help me get him out!'

The woman nodded, and together they began pulling at the naked body, trying to heave Marcus up and over the side of the bath.

There was no room for me, and for a moment I only stood, staring in horrified silence, as they finally wrestled the limp, bluish body up and over the side of the tub in a tidal wave of bathwater. Then Pieter Leidmann turned and spat at me over his shoulder, 'What are you doing? Why aren't you phoning anyone? Go! Get help!'

'I'm sorry.' I gasped. 'I – I'm going now. I'll call an ambulance.'

Then I turned on my heel and ran out of the suite, down the corridor, back towards my phone. But as I ran, I knew one thing for sure: Marcus Leidmann was beyond anyone's help. He was dead.

19

'Fuck.' Carrie was pacing up and down the little room. 'Fuck. *Fuck.* What do we do?'

The ambulance had come – and the police. And then, after the first officer at the scene figured out exactly who Marcus Leidmann was, a whole lot more police. Patrol car after patrol car after patrol car, until the driveway in front of the hotel was swarming with them. This, clearly, was what happened when someone important died.

Adeline LeBlanc had turned up from wherever in the hotel she had been staying, white and shaken, along with Marcus Leidmann's personal security guard, who looked distinctly worried – as well he might, considering his client had died on his watch.

Now Marcus's body had been taken away, Pieter Leidmann was presumably being interviewed, and I had been told in no uncertain terms not to go anywhere.

'I think there's only one thing we *can* do,' I said to Carrie. My nerves were jangling, the muscles in my jaw and neck were taut as wires, and I kept having to resist the urge to bite my nails. 'Sit tight and hope to hell the police don't realize you're here. I mean, they have no reason to search my room. As far as the hotel knows, I'm travelling solo. I just have to tell the truth about what I saw and let the police do their job.'

'But, Lo,' Carrie burst out, 'he's fucking dead! Don't you get it? If he's been killed, *I'm* the person with the biggest motive in all this. I'm suspect number sodding one in every single way.'

I felt the muscles at the back of my neck tense even further, and I forced myself to unclench my teeth.

'Okay, first of all, that's a big *if*. He could have had a heart attack, for all we know. And second of all, no, you're not.' I was surprised at the rush of protective anger I felt at Carrie's words, almost as if someone really were accusing her. 'You have absolutely no motive to kill him – in fact, it would be the stupidest thing you could do. Literally his only hold over you was his threat to turn you in to the police, and you'd just negated that by getting away from him. So why would you do anything to draw police attention? You're not named in his will; you have nothing to gain financially from his death. If anyone stands to gain from this, it's Pieter.'

'Wait, you can't be serious.' Carrie was staring at me. 'Pieter? But he loved Marcus. Do you honestly think it was him?'

'Honestly? I have no idea. Truly, no idea. But I do know it wasn't you.'

The problem was, Carrie was right. She *was* suspect number one – or, rather, she would be if the police ever figured out she was here. And I'd have been lying if I said the idea hadn't occurred to me as I stood there in front of Marcus Leidmann's dead body: *Did Carrie do this?*

But I'd spent every moment since returning to the room going over the confused back-and-forth I'd overheard between the police officer at the scene, the cleaner, and the hotel employee who'd turned up with Marcus's room-service order as they tried to piece together the timeline of Marcus's death. It had only been fragments, and I'd been trying to explain my own movements to a different officer in the adjoining room. But one thing I was certain of: the room-service girl had said repeatedly that Marcus had called down to order breakfast at 9:05, a few minutes after I'd seen Pieter talking to him at the bedroom door. She'd said it twice, brandishing the tray she was holding and the receipt on it.

Which meant that Marcus Leidmann must have been killed some time after that point. And from 8:55 right up until the discovery of the body, Carrie had been in the bathroom washing her hair next to where I was packing my clothes. No matter what, no matter how desperately she might have wanted Marcus Leidmann dead, she could not have killed him. *I* was her alibi – I had been standing outside the door myself; I'd even seen her in the bath. Which meant that out of all the people in the hotel, there were two I knew for certain were innocent: Carrie and myself. I just had to hope that the police believed that fact.

For the rest – who could say. There could have been any number of people in the hotel with motives for killing Marcus Leidmann, starting with his own son. Maybe Adeline LeBlanc too, for all I knew – I had no illusions that Marcus would be an easy man to work for, and I'd encountered enough predatory men to know that once they acquired a taste for exploitation, they rarely stopped at one pretty young woman. Hell, even Heinrich could have been involved. He was, after all, the one person with the strength to hold Marcus down under the water. I had no way of knowing. All I could do was stick to my story and hope to God the truth came out somehow.

For the moment, I was hanging all my hopes on Carrie's *if*. *If* he'd been killed. We didn't know for sure it was murder; it could have been a heart attack or a stroke. Or maybe he'd fallen over as he got into the bath, slipped under the water, and drowned. The possibilities were endless – and most of them were perfectly innocent. And I was hanging on to that thought as hard as I could.

I was just opening my mouth to say all this to Carrie when there came a knock at the door. My own heart sped up uncomfortably fast, and Carrie looked panicked. She pointed at the bathroom door as if to say, *Should I?*

I nodded vigorously and called, 'Just a second,' to the person outside the door. I watched as Carrie tiptoed across the bedroom and shut the bathroom door behind herself with infinite caution, though there was no way the person outside could have heard the *click,* still less realized what it meant. Then I took a deep breath and opened the door to the corridor.

Standing outside were a man and a woman, both looking slightly grim. Neither was in uniform, but they had an indefinable air of belonging to the police, and I wasn't surprised when the man pulled out a police warrant card.

'Good morning, Miss . . . ' He consulted a notebook, then frowned at me. 'Miss Blacklock, is that right?'

I nodded. 'Yes, I'm Laura Blacklock. Did you want to speak to me about Mr Leidmann?'

'If you don't mind. My name is Detective Sergeant Dickers' – he held out the warrant card, angling it so I could see the photo and verify his identity – 'and this is my colleague DC Wright.' He indicated the woman standing beside him, who put up a hand in greeting. 'I know you spoke briefly to one of my colleagues at the scene, but we'd like to take a formal statement from you, if that's all right. Would you like to do it here or downstairs? The manager's offered us a room.'

'Um, perhaps downstairs?' I said. If I were Carrie, I wouldn't relish being trapped inside the bathroom for however long the interview took, and there was always the unpleasant possibility that one of the officers might ask to use the toilet.

The male officer nodded and turned to go, but the female officer, DC Wright, put out a hand.

'Just one moment, Ms Blacklock – were those the clothes you were wearing at the scene?'

'The clothes?' I looked down at myself, then realized what she meant: were these the clothes I had wrestled Marcus out of the tub in. 'Oh, no, I changed.' It had been one of the first things I'd done, a mix of practicality – my clothes were pretty wet – combined with a kind of indefinable queasiness about having a dead man's touch all over me. 'They're in my suitcase. Do you want them?'

'Yes, please,' DC Wright said, and I went and grabbed the soggy little pile from my case, thanking my lucky stars I hadn't left the garments in the bathroom. DC Wright let me drop the pieces into individual plastic evidence bags, sealing each one as I handed them over.

'That's it?' she said, as I gave her the last bag. 'No jewellery, no wedding ring or wristwatch, anything like that?'

I shook my head. I hadn't worn a watch since school.

'I don't have one.'

Wright nodded, turned for the door, and I followed the pair of them out of the room, shutting the door firmly behind me. The Do Not Disturb sign clacked against the wood as I did and I hoped that Carrie had heard the conversation and would know she was no longer trapped – at least for the moment.

Downstairs, in a pleasant little study overlooking the gardens, DS Dickers reopened his notebook and cleared his throat.

'Right, well, thanks for speaking to us, Miss Blacklock. I understand this morning's events can't have been easy. If you could just take me through your movements, that would be great. We're just trying to build up a clear picture of what happened.'

'Of course,' I said. My heart was thumping uncomfortably hard in my chest, and I found myself praying I wasn't going to have a panic attack. It was a long time since I'd had a full-blown one – the last had been in the dark postnatal days after Eli's birth, before my anxiety meds had been adjusted. My current cocktail had seen me through Teddy's birth and all of COVID, and I'd remembered to take my dose before breakfast, but the pills weren't bulletproof.

Still, if being interviewed by the police about a sudden death wasn't cause for anxiety, nothing was.

'Um, well, I woke up around . . . ' Fuck, when had I woken up? I remembered Carrie checking her phone on the bedside table. 'Around eight fifteen, I think . . . and I went down to breakfast shortly after. I guess I got down there at about . . . eight twenty-five, maybe? I ate pretty quick – I was supposed to be checking out today, and I wanted to catch a train.'

The officer made a sympathetic face indicative of the fact that he knew I wouldn't be leaving anytime soon now and appreciated the inconvenience this was causing me.

'Um, then I went back up to my room. I got up to the landing at eight forty-seven – I remember that specifically because I was hoping to catch a train at nine forty-five and I remember thinking I had just under an hour to pack and check out.' My heart rate was settling a little. These were questions I could handle.

'And you said to my colleague that that was when you met Pieter Leidmann?' DS Dickers asked. I nodded.

'Yes, I met him coming out of his father's room. He'd been asking his father if he wanted any breakfast sent up.'

'And you heard the conversation?'

'Well, I mean, I heard them talking, but it was in Dutch or whatever it is they speak in Belgium. Flemish. I don't speak it, so I don't know what they actually said, but Pieter explained that his father always had breakfast sent up and he'd been asking him if he wanted him—' I stopped, realizing that my phrasing was becoming close to nonsensical. 'If his dad wanted Pieter, I mean, to order. But his father said no, thanks, apparently.'

The officer nodded.

'Gotcha. And then Pieter headed down to breakfast?'

'Yes, and I went back to my room. I got there . . . it must have been about eight fifty?'

'Eight fifty-one, according to the key-card data,' the female officer, DC Wright, said casually, and I felt a little prickle of shock run through me. Of course it made sense – but it somehow hadn't occurred to me that the hotel would have a record of every swipe of every door, and the realization sent a shiver running down my spine as I tried to figure out what, if anything, this information meant. Would the system know if the door was opened from the inside? Would they have a record of every time Carrie had let me into the room? Did that matter? Either way, the thought made me feel a bit sick, and I had to force myself back on track as I realized the police officers were waiting for the next step of the story.

'Um . . . so, um. Oh God, sorry, this is so weird.' I knew I was babbling. 'Right. I guess it must have been around quarter past nine, I heard a noise coming from the corridor. It sounded like a woman calling for help. I thought maybe she was ill or something.'

'Okay,' DS Dickers said encouragingly.

'And I, um, I followed the noise down the corridor and realized it was coming from Mr Leidmann's room. So I went in—'

'It wasn't locked?' DC Wright put in, and I shook my head.

'No.' I tried to cast my mind back, picturing the door, my hand pushing it open. 'No, it had been propped open with the security bolt – I guess it must have been housekeeping. They'd obviously come in to service the room.'

'No problem, carry on. What did you see when you got inside?'

'Well, nothing, really. No signs of a struggle or anything like that. I just followed the sounds through the bedroom. I think I called out and asked what was wrong, and a woman – I didn't get her name, but she's a hotel employee – she shouted back something about coming quickly.'

'And how would you describe the scene when you entered? What did you see?'

'I saw a woman in a housekeeper's uniform leaning over the bath and trying to keep Marcus Leidmann's head above water – I think the tap was still going, but there was water everywhere. I mean, really everywhere – it was all over the floor, seeping under the door.'

'And what did you do? Was it you who turned off the tap?'

'I think so.' I tried to remember. 'Yes, that was me. There didn't seem much point in leaving it going. And then, well, I tried to help the cleaner – help get him out of the bath, I mean. But we couldn't – he was too heavy. We were still trying when Pieter came in. I think he said something like "What's going on?" And then he said, "Go. Go and get help." Something like that. I'd left my phone in my room, so I ran back there and called 999.'

'Gotcha,' DS Dickers said again. He tapped his pen on the notepad. 'Just out of curiosity, you didn't think to call when you first got on the scene?'

'I did, but I didn't have my phone. And it seemed more urgent to get him out of the bath. I thought we might be able to save him – I didn't know he was dead until, well, until after.'

'And you didn't think to use the hotel phone?' Wright asked. 'The one in the room?'

For a second I couldn't recall – why had I run back to my own room? Then I remembered.

'It wasn't there. The room phone, I mean. It was one of those cordless ones, and the cradle was beside the bed, but the phone wasn't on it. I didn't bother hunting, I just went for my mobile. It seemed like the quickest option at the time.'

'Fair enough,' DC Wright said with a smile. 'Probably faster in the end, as you say.'

'Well, that's it, really,' I said. I was feeling a lot calmer now. The questions had been straightforward – a little picky, perhaps, particularly about the phone, but nothing I couldn't handle, and the officers seemed kind. The realization made me bold enough to ask a question of my own. 'Listen, I hope you don't mind me asking but . . . you seem like you're taking this pretty seriously. Is that just routine or do you think . . . ' I tried to come up with a euphemistic way of asking the question, but there didn't seem to be one. 'Do you think there was something wrong about Mr Leidmann's death? I mean—' I hurried on, aware that I was talking too much but somehow unable to stop myself. 'Isn't it possible that he just had a heart attack or something? Or is this just precautionary because of who he was?'

The officers looked at each other as if telepathically communicating about how much information to give out, and then DC Wright looked back at me and spoke.

'Well, I can't say too much about the investigation at the moment, but I can confirm we're treating the matter as a suspicious death at this stage.'

I felt the wind go out of me, like someone had punched me in the stomach, and suddenly the butterflies were back. It was exactly what I hadn't wanted to hear. This was a murder investigation. And Carrie and I were right in the middle of it.

'Just one more question,' DS Dickers said rather casually as I was trying to process the information DC Wright had just conveyed. I looked up at him. He was frowning a little, but he didn't look concerned. 'Just now, you mentioned *who he was* . . . am I right in thinking you and Mr Leidmann knew each other before this trip?'

Oh, fuck. I felt my heart speed up, not just back to how it had been when I sat down but faster even that that – uncomfortably, sickeningly fast. *Please don't have a panic attack, please don't have a panic attack . . .*

He had phrased it casually, almost like the question had only occurred to him because of what I'd just said, but I had a horrible feeling that this last-minute ambush, Columbo-style, had been quite deliberate. Either way, there was no point in lying about this. If they hadn't spoken to Pieter Leidmann yet, they certainly would soon. And he had no reason not to tell them the truth.

'We did,' I said at last, trying to keep my voice as steady as possible. 'I mean – well, *knew* each other is probably a bit of an overstatement, but I knew who he was, and yes, we'd met. I'm a travel journalist and a few weeks ago, he sent me an invitation to the opening of one of his hotels in Switzerland. I'd been hoping to get an interview with him, but it didn't really happen.'

'Huh,' DS Dickers said. He gave a little laugh, not unpleasantly, more in a kind of funny-old-world type way. 'And now you're both here at the same hotel in the UK. Was that intentional?'

'Oh God, no!' I gave a laugh that sounded slightly shaky to my own ears. 'No, total coincidence and a complete shock. Well, except that I suppose I cover the same kind of high-end travel sector he was trying to expand into, so I guess in a sense it shouldn't have been *that* shocking. I mean, we were all here for professional reasons, and high-end travel is a pretty small world.' I knew I was talking too much again. 'I believe Pieter was here on . . . I think he called it a spot of industrial espionage.'

'So you're here for work?' DC Wright asked quizzically. I felt my stomach shift and my cheeks heat a little. *This* was why I never told lies. I was unbelievably bad at it.

'Not work, exactly, I mean, I'm not being paid to stay here,' I said uncomfortably. 'It's more . . . well, it was a mix of convenience and professional curiosity on my part. I was supposed to be visiting my mum, but she's had to go into hospital, and I thought I'd treat myself. And like I say, I'm a travel journalist' – that was stretching it these days, but never mind – 'so I try to stay in interesting places. And I'd been told this place was quite interesting. I think Pieter booked it for the same reasons.'

'It's certainly pretty flash,' DC Wright said. She gave a laugh, showing her teeth. 'Wish my salary ran to hotels like this! My style's more package holiday on the Costa del Sol. Well, thanks so much, Ms Blacklock. You've been really helpful.'

'No problem,' I said, standing up. I could feel my top sticking to the back of my spine with sweat, and I hoped I hadn't left a mark on the seat. I held out my hand, and DC Wright, then DS Dickers shook it. 'Can you – I mean, obviously I'm happy to hang around as long as you need me, but I'm supposed to be leaving to visit my mum fairly soon. She's in hospital. Do you know when we'll be free to head off?'

DC Wright and DS Dickers looked at each other, and I could feel that wordless communication flowing between them again. This time it was DS Dickers who spoke.

'I'm afraid I can't give any guarantees on when the investigation will conclude, Miss Blacklock. But we understand the inconvenience, and if you can bear with us for a little while longer, that would be extremely helpful. We may well have some more questions, so if you could stay here until we let you know otherwise, that would be appreciated.'

'Okay,' I said a little reluctantly. 'I won't go anywhere.'

As I left the study, my phone clutched hot in my sweaty hand, I should have been relieved. I'd come through the police interview relatively unscathed and without making any major slips about Carrie. But I didn't feel relieved. I felt very, very worried.

From: Pamela Crew
To: Judah Lewis
Sent: Saturday 9 November
Subject: Urgent message – Lo arrested. Please call urgently

 Judah love please can you call me as soon as you get this? I didn't want to ring you in the middle of the night but it's very important. Lo has been <u>arrested</u>. There's been some terrible mix-up about a death at her hotel and they've arrested her for murder or something awful. I'm at my wit's end trying to organize a lawyer for her but I'm in hospital and it's all very difficult. Please can you call me as soon as possible? Any time is fine, I'll be up before you, I expect. Love to the boys and you.
 Love Pam (Granny) xx
 PS If I don't answer then I might have gone down for surgery. Just leave a message.

From: Judah Lewis
To: Pamela Crew
Sent: Saturday 9 November
Subject: RE: Urgent message – Lo arrested. Please call urgently

 Pam, I've been trying to call since your email came through and your phone is going straight to voicemail. So is Lo's. Please, please call me as soon as you're out of surgery. It doesn't matter what time – it's just after midnight here but there's no way I'll be going back to sleep.
 What the hell happened? Whose death? And what hotel? The one in Switzerland? I thought Lo was staying with you at the moment?
 Please call me as SOON as you get my messages. My mom has gone back to Connecticut but if you need me to

come to the UK, I can get her to come back and look after the boys and I could be on a plane within 12 hours.

PLEASE call me. I'm sorry, I know I already said that. You'll appreciate I'm going a little out of my mind here.

Judah x

PART
FOUR

PART FOUR

20

When I got out of the interview room, the first thing I wanted to do was call Judah. It was barely 6.30 a.m. in New York but I was desperate to talk to him. I just didn't want to do it in front of Carrie.

Instead, I made my way back to the entrance hall, the cozy oak-beamed room with the roaring log fire, but when I walked in, there was a plainclothes officer I recognized from the room upstairs sitting casually in an armchair. He was ostensibly reading the paper – but his eyes were on the door.

I wheeled round and began retracing my steps. I hadn't been planning to say anything incriminating, but I didn't relish the idea of talking to Judah in front of a cop. After some false starts with rooms that were either locked or occupied, I knocked on the door of a room signed as THE LIBRARY with a discreet little brass plaque. *Library* turned out to be something of an overstatement – there were a few bookshelves, but it was more like a little book-lined sitting room overlooking the gardens. Either way, I wasn't going to quibble with their description. Sinking shakily into an armchair, I opened up my phone and video-called Judah.

When he answered, it was with a thick, croaky voice that told me that he'd been asleep, and I couldn't see anything, so I knew he had the phone pressed to his ear.

'Lo?' He cleared his throat, and I saw his puzzled face come into view as he looked at the clock on the screen, then realized this was actually a video call. 'Oh, hey you. Is something wrong?'

'Judah!' I felt a sense of relief that was almost physical wash over me. I hadn't realized how much I'd missed his voice, his face, his presence. I fought the urge to reach out and touch the screen, as if I could stroke his stubble-roughened cheek. 'Oh my God, it's so good to talk to you. I'm okay, it's just – oh, Jesus, where to begin.'

'What time is it where you are?' Judah asked. He looked half asleep, though the room was so dark, it was difficult to see his face.

'It's half past eleven in the morning. I'm in the library of my hotel.' I swung the camera around to show Judah the leather armchairs and oak panelling. Judah gave a croaky laugh.

'Jesus! Where are you, Hogwarts?'

'I know, right?' I could feel the tension in my shoulders unwinding at the sight of his familiar face and sound of his voice. I wanted to reach out and hug him so badly it almost hurt. 'It's this place called the Old Manor. It's outside this cute little village – West Tyning?'

Judah had lived in the UK for almost ten years but I was never quite sure how often he'd ventured outside London. Now he shook his head.

'Never heard of it, sorry.'

'Don't worry, it's pretty small. But the hotel is kind of fancy.'

'Well, I'm glad you're treating yourself,' Judah said. 'But bring me up to speed on your mom. Did it turn out to be a fracture?'

'Oh God, Mum's not even the half of it.'

But before I could start trying to explain the whole tangled mess, I heard the unmistakable sound of a wail from Judah's end and then a thin rising cry of 'Daddeeee!'

'Aw shit,' Judah said irritably. The phone lurched as he dragged himself upright. 'That's Teddy. The phone must have woken him up. Can I sort him out and call you back?'

'Of course,' I said. My stomach was sinking, but there was no point in trying to unravel all this with Teddy wailing in the background. 'Look, it's important, but it's not urgent. It's a kind of . . . well, there's been a sort of fuck-up at the hotel that I wanted to talk to you about, but it's a long story. Complicated. Why don't you ring me back when you've got the boys off to school and we can talk properly.'

'Okay,' Judah said. He coughed, and then, as Teddy's voice reached an angry pitch, I saw him turn away from the screen and yell, 'Teddy, will you give me a break, buddy? I'm coming.' His face came back into view, his expression resigned. 'I'd better go get him. I love you, honey.'

'I love you too,' I said. 'When shall we talk?'

'I've got a Zoom straight after I drop the boys off, so can I call you after that? Say, ten my time? I've got an hour between meetings then, so you can explain the whole thing.'

'Sure,' I said. In the background I could hear Teddy had reached peak anguished fury. 'Daddy, where are you? I need you!'

'I'd better go,' Judah said again. 'Love you.'

'Love you,' I echoed, and then there was a click and the screen went dark. I looked at the clock on my screen, trying to calculate what Judah's 'ten my time' meant. That would be . . . 3 p.m. here. It felt like a long time to wait.

I tried Mum next – no answer on the home phone, and straight to voicemail on her mobile. I left a message explaining that there was a hold-up at the hotel that I needed to sort out but that I'd be over to her as soon as things here were straightened out and to *please call me*. Then, with a sigh, I put my phone away and climbed the creaking stairs to go and see how Carrie had fared. Hopefully she'd had the sense to come out of the bathroom. As I turned off the second-floor landing, I couldn't help casting a glance at the door to Marcus

Leidmann's room. It was closed, obviously, and I don't know what I'd expected – police tape, maybe – but from the outside, you couldn't tell anything was amiss. When I paused in the corridor, though, I could hear the unmistakable sounds of activity filtering through the ancient wood – the hum of voices, the sound of people walking around inside. I tried to imagine what they were doing. Dusting for prints? Measuring water spatter?

Then the sound of footsteps came nearer to the closed door, and I jerked myself out of my reverie and hurried away down the corridor. The last thing I wanted was to be found eavesdropping on a crime scene.

WHEN I LET myself into our room, I found Carrie pacing back and forth like a caged tiger.

'Fuck,' she said as soon as she saw me. 'You were ages. What happened?'

'Nothing much,' I said. I told her about the interview, summarizing the questions as best I could, and she sat on the side of the bed, chewing her nail. I felt the old anxiety coiling in the pit of my stomach, making my heart rate skitter uncomfortably, and thought, briefly, about taking another pill – but messing with my meds didn't seem the best idea right now.

'So they definitely think it's murder?' she said at last. I nodded.

'I think so. I mean, they weren't giving much away, but they said they're treating it as a suspicious death.'

'But how?' Carrie burst out. 'I mean, are we talking poison? Stabbing? Strangulation?'

'Not stabbing,' I said slowly. I had been thinking about this, trying to cast my mind back to the scene I'd walked in on. 'There wasn't really any blood apart from a scratch on his leg – I suppose he could have got that thrashing about, but it wasn't anything that could have been fatal. And not strangulation either, I don't think – I think there'd be bruising around his throat, although I'm no coroner. Poison or drugs . . . well, I guess either of those could be a factor. I suppose they'll find out at the postmortem. But I think if he *was* murdered, he must have been drowned.'

'What makes you say that?'

I shrugged. 'I mean . . . it's all guesswork, of course. Partly the fact that they seem so sure it wasn't a natural death – if it was poison, I don't see how they'd know that yet. But mainly the amount of foam that was coming out of his mouth. There was a lot.' I felt a little sick at the memory of it, Pieter cradling his father's naked body, the pinkish foam cascading down his chest. 'It's a pretty conclusive sign of drowning, apparently. I researched it once for a piece.'

'Could you really drown someone in a bathtub?' Carrie's expression was sceptical. 'They're not *that* deep.'

I shrugged. 'I don't know. Maybe if you surprised the person – or you were very strong.' I thought of Heinrich, of his huge hands and the impression I'd had of coiled strength, and shivered.

'I guess. And if the bath was very full . . . but they let you go? We're free to leave?'

'Not really,' I said reluctantly. 'At least, I'm not. They were very emphatic that I shouldn't go anywhere until further notice. And I saw a plainclothes officer in reception, so I assume if I try, I'm going to find myself quietly escorted back to my room.'

'*Fuck*.' This time it was with a different emphasis. A kind of frustration and fear.

'And there's another thing you should know,' I said, and I told her about the key cards and the fact that the hotel had a record of every swipe.

'Shit,' Carrie said. Her face had gone pale, as if she, like me, was running over the last forty-eight hours and trying to think whether we had done anything incriminating. 'But I mean . . . that's good in a way, right? It should back up your story – when you went down for breakfast, when you came back. The fact that you didn't leave again until we heard the shouts. The door lock records will back that up?'

'I think so,' I said slowly. 'I mean . . .' I walked to the window of the room, the one overlooking the garden, opened it, and stared out. It was an old-fashioned window with a rickety iron frame and diamond-shaped leaded panes, and someone very athletic could just about climb out – but I didn't see where that would get them. The wall was sheer, with no creepers or balconies. We were three storeys up, and no one but a professional acrobat could have inched along the golden sandstone blocks to Marcus's room. Even then, they could hardly have avoided being seen by one of the other guests. It just wasn't plausible. 'Yes, I think so. There's no way you could get out of this room without using the door.'

'Where does that leave me, though?' Carrie said, a little blankly. 'I mean, I can't stay in here forever, can I? I have to get away.'

'I don't think you can,' I said. 'Not right now, anyway. Look, I understand the feeling.' Of being trapped in a prison of my own devising? Hell yes, I understood that feeling, as Carrie should remember. 'But we know they've put at least one police officer on the main door. I'm pretty sure they'll have people in the car parks. I think we should sit tight, wait until this all calms down – I'm sure they'll let me go tomorrow. After all, the hotel will need the room. They can't keep the place locked down forever.'

'Ugh.' Carrie raked her fingers through her dark hair and then swore as her huge ring tangled with one curling tress. 'Oh, for fuck's sake!' She began to yank, ripping the hair at the roots, and I stepped forward and grabbed her wrist gently, stopping her.

'Carrie, seriously – calm down. Listen, you must be starving. You had no supper last night and no breakfast this morning. Let's get you some food, and everything will look better.'

'But I can't go down to the bloody restaurant, can I!' Carrie exploded. 'This is a fucking shitshow, Lo!'

'We'll order room service,' I said. I was untangling the long strands from around the sapphire, and I kept my voice as soothing as I could without veering into patronizing. Somehow, calming Carrie was helping me calm myself. 'I mean, I will. I'll order a massive lunch, enough for two – they can't prove I'm not just a greedy guts. Look.' I leaned over and grabbed the room-service menu, shoved it into Carrie's lap, then returned to trying to free her ring. 'What do you want? I'll phone down as soon as you've picked.'

Carrie was staring down at the menu, leafing through its stiff pages with a frankly longing look on her face.

'Oh my God, chicken liver pâté with brioche bread, Roquefort and walnut salad, filet mignon with truffled fries . . . this all sounds amazing. I want it all.'

'So have it all. What do you want?'

'I want the lobster bisque . . . no, wait, the smoked salmon terrine, and then . . . fuck it, I'm going to have the house burger with blue cheese and the truffled fries *and* onion rings. And a large Coke. *Fat* Coke, not diet. And a slice of tarte citron.'

'Done,' I said. The ring was free, and I dropped Carrie's wrist and went over to the phone to put through the order.

THE KNOCK ON the door came surprisingly quickly, well within the half hour the kitchen had promised. Carrie slipped into the bathroom in a move that was fast becoming routine, and I went across and opened the door.

I'm not sure who I'd been expecting, but the blonde girl standing there with the tray of food made me do a double take. It was the same employee I'd seen talking to police in Marcus Leidmann's room, the one who'd turned up with his breakfast halfway through proceedings.

'It's you!' I said, and then when she looked puzzled: 'Sorry, I don't know if you saw me, but I was in the next-door room when you were being interviewed. I'm the one who helped out the poor cleaner. I'm so sorry, this must be a complete nightmare for the hotel — and for you.'

'Oh my God!' The girl let out a shocked giggle. The effect wasn't super-professional, given we were talking about a dead guest, but she looked about twenty-two, twenty-four at most, and I tried to imagine myself being flung into the centre of a murder investigation straight out of uni. Then again, I'd been only a few years older when I boarded the *Aurora*. 'Yeah! Of course! Sorry, I did see you talking to the police but I hadn't put two and two together. Not being funny, but it's a total nightmare. Poor Tana — she's the cleaner — she was in bits after she spoke to the police. Our boss had to send her home.'

'I'm not surprised,' I said. 'Are you okay?'

'Oh, I'm tough as old boots, me. My boss said I could go home too if I wanted to, but I thought if I did that I'd just sit around thinking about what happened, so I said I'd rather be here. I'm so sorry, I didn't recognize you. Are you . . . like, did you know him?'

'Not really,' I said. 'I mean, I knew who he was — he was a famous businessman, did you know that?'

The girl nodded. 'Yeah. They were talking about him in the kitchen after. German or something? And really rich, apparently. That's what my boss said, anyway.'

'Belgian. And yes, really, really rich.'

'And you were the one who found him?'

'Not exactly.' I wasn't sure how much I was supposed to say, but fuck it, the police hadn't told me to keep this to myself. 'It was the housekeeper who found the . . . well, his body, but I heard her calling for help.'

'Nightmare,' the girl said earnestly. She shifted her weight, and I realized that she was still in the corridor holding the heavy tray.

'I'm so sorry. I shouldn't be keeping you standing around like this. Come in. Please.'

The girl edged past me into the room and began clearing a space on the cluttered coffee table. As she did, I realized with a wince that there were two coats flung over the armchair to her left, two glasses of water beside the bed . . . but fortunately the girl didn't seem to notice, or if she did, she didn't appear to realize what it signified. Still, I made a note to clear one of each away in case the police came by again.

'You were the one who took his order?' I said as the girl began taking off silver covers and arranging napkins. She nodded and straightened up, rubbing the small of her back.

'Yeah. He rang down from his bath. The police asked about it loads. What did he order, how did he sound. Luckily we record all the orders in case there's a mistake, so I could just play them the tape.'

'And how did he sound?'

The girl shrugged.

'Completely normal, that's the mad thing. You'd never have thought he'd have a heart attack ten minutes later.'

'You think it was a heart attack, then?'

The girl opened her eyes very wide.

'Don't you?'

Now it was my turn to shrug. 'The police told me they're treating it as a suspicious death.'

'Oh my God.' The girl's hand went to her mouth. 'They don't think it was the food, do they? God, the chef will go spare.'

I shrugged again. 'I have no idea, but I doubt it. I mean, from what you said, he sounded fine when he called down, and I imagine if it was something he ate at dinner, it would have taken effect a lot sooner, and his son would have noticed something.' There was silence as the girl apparently considered this, and then she seemed to snap herself back into being an employee and fished in the pocket of her apron for a leather-bound folder.

'Sorry, if you don't mind signing here...'

'Of course,' I said. I signed, added a hefty tip for good measure, then said, 'Well, gosh, I know it sounds weird, but it was actually really nice to talk to someone who was there too. I've been going a bit mad stuck up here by myself – the police told me not to go anywhere.'

'Oh my God, totally,' the girl said. She took back the folder and looked at me, sympathy in her face. 'I totally get it.'

'My name's Lo, by the way,' I said. 'Lo Blacklock.' I held my breath. This was the moment. I couldn't ask outright, but...

'Bella,' the girl said, and I let out a little inaudible exhalation of relief. 'Bella Mutter.'

'Well, great to meet you, Bella,' I said. 'And, um, thanks. Thanks for letting me rattle on.'

'You're welcome,' Bella said. She looked down at the signature page of the bill and then blinked when she saw the tip I'd added. 'Oh, wow, I mean, no, thank *you*. Anything you want, Miss Blacklock, just let me know.'

'Thanks so much, Bella,' I said, and Bella smiled.

'No problem. Just call down when you're done with the tray, yeah?'

'I will,' I said. I watched as she backed out of the door with a little wave. It clicked shut behind her and as it did, the bathroom door creaked open and I saw Carrie peering out.

'Well, she seemed pleased. How much did you tip her?'

'Were you watching?'

'Through the crack in the door, yeah. Judging by her face, you've been in the States too long, mate. Remember that's going on my bill.'

I could tell from her tone she was joking, but there was an edge of irritation in there too, and I realized uneasily that she was probably worrying about this extra, unplanned stay and how to fund it out of her dwindling stash of cash.

'I thought it was worth the investment. It might be handy to have someone on our side on the staff – but don't worry, I'll contribute. To all of it, I mean, not just the tip. I know you weren't exactly expecting all this when you booked us in.'

'The fuck I was,' Carrie grumbled. She shut the bathroom door behind her and sat down at the coffee table, a look of frank greed on her face. 'Though I reckon we've got a pretty good case for getting the police to stump up for the extra night. It's not like either of us *chose* to stay on.' She took a huge bite of the burger, closed her eyes briefly, and said, though a mouthful of meat and cheese, 'Bloody hell, whatever you tipped her, I reckon it was worth it. This is fucking incredible.'

I laughed.

'Can I have a chip?'

'*One*,' Carrie said, but she was grinning now, and I could tell that the food was already having an effect, making the whole situation feel a little more bearable. I watched as she hoovered up the burger in what felt like a ridiculously short time, then turned to tackle the terrine with no apparent loss of appetite. She was just starting on the tarte citron when there came a knock at the door. We both froze, looking at each other.

Again? Carrie mouthed and I shrugged helplessly. Was it the police? The knock came again, harder this time. It sounded too peremptory to be Bella. Housekeeping, maybe?

'One second!' I yelled, hoping that whoever it was didn't have a key card. 'I'm – I'm just in the middle of something.' I pointed frantically to the bathroom, and Carrie rolled her eyes.

'Fine, but I'm taking the tart,' she hissed.

'I don't care, just go,' I whispered back. Then, 'Who is it?' in a normal tone.

'Police.' The voice was male and deep, not the same as the officer I'd spoken to that morning. I felt my stomach flip. Not again.

'Okay,' I yelled. Carrie was in the bathroom now, the door defiantly just ajar. I stalked over and slammed, not trying to hide the sound. If they thought I'd been on the loo, so much the better. Just before it shut, I saw Carrie raise two fingers up at me, and I rolled my eyes. She was acting like a moody teen. 'Just coming!'

As I set my hand on the latch, I took two deep breaths. My heart rate was spiking to the point where I felt a little sick, though I couldn't tell if it was anxiety or irritation at Carrie. Maybe both. It was skittering and skipping beats in a manner that felt worryingly close to my old, bad panic-attack days. Should I take a double dose of my meds? An accidental overdose would hardly improve matters.

At last, realizing that I couldn't put this off any longer, I twisted the latch and pulled open the door.

This time, a single officer was standing outside – at least, I assumed he was an officer; he was wearing plainclothes, like the two detectives this morning.

'Laura . . .' He looked down at something in his hand, then up at me with a pleasant smile. 'Blacklock, is that right?'

'Hi, yes, can I help? I did already speak to your colleagues this morning – I think I told them everything I knew.'

'Of course, but actually, they weren't my colleagues.' He had a very slight Italian accent, I noticed, almost imperceptible. 'I am here from Interpol. My name is Inspector Filippo Capaldi.'

My heart rate did another sickening spike. I supposed it was only to be expected – the death of someone like Marcus Leidmann was always going to be a major international incident. But somehow, hearing the word *Interpol* only underscored the nightmare that this was turning into. Interpol. Fuck. Were they more or less of a big deal than the UK force? I had no idea how they worked.

I realized that I was staring, stricken, and also that Inspector Capaldi was speaking, and I hadn't heard a word he'd said.

'I – I'm sorry. I wasn't – what did you say?'

'I said, may I come in?' He gave a smile – clearly trying to be reassuring, and stupidly it worked, even though I didn't think a smile would have any bearing on his intent to arrest me.

'Oh, I – I mean, of course.'

I glanced behind me at Carrie's abandoned lunch strewn across the coffee table. Thank God there had been only one set of plates.

'Sorry it's a bit of a mess. I was just eating. We could go downstairs if you prefer?'

But Inspector Capaldi didn't take the hint and waved away any suggestion that the room was untidy with a very Italian hand gesture.

'Please. I can assure you, I have seen much worse.' He followed me into the room and indicated one of the two armchairs on either side of the coffee table. 'Do you mind if I sit?'

I nodded, moved Carrie's tray to the door, then took the other seat. Now that we were sitting opposite each other and I could study him properly, I could see that he was young for an inspector, and very handsome, almost improbably so for a police officer, though on reflection, I guessed there was no reason the police couldn't be as good-looking as people in any other profession. I also had the faint feeling of having seen him somewhere before. I quickly realized that was because he must have been at the crime scene earlier this morning, though I hadn't spoken to him. His voice was completely unfamiliar – with that very slight accent, though, he'd clearly been in the UK long enough to smooth it out to something almost undetectable.

'I am really very sorry to intrude, Ms Blacklock. I know you've answered a lot of questions already, and I won't take up too much more of your time. I mainly just wanted to ask a couple of things about your connection to Pieter and Marcus Leidmann. Am I right in thinking you're a financial journalist?'

My eyebrows went up at that. Clearly this man had done his homework.

'A travel journalist. But yes, I had a sort of semi-commission from the *FT* for a profile on Marcus Leidmann if I could get one. Obviously . . . '

I trailed off.

'Obviously that won't be possible now,' Inspector Capaldi finished with a rather grim smile. 'But you *did* speak to him in Switzerland, yes? You had a meeting?'

There was no point in denying it. He must have talked to the Leidmann Group press office. I nodded.

'Briefly. It wasn't enough for a profile, to be honest. I got the impression his PR person stepped in to put a stop to it when he said something indiscreet.'

'Indiscreet?' The officer raised one eyebrow, and I bit my lip, kicking myself. Had I just spoken out of turn? Still, if Marcus Leidmann really had been murdered . . .

'Look,' I said a little reluctantly, 'this is probably nothing but . . . he was talking about the succession. Of the Leidmann Group. I'd got the impression from previous interviews that it was pretty much a done deal that the CEO position would pass to Pieter but . . . Marcus gave me the idea that perhaps that wasn't completely set in stone.'

'What do you mean?' Capaldi had pulled out a notebook and now his pen was poised. I sighed. From everything Carrie had said, Pieter seemed like a perfectly nice guy. And more concretely, I didn't see how he could possibly have anything to do with his father's death – he had been downstairs in the dining room in the narrow window of time when his father had died, and apparently there were multiple witnesses to prove it – but on the other hand . . .

'I was talking about the fact that the Leidmann Group was – is, I suppose – a family business. I said something about it passing to Pieter. And Marcus interrupted me and said . . . I think his exact words were *Well, as to the succession, that's undecided.* Something like that. But actually . . . ' I paused, realizing something else, something that hadn't occurred to me until just now. 'Actually, that wasn't when Adeline stepped in. That was a couple of remarks later.'

'Adeline?'

'Adeline LeBlanc. She's . . . I don't know. Head of international relations or something. She's staying here in the hotel.'

Inspector Capaldi nodded, made another note, and said, 'And what was he saying then? When she did step in?'

'He was talking about his wife, Pieter's mother. He called her . . .' I paused, trying to remember the exact phrasing. 'He said she was *a rather limited person*. It struck me as . . . frank. And kind of cruel, if I'm being honest.'

'And that was when Miss LeBlanc stepped in to stop the conversation?' Capaldi tapped his pen on the page. 'Interesting. And he said nothing else, nothing about his relationship with Pieter or his plans for the company?'

'No, nothing.' I was puzzled now. 'But they travelled to the UK together. Their relationship must have been reasonably solid. Don't you think?'

Capaldi said nothing, he just shrugged and smiled again, a rather charming smile. Then he stood.

'Well, thank you, Ms Blacklock. But listen, if you have any information, and I do mean *any* – if *anything* at all occurs to you, any suspicions, or if you remember anything that could cast light on the case, would you please call me? I will give you my personal mobile number . . . one moment.' He wrote something on a page of his notebook, tore it out, and handed it to me. I looked down at the page. *Filippo Capaldi*, it said in neat handwriting, followed by a UK mobile number. I nodded, folded the page, and tucked it in my pocket.

'Of course. But Inspector—' I stopped, unsure how to ask what I wanted to ask. I didn't imagine he would give me any information about the case.

Inspector Capaldi was almost at the door, his hand on the latch.

'Yes?'

I made up my mind. I had to say something.

'Look, I'm sorry if this is out of line but . . . you don't seriously suspect Pieter, do you? He was at breakfast the whole time. I saw him go down and from what—' I stopped. *From what Bella told me* was what I had been going to say, but I didn't want to admit that I'd been sniffing around, asking questions. I'd done enough of that on board the *Aurora*, and it hadn't done me any good. 'From what your colleagues were saying, the window of opportunity was very small, and Pieter was downstairs the whole time.'

'I'm sure you'll understand that we can't comment on that at this time,' Inspector Capaldi said. 'But thank you, Ms Blacklock, for your openness. It is much better to be frank about these things, I find. Honesty is always the best policy.'

And then he opened the door, tipped an imaginary hat, and let himself out.

As the door closed, I slumped back into my chair, letting out a deep shuddering breath and wondering what I had just done. Had I just made Pieter Leidmann the number-one suspect for a crime he hadn't committed? I could only hope that Filippo Capaldi was right – that honesty really was the best policy. Because the last time I'd stuck my neck out about what I'd seen, the person who'd ended up paying the price was me.

21

'Well, my ankle's definitely broken.'

My mother spoke without preamble as if we were halfway through a conversation, though in point of fact I'd only just picked up the phone.

'Okay.' I tried to rearrange my thoughts. I'd been lying on my bed, counting down the minutes until three, when Judah was supposed to call, and perhaps it was because I'd been waiting for the *dring-dring* of my phone or perhaps it was just because my nerves were already on edge, but either way, the shrill of my mobile had sent my adrenaline spiking and my heart rate through the roof. Now I was trying to steady my breathing and keep the anxiety out of my voice. 'I'm really sorry to hear that, Mum. What does that mean? A cast?'

'It means I've got to be transferred to Watford for an operation, apparently. Hopefully some time this afternoon, if they can get hospital transport. So that's why I was ringing, to say don't come here.'

'Well, you hadn't actually told me where you were.' I tried to keep my voice as neutral as possible, but I could feel the tension creeping in. Over on the other side of the room, I could see Carrie laughing at me and I shook my head sternly. 'That's why I kept texting you, asking you to phone me. But anyway, that's not important now. Shall I come to Watford? Do you need clothes and stuff? What time will you be there?'

'Honestly, who knows. You know what hospitals are like – the patient is the *last* person to get told anything.' My mum's tone was tart, and I felt a momentary flash of sympathy for the nurses who'd presumably been on the receiving end of this for longer than I had. 'But they're talking like I should be there by this evening and maybe going into surgery tomorrow.'

'Okay,' I said. My heart rate was calming now. 'That sounds good. Shall I try to pop over this evening, then? I could pick up some pyjamas for you on the way – I think there's an M&S not far from the station.' I had no idea how the police would react to me leaving the hotel, but surely they'd have to let me see my elderly hospitalized mother? It wasn't like I was fleeing the country.

'Well, you'd better let me get there before you book any trains. And check the visiting hours for the ward. But yes, that sounds like a plan. I'll phone you when I know which ward I'm on.'

'Okay. I love you, Mum.'

'I love you too.' My mum's voice had softened, and I shut my eyes. I knew that this tough, no-nonsense *I don't need any coddling* attitude was probably just my mum's way of dealing with her own fear, her own anxiety over what must feel to her like her body's betrayal. A trip and fall. It was the classic old-person accident, and for someone like my mum, who'd never thought of herself as old, it probably felt like a terrifying slide into old age. 'I'm sorry if I've been a bit grouchy, love. I know you've been worried. And I know this wasn't what you imagined when you planned the visit – me in hospital and you stranded in a hotel.'

'It doesn't matter.' I felt tears pricking at the back of my eyes. 'Honestly, Mum, it really doesn't. I just want to give you a hug. I've missed you.'

'Well.' My mum's voice was brisk, but I heard the crack in her tone and felt my own throat tighten in sympathy. 'Well, anyway, I'm really looking forward to seeing you. I'll call you when I know where I end up.'

'Okay. Lots of love, Mum.'

'Lots of love.'

There was a click, and the line went dead.

'That sounded like good—' Carrie began, only to be cut short by a knock at the door.

For a second, we both sat there staring at each other, wondering who it could be. The sound had sent my pulse skyrocketing again, in spite of the fact that I knew it was probably just housekeeping come to offer us more towels.

Should we ignore it? I mouthed at Carrie. The Do Not Disturb sign was hanging on the doorknob, so they weren't likely to come bursting in – but then the knock came again, and this time, I heard a male voice say:

'Miss Blacklock, could you please open up? It's the police.'

Fuck. I looked down at my phone. It was 14:54. Could I get rid of them in six minutes? It seemed unlikely.

When I looked up, I met Carrie's worried gaze. Then she shrugged, made her way quietly to the bathroom, and shut herself inside with a soft click. I took a deep breath and swung my legs over the side of the bed.

Somehow, in the long, comforting years of staying home with the boys, I had forgotten what stress – real stress – felt like. Now it was back, and I remembered all too well the sour taste in my mouth, the skittering heart, the clammy palms. If the police didn't leave me alone soon, I was going to have to get my medication adjusted. Maybe beta-blockers would work. But somehow this whole business had thrust me back into a nightmare I thought I'd left behind, a nightmare of dead bodies and locked doors, and I knew that I couldn't go on like this: sick with anxiety every time there was a knock on the door, my head pounding with a constant low-level stress headache that never quite went away.

At the door, I raised my hand to the security latch and saw, with a kind of detached interest, that my fingers were shaking – just a little. Nothing that anyone else would have noticed but enough to make me realize that I was a lot more on edge than I had been admitting, even to myself.

Then I pulled back the latch and opened the door.

Outside were the two plainclothes officers from earlier – Dickers and Wright – and alongside them two uniformed police officers. I was about to open my mouth to ask if they wanted to speak to me again when one of the uniformed officers stepped forward.

'Laura Blacklock?'

I nodded.

'I am arresting you on suspicion of murder. You do not have to say anything, but it may harm your defence if you do not mention, when questioned—'

The rest of his words were lost. I could hear my heart thumping in my ears, incredibly loud, and above it my own voice saying, as if from a long way away, 'I'm sorry, what? There must be some mistake.'

'Do you need anything?' the female officer was asking, and I stammered out something about my phone, my room key. An officer picked up both, and my arm was taken in a very firm grasp, one that meant business. One that I could tell was going to end up with me in handcuffs if I squirmed.

I had just enough time to think, *Carrie, what will Carrie do?*

And then the door of the room slammed behind us, and I found myself being led away along the same corridor I had run down only ... God, was it only this morning?

As I stumbled down the stairs, through the entrance hall, and out to the waiting police car parked outside the front entrance, all I could think of was my mum on her way to Watford General and Judah, who would even now be settling himself down with a coffee, picking up the phone, ready to call.

And sure enough, as the police car drew away, the gravel of the neatly combed drive spitting under its tyres, I heard my phone, far away in some police evidence bag, begin to ring.

It might as well have been at the bottom of the Atlantic Ocean, for all I could do. I couldn't answer it – and I didn't think the police officer was likely to hand it over for the asking.

All I could do was sit there as it rang and rang, and Judah wondered what on earth had happened and why I wasn't picking up.

As the car swung out of the driveway into the narrow country lane, I looked back at the Old Manor and felt a lump rise in my throat – not quite tears; something else. A feeling of terrified overwhelm at the idea of everyone who was depending on me, waiting for me, stuck in hospital without me – while I was being driven off to God only knew where.

What had I done?

22

It must have been well gone four by the time we got to the police station. I was booked in, swabbed and fingerprinted, photographed, read my rights, and taken to a small featureless cell, where I was just . . . left. And left. And left.

After what could have been an hour but might have been two or more because without my phone I had no real idea of the time, I was starting to climb the walls. Was this some kind of psychological torture? Were they softening me up for interrogation? It no longer seemed implausible.

The room was hot and windowless, and my claustrophobia, never that far away, had started to close in around me. My headache had only intensified since I'd left the hotel, and I had nothing with me – no paracetamol, certainly none of my anxiety medications, nothing.

At last, unable to take the silence and the waiting any longer, I walked to the door and banged on it. After a few minutes, a hatch in the door opened. Through the gap, I could see a uniformed officer standing outside.

'They'll be with you shortly,' he said before I could speak. His tone was bored.

'That's what they said when they dropped me off,' I snapped back. 'I'm dying here – could I at least have some water?'

'Didn't they give you any?' The officer peered into the cell, then seemed to mentally shrug when he saw there was none. 'All right. I'll be back.'

He disappeared, and I went back to the narrow little bunk and put my head in my hands.

At the sound of the door opening I jerked upright – but it wasn't the young officer. It was DS Dickers and DC Wright. They weren't smiling anymore. In fact, they looked pretty grim.

'Thank God.' I stood up as they came in, but DS Dickers made a motion for me to sit down, and I obeyed. 'Listen, this has all been a horrendous mistake. I don't know what you think—'

'If it's all a mistake, then we'll be able to get that sorted out,' DC Wright said pleasantly. 'We're going to take you to an interview room, and you'll get every opportunity to have your say then.'

THE INTERVIEW ROOM turned out to be a different room from the one we'd been in before, in a different part of the station, but it was equally bare. DC Wright showed me to a hard plastic chair, then seated herself opposite, clicked on the recorder, and spoke into it, giving a brief summary of the date, time and purpose of the interview, rereading the caution she'd given to me earlier.

'And can you please confirm for the recording that you don't want a lawyer present at this interview, Laura?' she finished.

I shook my head somewhat impatiently. Hanging around for some hotshot lawyer to advise me to say *No comment* to every question was not going to get me out of here any faster. The truth was that I had nothing to hide, nothing to do with Marcus Leidmann's death, and no conceivable reason to kill him. The truth was about the only thing I had going for me.

'No, I don't need a lawyer. This is all a huge mix-up. I barely knew the guy.'

DS Dickers and DC Wright exchanged a glance at that, then DS Dickers leaned across the table. He was holding a folder, I saw. Holding it closed, one hand over it, pressed against the table, as though it contained something important.

'Okay, Laura, let's start with that. I'm going to forget all that stuff you told us this morning. Let's begin at the the beginning. Tell us how you really knew Marcus Leidmann.'

I took a deep breath. The only way out of here was through. And whether Inspector Capaldi was right or not, honesty was about the only thing I had going for me. And I had *not* hurt Marcus Leidmann. I hadn't even laid a finger on him. So the truth couldn't hurt me. The problem was, it could hurt Carrie.

'I told you.' I tried to make my voice neutral, smoothing over the tremor that might have been anger or anxiety – even I wasn't completely sure. 'I was invited on this press trip as a guest, and I was hoping to interview him for the *FT*. I had a loose commission but no firm promises from his office. I got a few minutes with him in Switzerland but not really enough for a profile. That's literally it. I barely knew him.'

'Listen.' Dickers gave me a look that was halfway between exasperated and something else, something close to . . . weary? It was the look of a head teacher who's caught a naughty schoolkid out in a lie and is irritated that he has to go through proving it. 'Laura, we both know that when the forensics come back, your DNA is going to be all over that room and all over Marcus Leidmann's body. So why don't we take that as read, and you give me the real answer? How did you know him?'

'Is that why you swabbed me?' My voice had gone up an octave, and I felt close to bursting into tears. 'Of course my DNA'll be all over his body! I helped get him out of the fucking bath. All that will prove is that I was telling the truth. Didn't you read my statement? The cleaner can corroborate all of this.'

'I did read your statement,' Dickers said. He sat back, folding his arms, his chair tilting in a way that made me want to push him over backwards. 'I was there when you gave it, if you recall. It's a shame it turned out to be a pack of lies.'

'What?' I wanted to stand up, pace around the cell, but I restrained myself. I had a strong suspicion I might end up in handcuffs if I did. 'What did I lie about?'

'Well, to begin with, you gave me the same story that you told the Leidmanns – that you were staying at the Old Manor because your mum was in hospital just up the road, and we know that's not true.'

I felt my cheeks flare. Oh. Okay, that *was* a lie. And it now felt like a very stupid one. Dickers waited for me to respond, then, seeing that I wasn't about to, he gave a smirk and continued.

'Second, we know you lied about when you left your room and went down to breakfast. We have the door-lock information from the hotel and it directly contradicts your account of your timings.'

'What?' Now I was puzzled. 'What are you talking about? I guess I might have got the times a few minutes wrong; I wasn't paying attention to the clock. But what does that matter? He wasn't killed when I was at breakfast, you know that.'

'Third,' DS Dickers said as if I hadn't spoken, 'you lied to us about your wedding ring. You claimed you don't own one and we have evidence that in fact you do.'

'*What?*' I said again, this time with a mixture of exasperation and bewilderment in my voice. What did all these facts have to do with one another? Did he honestly think he was building a case here? 'I never said I don't have a ring.' Then, suddenly, I remembered the conversation with DC Wright as she bagged up my clothes, and realized what he was on about. 'Hang on, I said I don't have a *watch*. I do have a ring, I just don't wear it – look.' I held out my bare hands, my fingers spread. 'Not every day, anyway. But what's my wedding ring got to do with any of this?'

'And finally—' DS Dickers spoke with the air of someone producing a trump card with grim triumph. 'Any idea what these were doing on Mr Leidmann's phone, Laura?'

He opened the folder and slapped a grainy black-and-white photograph down on the table.

For a long moment I stared at the printout, unable to figure out what he was asking. It was a picture – it looked like a still from CCTV – of a man and a woman. They were standing in front of a a grandly panelled door, and the man was bending over the woman, plainly kissing her. You couldn't see their lips, but from the tilt of his head and the angle of hers, it was pretty clear what was going on. The man had one hand curved possessively around the woman's shoulder, the other around her waist. The woman had her back to the camera and was simply standing, hands loose by her sides, as if made limp by his touch. You could just see that on the third finger of her left hand, she was wearing a ring.

It was a startlingly intimate, almost erotic image, and for a moment I couldn't understand why DS Dickers was showing it to me.

Then, with a feeling almost like an electric shock running through me, I realized.

The door wasn't just any door – it was a door in the Grand Hotel du Lac.

The man wasn't just any man – he was Cole Lederer.

And the woman. The woman wasn't just any woman. She was me.

For a long moment I said nothing, I just sat there, staring down at the photo, unable to believe my eyes. My heart was pounding so hard in my chest, I thought I might be about to faint. This picture – this black-and-white printout from Marcus Leidmann's phone – was a still of the moment Cole Lederer had kissed me outside my hotel room, a few nights ago.

Cole had kissed me on the cheek – but from the angle of this photograph, you wouldn't know that. His head was bent possessively over mine, and you couldn't see anything except the top of Cole's head and the way mine was flung back, seeming almost to welcome his mouth. And what had felt at the time like a fairly innocuous, even brotherly touch on my shoulder looked very, very different in black-and-white – it looked like a man taking a woman, and definitely not against her will.

This picture, presumably taken from a security camera I hadn't even known existed in the corridor of the hotel, looked very, very bad for me. It was the kind of picture I would have been ashamed to show Judah – though I would have, if it came to it. And I hoped he would believe me when I told him how I had really felt that night in the corridor. The way Cole's lips had landed gently on my cheek, not possessively, giving me every opportunity to push him away if I'd wanted to.

But that's worse, a little voice whispered in the back of my head. *You do get how that's worse, right?*

'For the benefit of the recording, I'm showing Ms Blacklock CCTV photographs, marked twelve A, twelve B, and twelve C, which appear to be the suspect engaged in a romantic tryst with an unidentified man,' DS Dickers said, his voice neutral. 'On her wedding finger, she is wearing what appears to be a ring with a large stone.'

'I—' I tried. My throat was dry and I swallowed and managed, 'It – it's not what it looks like.'

'Oh, please!' It was DC Wright, and there was genuine amusement in her face, an expression I didn't think was faked. For a moment I thought she was going to laugh – but then she seemed to get hold of herself and smoothed out her expression into something more neutral and professional. 'Well, in that case, Laura, why don't you give us your version of events? What's really going on in this photo?'

'He's kissing my *cheek*.'

Wright didn't even bother to reply; she just gave me a look that said *Pull the other one*.

'Look,' Dickers said, and his voice was gentler than it had been a moment ago, almost kind. 'What you do in your own time is no one's business but your own. If you're a married woman having a fling on a press trip—'

'It wasn't a fucking fling!' I protested, my voice almost cracking, but Dickers ignored me and carried on, raising his voice over my words.

'None of that's a crime and we're certainly not going to go telling any tales to your husband. But if there's a reasonable explanation for why one of the world's richest businessmen travelled halfway across Europe to ambush you with this photo – and that's not all we found on his phone, by the way – you'd better come out with it. Because I can't see one, and at the moment, it looks very bad for you. How well did you know him exactly? Were the two of you having an affair, and Marcus found out he wasn't your only extracurricular activity?'

For a long moment, I said nothing. I just sat there staring down at the printout lying on the table between us, at my own head flung back in what looked a lot like ecstasy. At Cole's, bent over mine with possessive passion. I could hear my heart thudding in my chest, my shallow breaths hissing between my teeth. I felt, suddenly and surely, that if this continued, I was going to have a panic attack. Or throw up. Maybe both.

'I want a lawyer,' I managed. Above the roar in my ears, I heard Wright sigh. 'I'm not answering any more questions until I have one.'

There was a silence, and then Dickers bent over the recorder.

'Interview terminated at ten forty-six p.m. at the request of the suspect.' Then there was a click, and the recorder shut off.

Wright stood up. Her face was . . . not bored, exactly, but like someone whose chess opponent has just made a move that is going to draw the game out to tedious length.

'All right, then, Laura. We'll call your lawyer. Do you have one in mind or do you want us to contact the duty solicitor?'

Fuck. No, I didn't have a lawyer in mind. How did I go about finding one in a jail cell in the middle of the night? Judah was more than three thousand miles away and had only the sketchiest idea about the British legal system. My dad was dead. I had barely been in contact with any of my UK friends since COVID and I couldn't imagine phoning any of them up in the middle of the night to demand that they come and sort this out for me. What on earth was I supposed to do? Legal aid? Did I even qualify anymore? I wasn't a UK resident, after all, though I had no idea if that made a difference.

There was always my mum, of course. But I wasn't sure what an elderly, hospitalized woman with a broken ankle would be able to do.

I made up my mind. Judah was my best option, and if he couldn't help me, he'd know someone who could. It must be late afternoon in New York. Would he pick up? I just had to hope and pray he would.

They brought a phone to the interview room and offered to fetch my mobile to look up Judah's number, but I didn't need it. I'd written it on enough forms that I knew it by heart.

It was Dickers who dialled. He held the phone to his ear, then looked across at me and spoke.

'It's going straight to voicemail. Do you want me to call someone else?'

I felt my shoulders slump. Of course it was going to voicemail. When we spoke earlier, Judah had said he only had an hour's gap between meetings. Presumably he was stuck in one right now with his phone on Do Not Disturb.

The problem was, Judah barely ever checked his voicemail – as a working journalist, his messages were usually overrun with spam and pitches from enthusiastic PRs. Our arrangement was that if something was urgent, I'd follow up the missed call with a text and he'd ring me back. It was a system that usually worked well – but now seemed monumentally stupid.

'Can I send a text?' I asked, and Dickers shook his head.

'Sorry. This phone doesn't have that capability. I can try someone else if you like.'

Fuck. *Fuuuuck.* Was there really no other option? Ben Howard? I wasn't sure if I still had his number – but in any case, the thought made me shudder.

No. There was only one possible person I could call – and regardless, I needed to let her know what had happened and why I hadn't turned up at Watford General as I'd promised. My mum had been pushed clean out of my head during the interview, but now the idea of her sitting there, wondering where I was, well – it was too much to bear.

Slowly, reluctantly, I recited my mother's mobile number and watched as Dickers dialled it.

I could hear the ringing through the handset, and I found myself internally begging, *Pick up. Please pick up.*

Then Dickers spoke.

''Fraid this one's gone to voicemail too. Do you want to leave a message?'

He was holding out the phone. At least my mum *did* check her voicemail. Or she would if she ever turned her phone on. And surely, surely, when I didn't turn up tonight, she'd think to check?

I drew a deep breath, then took the handset from Dickers and spoke into the receiver, trying my very best not to let my voice sound as scared as I felt.

'Mum, hi, it's Lo. Listen, I'm so sorry that I wasn't at the hospital this evening. I hope you weren't too worried. There's been—' Fuck. How to describe the nightmarish spiral of events in a way that wouldn't give my poor mother a heart attack? 'There's been a horrible mix-up. I've – well, I've been arrested. Long story, but I need a lawyer. Urgently. Phone Judah, he'll know what to do. Don't worry about time zones, just call him – but don't leave a message. If he doesn't pick up, then text or email. Tell him I'm at West Tyning police station and the number is . . . ' I paused and looked up at Dickers, and he wrote down a number hastily on a scrap of paper and shoved it across the table. I read it off, then said, 'And don't worry, it's all going to be okay, but – well, look, just call. I love you.' Then I hung up and passed the phone back to Dickers, who nodded.

'Right. Well, am I to take it that you're refusing to answer any more questions until your lawyer gets here?'

I nodded. 'I am.'

'Well, in that case, one of my colleagues will show you to your cell.'

I closed my eyes. Then I opened them, pushed back my chair, and followed DS Dickers to the door.

As a uniformed officer walked me down the echoing central corridor of the custody suite, my elbow firmly in his hand, I couldn't help reflecting on the irony of that word, *suite*. It covered so many possibilities. From the first-class suite on Swiss Air to the palatial Monte Rosa suite in the Grand Hotel du Lac to the junior suite at the Old Manor Hotel and, finally, to this – a cell in the custody suite at West Tyning police station.

It was a pretty steep fall.

The question was, how much further did I have to go?

23

I was trapped. Locked in a cell, deep underwater, where no one could hear my cries.

There was no way to escape; I could only run from side to side in the little room, scrabbling at the locked door with my nails, tearing back the orange nylon curtains to find no window behind – just a blank plastic panel, cruelly mocking.

Desperately, I cast around for something, anything to help me break out of my prison – a piece of wood to pry open the door, something heavy to batter the lock. But there was nothing – only a metal bunk, bolted to the wall, and a rubber tray on the floor.

The door was fitted and flush with no helpful crack I could get my fingers into, no gap at the bottom I could peer beneath or shout into.

And as I scratched at the unforgiving plastic with broken, bloody nails, I realized: there was no way out. I was utterly and completely trapped. And the knowledge threatened to overwhelm me.

When I woke up, it was, as always, with a huge wash of relief. I lay there, my eyes closed, feeling my heart pounding and the blood singing in my ears. It was just a dream – the bad old dream I'd had more times than I could count. Just a stupid, recurring nightmare –

a memory of a horror I had long since escaped. I was safe at home, where no one could hurt me.

Except... was I? Even before I opened my eyes, I could tell something was wrong. I wasn't in my comfortable bed at home, Judah lying beside me, a pair of little toddler feet jammed into my stomach. I was alone, lying on a thin, hard mattress, with pain in my back and hips. The room smelled not of toddler sweat and fresh sheets but of toilet bleach and industrial cleaner. And the sounds were wrong too – there was no friendly rattle from our old air-conditioning unit, no honking of horns or wail of sirens in the New York night.

No, here there was only the clang of doors, the sound of footsteps, the shout of male voices raised in anger.

'If you don't calm down—' I heard, and then something I couldn't make out.

My heartbeat began to quicken again, and I sat up, opening my eyes with a feeling of dread as the events of the day before came flooding back. There was no fake window, no beige panel behind nylon curtains. And the door wasn't plastic. But there was a door. It was metal and fitted with a peephole that looked in and not out. And it was very much locked.

My dream hadn't been just a dream. I *was* trapped. I was locked in a cell. And I had no idea how I was going to get out.

For the first time in ten long years, my nightmare had come true. And this time there was going to be no awakening.

It was at that moment that I knew – this was it. I was going to have the panic attack I'd been fending off for hours, days. And even though I knew what was happening, knew what was coming, I was somehow powerless to stop it.

I felt my pulse speeding up, its beat loud in my ears; I felt my poor heart squeezing and squeezing like my life depended on it. I felt my breaths coming sharp and shallow, flooding my body until my palms prickled with sweat and my fingers went cold and numb and all my extremities tingled. I felt the screaming pulse of adrenaline saturating every cell in my body, and I lay back down and gave in – the way I imagined a drug taker must when they shoot up an accidental overdose, giving themselves up for the ride, however terrifying, because they have no other choice.

As I lay there, curled up on the bunk, my hands between my clenched thighs, trying to breathe, I felt my own consciousness floating away, dissociating in a way I hadn't done for . . . well, for years. It was like I was looking down at myself from a huge distance, feeling a kind of pity for this poor, crouched, panting creature with her cold-as-clay skin and her sweat-drenched clothes and her eyes rolling back in her head as her lids fluttered closed.

Could she hang on to consciousness? I didn't know. I wasn't sure I really cared even as I watched her clench her fists and bow her head and count her breaths the way she'd been taught. *One. Two. Three. Breathe in. Three. Four. Five. Breathe out.*

Poor Lo. Poor, stupid thing. She was probably going to go to jail for this – for someone else's crime. They would stand her up in court and show the photos of her kissing another man and explain how she had killed Marcus to protect her infidelity from coming out, and she'd be convicted. Because who was she, after all, but a flaky, unreliable woman who couldn't hold her drink, couldn't remember to take her meds, couldn't control her emotions, couldn't be trusted at the end of the day.

And she would rot in a cell far away from her husband and her children for a murder she didn't commit.

I don't know if it was that thought, the thought of the boys and how they would react if they saw me like this, or maybe the thought of Judah, or maybe the injustice of it – the fucking ridiculous injustice of me lying here, locked up for a crime I not only hadn't committed but *couldn't* have committed. But suddenly, I wasn't just panicked – I was angry. And the anger was overriding the fear. My heart was banging with a different rhythm. My fists were clenched, but not to ward off a blow – because I wanted to hit someone.

I pushed myself up. I raked my hair off my forehead. I forced myself to breathe. *One. Two. Three. Breathe in.* I was not going to rot here. That was just my paranoia talking. They couldn't lock me up for a crime I hadn't committed. Eventually, this night would be over, my mum would pick up her fucking messages, and a lawyer would come and point out the absurdity of this situation. And everything would be sorted out and I would fly back home to hug my babies and breathe in the smell of their warm skin and kiss Judah, and all of this would be just another bad dream to add to my already impressive tally of nightmares.

I would not crack. I would *not*. I just had to make it through this night.

24

'Blacklock. Laura Blacklock.'

The voice was bored, male, and accompanied by a thumping on the steel door of the cell. I sat up, my heart pounding a mile a minute, but not with fear this time, not with the consuming, sickening panic that had gripped me in the middle of the night. This was just the zero-to-sixty jolt of consciousness that had me up and running to the boys when one of them cried out in the night with a bad dream.

'Yes!' I called back. My heart rate was steadying, and I pulled my draggled hair off my face and straightened my clothes. 'Yes, I'm awake.'

Without a window in the cell, I had no idea what time it was, but the light was on, and I felt like I'd slept for not just hours but days.

I swung my legs over the side of the bed, trying to counteract the sudden sickness that swept over me, and as I did so, I saw a movement in the peephole, as if someone had peered in to assess the situation inside the cell. Then there was the sound of a key in the lock, and the door swung open.

'Your friends are here. Along with a lawyer.'

My friends? I frowned, puzzled. Which friends? Had Mum called someone? 'Did they give their names?'

'The solicitor is . . . ' He consulted a piece of paper in his hand. 'A Mr Daniel Winterbottom from Callahan, Hennessey and White. I take it you want to see him?'

The name meant absolutely nothing to me, but the answer was hell yes. If he was going to help me sort out this nightmare, then yes, I wanted to see him.

'Yes. Yes, please. Is he – are we going now?'

The officer opened his mouth to make what looked like a sarcastic remark, but then I could almost see him swallowing it back, perhaps out of pity for the dishevelled, desperate woman hunched on the bed in front of him.

'Yes, he's here now' was all he said. I felt my heart speed up, this time with a burst of hope. Maybe this was all going to be okay.

'Do you mind if I use the bathroom before we go?'

The officer nodded and withdrew. I peed in the stainless-steel pan situated unglamorously opposite the bed, washed my hands, and tried my best to pull my clothes straight and tidy my hair. There was a mirror, but it wasn't proper glass, just a kind of polished steel panel that didn't really reflect much of anything at all. Still, the misty silhouette staring back at me looked as presentable as I could make her, and without a comb and some deodorant, I wasn't going to get much better. Taking a deep breath, I banged on the door and waited for the officer to come get me.

'**RUN ME THROUGH** the situation with the photograph again.'

Mr Winterbottom ('Call me Dan') had turned out to be around my age or maybe a few years younger, with a neat designer beard and a suit that made me feel even scruffier and more crumpled than I already did. He had the clipped, slightly ambiguous accent of someone who's been to a fancy private school but doesn't want that fact to be too obvious, and I liked him from the outset.

For the past half hour, maybe more, he had taken me patiently through my story – or at least, the slightly edited version of it that left out Carrie – and now he was looking appropriately outraged on my behalf.

'So what you're saying is you spent a total of, what, thirty minutes with this man, and the only evidence against you is the fact that he had a photograph of you?'

'As far as I can see, yes.' I could have cried with gratitude that Dan saw the situation as being as fucked up as I did. 'And the thing is, the police must *know* I couldn't have killed him. The door-lock information will prove that – I didn't enter or exit my hotel room from the time I got back from breakfast, to the time I heard the cleaner screaming.'

'And the door locks, they don't just record key passes, they record every time the door is opened or closed?' Dan had his pen poised.

I frowned, trying to remember back to what DS Dickers had said when he accused me of lying about my breakfast timing, and then nodded.

'I think so. I mean, the police will know for sure, but when they interviewed me earlier, they definitely implied they could tell when I'd *left* the room, not just entered it. I think the lock must record whenever it's opened from the inside as well as when it's swiped. So if that's true, they must be able to tell I didn't leave the room.'

'Okay.' Dan tapped his pen on the paper, then pushed back his chair. 'Look, I don't want to make any promises I can't keep, but this seems pretty thin to me. That CCTV photo is evidence that *he* might have been obsessed with *you*, but it's definitely not evidence of the reverse. And just to check – he'd never contacted you before this trip? Never met you or shown any particular interest in you?'

I shook my head.

'No, although . . . ' I stopped. Should I say this? It was opening a fairly giant can of worms as far as the police went, but it was probably better for the information to come from me before Wright and Dickers dug up a garbled version online and added two and two together to make five.

'Although?' Dan prodded.

I took a deep breath. No way back now.

'Well, I don't know how to say this without sounding like an asshole—' *Asshole. Very American, Lo.* 'But I guess I am – was – kind of a public figure at one stage. I was involved in a high-profile disappearance a few years back. On board a cruise ship, the *Aurora*. Did you hear about it?'

'Vaguely,' Dan said in a way that I could tell meant that he had no idea what I was talking about but didn't want to sound rude.

'Well, I was involved in the case – I mean, I wasn't a suspect, I was a witness – and I ended up writing a book about it. It was a fairly big seller and I got . . . well, I got some pretty odd correspondence about it afterwards.' *Odd* was understating the issue. The emails had been everything from marriage proposals to begging letters to accusations that I'd made the whole thing up. One guy had low-key stalked me for a while, though thankfully that seemed to have tapered off. 'I wouldn't have put Marcus Leidmann down for an online weirdo, but the fact is that when I got to Switzerland, I found three other people from the *Aurora* staying at the hotel as well, and if I'm honest . . . that freaked me out a little bit.'

'Interesting,' Dan said. He tapped his pen on the paper again. 'And those other people. What were their names?'

'Alexander Belhomme, the food critic,' I said, watching as he wrote them down. 'Cole Lederer – he's a freelance photographer. He's, well, he's actually the guy—' I swallowed, remembering the intimacy of the photo Dickers had slammed down on the table, then forced myself to spell it out. 'He's the guy in that photo. The one the police had. And the third person was a journalist called Ben Howard.'

'I *see*,' Dan said, and now he didn't just look interested, he looked positively intrigued. 'Well, well, well. Let me see what I can do, Laura. Keep your fingers crossed. I'll be back.'

And then he banged on the door of the interview room and disappeared.

THE NEXT HALF hour – it could have been more – felt like a very long wait. I spent a chunk of time pacing the length of the room before realizing that its narrowness and the repetitiveness of the action was making me feel worse. I sat back down and tapped my fingernails on the edge of the bunk in a staccato rhythm that also began to make me feel a little crazy. Then at last I put my forehead on my knees, shut my eyes, and begged for all of this to end.

I don't know how long I had been in that position – head down, eyes closed, counting the minutes until I was dragged back to my cell – when the door was flung open without warning and I sat up, pulse spiking in a way that made me feel almost dizzy.

'Laura!' It was Dan, and he looked delighted with himself. Behind him was DS Dickers, who looked extremely pissed off. 'I'm happy to say that I've had a chat with the good detective here, and we've agreed that you'll be released on bail. Now the only question is accommodation. Am I right in thinking that you don't have a permanent residence in this country?'

I shook my head, unsure where this was leading. 'No, but I could go back to the hotel?'

'She can't re-enter the crime scene,' Dickers said to Dan a little irritably, as if this was a conversation the two of them had already had. 'Are there any relatives you could stay with?' he asked me directly.

I opened my mouth to say 'My mum,' then shut it again. I could stay at my mum's house, of course I could. The problem, and it was a big problem, was Carrie. She was very likely still at the hotel.

I had to find a way to get back there, if only to collect my stuff. I couldn't risk the police going in to collect my things and running across her.

'I might be able to go to my mum's,' I said at last, 'but she's in hospital and I don't have a key. Is there any way I could stay at the hotel tonight, then relocate tomorrow?'

'Look.' Dan turned to Dickers with the air of someone being reasonable to the point of magnanimity. 'We both know you haven't declared the whole hotel a crime scene, and my client doesn't have anywhere else she can stay tonight. Why not let her go back to the hotel under instruction not to speak to any of the other witnesses?'

For answer, DS Dickers beckoned to Dan, and the two of them stepped out into the corridor, the action only slightly undermined by the fact that I could still hear them arguing through the door.

Eventually, from what I could make out, it was agreed that I'd surrender my passport, and would be allowed to go back to the hotel for one or two nights as long as I didn't speak to anyone involved in the case. Which was A-OK by me. In fact, I would have agreed to almost anything if it meant getting out of here.

At last, it seemed like the deal had been struck, and Dan, still beaming, came back into the room to tell me about the conditions, pick up my possessions, sign various legal undertakings, and escort me out of the police station.

It was done. I was going – well, if not home, at least somewhere with a shower and a toilet with a door.

I could have cried with relief.

'WHAT. THE. FUCK.'

'Surprise!' Ben's face was smiling but nervous. He and Cole had both got up as I entered the reception area of the police station. Now I stood, glaring from one to the other, utterly robbed of speech. I wasn't sure whose presence made me more uncomfortable – Ben, the man who was at least partially responsible for my last bout of being disbelieved by investigators, or Cole, who was the main reason I'd just spent the night in a prison cell. A horribly vivid image of that photo flashed into my mind – Cole cradling me in his arms, my head flung back as if sinking into his kiss. I felt my cheeks flush with mortification. Should I tell him about the photo?

Yes. No. Maybe.

Not now, anyway. Not in front of Ben. I couldn't think of a worse audience for a conversation I really didn't want to have. *So there's this photo . . .*

'I take it Dan didn't tell you we were here?' Cole said a little wryly, breaking into my frozen indecision, and I shook my head.

'No, he didn't.'

'Sorry!' Dan's voice came from behind me, his cheerful tone belying the apology. 'I believe I *did* tell the custody suite officer to mention that you had friends waiting in reception, but perhaps he didn't pass the message on?'

I opened my mouth to contest this, then remembered, actually, the officer *had* said something to that effect. But no wonder Dan had looked intrigued when I'd mentioned the names of the other three passengers from the *Aurora* I'd met in Switzerland. Two of them had been waiting for me just a few feet away. And I had to assume that Dan, at least, had seen the photo.

'How?' I demanded, turning from one to the other, and Ben pointed to himself.

'I got a text message from your mum.'

'And I got a frantic call from your husband,' Cole said. 'I was the person who contacted Dan – he's a friend of a friend – and we arrived around eight thirty this morning and found Ben already here.'

'I'd been here since seven, but they wouldn't let me in,' Ben said. 'Apparently you have to be a lawyer or some bollocks like that. I thought about saying I was your husband, but I thought that might backfire when they found out I wasn't.'

He laughed, but I felt like I'd had a stab to my heart at the idea of Ben pretending to be poor frantic Judah. For Judah to phone Cole – he must have been going out of his mind.

'I'm sorry,' I said. 'Before we do anything else, I have to talk to Judah. That's my husband,' I added for Dan's benefit.

Dan nodded. 'Look, let's get out of here – I doubt the police officers want us clogging up reception, and you can phone your husband. Then maybe we can find a spot to debrief.'

25

It was ten, maybe twenty minutes later that I put the phone down on what had been a surprisingly upsetting call with Judah. I'm not usually a crier – I don't process stress like that; instead, I turn it all inwards – so I had shocked myself by bursting into tears when I heard his voice on the other end of the phone, and Judah had spent most of the rest of the call trying to talk me down and saying comforting things about Dan's expertise, my rights as a US citizen, and the fact that I definitely wasn't going to go to jail for a crime I hadn't committed.

What made it worse was that I desperately wanted to tell him about Carrie – he was the one person I would have completely trusted with the news – but with Dan, Cole and Ben hovering awkwardly on the other side of the car park, I felt I couldn't. And in any case, I had a horrible feeling that Judah would tell me to turn Carrie in to save myself.

At the end of the call, I asked Judah to put the boys on the line and heard him hesitate.

'Are you sure? I can, but it's only five a.m. here. They're still asleep.'

'Five? God, I'm so sorry. Why didn't you tell me I'd woken you up?'

'Because I wasn't asleep, you idiot,' Judah said, but his voice was affectionate. 'I've been pacing all night. And look, I'll wake the boys, of course I will, I just – if they're cranky or whatever, I don't want you to end up feeling worse.'

'No,' I said reluctantly. 'No, you're right. They'll wake up grumpy and they either won't want to talk to me, or they'll be sad I'm not there, and whichever it is, it'll make me feel like shit.' I shut my eyes, wishing, wishing I could transport myself across the ocean, creep into their room, slide into one of their toddler beds with my knees crooked and my feet sticking uncomfortably off the side the way I did when they had a nightmare. An idea occurred to me. 'Listen, don't wake them, but would you . . . would you just put the phone next to them for a minute?'

'Of course,' Judah said, and I heard the sound of his footsteps as he padded across the polished wooden floor of the apartment, gently opened the boys' bedroom door, and knelt down between their beds. Then I heard a soft rustle as he placed his mobile on one pillow, and faintly, very faintly, I heard little-kid snuffling snores. I knew instantly and without a single doubt that I was listening to Teddy.

My heart seemed to swell in my chest and I put my hand over my mouth, stifling the sobs that threatened to break through. It wasn't just that I didn't want to wake Teddy – I could have muted my phone – it was more that I didn't want to lose a single one of his soft breaths. I stood there in the car park, my eyes closed, the tears leaking out the corners and running down the side of my nose, and I swallowed against the pain in my throat as I listened to the sound of my little boy sleeping.

'That was Teddy,' Judah whispered very quietly into the receiver. 'I'll put you next to Eli now.'

There was another rustle and then, as silence fell again, I could hear Eli's gentle breathing. His was softer and more regular than Teddy's but just as sweet. I wished more than I had ever wished anything that I could put my nose in the top of his head and breathe in his little-boy smell, the smell of no-more-tears shampoo and something that was completely his own that I would have known even if I were blindfolded, even if a million kids came up and hugged me.

I could have stood there all day, I would have, no matter that this was costing me an arm and a leg in transatlantic call costs, but after what felt like a heartbreakingly short time, I heard the rustle of the phone again and the sound of Judah tiptoeing out of the room.

'Better?' he asked when he was back in the main room. His voice was gentle, and I had to swallow hard against the lump in my throat before I could reply.

'Better,' I managed. 'Sorry. I'm not crying.'

'I know you're not.' It was a lie, and we both knew it, but neither of us cared. 'Now, listen, are you *sure* you don't need me to come? My mom could take the boys. I could be with you in eight hours. Twelve, maximum.'

'No,' I said, my voice stronger now. 'No, I really mean it. The only thing that's making this bearable is knowing that you're taking care of the kids. If I had to worry about them as well as everything else . . . I'll be fine. Dan's got me out. This is all going to be sorted.'

'It is,' Judah said firmly. 'But if you change your mind, just say. I will drop everything. You don't need to do this alone.'

'I know.' My voice sounded stronger in my own ears. 'I love you.'

'I love you too, honey. Keep me posted, okay?'

'Okay,' I said. Then I hung up, scrubbed my damp cheeks with the sleeve of my sweater, and walked across to where Ben and Dan were waiting. They tactfully pretended not to notice my red eyes.

'Cole and I are starving,' Ben announced, 'so he's gone to find a café. Could we tempt you to some breakfast?'

I hadn't thought about food, but as soon as he said the words, I realized my mouth was watering. I hadn't eaten since breakfast yesterday, and I was famished.

'Actually, yes.' I wasn't sure what the etiquette was with your lawyer – I'd never had one before – and I was pretty sure that Dan's billables wouldn't include bacon sandwiches, but it felt rude not to at least ask. I turned to him and said, 'Dan, would you like—'

But Dan was already shaking his head. 'Thanks, but I won't. I need to get back to the office and make a start on the paperwork. We'll set up a time for a proper debrief, but don't worry, I'm sure we can get this sorted out. That door-lock information you mentioned.' He patted his bag. 'It's pretty hard to see how that fits in with the police timeline.'

A thought occurred to me. 'If this isn't allowed, then don't worry, but can I . . . could I have a copy of that?'

'Of the door-lock printout?' Dan looked surprised, then seemed to consider the request. 'I mean, I don't see why not. Hang on.' He fiddled with his case for a minute, then took out a small handheld scanner the size of a compact umbrella and a couple of sheets of paper. He ran the sheets through a slot in the scanner, then pulled out his phone. 'What's your email address?'

I read it off to him, and a minute later I felt my phone buzz with an incoming message.

'Done,' Dan said. He snapped the case closed, then hitched his other bag further up his shoulder and smiled. 'Anything else before I shoot off?'

I sighed.

'Well, I mean, I have loads of questions – like when the hell am I going to be able to get back to my kids – but I guess the main one is what on earth happened to him? To Marcus, I mean. I asked DC Wright about it and she was really noncommittal, just said they were treating it as a suspicious death. Did he drown? Did someone poison him?'

But Dan just shook his head.

'I'm sorry, I don't know, Laura. The police clearly believe he was murdered, but until we get the postmortem, I don't have much more information than you do. But look, I'll call you as soon as you're back at the hotel. You've got my number, yes?'

'Yes,' I said. 'And, Dan, thank you so much. I'd probably still be rotting in that custody suite if it weren't for you.'

'No worries at all,' Dan said. He gave me a smile, a rather nice one. 'Take care, okay?'

And then he walked across to his car, and I turned and followed Ben to the café.

THE CAFÉ TURNED out to be the same place I'd bought the sausage roll . . . was it only two days ago? It felt like a lifetime. I slid into the seat Cole had saved for me, the gingham tablecloths, the pink-and-white-striped cushions, even the cakes under their glass domes, all of that was exactly the same as my last visit, but I felt like a totally different person, ten years older than when I'd last sat at this table.

I ordered a double-shot cappuccino and a bacon sandwich with extra HP Sauce, and as the waitress walked away, I felt myself slump in my seat – overcome by the roller-coaster of the past few days.

'Hey.' Cole put out his hand, squeezed my wrist. 'Hey, Lo, it's going to be okay. Yes?'

'Sure,' I said, though I wasn't certain I believed it. I was remembering the sound of Judah's voice, Teddy's quiet snuffles, Eli's soft breathing, and it felt like my heart was going to crack. 'Yeah. Absolutely.'

Perhaps Ben could tell that I was close to breaking down in tears because he cleared his throat and spoke with the air of someone trying to change the subject.

'That portable scanner of Dan's was pretty fancy, huh? Never seen one like that before.'

'Portable scanner?' Cole looked mystified, and I realized that he hadn't been present for the conversation about the door locks. I explained, and his expression changed from puzzled to intrigued.

'Well, that sounds interesting. What does it show?'

'I don't know.' I pulled out my phone, opened up the email Dan had sent to me, and clicked on the PDF attachment. The screen filled with a slightly wonky computer printout, annotated by hand in pen.

LARK		CHAFFINCH	
8:26	0	8:30	0
8:31	0	8:36	0
8:51	G469	8:49	0
9:17	0	9:15	S14
9:18	0	10:04	S02
9:22	G469	10:09	0
9:23	0	10:11	0
9:27	G469	10:22	0
9:41	0	10:23	0
10:38	G469	10:23	0
10:51	0	11:28	S02
11:47	G469	11:59	S02

At the top was written in blue ballpoint pen *G469 = LB, S14 = maid, S02 = us.* I stared at it blankly, then looked up to see Cole and Ben peering over my shoulder, looking equally puzzled. Ben had put on reading glasses that were new since I'd last seen him.

'What does it mean?' Cole asked. 'I take it Lark and Chaffinch are the rooms?'

'Yes, mine is Lark. I guess Chaffinch must be Marcus's. And I suppose . . . hang on.' I frowned, staring at the times, then back at the annotations, trying to piece together the times and the numbers. 'Wait, this is starting to make sense. The times must be a list of when the door lock was activated, and G469 must be my key card. It says here "G469 equals LB" – that must mean Laura Blacklock.'

'But what are the zero entries?' Cole asked. He was squinting at the screen, his eyes screwed up to try to make out the small print. 'God, this is so tiny. I wish I had my tablet.'

'You need reading glasses, mate,' Ben said. 'Hang on a sec.' He felt in one pocket of his coat, then in another, and finally drew out a crumpled piece of paper. It had print on one side, but the back was blank, and he smoothed it out against his napkin, then handed it to me along with a pen. 'Why don't you copy it out, Lo. Then we can all see properly.'

I nodded and began transcribing the list, one entry at a time, in handwriting as clear as I could make it. When I was finished, I pushed it across the table and watched as Cole and Ben went slowly down the two columns, trying to make sense of the codes.

'So, the zero entries,' I said, 'I think they must be when the door was opened from the inside, without a card. 8:26, that would correspond to when I went down to breakfast. And 8:51 was when I came back and swiped myself in.'

'And what about 8:31?' Ben asked. His voice was casual, but I felt my stomach flip, realizing the mistake I had just made. *Now* I understood that throwaway remark DS Dickers had made about me lying over when I went down to breakfast. By 8:31 I had been downstairs helping myself to the breakfast buffet. That entry must have been Carrie opening the door from the inside, presumably to check if I really had put out the Do Not Disturb before she went to take a bath. Unfortunately, there was no way I could admit that, and to Dickers and Wright, it must have looked like the first entry, 8:26, was me checking for a newspaper or putting out the Do Not Disturb sign, and the second entry, at 8:31, was when I actually left the room. It was a discrepancy of only a few minutes in my story, but it *was* a discrepancy, and in a case that might boil down to a few minutes here or there, I could understand why Dickers had picked up on it.

In any case, I could not admit the truth to Ben and Cole. Fessing up to Carrie's role in this, even just to Ben and Cole, would be insanely stupid and might land me back in a prison cell. And besides, I had done all this for her, for Carrie, the woman who had saved *my* life almost a decade ago. I wasn't about to throw all that away by betraying her secret.

'Oh . . . ' I said slowly. 'I don't know. Maybe I went out later than I thought. But look, 9:17, that's when I heard the screaming from the corridor – that's me opening the door from the inside.' I glossed over the 9:18 entry. Presumably that had been Carrie peeking out to see what was taking me so long, but it was close enough that it didn't look like an error in my story. 'Then 9:22, that's when I ran back to get my phone. Then I called 999 and went back to Marcus's room to check on Pieter and the cleaner, and the rest is me going back and forth from there and being interviewed by the police.' Thank God the rest of the timings matched up with my story, but as I looked down the list, I realized that if the police had probed any further back, things could have got very sticky indeed. How many times had Carrie opened the door for me from the inside without making me use my key? That would have been very hard to explain. But the printout seemed to cover only the morning of Marcus's death. I had to hope they wouldn't check anything earlier. I also had to hope that Carrie hadn't done anything stupid in my absence.

'Okay, that makes sense,' Cole said. He was running his finger down the second column, the one marked *Chaffinch*. 'So, if this is Marcus Leidmann's room . . . 8:30, 8:36, what's that? Him opening the door to someone?'

'I guess . . . maybe picking up a newspaper.' I tried to think and then realized. 'Oh, wait, I guess the 8:36 one must have been him letting in his son. Do you remember I met Pieter coming out of his father's room? That entry must be Marcus letting Pieter into his room, and then the 8:49 entry, that must be Pieter leaving his father's room to go down for breakfast. That corresponds to when I met him on the landing, when I was coming back from breakfast and he was going down. You can see we chat, and then two minutes later, at 8:15, that entry is me swiping back into my own room.'

'Okay, so that all adds up,' Ben said slowly. 'But what's this?' He pointed at an entry a couple of lines below where Cole had stopped. 'This entry, S14, is that the killer?'

But I was frowning, looking back at the scan on my phone, trying to make sense of the annotations at the bottom.

'I don't think so. There's a handwritten note here on the original that says S14 is the maid. I guess the *S* prefix must mean they're staff cards, as opposed to *G* for guests. So that must have been the cleaner swiping herself in to service the room. That would tie up with it being two minutes later that I heard the screams and ran down the corridor. The window for Marcus's death has always been after 9:05, when he made the room-service call, but before 9:15, when the cleaner discovered the body. That's the whole point from the police perspective – that's the period that I don't have an alibi for because I was in my room. But that means the door wasn't opened at *all* in that window. How did the killer get in?'

But Cole was still looking at the 9:15 entry, his face puzzled.

'There are no entries for forty-five minutes after 9:15. What happened to you getting in, then running back and forth from your room, making calls? Why is that showing up on your room but not Marcus's?'

There was a moment's silence while we all stared at the page, and then I realized.

'Oh, I know. It's because the door never closed. It was propped open. The cleaner put it on the latch. I guess it must be hotel policy while they're cleaning, but it means that the door only shows one initial opening, at 9:15, when she swiped herself in. All the subsequent openings and closings never registered, because the lock never engaged.'

'Ah . . . ' Cole drew the syllable out. 'Okay, that makes complete sense. So it was on the latch from 9:15 until, well, I guess around 10 a.m. And "S02 equals us" at 10:04 – presumably *us* means the police?'

'Yes, I guess the hotel must have given them a staff swipe card so they could secure the scene and still get access to the room.'

'But hang on.' Ben was looking like he was putting two and two together and finding the exercise difficult. His brow was furrowed, and he reached up and rubbed the skin under his reading glasses. 'Hang on . . . wait, doesn't that mean that that could apply to *all* the times? I mean, you're saying that the door wasn't opened between Pieter leaving at 8:49 and the cleaner turning up at 9:15, but how do we know that? Couldn't Pieter have left the door propped too? What if someone got in?'

There was a long silence while both Cole and I considered this. It was a good point, and I was desperately trying to cast my mind back to the end of the conversation I'd had with Pieter to recall whether he had shut the door or not.

'I can't be a hundred per cent sure,' I said at last, 'but I'm as certain as I can be that the door *was* shut. I remember Pieter standing there as we were chatting with his hand on it and then walking away and the door swinging closed. I really think I would have noticed if the door hadn't shut properly. I mean, it makes a distinct sound, you know? And you can see it – the latch, I mean. I noticed it immediately when I arrived to investigate the screaming; you could see the security latch was sticking out, preventing the door from closing. It's like a kind of silver bar – it's pretty noticeable.'

'But what if it wasn't the bolt,' Ben argued. 'What if it was something else, just a wrinkle in the carpet, so it *looked* closed but actually wasn't?'

I considered this, biting my lip as I tried to figure out whether what Ben was suggesting could be true. In one way I hoped it wasn't, because that was at the heart of Dan's argument to the police, the argument that had got me out of that cell. If Pieter Leidmann had shut the door as he left, if no one had entered the room during that period, the only period I *didn't* have an alibi for, then I couldn't possibly have been the person who drowned Marcus Leidmann.

The problem was, if Dan's assertion was correct, if the door really *had* been closed the entire time, from Marcus Leidmann's room-service call at 9:05 right up until the cleaner opened it at 9:15, then it left only one possible killer: the cleaner. And I just didn't believe that. I had been in that room; I had seen her shock and anguish as she tried, desperately, to help Marcus, wrestle him out of the tub, save his life. And more than that, where was the motive? Why on earth would some random hotel cleaner kill one of the most prominent businessmen in Europe – someone she'd had no idea would be staying in the hotel until that very day?

I was still sitting there, trapped in this mental round-and-round, when a rather bored female voice came from behind my shoulder.

'Bacon sarnie, extra HP, full English, beans on toast?'

I twisted round in my seat to see a woman standing there with a tray laden with food and felt my stomach growl.

'Yes! Bacon sandwich! That's me.'

I folded the paper hastily and put it in my pocket, and the woman banged the plate down in front of me, waving aside my attempt to take it with a curt 'Too hot.'

The plate was indeed hot. So was the sandwich. It was also frankly incredible. The bread was two thick, fluffy doorstop slices, the bacon was crisp and moist and blisteringly smoky, and the whole thing was spread with real butter and enough brown sauce to make my eyes water. I found myself wolfing it down with scant good manners, completely ignoring Cole and Ben's chitchat as they ate their own breakfasts.

It was only when we'd cleared our plates and downed our hot drinks that I realized something: I hadn't thought of Carrie this entire time. Was she still waiting for me, stuck in the hotel room, unable to get in or out without triggering the lock? What if I was sitting here stuffing my face while she hadn't eaten since yesterday morning?

I had to get back. I had to make sure she was okay. And then I had to figure out how to get us both out of this mess.

26

It was the strangest experience, walking into the reception area of the Old Manor with clothes crumpled and stained with sweat and my hair tousled from a night in a prison cell – no one batted an eyelid, not Cavendish at reception, not the two tweed-clad old men snoozing by the fire. Had they even moved since the first day?

I passed through the entrance lounge and began to climb the stairs, my phone clutched in one hand and the room key in the other, my heart beating faster as I rounded the first landing. I had no idea what I might find – a furious, starving Carrie pacing the room ready to tear a strip off me? The whole corridor marked off by police tape and guards?

I knew the second wasn't true the moment I turned off the main staircase. The second-floor corridor looked exactly as it had the night we'd arrived – completely quiet and undisturbed. The only clue that anything was out of the ordinary was a discreet DO NOT ENTER sign on the door of Marcus's room, presumably to remind the cleaners.

What was more puzzling, though, was that when I got to my own room, the Do Not Disturb sign was gone.

The sight gave me a sharp, uneasy pang, wondering what might have happened. Had someone searched the room? Had Carrie been found?

There was only one way to find out, and I tapped the key card on the reader, mentally imagining the entry on the computer downstairs: *12:32 – G469.*

As the door swung open, I held my breath, bracing myself for – I wasn't sure what. But there was nothing there. The room was empty, the bed neatly made, the carpet freshly hoovered, the towels in the bathroom hanging in fluffy white rows on the heated towel rail.

Just to be sure, I went right into the bathroom and stared around, even peering into the shower stall. Then I went back to the bedroom and checked the wardrobe. I knew I was being insane. It was an ordinary Victorian wardrobe with two carved mirrored doors, not a walk-in or anything fancy. Carrie might just have been able to fit inside, but she couldn't have stayed there long.

It was the wardrobe that convinced me. Because not only was there no Carrie inside, there was also no suitcase. Her tote bag was still there, lying crumpled and empty on the floor of the wardrobe. And my clothes were still hanging on the rail along with my raincoat. But my wheelie suitcase had disappeared, along with all Carrie's clothes.

She had gone. Left. Vanished into thin air. And I had no idea when or where.

And most important of all, my break-glass-in-case-of-emergency alibi – the one person who could testify to the fact that I had never left the room during Marcus's murder – had disappeared with her.

With that realization, something, some shred of reassurance that I hadn't even known I was still clutching, seemed to leave my body, and I found myself slumping down in one of the armchairs, putting my face in my hands. I felt utterly and completely exhausted, and yet at the same time, a small part of me was relieved. Because although Carrie had been my last-ditch alibi, she had also been my greatest liability. With her gone, I could finally stop worrying about her and start worrying about myself. And my mum. Who I still hadn't called.

Pulling myself together, I took my phone out of my pocket and dialled my mother's mobile, and this time, by a miracle, she answered on the first ring.

'Lo?' She was still doing that stage whisper she had before. 'Oh my goodness, where are you?'

'I'm back at the hotel. The lawyer got me out on bail.'

'Oh, thank heavens it's all sorted out. When I got your message I nearly had a heart attack. What on earth happened?'

'Well . . . ' I took a deep breath, wondering how much to tell her. *All sorted out* was a pretty big overstatement, but at the same time, it was probably better if my mum thought that was in fact the case, or close to it. 'It's a long story, to be honest. There was a death at the hotel and I happened to be one of the first people on the scene. I guess the whole thing looked a bit suspicious to the police, but I . . . well, I hope it's fixed. Or at least on the way to being fixed. I can give you the full version when I see you. More importantly, have they operated on your ankle yet? You said yesterday that it might be today.'

'No.' My mother's voice was frustrated. 'I've been on nil by mouth since last night but I keep getting pushed down the list. I'm absolutely starving and I'm gagging for a cup of tea but they won't let me have one so I've got a terrible headache. The woman in the next bed went down for her hip hours ago, so goodness knows what's going on.'

'Shall I come over?' I wasn't sure how the police would feel about me leaving the Old Manor but presumably they couldn't stop me. 'Maybe I could talk to the nursing staff, try to find out what's going on?'

'I don't think you'll be able to do anything,' my mum said a little wearily. She sounded like she was fed up, and I didn't blame her. I remembered the endless hurry-up-and-wait of being in hospital having Eli. The way everything was an emergency until it wasn't. The way the patient was the last person to be told anything. 'And I don't think there's any point in you visiting because I'm hoping I'll be in surgery.

Well, at least, hang on. There's a nurse going past. I'll ask her if she knows anything.'

There was a scuffling sound as if Mum had put her phone down on the bed, and I heard muted voices, then my mum came back on the line.

'They're saying it's still going to be today, but who knows. I think it's probably better if you stay put until I know what's happening. When's your flight?'

'Monday,' I said. 'But I can put it off, so don't worry about that.' I didn't bother mentioning that the police had my passport, so at this point flights were pie in the sky. 'Look, why don't I—'

'Oh!' My mother's voice was sharp, and there was a note of hope in it that I hadn't heard before. 'Hang on, there's a chap coming with a trolley. I think this could be my pre-op medication. Listen, I'd better go. Love you, darling!'

'Okay, but, Mum, keep me posted, okay? Text me if you're going down to surgery. Mum?'

But she had already gone.

I hung up and lay back on the bed, wondering what the hell I should do. Should I go to St Albans? I didn't have a key to my mum's house, but perhaps I could find a cheap hotel. The problem was, I had been released from custody on police bail, and Dickers had told me in no uncertain terms not to go anywhere. The two addresses I'd given him were here and my mum's house. Was I legally allowed to stay anywhere else? The last thing I wanted was to accidentally run afoul of my bail conditions and get hauled back to the station on a technicality.

Christ. How on earth had it got to this? And how was it that I, out of everyone in this fucking hotel, was the police's number-one suspect? There *must* be other possibilities. Carrie was the most obvious suspect, and if I hadn't been standing right outside the bathroom door the whole time, I would have been pointing the finger at her myself. But there was no way she could have got out of our room and down the corridor to Marcus's in the time frame of the murder. The same thing appeared to apply to Pieter, and I had to assume the police had looked into Adeline and Heinrich. But none of those names explained the fundamental impossibility of someone getting into Marcus's room around the time he was killed without triggering the door lock. Could the lock times be wrong? Could someone have been hiding out in the room all along? But if so, when did they get out?

There was a pen and paper on the bedside table and I sat up and wrote down a list of names along with two columns – one for motive, and one for opportunity.

	Motive	Opportunity
Me	Supposedly the photos	No, but the police don't know that
Pieter	Beneficiary in the will?	No, at breakfast during the crime
Cleaner	None known	Yes, could 100% have killed Marcus
Heinrich	Paid by Pieter???	Possibly, if door-lock info is wrong
Adeline	Ditto	Ditto
Carrie	Hell yes	No
Unknown	???	? But door lock still a problem

Setting aside the idea that a random hotel cleaner had a grudge against Marcus and had decided to act on that grudge in a way that was practically suicidal – which seemed extremely improbable – the more I thought about it, the more it seemed like Ben's suggestion, that the door had not been properly locked when Pieter went down to breakfast, was the only one that made sense. Because there were two inarguable bookends to the crime: the time Marcus Leidmann had phoned down for breakfast, and the time the cleaner had discovered the body. And according to the log, no one had accessed the room during that period. Which meant that either someone had been hiding out in the room all along – which seemed unlikely – or the door-lock data *must* be wrong.

On the other hand, if Pieter hadn't closed the door properly, then both Heinrich and Adeline were distinct possibilities, and Pieter Leidmann might be one too if he had slipped away from breakfast for a moment. In fact, if that had been his plan – to loiter in the corridor until someone could establish him leaving the room, then double back – it could also explain *why* he hadn't pulled the door completely closed, something that was hard to put down to carelessness.

The other possibility . . . I stared down at the page, and then across at the list of lock entries on my phone, feeling a vague theory beginning to form at the edge of my mind. The other possibility was that the door-lock information was right but one of the times that fixed the window of the murder was wrong. The discovery of the body – that was fairly fixed. There was the lock swipe at 9:15, showing the cleaner's entry, corroborated by her screams at 9:17 and my own discovery of the crime scene a few moments later.

But the other timing . . . the room-service breakfast call . . . was there any way that could have been faked? It was only a phone call, after all. If someone with a plausible accent had rung up and asked for Marcus's usual breakfast, could the staff really tell?

My heart was beating fast now, and I put down the piece of paper, picked up my phone, and dialled Dan. He answered on the first ring, his tone a little distracted.

'Hello, Daniel Winterbottom, CHW Solicitors?'

'Dan? It's Laura Blacklock.'

'Laura! Good to hear from you. Are you back at the hotel?'

'I am. Thank you so much for earlier.'

'My pleasure. Listen, sorry I haven't been in contact to set up our meeting, I wanted to get a good handle on the paperwork and this business with the door lock before—'

'It's fine,' I said, interrupting his apologies. 'Honestly, please don't worry about not ringing, but listen, that door-lock information is why I wanted to phone you. I've been sitting here with the printout, and the more I look at the timings, the more the police case just doesn't make sense. Not just for me, I mean, but for anyone. There's no way anyone could have entered the crime scene in the time they're talking about. Which made me wonder – is there any possibility that room-service call was a fake?'

'The room-service call?' I heard Dan shuffling through papers and realized that this was all new to him; he hadn't been at breakfast when we discussed it. He probably had no clue what call I was referring to.

'It's how they pinned down the window of time for the murder,' I explained. 'The police assumption was that Marcus must have been alive at 9:05 because he called down for room service. But I was wondering . . . what if he wasn't? What if someone with a Belgian accent had rung up pretending to be him?'

'It's a thought.' Dan sounded intrigued. 'It's definitely a thought. I mean, you're right, none of the staff would know him. When you say "someone with a Belgian accent", are you thinking about the son?'

'Pieter? Maybe, or maybe the bodyguard. Or anyone who could do a convincing male voice with a Belgian accent, really.'

'But if the call *was* faked . . . ' I could hear Dan leafing slowly through the sheaf of papers the police had provided, his voice a little puzzled. 'Then what does that mean for the window of opportunity? Are we pushing it back to when you saw Pieter in the corridor talking to his father? 8:52 or whatever that was?'

'I guess,' I said, looking down at the list of lock times. With a sinking feeling I realized what Dan was about to say right before the words came down the phone.

'Because the thing is, that doesn't really change much. There are no other lock activations in the earlier period either. It gives Pieter Leidmann a slightly worse alibi, because in theory, he could just about have left the door on the latch, then ducked back in after seeing you, but it's pretty tight for him getting down to breakfast in dry clothes just a few minutes later. I mean, don't get me wrong, it's a loophole, and I'll take it, but I'd prefer a slightly bigger one.'

But something else had occurred to me as he was speaking, something that had me clutching the phone so hard, I thought the case might snap.

'Dan, wait, wait just a second, what you just said about Pieter . . .'

'About the worse alibi?'

'No, earlier. When you said "you saw Pieter in the corridor talking to his father," I actually didn't.'

'You didn't see him?' Dan's voice was really puzzled now. 'But your statement to the police—'

'No, I saw *him*, I saw Pieter. But I didn't see his father. Or hear him. I only heard Pieter calling back over his shoulder. I don't think I heard Marcus reply at all.'

'Oh, my word.' Dan's voice was tinged with a very real excitement as he realized what I was saying. 'So if Marcus Leidmann was already dead when that call came through . . .'

'Then he could have been already dead when Pieter Leidmann was having that conversation. Pieter could have killed him at any time.'

'Okay,' Dan said. His tone was full of a brisk purpose. 'Now, *this* is a loophole. This could be what we need to get the police to drop the charges against you. Leave this with me, Laura. I'll get back to you as soon as I can.'

'Oh, Dan, wait—' I said, but he'd already hung up. I'd been going to ask him whether I was allowed to leave the Old Manor, whether I needed to get permission from the police if I went to a hotel in St

Albans instead of my mum's house as I'd told them. But he was gone, and when I rang back, the line was busy.

Instead, I put my mobile phone back on the night table and sat there for a long moment, staring into space, trying to figure out what all this meant, the cat-and-mouse-and-cat game that Pieter, Marcus and I might have been unwittingly playing. Because if I was right, then the whole time that Marcus had been pursuing Carrie, trying to get his revenge on a mistress who had escaped his clutches, Pieter had been working on a very different plan, one that ended with his father's lonely death in a strange country. It was hard to reconcile the mild-mannered grey-suited man I'd met with the idea of a ruthless killer – was it really possible that the kind, gentle person who'd enquired tenderly about my mother had cold-bloodedly drowned his only living parent in a hotel bathtub just hours later?

Even though I'd blithely jotted Pieter's name down on my list of possible suspects, taking the notion seriously was a lot more difficult. He seemed too *nice*, and his relationship with Marcus seemed . . . well, it seemed loyal and supportive, at least on Pieter's side. But I kept coming back to that interview in the forest with Marcus, the interview where Marcus had suggested, or at least heavily hinted, that he might be about to disinherit his only son. Maybe I wasn't the only person he'd spoken to about that. And maybe that loyalty had finally snapped.

Slowly, very slowly, I picked up the list of suspects I'd drawn up before I'd called Dan and scratched out the words next to Pieter's name. Then I picked up the pen and wrote a new entry. *Pieter. Motive: About to be cut out of the company. Opportunity: Maybe . . . yes?*

I was just putting the notepad back where I'd found it on the bedside table when I noticed something. A book that had been lying underneath it.

It was a children's book. It would have been completely inconsequential to a hotel maid or anyone else searching the room, but it wasn't inconsequential to me, for two reasons. First, because it hadn't been there when I left. And second, because I recognized it – even though it was more than ten years since I'd last seen it.

It was a copy of *Winnie-the-Pooh* and it had once belonged to me. I recognized the little rip in the cover – I even recognized the slight brown spatter across the edges of the pages. The droplets looked innocuous enough; they could have been tea or hot chocolate. But they weren't. That spatter was blood. And the last time I had seen the book had been in a cabin far below decks on a boat in the North Sea – a boat where I had once expected to die and where Pooh had become an unexpected lifeline.

I had left the copy behind when I fled – unable to save anything except my own skin – and now it had ended up here. The question was how.

The answer, the only possible answer, was Carrie. She had told me once that this was her favourite book and that, when she was a little girl, her mum had nicknamed her Tigger, telling her, *You're like Tigger, you are, no matter how hard you fall, you always bounce back.* Maybe it was that memory that had made her snatch it up, taking it with her when she made her escape from the boat where both of us had almost died.

For ten years, she must have carried that copy with her across Europe. Was it the link with me? Or the link with what she had done? I wasn't sure. Either way, the book had clearly meant enough to her that she had kept it with her as she moved cities and countries and as layer after layer of the old Carrie was stripped away. And now, here, in a luxury hotel in England, she had finally abandoned it. But why?

I picked it up and leafed slowly through it. Nothing on the title page. Nothing on any of the inside pages as far as I could see. I was about to put it back when one last thought occurred to me. I pulled off the dust jacket – and there it was. A little message written in pencil on the back board.

Dear Pooh, thanks for everything. This time it really is goodbye. Love, Tigger.

So. It was true. She was gone – really gone. Carrie had hit rock bottom, just like she had before, and once again she had bounced.

27

After a long bath, one that washed away every trace of the police cell, I got dressed in clean clothes, picked up my room key and coat, and set out to get some much-needed fresh air.

The rain was lashing against the leaded windows of the stairwell as I went down, and when I passed through the lounge, Cavendish stepped out of his little concealed cubbyhole holding a long, dark green golf umbrella with a curved wooden handle.

'Umbrella, ma'am?'

'I mean, I'm waterproof,' I said with a smile, pointing to my raincoat and hood. 'But thanks anyway.'

I didn't go far, just around the gardens, which were beautiful even in the rain – crystal droplets forming on the autumnal spider webs that stretched across the yew hedges, rain dripping off bare spiked seedheads of flowers whose petals had dropped back in the dog days of August, and little puddles pooling on the dark green holly leaves. I might have walked longer, but the rain was not showing any signs of letting up – in fact, the intensity of the drumming on my hood was increasing – so after fifteen or twenty minutes I retraced my steps across the soaking croquet lawn, picked my way down through the rock garden, and took a shortcut through the shrubbery – only to come face to face with the last person I wanted to see: Pieter Leidmann.

He wasn't in handcuffs, but it looked a lot like he was being escorted to the police station, and not entirely voluntarily. There were two uniformed officers, neither of whom I recognized, walking either side of him: a man in a suit who looked a lot like a lawyer in front; and, following behind them all, towering over even Pieter's considerable height, was his father's bodyguard Heinrich, his grey eyes as cold as I had ever seen them.

For a moment I just stood there, unsure what to say. *I'm sorry about your father. PS: Did you kill him?* The police warning about interfering with witnesses flashed into my head – was I even allowed to speak to him?

Then I realized I was blocking their path, and I stepped aside with a stammered apology. Pieter said nothing. He didn't acknowledge me. He didn't even blink. He just carried on walking, his eyes straight ahead, as if I weren't even there. But Heinrich – Heinrich turned his head as the group approached, fixing me with his cold flint-coloured gaze – and I felt a chill run through me.

This was a man, I was suddenly sure, who would stop at nothing to protect his employer. Once upon a time that employer had been Marcus Leidmann. But judging by the way he was towering over Pieter, that loyalty had very much transferred. What was it they said when a monarch died? The king is dead – long live the king!? Pieter Leidmann looked a lot like he had inherited Heinrich along with the throne. And my little theory had just put Heinrich's new king squarely on the police's radar.

I stood there as the little group drew level, holding Heinrich's unyielding gaze as steadily as I could. He kept his eyes fixed on me, and there was something in them . . . an expression that made me shiver in spite of my warm coat. Calling it *dislike* wasn't nearly strong enough. It was closer to . . . well, it was closer to hate.

He kept his eyes locked on mine as the five men passed me, and as they moved up the path, he continued staring over his shoulder at me with unconcealed malevolence. He had said nothing, not one single word, but the threat was clear: *Put my employer in the firing line again, and you will regret it.* All of a sudden, I understood Carrie's shiver when she spoke of him and her half-joking remark that he was a man who knew where the bodies were buried.

And then he snapped his head forward, and all five of them disappeared around the bend that led towards the car park – and, I assumed, the waiting police car.

When at last I heard the sound of an engine starting up, it was as if a spell had been broken. I let out a shaky breath – yes, that one, the one I didn't know I'd been holding – and began the slow walk up the gravel path to the house.

Did they know? Did Pieter know that *I* was the person who had set the police on his trail for the murder of his father?

I had no idea. I only knew that I had just crossed someone who was now one of the most powerful and wealthiest men in Europe, and that suddenly felt like a very bad idea indeed.

IT WAS A couple of hours later, as I was sitting by the window in my room, a hot cup of coffee steaming gently on the windowsill, that my phone rang. I glanced over at the screen and saw it was a withheld number.

For a moment I debated not answering. Was it spam? But it might be the police with an important update or some quirk of international dialling.

In the end I picked it up. 'Hello?'

'Laura Blacklock?' The voice was deep and flat, no accent that I could make out.

'Yes?'

'Be careful what you say to the police.'

'*What?*' The adrenaline that shot though me was like bolt of electricity – fear, anger and surprise all tangled up together. 'I'm sorry, what the fuck did you say? Who is this?'

'You heard me,' said the voice. Then there was a click, and the call ended.

I stood there, my heart pounding with fury, glaring down at the screen like the NO CALLER ID on the display could magically tell me something I didn't already know. It was Pieter – I was sure of it. Not the caller – he would have been careful about that. He was undoubtedly being interviewed by the police right now, carefully giving himself an alibi for his threats. But it was someone on his staff. Maybe even Heinrich.

For a second, I fought the urge to throw the phone across the room, smash it into the wall, and stamp on it. But my more rational side knew that was ridiculous – this was (a) my lifeline to Judah and the kids, and (b) an eight-hundred-dollar phone. Destroying it would be the definition of cutting off my nose to spite my face.

But as I stood there, my heart still thudding with the aftermath of the shock, I noticed there was something else listed on the call history screen. There was a missed call. It was from Dan's mobile.

My fingers were trembling as I pressed the icon to call him back. Had the police charged Pieter? Maybe that was why I'd had that threatening call. Even better, had they dropped the charges against me?

'Dan?' I said as soon as he picked up. 'It's me, Lo. Laura, I mean. You called me?'

'I did,' Dan said. He sounded . . . not as jubilant as I would have hoped. 'Did you hear they took Pieter Leidmann in for questioning again?'

'Yes.' I took a sip of coffee, as much to steady my nerves as anything. 'I mean, I didn't know for sure, but I saw him leaving the hotel accompanied by a bunch of officers. And I had – well, never mind that now.' I doubted Dan could do much about the strange call. I was pretty sure that Pieter Leidmann's people would have covered their tracks very carefully. And stripped of its context, without the flat, menacing tone of the caller, *Be careful what you say to the police* sounded less like a threat and more like good legal advice. What I needed to know was how this affected my case. 'Are they arresting him?'

'I don't think so. In fact, I'm pretty sure they let him go. That's what I wanted to tell you.'

'Fuck.' I felt the air go out of me and sat down on the bed. The hand holding the coffee cup was shaking very slightly, I saw, little vibrations going across the surface of the liquid. 'Does that mean he's coming back here?'

'That's certainly a risk, yes. He may have moved to a different hotel, but I imagine he's been told not to leave the country, so it's not impossible that he's still in the vicinity.'

'*Fuck.*' I put the coffee cup down on the saucer, hearing the rattle of china against china, then rubbed my eye sockets with my free hand. 'Do you think he knows I was the one who pointed the finger?'

'No!' Dan said, his voice reassuring. 'No, absolutely not.'

But I was remembering the cold fury in Heinrich's eyes and the flat menace in the voice of the caller, and I wasn't so sure. You didn't have to be Sherlock Holmes to realize that I was the person who could put Pieter Leidmann at the crime scene and that any arrest probably had something to do with what I had told the police. I wished now that I'd been quicker on my feet and had managed to record the anonymous call. If it happened again, I would – but at the time, the last thing I'd been thinking about was keeping the caller on the line long enough to get him on tape.

'Listen, Dan,' I said. 'I meant to ask you this earlier, but can I leave? The hotel, I mean. Or do I have to stay here because of my bail conditions?'

'You can certainly go to your mum's,' Dan said. His voice across the phone line was a little tinny. 'I wouldn't go anywhere else, though. The last thing we want is to spook them into thinking you're fleeing the country. But Dickers made it clear he'd be okay with your mum's as an alternative to the hotel, and you gave him the address, didn't you?'

'I did, but the thing is, my mum's in hospital, and I don't have a key to her house. I was thinking I might go . . . well, I don't know where exactly. Maybe a hotel in St Albans. I haven't figured it out yet, but the idea of staying here waiting for Pieter to possibly come back . . . it's not exactly thrilling me.'

'I can totally get that.' Dan's voice was understanding. 'And I'm sure Dickers will too. You're not under a bail condition to remain at the Old Manor, but it would be a good idea to let him know before you make any sudden moves. Look, I assume you're not going anywhere tonight, so why don't you let me know your new address tomorrow, when you've figured out where you're going, and I'll give him a ring and make sure it's all ticked off.'

'Okay,' I said. Dan's words should have been reassuring, but somehow the reminder of how much I was still at the police's beck and call was not. The idea that Pieter had been let out after just a few short hours . . . 'Do they really think he didn't do it?' I said. 'Pieter, I mean. They seemed to let him go so quickly compared to how they treated me. Does that mean they've ruled him out completely?'

On the other end of the line, I heard Dan make a kind of noncommittal sound.

'I wouldn't go that far. I'd say it's more likely his lawyers have made short work of them with the recording.'

'Recording?' I was puzzled now.

'Oh, sorry, sorry, I forgot I hadn't spoken to you since they sent it over. It's the recording of the room-service order. I requested a copy of it, as it's fairly germane to your alibi, and . . . well, I'll play it for you. See what you think.'

There was a brief scuffle at the other end, then a click, and I heard a woman's voice come over the telephone, a little distorted.

'Hello, Old Manor Hotel room service, how may I help?'

'Hello.' It was a man's voice, and as soon as he spoke, I felt the coldness in the pit of my stomach harden into something heavy and full of dread. 'Hello, this is Marcus Leidmann. May I order some breakfast.'

The request was phrased as a question, but there was no interrogative uplift. It was spoken by someone who had absolutely no doubt about whether his commands would be obeyed. It was also . . . well, if it wasn't Marcus, it was an astonishingly, *astonishingly* good impression. I had only spoken to Marcus a few times, and yet the force of his personality, the gravel in his voice, the curtness of his remarks, they were all unmistakable. *She was a rather limited person.* I fought the urge to compare the voice coming down the phone to my own recording of the man I'd interviewed back in Switzerland and instead forced myself to sit quietly and listen.

'Of course, Mr Leidmann. What would you like?'

'I would like my usual order. Coffee. Two eggs. Orange juice.' There was a background noise to the recording, a kind of low roaring that made it sound like there was traffic in the distance, though that could have been a defect on the tape.

'Of course. Will there be anything else?'

I heard an odd sound. Could it be a splash? There was a short pause, then Marcus said, curtly, 'No.'

There was another, briefer, pause, and the girl at the other end of the line said, 'Well, no problem at all, Mr Leidmann. That will be up with you in about twenty minutes. Is there anything else I can help you with?'

Then the call cut out.

There was a short silence, then Dan came back on the line.

'I'll get an expert on it, but I've googled a couple of interviews with the guy, and I have to say, I think it sounds like him, don't you?'

'Yes,' I said flatly. There was no point in denying it. It did sound like him, unfortunately. It sounded exactly like him and absolutely nothing like Pieter. 'Yes, it sounds like him.'

'And further to our idea of Pieter being the person to make the actual call, there's two problems with that. First, I've gone through the witness statements the police sent over, and the hotel staff are very clear that he was at breakfast the whole time, in full view of about a dozen guests and staff members. And second, the call came from the hotel-room phone, apparently. The police have checked that out. It was a cordless, and it was found in the bottom of the bathtub, which would tie up with the background noise. You can hear a tap running.'

Suddenly the low roaring sound on the recording and the splashes made sense. Of course – he had been phoning from the bathroom. Fuck. It all tied in. It even backed up what Pieter had said in the corridor about his father's intention to have a bath and order breakfast. Had I got this completely wrong?

Dan could evidently hear my doubts over the phone because he said, 'Look, Laura, don't worry. In some ways this is good for us. If Pieter sticks to his story that he did shut the door properly – and that's what his initial statement suggests – it's going to be very hard for the police to explain how anyone got entry to the room during the period they're looking at, particularly someone like you with no access to the lock system and logs. It makes it much more likely it was someone on the inside. If it comes to court – and I don't think it will – that's going to be my line.'

'Someone on the inside?' I was puzzled. 'You mean someone at the hotel was in on this?'

'Look, the way I see it, there's two possibilities here. One, the door didn't lock for some reason, and Pieter Leidmann seems pretty adamant in his statement that's not the case. It's not a lie that would help him, on the face of it, so I can't see why he'd make that part up. Or two, it *did* lock, and someone tampered with the IT system to erase the records between nine oh-five and nine fifteen. And that pretty much has to be someone at the hotel. The idea of some random guest managing to infiltrate the system and tinker with the settings – well, it's just not plausible.'

'Huh.' It was an angle I hadn't considered, and I paused while I took it in. 'You're right.'

'Anyway, "Don't panic," as Douglas Adams would say, and leave it with me. Are you holding up?'

I considered the question. Was I? In some ways I felt like I was doing okay. I was putting one foot in front of the other, not dwelling on what could go wrong. I hadn't even had a proper panic attack about all this, which was considerably more than I thought I could have managed five years ago.

But every time I thought about Judah or the boys, I wanted to burst into tears. And if I thought too hard about the charges stacked against me, about the fact that Pieter Leidmann's high-priced lawyers had taken about five minutes to wriggle him off a hook that I was still stuck on – well, it made me want to curl up in despair.

I couldn't admit that to Dan, though. Not least because he was the person trying his best to help me, and the comparison with the high-priced lawyers wasn't likely to go down well with him.

'I'm okay,' I said at last. I wasn't sure my voice was totally convincing. It sounded wobbly. Thinking of Judah and the boys had been a mistake. But the words, at least, were positive. 'Truly. I'm okay. I just – I *really* want to get this sorted out.'

'I know,' Dan said. He sounded bolstering. 'And we will. Hang in there, okay, Laura?'

I nodded, forgetting he couldn't see me, and cleared my throat of the frog that was suddenly lodged there and said, 'Yeah. I will. Thanks, Dan. Bye.'

And then I hung up the phone and put my head in my hands and tried not to give way to the tears that were threatening to overwhelm me.

I don't know how long I sat there. Ten minutes, maybe. Then I sat up, shook back my hair, and pulled the piece of paper towards me – the list I had left on the bedside table.

	Motive	Opportunity
Me	Supposedly the photos	No, but the police don't know that
Pieter	About to be cut out of the company	Maybe... yes?
Cleaner	None known	Yes, could 100% have killed Marcus
Heinrich	Paid by Pieter???	Possibly, if the door-lock info is wrong
Adeline	Ditto	Ditto
Carrie	Hell yes	No
Unknown	???	? But door lock equally a problem

Once more, this time with a heavy heart, I scratched out Pieter's entry and amended the line under Opportunity to *Probably not*. Then, at the bottom, I added another entry.

	Motive	Opportunity
Hotel employee	??	Yes, could have altered the lock info

I folded up the list and tucked it inside the copy of *Winnie-the-Pooh* that Carrie had left on the bedside table. And then, thinking I might as well put all the information in the same place, I dug in the pocket of my jeans, fishing for the piece of paper I had copied the door-lock information on to.

When I pulled the paper out of my back pocket, my first reaction was that I had got the wrong sheet. What I was holding was not a handwritten list of door-lock times but a printout of a Eurostar ticket, presumably left over from when I'd travelled back from Paris with Carrie. I was about to throw it in the bin and look in my other pocket when I realized – I hadn't been wearing these jeans the day I'd travelled back.

Slowly, I unfolded the paper, and there, on the blank side, it was: the list of times and key cards.

But I wasn't interested in the list anymore. I turned the page over and looked at the other side, at the ticket information.

It was a Eurostar ticket for the same route Carrie and I had taken – Paris to London, St Pancras, Wednesday 6 November. Even the time was the same. It was exact same crossing. Only two things were different. The ticket was regular economy, not the premier economy Carrie and I had taken. And the name – the name on the ticket was not mine or Carrie's, but it was still a name I knew well. Horribly well, in fact.

It was Benjamin Alan Howard.

Ben fucking Howard.

What the hell had he been doing on the same train as us?

I stared at it, trying to make sense of it. Was it possible he had been in the same train, the same station, probably on the same TGV, for all I knew, and hadn't mentioned it? How could this possibly be a coincidence?

My heart was thudding in my chest and I reached out to grab my mobile, phone him, demand an explanation – and then stopped. No matter what was really going on, he was going to say the same thing: that there was an innocent explanation, that he'd always been going to take that train. After all, he had caught the Eurostar out, why wouldn't he have caught it back? And yes, it was a day early, but

I hadn't asked him about his schedule. I hadn't asked him anything at all. If I'd bothered to enquire, he would have told me that he was leaving Wednesday, always had been. He had an urgent deadline back in London.

And, most persuasive, as far as I was concerned, if he really *were* tracking me, would he honestly have been stupid enough to hand over his Eurostar ticket?

That version of events was possible. More than possible. I could even hear the explanations in Ben's indignant tone. The problem was, hearing them from his lips would be useless. I would have no better idea than I did now whether he was telling the truth or not. I would be, in fact, in the exact same position – uncertain of Ben's motivations, unsure of what was really going on, unable to trust him. The only difference would be that Ben would know I had this information.

No. It was better to hug this to my chest. At least for the moment.

But one thing was for sure – I was no longer able to trust Ben. And now I took out the sheet of paper from the copy of *Winnie-the-Pooh* and added a final line at the bottom:

Ben Howard   ???   ???

BBC News
Monday 12 November

Sussex Police announced today that they are urgently looking to question the woman pictured above in connection with the recent death of financier Marcus Leidmann at a West Sussex luxury hotel.

The woman, described as being in her early forties, white, and of slim build, is approximately 5ft 6in or 170cm tall, with dark eyes and dark hair, which she may have dyed.

She is thought to be travelling under the name Lo, or Laura, Blacklock but may be using an alias.

The suspect is wanted for questioning in connection with the murder of Mr Leidmann, and the police have urged members of the public not to approach her but to report sightings or any additional information to Sussex Police on 101 or by calling Crimestoppers on 0800 555 111.

PART
FIVE

PART FIVE

28

I didn't sleep well that night. It wasn't just the stifling heat of the hotel room, the radiators working too enthusiastically to combat the chill outside. It wasn't just the thought of Pieter Leidmann roaming around the English countryside and likely wishing me dead. It wasn't even the fact that I was beginning to suffer from serious cabin fever – in the end I'd decided to stick it out just one more night at the Old Manor and get my mum's keys in the morning, which had seemed logical at 5 p.m. but now seemed like a pretty terrible idea.

No, it was everything. Carrie was gone. I was alone, trapped in this room, with the four walls pressing in on me, and the terrifying notion that without my passport, I was completely stuck here, thousands of miles away from my husband and children. What on earth was I going to do? Could they seriously keep me here until the trial?

It didn't help that neither Judah nor my mum were answering their phones. Judah in fact had been out of contact for the past several hours, which was extremely unlike him, my calls going to voicemail and my messages still marked as unread. My mum . . . well, that was less surprising, although she *had* promised to let me know when she was out of surgery. In the end I had resorted to phoning the ward, who were chilly about the idea of giving out information but thawed slightly when I said Pamela Crew was my mother and that I was desperate to know she was okay. In the end the ward sister admitted that my mother was out of surgery and the operation had gone well but said that she was sleeping off the anesthetic, and I hadn't had the heart to demand that she wake her up.

Judah, though . . . It was honestly a little hard to accept that he had left me on unread for . . . I checked my phone, squinting at the bright screen in the darkness. The most recent message squatted there, painfully vulnerable, as close to a cry for help as I was ever going to make: *I'm not doing great. Do you have time to talk?*

It had been five hours since I sent the message and it was showing as not just unread, but undelivered. Had his phone really been turned off the entire time? Or did he just not care that his wife was three thousand miles away, facing criminal charges for a murder she hadn't committed?

I rolled over in bed, turning the pillow to the unused side in a vain attempt to cool my hot cheeks, and trying not to think about everything that could go wrong. In the daytime, Dan's cheerful assurance that this would all be sorted out very soon was persuasive. But here, now, alone in the silent pressing darkness . . . I was not so sure.

I was just drifting off to sleep when a sound made me sit up in bed, my heart pounding wild and hard in my chest. I hadn't imagined it, had I? It was a soft *tap, tap, tap* on my door. Not the confident rap of a hotel staff member on official business or the peremptory bang of the police come to drag me back to a cell – at least, I devoutly hoped not.

For a long moment I just sat there, my heart thumping in my chest like a war drum, and then it came again, a little louder this time. *Tap, tap, tap.* Was it . . . Carrie?

The thought made me turn on the reading lamp and jump out of bed, grabbing for a robe, but I was only halfway across the room when I heard another sound: a voice, muffled by the door – and it was male.

That made me stop in my tracks. I couldn't quite make out the words – whoever it was had spoken quietly, maybe to an associate, or maybe they were trying to figure out if I was awake without disturbing the other guests. But if it wasn't a hotel employee or the police, I couldn't think of an innocent explanation for why a man would be trying to gain entry to my hotel room at . . . I checked my phone: 12:49 a.m. Fuck. This wasn't good.

For a second, I thought about phoning the front desk, asking them to send someone up. But what if it *was* Carrie and I'd made a mistake about the voice?

What if it's not Carrie, whispered back my subconscious. *What if it's Pieter Leidmann with Heinrich standing right behind him, ready to make you regret you ever said anything about him to the cops?*

I shook myself. This was stupid. There was every likelihood that Pieter Leidmann was long gone – I certainly wouldn't have stuck around following his arrest if I were him. Even if he *was* still here, he would be extraordinarily stupid to try anything in a hotel full of guests and witnesses. And there was a perfectly good security peephole in the middle of the door. Maybe, just maybe, I should use it instead of indulging in paranoid fantasies about men come to menace me in the middle of the night.

Moving with infinite caution, I tiptoed across the rug, trying not to let the centuries-old floorboards creak any more than necessary, and stood in front of the door. Then, taking a deep breath, I put my eye as close to the security peephole as I could, and only after I was in position did I swing the cover aside so that no one standing in the hallway would detect the movement or the little flash of light from within.

It took a few seconds for my eyes to adjust to the brighter light of the corridor. The first thing I saw was that whoever was outside, it wasn't Carrie. There was absolutely, definitely a man standing in front of my door, but I couldn't make out who. He was alone and facing away from me, looking back the way he'd come as if deciding what to do, and the fish-eye lens distorted his stance, making it hard to see his true build. It was someone tall, I was sure of that, though probably not Heinrich. I thought even through the fish-eye lens, I would have recognized those broad, hulking shoulders. And I was fairly sure it wasn't Pieter; the hair wasn't right – it was curly and dark and streaked with grey at the temples. In fact, it looked a lot like . . .

I sucked in a breath and spoke through the door, my voice a shaky, incredulous whisper.

'Judah?'

He swung around to face the peephole, his expression . . . well, I couldn't make it out, but some kind of mix of relief and surprise.

'Lo?'

'Oh my God.'

I found my fingers were fumbling as I tried to fling open the door. First, I forgot that I'd engaged the security latch when I went to bed, and the door banged against it, then when I tried to close it again so I could remove the latch, I managed to slam Judah's hand in the gap, making him yelp and swear. But at last, the door was open, he was inside, and I was in his arms, breathing his familiar scent and sobbing out questions that weren't even really questions – things like 'What the fuck?' and 'How?' and 'Why didn't you call?'

'I'm so glad to see you,' he kept saying. His face was pressed into my neck. 'Oh my God, I'm so glad to see you, Lo, I was going nuts. What the hell is happening?'

'Is your hand okay?' I pulled away, holding his face between my hands, kissing him, and then pulling back to ask it again. 'And where are the boys?'

'My hand's fine. And they're fine, they're at home. I told you, I asked my mom to come back down to look after them.'

'And I told *you* I didn't want you to leave them!'

'Lo, honey, they put you under *arrest*. There was no way I was going to sit back and let that happen – the more I thought about it, the more I realized how nuts that was, that I was sitting on my ass in Manhattan while you were rotting in some British jail cell.'

'Judah, I love you.' I was smiling in spite of myself, smiling in spite of the fact that he'd ignored everything I'd asked of him, abandoned our kids, and flown halfway round the world when I'd expressly told him I *didn't* want him to. But I didn't care; it was so good to see him. 'I love you, but you're not a lawyer! What do you think you're going to be able to do that Dan can't?'

'I have no idea.' He looked serious. 'Drag the fucking US consul in by his ear if I have to. But I couldn't sit there and let you go through this alone. The boys will be fine, you know they will.'

I nodded. I did know it, even though part of my heart was hurting for how confused they must be. First Mummy flew off into the blue, and for who knew how much longer, and now Daddy too. I could all too easily imagine Teddy waking up in the night, crying, asking where we both were. However, with my rational head on, I knew that if they did wake up, Gail would be perfectly competent to comfort them – and that in the daytime she was almost certainly giving them Pop-Tarts and Cheetos and all the processed snacks I didn't allow and letting them watch *Bluey* from dawn until dusk. In all probability they were not crying out in the night for me but were happy as pigs in mud.

And maybe, if I were honest, that was part of what was making my heart ache too: the idea that my little boys were growing out of wanting me 24/7, that soon they wouldn't need me like they had when they were babies and toddlers. And that was okay.

I cleared my throat.

'You're right. They will be fine. I know that. I'm just – oh God, I'm going to cry.'

It was the second time in as many days. I felt the hot prickly tears welling up in my eyes, the sobs hard in the back of my throat, and when Judah put his arms around me and I rested my forehead on his shoulder, they came – proper sobs, in a way I hadn't cried in years, maybe not since I was a pregnant hormonal mess.

'I miss them so much, Judah. I just want to go home.'

'I know, honey.' He held me, his cheek warm against the top of my head. 'I know. I got you. I've got you.'

'It's all such a fucking mess. Part of me thinks no one killed him, you know? Maybe the old bastard had a heart attack and died.'

'Lo, honey, what actually happened?' Judah pulled back, wiping my tears, and I shook my head.

'I have no idea.' I realized, for the first time, that I hadn't told Judah the full story, from start to finish. In fact, I hadn't told *anyone* the true, unexpurgated story, the one that included Carrie.

Maybe it was time to do that. Maybe I needed to get the stupidity of what I'd done off my chest.

I took a deep breath.

'Judah, there's something I have to tell you. Something I haven't told anyone – not even the police.'

His face went pale, and he sat down on the edge of my bed, but he was still holding my hand.

'What is it?' He swallowed. 'You – you didn't actually kill the guy, did you?'

I laughed at that, a short, shocked laugh that had me clapping my free hand over my mouth. 'What? No. Fuck, Judah, how can you ask that?'

The relief on his face told me that he had actually thought it was a possibility, and I wasn't sure how I felt about that – but he hadn't let go of my hand, and that was something.

'Then what? Spit it out, Lo, you're concerning me.'

'You're not going to like it.' I felt suddenly scared. Not just of Judah's reaction, but of the reality of what I'd done – and the strong possibility that he was going to make me tell someone and face up to that reality.

'Lo, *say it*,' Judah said. His face was really worried now, and I knew that I had to just rip the Band-Aid off.

'Okay. Listen, and please just hear me out before you go off the deep end.'

Judah nodded, and now I could see he was puzzled as well as worried. Did he think I'd had an affair? I thought of those photos and realized I needed to tell him about those too, but that could wait. Carrie was more important.

'Carrie's back,' I said, and watched as all the emotions I'd expected – shock, confusion, blank rage – flickered across his face, along with some I hadn't, like a kind of hurt disbelief.

It took a good hour to go through exactly what had happened – from the note on the bed back in the Grand Hotel du Lac to Carrie's impassioned late-night plea in suite 11 to our mad dash across Europe and, finally, to us both ending up here, in the Old Manor, and Marcus's death.

'It's her,' Judah said as soon as I'd finished. 'It has to be. How could you be such a—' He stopped, biting back the words I knew he'd been going to say. *Such a soft touch. Such a fool. Such a gullible idiot.*

A part of me wanted to take offence, but it wouldn't do any good. He was right to be hurt that I hadn't told him. He was right even to be angry. I had, if not exactly lied to him, at least kept a secret that was bigger than anything else I'd ever concealed our entire marriage.

But more than that – he was right in a different kind of way. I didn't think Carrie had killed Marcus Leidmann, but she had landed me in another life-or-death situation and walked away scot-free –

and it was my own soft heart that had allowed that to happen. Maybe I had been an idiot.

But there was no point in dwelling on that. I shook my head.

'I knew you'd say that. And maybe you're right about me being stupid to trust her again. But you don't understand, it's not like I'm trusting her word on this. I was right here when Marcus was killed. And I saw her in there – she was naked, Judah. In the bath. She was in there the whole time. I could hear her splashing around, I was even talking to her through the door at one point.'

'That could have all been part of her plan. She could have, I don't know, climbed out the window.'

'Are you joking?' I tried not to laugh, but there wasn't much amusement in my voice, only weariness. 'Judah, honestly, come into the bathroom and take a look.'

Reluctantly, knowing I was about to shoot his very convenient theory to pieces, Judah pushed himself off the bed and together we walked through into the little bathroom. The first thing he did was try the window – but it had a limiter fitted, meaning it could only be opened a few inches. He spent some time fiddling with the device, trying to see if he could get it off, then gave up and went back into the bedroom to do the same thing I had done just a few days before – peer out of the bedroom window at the long expanse of sheer golden stone separating my bedroom from Marcus Leidmann's.

I could tell from his silence that he was coming to the same conclusions I had – that no one but a professional climber armed with ropes, crampons and belay anchors could have scaled the side of that building from my window.

'Fuck,' he said at last, and I knew that was his way of telling me I was right, and he was wrong – there was no way Carrie could have killed Marcus.

'See?' I said. 'It's just not possible. She's the one person – apart from me – that absolutely couldn't have killed him.'

'Then,' Judah said, a little stubbornly. I frowned.

'What do you mean?'

'I mean, she couldn't have killed him *then*. Killing him at nine fifteen while you were in the bedroom listening to her in the bath – that's impossible, I'll give you that. But the time of death rests exclusively on that phone call. It seems pretty sus to me. In fact, it seems like it's set up to give Carrie an alibi.'

'I've already explained to you, Dan and I looked into that theory, and much as I'd like someone else to have made that call, it's just not possible. It was Marcus speaking. I mean, I played you the recording.' I was starting to feel frustrated. I understood why Judah didn't like Carrie – well, that was an understatement – but his refusal to look the evidence in the eye was more than a little annoying. However much he wanted Carrie to be guilty, the facts just didn't stack up, any more than they stacked up to condemn my own pet villain, Pieter Leidmann. Both of them were ruled out by the phone call, and Judah's inability to accept that was beginning to grate. 'I can play you my interview with him as well so you can compare the voices, but I'm telling you, it's him. I met the guy; his tone is pretty unmistakable. And not only is it his voice, but the call was placed on his own room phone, which was found at the bottom of the tub. So please tell me how anyone else could have done that?'

'The reception on those cordless phones stretches pretty far,' Judah said, but with the air of someone who knew he'd lost. I shook my head, trying to be annoyed with him for refusing to accept what I'd already spent hours figuring out – but really, I knew that he was only trying to help, willing himself to find a solution to this whole mess, one that ended up with someone else behind bars, not me.

'Look, let's go to bed,' I said at last. 'It's late, I'm shattered. You must be tired from traveling all day. Let's go to bed, and we can talk about this in the morning.'

But Judah put his arms around me, shaking his head.

'I'll go to bed,' he said, and then he kissed me on the side of my neck, his lips soft and warm. 'But I'm warning you, I'm not tired. I'm on East Coast time. It's barely nine o'clock for me. And I haven't seen my wife for a week.'

In spite of myself, in spite of my tiredness and everything I'd been through, I felt my own lips curve in a smile as Judah's mouth moved over my collarbone and down my shoulder, pulling aside my robe. Yes, everything was a shitshow. Yes, I might still be facing charges for a crime I hadn't committed. But tonight was the first night Judah and I had spent alone together since Eli had been born. Maybe a good night's sleep could wait . . . for a little while.

29

I woke up tired, relieved, and sore in the best possible way, wondering why I felt so shattered and also so content.

Rolling over to squint at my phone in the thin autumn sunshine gave me the answer to both those questions. I was tired because it was 7 a.m. and I'd had barely four hours of sleep the night before. I was relieved because however awful things were, my husband was lying in bed next to me, his arm over my waist, looking as irresistible as I'd ever found him. The curly hair at his temples was more silver now than dark, and I could see the lines at the corners of his eyes, relaxed in sleep but too ingrained ever to fade completely, but none of it mattered to me – I had never wanted him more than I did now.

Knowing that it was 2 a.m. to his body clock, I swung my legs over the side of the bed and stretched, then went through to run myself a bath. I was up to my hips in bubbles, scrolling my phone, trying not to think about the day ahead – would Dan come back with news about the charges? Would I finally be able to get away from here and see Mum? – when something occurred me to me. For a moment I just lay there stock-still in the rising water with my finger poised where I'd been about to click. I could hear the low roar of the extractor fan and the thunder of water from the taps.

'Judah?' I called. Nothing. 'Judah?'

Then I got up. I wound a towel around my naked, dripping torso and walked through into the bedroom. Judah was still lying on the bed, out cold, his bruised hand cradled on his pillow.

'Judah,' I said urgently.

He shook his head, burying his face in the pillow as if to shut out both the morning sunshine and me.

'Jude. Wake up. I need to try something.'

'What is it?' At last he sat up, blinking and disoriented. 'Fuck, what time is it?'

'Almost eight. Listen, I want you to make a call to our room.'

'What?' He frowned in confusion, then rubbed the sleep out of his eyes with his unbruised hand. 'But we're both here.'

'Just – look, it'll make sense, I promise. Just do what I'm telling you. Call our room from your mobile.'

Judah made a face but did as I asked, likely, I thought, because he was too jet-lagged to argue. There was a brief pause while the front desk put him through, and then our room phone rang and I picked it up.

'Okay, hold that thought.' I hitched the towel more firmly around myself. 'Stay on the line.'

'Lo, what the fuck is going on?' Judah said wearily, lying back on the pillow. 'Can this not wait?'

'No. Stay on the line. Tell me if I'm breaking up. Okay?'

'Okay,' Judah said fatalistically, and I picked up the room key and let myself out into the corridor, devoutly hoping I wouldn't run into any of the other guests.

'Can you hear me?' I said into the room phone as I walked away from our room, up the corridor.

'Yes.' I heard Judah's voice come down the line, a little crackly and considerably grumpy, but clear enough. 'Yes, I can hear you.'

'How about now?' I was level with Marcus's room.

'Yes, I can still hear you. How long are we going to keep this up for?'

'Almost done.' I was in the stairwell now, well past Marcus's room. 'Can you still hear me?'

'Just about.' Judah's voice was very crackly now; the reception starting to become patchy. 'You're breaking up a little, but I can make out what you're saying.'

'And how about – oh, shit.' I had turned the corner past the stairwell into a different wing of the building and had almost run into an elderly man and his wife, who looked considerably startled to see a half-naked woman in a towel. 'Sorry, sorry, wrong corridor.'

Stifling my laughter, I did a hasty 180 and half walked, half ran back down the hall to Lark, where I swiped myself in and put the room phone back on the cradle with a click. Then, ignoring Judah pulling the spare pillow over his head, I picked up the copy of *Winnie-the-Pooh* from where it was lying on the bedside table, pulled out the list of lock times, and stared at it with fresh eyes.

'Lo,' Judah's voice came, muffled, from beneath the pillow, 'do you have *any* intention of explaining this or are we just playing ding-dong-ditch with unsuspecting hotel guests?'

'Shh,' I said. 'One sec, I need to . . . '

I was staring at the list, at the times, watching entries that hadn't quite added up slide into focus, and things I'd never been able to explain make sudden sense. There was a strange feeling in my stomach – a mix of triumph . . . and dread. And suddenly – I knew. I knew exactly how Marcus had been killed, and when. And I knew who did it. I just had no idea how I was going to get myself out of all this.

'I've got it,' I said at last. The triumph was ebbing away, and now I felt mostly anger. My voice when I spoke again was cold. 'I know how she did it.'

'How *who* did it?' Judah had cast aside the spare pillow, and now he had his forearm over his eyes, blocking out the sun. 'You're making no sense.'

'Carrie. You were right, Judah. It *was* her all along. And I know how she did it – how she made the phone call on Marcus's room phone.'

'What?' Judah sat up, suddenly wide awake. 'Are you kidding me?'

'No. It was what you said last night – about the reception being pretty good on those phones. I suddenly realized how she could have done it – how she could have made that call right under my nose.'

'But—' Judah was speechless. 'But, Lo, are you saying she killed him?'

I swallowed.

'I think . . . I think I am. I just have no idea what to do now.'

30

It took a long time, going back and forth through the list of key-card entries, to explain my theory to Judah, but at last he was in agreement – it was the only possible way of making sense of every single entry, of the phone call, and of Carrie's own behaviour.

It explained everything, every last key swipe, every single detail, and in some ways it was the perfect get-out for me – the only problem was that there was no way I could convey any of this to the police without confessing to my own part in the plot, to the fact that I'd helped a wanted criminal escape across Europe and, however unwittingly, get away with a second murder.

If I'd told DS Dickers and DC Wright about Carrie when they first came to my room, if I'd explained everything, who she was, what she'd done, she would be in a cell right now, and I would be off the hook. Instead, she had slipped through all our fingers – and I had no idea where she could be.

'You don't know who her mum is?' Judah said. I shook my head.

'She never spoke about her family. I don't even know if Carrie is her real name. She said it was, but she has a pretty elastic relationship with the truth.'

'If only—' Judah said, then bit his lip. I knew what he'd been going to say, and in all honesty, in his position, I wasn't sure if I could have held back the *I told you so* that was clearly hovering on the tip of his tongue. I sighed.

'It's okay, you can say it. If only I'd shopped her into the police when this whole thing started. If only I'd told you. I mean, I didn't because I knew what you'd say: *You can't trust her, tell the police, turn her in*, and guess what, you were right. Stupid fucking Lo.'

'You're not stupid,' Judah said, with a sigh. He pulled me into his side, kissing the top of my head. 'We just have to figure out what to do. And actually that wasn't what I was going to say. I was going to say, if only there was some way of tracking her down. She had a mobile phone, didn't she?'

'Yes.' I was thinking hard. 'A burner. But I have no idea what the number was. She never gave it to me. Could the police figure something out from the phones that connected to the hotel Wi-Fi?'

'Maybe...' Judah looked dubious. 'I don't know if they can find out a phone number from that, but maybe an IP address. Depends on if she actually hooked into the Wi-Fi, though. If she was being really paranoid, she might not have. Look, Lo, I think you have to hand this whole thing over to the police and just take the rap.'

'There's a good chance I'm looking at prosecution, you know that, right?' I looked up at him, and he nodded soberly. 'Obstruction of justice or something. Fuck.' I thought about explaining all this to Dickers and Wright and felt sick to my stomach.

'Hon, it'll be okay,' Judah said, but I shook my head. With his arm hard around me, that felt true, but I knew it wasn't. Not for certain, anyway.

'We should pack,' I said at last. 'I'm going to see Mum today, and I can get her key while I'm there. I never thought I'd say this about such a nice place, but I can't wait to get out of here.'

'Actually, that reminds me,' Judah said. He looked puzzled. 'I was going to ask you, and I forgot. Where's your suitcase? It's not in the wardrobe. Did they put it somewhere?'

'Oh, that.' I felt another wave of irritation rise within me. 'You can thank Carrie for that. Again. Her bag broke, so she pinched mine.'

Judah let out a short laugh, more shock than mirth.

'You're kidding me. That was her parting shot? She stole your suitcase?'

'Yup. The woman's shameless.'

I gave a shrug, and went to stand up, but before I could do so, I felt Judah grip my arm, his fingers digging into my biceps.

'Wait,' he said slowly, 'you're telling me she took *your* bag?'

'Yes,' I said a little impatiently. 'That's what I just told you.'

'But – Lo – this solves everything.' There was a rising excitement in his voice. I frowned.

'What? What does it solve? I'm stuck with a stupid designer tote with a broken strap.'

'I put an AirTag in all our bags.' Judah was sitting bolt upright now, his eyes wide. 'Last summer, when everything was melting down and all the airlines were losing luggage. Don't you remember?'

I opened my mouth to say no, then realized I did remember. I remembered Judah buying the tags – little silver things that looked like tiny flying saucers – and setting them up on our phones before we went to the lakes. I hadn't bothered to get involved beyond feeling faintly annoyed when Judah was away and the AirTag in the kids' suitcase started pinging out of the blue. Now I wished that I'd paid more attention to how they worked.

'So what does that mean?' I asked.

'It means we can track her – at least, it does if she hasn't had an alert and disabled the thing. How long ago did she leave?'

I began working back, counting in my head.

'I think she probably left early yesterday,' I said at last. 'Though

I'm not certain. It was sometime while I was at the police station, so I can't be sure.'

'So we're talking twenty-four to thirty-six hours, max?' Judah had picked up my phone and was scrolling through the apps. 'I think they start alerting about twenty-four hours after they've lost contact with their home device. So we'll have to pray she hasn't had a notification on her phone and figured it out.'

'Would it work on her phone, though?' I asked, a little doubtfully. 'She had a really cheap phone. One of those twenty-pound Androids you get at train stations. It wasn't an iPhone or anything fancy.'

But Judah was shaking his head.

'Wouldn't make any difference. It's an anti-stalking measure. I think in theory any phone in the vicinity of an unclaimed AirTag *could* get an alert, though it depends how new the phone is. And whether Carrie realizes what it means.'

He had opened up the Find My app on my phone while we were speaking, and now he clicked on a little suitcase-shaped icon labelled *Lo's Case*. A map popped up. A little blue dot in a tiny house entirely surrounded by streets. Judah scrolled out and out. I saw the green splotch of a park. Then a primary school. Then the text *Woodingdean*. It took me a minute to place it – a small town near Brighton, which became apparent when Judah scrolled out a little more and the blue of the sea came into the frame.

'Huh,' Judah said. He sounded a little disconcerted. I was feeling something similar. I'm not sure what I had expected – anything from the Ritz to halfway to Dubai; neither would have surprised me. But a small town off the Sussex coast was not up there.

'Do you think it's her mum's house?' I asked. Judah had pulled up Google Street View and was frowning.

'Could be. It's a *really* unremarkable little house. Just a normal south-coast bungalow.'

He showed me the stretch of road. Small, single-storey houses lined a suburban street, modest little things that looked a lot like the bungalow my grandma had retired to before she went into a home. It was probably smaller than our flat in New York and undoubtedly cost a fraction of the price.

'So what do we do?' Judah asked at last. 'Call the police, I assume?'

'I don't know.' I sat there staring at the picture of the house, willing . . . I don't know what. Maybe for Carrie to step out of the front door, give me a wave, tell me what the hell was going on. 'I just . . . I know it's crazy, Judah, but I feel like I *have* to at least get her side of the story. What if I'm wrong? What if I've put two and two together and made five, and instead of getting justice for Marcus, I end up sending innocent people to jail? She could still have nothing to do with all this. It could be all Pieter.'

'It could,' Judah said, but the scepticism in his voice undermined his words. He wasn't convinced.

'And there's another reason why I need to be sure,' I said. I could hear the pleading note in my own voice, and I tried to push it down, frame this argument in the clearest, most logical way. 'Because, listen, if I call the police on Carrie, I'll be putting myself in the firing line in the process. Getting her arrested might get me off the hook for Marcus's murder, but there's a very good chance I'll end up in jail anyway – obstruction of justice or something like that, maybe even accessory to murder if they don't believe my version of events. If Carrie's guilty – well, then, I'll just have to suck that side of things up. But this is only worth doing if I'm absolutely, completely sure I'm right. Otherwise, I might end up putting two innocent people behind bars and letting the real culprit off the hook. I'm not being selfless here, Judah, I swear. I'm looking out for myself as much as Carrie. If she's done this, I'll pay the price for helping her. But I need to be sure.'

Judah sighed. As much as he had no sympathy for Carrie, I could tell that my argument had hit home.

'Okay, that makes sense, I guess. What do you want to do, then? You want to go see her?'

'I think I have to,' I said. 'I'm sorry, Judah – I know it's risky, but I think I have to at least hear her out. But, listen, the second she pulls any bullshit, I'm going to be on that phone dialling 999. If she doesn't have a good explanation for every single thing she's done, every single entry on that door lock, every single point on the timeline, then I'm on the phone before you can say *knife*, I swear.'

'Okay,' Judah said again. This time his voice was resigned. He knew when he was beaten. 'When do we leave?'

I put my arms around his neck, kissed his soft beard.

'As soon as I've finished packing.'

31

Less than two hours later, Judah and I found ourselves standing beside Judah's hire car in a windswept suburban road somewhere near Brighton. The sea was at our backs, and in front of us was a low brick house with UPVC windows and a neat garden dotted with geraniums.

The flashing dot on my phone was unmistakable – my suitcase was in that house.

The only question was, was Carrie?

I took a deep breath and found my hands were trembling. This was it. I was about to discover whether Carrie had betrayed me and left me to shoulder the blame for a plot she'd cooked up.

'Ready?' Judah said. I swallowed.

'I'm not sure. Listen, Judah – I think – I think you should hang out here. Just in case.'

'Just in case what?' Judah's expression was sceptical.

'Just in case she makes a run for it.'

'You want me to wait outside? And what if she doesn't run for it? What if she just whacks you in the head with a baseball bat and watches you bleed out?'

'Judah . . . ' I gave him a look. 'Don't be dramatic. She's not going to hurt me.'

Though even as I said the words, sharp memories were surfacing — Carrie hitting me over the head from behind on a darkened stairwell. Carrie smacking my face into a metal door. And me, for my part, trying to attack her with a shard of sharpened plastic. She *had* hurt me. She had hurt me badly, and more than once. Could I really trust her? I was about to find out.

The problem was, I didn't think Carrie was going to confess to anything with Judah glowering from the corner of the living room, arms folded. No. I had got myself into this, I had to get myself out.

'Look, the whole point of this is to find out the truth — and I don't think I'm going to get that unless Carrie feels safe. And I don't think she'll feel safe with you standing over her. More likely she'll leg it when she sees a strange man there.'

'Okay,' Judah said. He didn't sound in the least persuaded, but as if he knew I wasn't going to be talked around. 'If you really don't want me to come in, I won't. But I'm going to stand here watching that window, and if I hear so much as a peep from you, I'm dialling 999. Okay?'

'Okay,' I said. 'And maybe . . . well, look, I'm not saying she's going to do anything, but if you haven't heard from me in ten minutes or so, maybe send me a text, and if I don't reply, come knocking.'

'If you don't reply, I'll be kicking the door down,' Judah said. He was smiling, a wry, resigned smile, but I could tell there was real anxiety under the surface.

'Okay. Thank you for trusting me.' I stood on tiptoes and kissed his bearded cheek, and then, something about the pose made me remember the photo, the one on Marcus Leidmann's phone. I took a deep breath. This wasn't the time, but there might never be a better one.

'Judah, listen, before I go in, there's something else. Something I left out, and I need to tell you.'

'Go on,' Judah said. His voice was neutral, but he didn't look overly concerned.

'Marcus Leidmann had a photo. A photo of me and, well, Cole Lederer. And it looked . . . compromising.' I swallowed hard. Judah's dark eyes were fixed on me, a furrow between his brows. I found myself hurrying on, the words tumbling out. 'It wasn't, I swear it wasn't. He kissed me on my cheek and that was it. But the way it was framed, the way the camera was angled, it looked bad. It looked like more, and I just – if it came out—'

'Lo—' Judah put a hand on my cheek, and his voice was gentle. 'Lo, it's okay. I know you, remember? I *know* you. And if you tell me there's nothing between you and Cole, I believe that.'

'There was *nothing* in it.' I stared up at him, at his knitted brows, at his hawk-shaped nose. I put my hand up to his cheek, holding his gaze, unconsciously mirroring the way he was holding me. 'Do you understand? Nothing. I love you. I've always loved you. But it was part of the police case against me – that, I don't know, that I knew Marcus somehow. That he was spying on me and had all this kompromat on me for some fucked-up reason of his own. I need you to know it's not true. Whatever that photo looked like, there was nothing in it.'

'I know,' Judah said again. He bent down and kissed me, his lips soft and warm. 'I believe you. One thing I love about you Lo, is you're honest as the day is long. I just worry—'

He stopped, and I found myself holding my breath, wondering what he was going to say. When he didn't speak, I prompted him.

'You worry?'

'Look, your honesty, your complete commitment to the truth, that's part of what I love about you. But I sometimes worry that it makes you . . . vulnerable. To people like Carrie.'

I shut my eyes. It was a fair point. I *was* honest, maybe too honest sometimes. And it had got me into trouble more than once, my inability to shut up about what I saw, to brush anything under the rug. My inability to lie to save my own skin.

Now, my inability to walk away from the truth had led me here, to confront Carrie. And maybe that was going to turn out to be another terrible mistake – I just knew that I couldn't let this go. If Carrie *had* killed Marcus, I needed to know. I needed her to face justice, no matter what the cost to me.

I thought, suddenly, of Inspector Filippo Capaldi. What was it he'd said? *Honesty is always the best policy.* A cliché, sure, but somehow, in his slight Italian accent it hadn't sounded like one. It had sounded wise and true. I just hoped to God he was right.

'Okay,' I said at last, squeezing Judah's hands. 'Wish me luck.'

'You're really going to do this?'

'I'm really going to do this.'

He let go of my hands, and I felt his gaze on my spine as I walked up the garden path to the neat front door and raised the knocker.

32

The woman who answered the door wasn't Carrie. She was old, in her eighties or nineties, and looked very fragile. One thin, mottled hand was holding on to the doorjamb, the other clutching a heavy walking stick. I felt a jolt of doubt. Had I made a mistake? Had the Find My tracking dot led me to the wrong house?

'Oh, hi,' I said nervously. 'Um, my name is Laura. Is – is Carrie here?'

The woman turned, awkwardly, facing into the house, and for a moment I thought she was going to call for some kind of carer, someone who'd point to the No Solicitors door sign and tell me to sling my hook. But instead, she drew a breath and called out in a frail, croaky voice, 'Caz, love? You've got a visitor.'

I felt my heart speed up. I glanced over my shoulder at Judah, who gave me the slightest thumbs-up gesture. And then I turned back to the doorway, to the sound of bare feet coming down the carpeted stairs, and saw . . . Carrie.

She had changed out of her designer wear and was dressed much closer to how she had been when I'd first met her all those years ago – jeans and a faded T-shirt, though this one was Nirvana, not Pink Floyd. Her face was free of make-up and her hair was scraped back in a high ponytail that made her look simultaneously much younger and somehow also older. With her dramatic, careful make-up wiped off, her face looked sweeter, more vulnerable, less sophisticated. But without the contoured foundation and the blow-dried hair framing her features, I could see the lines around her eyes, the hollows in her cheeks, the tiny white scars of what must have been a long-ago facelift.

'Lo!' Carrie said. She looked – for the first time since I'd seen her in Switzerland – taken aback. Even shocked. Then she seemed to pull herself together. 'What are you doing here?'

'Can we talk?' I gestured to what I assumed must be the living room. Carrie took a deep breath, and then nodded.

'Gran, can you give us a minute? I need to talk to my friend.'

'Well, I think it's very rude,' the old lady grumbled, 'to shove me out of me own living room without so much as an introduction. I'll be in the kitchen if you need me.'

Carrie gave a laugh, a slightly strained one.

'Gran, this is Laura. Lo, this is my grandmother. Okay? Introductions complete. Now go on, Gran, I'll come through in a sec, make you a cup of tea.'

'I'm perfectly fit to make my own tea,' she said a little haughtily. Then, to me: 'I don't have carers, you know. I'm ninety-two and still managing on me own.'

'I can see,' I said politely. Carrie watched as her grandmother tottered along the hallway to the kitchen, then closed the door behind her. Carrie turned to me.

'What the fuck are you doing here? How did you find me?'

'You took my case,' I said, a little sourly. 'It had a tracker in it. As for why I'm here, we need to talk. I know, Carrie.'

'Oh, quit the amateur dramatics,' Carrie said, rolling her eyes. She turned and opened the door into what was indeed the living room. It was a small room, with two oversize velour couches and an armchair that were much too big for the space. Carrie closed the door behind us, pushed her way between the couches, and slumped into the one opposite the TV. I took the one opposite the window, the better to keep an eye out for Judah if I needed to. You couldn't see much through the net curtains, but just knowing he was out there was comforting. '*I know*,' she said in a deep, foreboding tone. 'What next? *Fly, all is discovered*?'

I gritted my teeth. I had promised myself I wouldn't lose my temper, and I intended to keep that, but this was Carrie at her most infuriating. What did she want me to say? *Time's up, bitch*?

'I know how you did it.' I took a breath. 'How . . . how you killed Marcus.'

The words acted like an electric shock on Carrie. She sat bolt upright, glanced towards the closed living-room door, then swung back to glare furiously at me.

'Seriously? Could you maybe shout that a little louder, perhaps get some kind of loudhailer? What if my gran had heard you throwing accusations like that around?'

'She's two rooms away,' I said, but I lowered my voice to a hiss. 'And maybe you should have thought of that before you helped kill a man, then left me to carry the can. How could you, Carrie? I *helped* you. I gave you my fucking passport, for God's sake! And this is how you repay me?'

'I don't know where you're getting this from, but you're making a mistake,' Carrie said firmly, but there was something unconvincing in her face, a pinch between her brows that told me that she wasn't as confident – or as innocent – as she was making out. 'You of all people know I wasn't anywhere near Marcus's room when he died. You were right outside, for fuck's sake. *You're* my alibi.'

'First, most people try not to land their alibi in jail. Second, that's not when Marcus was killed, and you know it. Why don't you tell me the truth, Carrie? You owe me that, at least.'

'Well, if you've got it all worked out, why don't *you* tell *me*,' Carrie said. Her tone was defiant, but her expression was an odd mix of sulky and something like worry, and I knew that what I'd said must have hit a little too close to home – either with the accusation that she was involved in what had happened to Marcus or with the reproach over the way she'd abandoned me. Maybe both.

I took a deep breath. I had to hope to God that the scenario I'd constructed was right – because if it wasn't, and Carrie knew it, she would know that she had me. As Capaldi had said, the truth was the only way out of this – I just had to hope that this *was* the truth.

'Okay, I will tell you. I'll tell you what I think really happened that morning. I think you and Pieter planned this whole thing together. You and me running away, holing up at the Old Manor under my identity so no one could track this back to you. Marcus following. Pieter coming along to make sure it all played out as planned. I don't know who tipped Marcus off about where you'd gone – probably Pieter; he was always the person in charge of making sure his father turned up in the right place at the right time – but you knew Marcus. You knew what kind of man he was, and I think you were telling the truth when you told me that he'd never let you go. As soon as he found out where you were, he set off to track you down and make you regret ever leaving him. But what he didn't know was that he was walking into a trap that you had set. After all, you were in the perfect situation – in a remote location, with the man you wanted to kill, and no paper trail to tell anyone you were ever there.'

'Go on,' Carrie said. Her voice was wary, and I felt a surge of triumph. I was on the right track. But the next part was the difficult bit, the part I wasn't sure of.

'On the day of the murder you waited until I'd gone down to breakfast. Then you left our room, leaving the door on the latch, and went down the corridor to Marcus's room. I don't know how you got in – maybe Pieter was already there, maybe Marcus let you in. I think probably the first one, given Marcus was in the bath when you found him. You walked in – and this was the part I could never explain in the police's version of events. Because if anyone else had walked in on Marcus naked in the bath, there's no way he would have lain there and waited for that person to drown him. Even if that person had been Pieter. If anyone else had come in unexpectedly, Marcus would have leaped up and out, grabbed a towel, told them to get the hell out of his room. But his mistress, the woman he loved, telling him she'd seen the error of her ways, telling him she was ready to come back to him, live with him again – that I could see. I could see Marcus smiling, lying back, revelling in the moment . . . until you grabbed him around the ankles and pulled him underwater.'

'A nice story,' Carrie said shortly, 'but how do you explain the fact that Marcus was alive and well and calling for room service when you came back from breakfast?'

'I'm getting to that bit. After Marcus was dead, Pieter tidied up the room and did his bit to create an alibi by faking a conversation with his father – a conversation that I obediently relayed back to the police. Then he went down to breakfast, making sure as many people as possible saw him, and you went back to our hotel room, taking Marcus's cordless room phone with you. The reception on those things is really very good, as I found out when I tried out the same distance yesterday. You got into the bath, and you made a room-service call ordering his usual breakfast.'

'Using my extensive training as a male impersonator?' Carrie said sarcastically, and I shook my head.

'He always ordered the same thing. Pieter even told me that. In fact, that was what tipped me off to the idea of it being a recording – because why would he say the usual when he was staying somewhere he'd never been before? You must have recorded him, saved the recording somewhere online, and hoped the conversation would go the same way. It almost did, but there's a strange gap on the recording where the person at the other end of the line asks Marcus a question, and you had to scramble to find the right response. I couldn't understand it at the time. It's a yes-or-no question, really simple, and Marcus leaves an odd gap before he says "No." That's because it wasn't on the original recording – the person on that call probably knew exactly what Marcus always ordered and didn't ask if there was anything else. You had to hastily scroll down your prepared recordings to find one that answered the question, and it took you a second.'

'Okay.' Carrie's voice was steely now. She was sitting opposite me, leaning forward, her expression grimly transfixed. 'This is all very interesting, Lo, but you said yourself that the phone used in the room-service call was found at the crime scene. Any explanation for how I got that back there between making the call and you finding Marcus dead in the bath? You were standing outside the bathroom the whole time, if you remember. Or maybe I threw it out the window and the wind caught it and blew it into Marcus's room?'

Her tone was sarcastic, but I ignored the jibe.

'You didn't take it back,' I said simply. 'Pieter did, while I was busy trying to get his father out of the tub. When he came up from breakfast, he collected the phone from you – that's the nine eighteen entry on the key locks – and then went to his father's room to "discover" the body. In the kerfuffle of us trying to get Marcus out of the bath, he must have dropped the phone in the tub. The poor cleaner and I weren't exactly concentrating on what Pieter was doing.'

'The nine eighteen entry?' For the first time, Carrie's expression was puzzled, and I realized I hadn't told her about the door-lock information. She had been gone when I got back from the police cell.

'Never mind,' I said. 'It doesn't matter – just something the police told me. But you haven't said what you think of my theory. It's pretty good, isn't it?' I was watching her face carefully. 'I mean, it explains everything – even some details that kept me puzzled right up until the end.'

'It is pretty good,' Carrie said. She sat back, folded her arms. She was trying for nonchalance, I could see that, but I also knew that folding my arms was what I did when I didn't want people to see my hands shaking. 'But it is *just* a theory. I mean, who's to say Marcus didn't just have a heart attack and drown in his own bath? Why are you so convinced he was murdered?'

'*I* wasn't convinced,' I said. I leaned forward, the springs of the old velour couch squeaking as I did. 'But the police are, for some reason. I don't know why for sure, but I have a theory.'

'Oh, great,' Carrie said sarcastically. 'Another theory. Please, do go on.'

'So the thing is, the police kept asking me about my ring. And I couldn't understand why.'

'Your ring?'

'My wedding ring. They were very triumphant that although I told them I didn't normally wear it, I had it on in one of the photos. They kept trying to get me to admit I was wearing it at the scene. Only I wasn't.'

'What?' Carrie's face was puzzled again. 'What's your ring got to do with any of—' She looked down at her own knuckles, at the big glowing sapphire on her left hand, and her face clouded. 'Fuck.'

'Fuck is right. He had a cut on his leg, I remember noticing it, but I didn't think anything of it at the time – it wasn't the kind of injury that could have killed anyone. But I think the police *did* notice it. And I think they knew what it meant.'

I was watching Carrie's face, and she said nothing, but her expression had changed from sulkily sarcastic to something closer to alarmed.

'There was this case,' I said. My voice was shaking a little now, but I tried to keep it steady. 'I remember hearing about it on some history podcast. They called it "the Brides in the Bath". Do you know the one I mean?'

'I have no idea,' Carrie said. She was doing her best to sound bored, but I could tell she wasn't. Every muscle and nerve in her body looked tense as wire.

'Okay, well, it doesn't really matter, but it was this Victorian serial murderer who'd marry these rich women and then kill them by drowning them in the bath. He supposedly did it by playfully grabbing their ankles while they were in the tub and hauling their feet up – their upper body slid under the water and they blacked out almost immediately. Even if you saw it coming and had the foresight to hold your breath, I don't think you could pull yourself up and out of the water. It would take tremendous upper-body strength – and there were no grab rails on Marcus's bathtub that I can remember. The sides were smooth and very steep.'

Carrie said nothing. Her arms were folded again, but this time she had tucked the hand with the big sapphire ring under her upper arm, as if she wanted to hide it.

'I think that's what you did,' I continued. I kept my gaze on her, trying to gauge her reaction. 'Maybe you and Pieter together, I don't know. It was a good plan – very hard to prove he didn't naturally drown. But you must have forgotten to take off your ring, and it scratched his ankle. *That's* how they were so sure it wasn't an accident. There's plenty of injuries you could sustain in the bath if you were flailing around, but a long cut on your ankle isn't likely. There was nothing sharp in that bathroom. I'm right, aren't I? That *is* what happened?'

'*Fuck*,' Carrie said, and suddenly all the tenseness seemed to have gone out of her, like a pricked balloon. She let her arms drop and bent over, her head bowed as if in defeat. 'Fuck. Fuck. He was so heavy, that was the thing. I didn't think he'd be so heavy, and so slippery too – even with Pieter hauling on one leg, he was so heavy, and he was kicking and thrashing . . . I lost my grip; I didn't even notice my ring had turned around. And I thought we'd been so fucking clever.'

'So I *am* right?'

I tried to meet her eyes as I said the words, but Carrie wouldn't look at me. She just put her face in her hands, shaking her head, but I knew, I knew in that moment the answer was yes. I was right. Right on every point. What I had told Judah was true – this was the only way it could have happened. The only way that could explain everything.

'How could you, Carrie?' I leaned forward, and there was a note in my voice I didn't like – it was a kind of grief. I had wanted to be stern, logical, steely. But instead, I found myself wanting to cry. 'How could you betray me like that? I saved you – I saved your life. I did *everything* for you. Was it always part of the set-up, that you'd leave me to carry the can? Was that why you were so keen on doing everything under my name? Was I just some fucking dupe to you?'

'What?' Carrie looked up at that, and I saw her eyes were red and there were tears on her cheeks. 'What? No! How could you think that?'

'How could I *not* think that, given you let me get dragged off to a police cell and then ran away, leaving me to hold the baby?'

'No, Lo, that's not what happened, you have to believe me!' There was a crack in Carrie's voice, and she looked so close to the girl I'd first met all those years ago, the steely, frightened girl fighting for her life, that my heart wanted to break. 'That was the only part of the plan that didn't work. You were never supposed to be here.'

'What?' I couldn't keep the scoff out of my voice and probably my face. 'Pull the other one, Carrie. You *invited* me, remember? Never supposed to be there? You practically dragged me to the fucking hotel!'

'For one night!' Carrie cried. 'Remember? It was only supposed to be for one night, you were supposed to be going to your mum's, and then she went and *actually* broke her bloody leg. You were never supposed to be in the hotel when Marcus arrived. That was the plan. You were supposed to be far away with your mum giving you a cast-iron alibi, and I was supposed to disappear into thin air after Marcus's death. But when your mum broke her leg or her ankle or whatever it was and you announced you were staying – I didn't know what to do. I tried to head you off at the pass, but you wouldn't have it. I just had to go on with the plan and hope that Pieter and I could change it enough to come up with an alibi that worked for all three of us. And I really thought I had. If it hadn't been for that fucking ring, they would have had no way of knowing that he didn't just pass out in the bath.'

'Shit.' I remembered Carrie's expression in the mirror when I'd told her I had decided to stay for another night – even at the time, I'd thought she looked put out, disconcerted, as if I'd just messed up some vital plans of her. Little did I know, I had – plans more vital for both of us than I had any way of knowing. And I could understand why Carrie hadn't known what to do. She'd tried to persuade me to go to my mum's, but not very hard, and I could see her dilemma – I might have had just as much difficulty proving an alibi if I were staying at my mum's house alone. Her whole plan had rested on my being with my mum from the moment I left the hotel to the moment I returned to the US. When that plan failed, I could see why she'd felt it was better to let me stay at the hotel, where she could keep an eye on me, make sure I was out of the way for the actual murder. And it had so nearly worked.

'Lo, you have to believe me.' Carrie's voice was shaking with emotion, shaking with a sincerity I'd barely ever heard before. 'You have to believe me, it was never meant to work out like this. And I didn't run away from *you* – I ran because the police came to search our room. I nearly didn't make it out. I saw that twat Dickers coming up the driveway and heard him talking about a search warrant. I only had just enough time to stuff things into a case and run down the fire escape.'

I let out a shuddering breath and sat back against the worn cushions of the couch. I wasn't sure what to do. A part of me was more relieved than I could properly express that Carrie *hadn't* deliberately betrayed me. Because in a way, that was what had hurt the most – the idea that I could have been so wrong about her. That she had lured me across the Atlantic and then the Channel not to save her but to be her patsy. That had pained me almost beyond bearing – in a way I only truly realized when the pain stopped.

But the fact that she hadn't done that left me in a different quandary. Shopping Carrie to the police when I thought she'd framed me for murder – that was one thing. But turning her in in cold blood when she'd done all she could to protect me – that was something altogether different. And yet I knew what Judah would say if he were here in this room instead of standing outside. He would point out that, all of that notwithstanding, she was *still* a murderer. She had killed a man, and not in self-defence, as she had before, but coldly, with calculation, premeditation and deliberation.

He was abusing her, I found myself arguing back in my imagination. *He was blackmailing her, holding her past over her head to keep her a prisoner, tied to him, however much she wanted to escape.*

You have only her word on the abuse, the imaginary Judah retorted. But that was a bridge too far – even in my own imagination. Because it was true – I had only Carrie's word for that part of things. But I still believed her. I didn't think you could fake the fear in her face when she'd talked about Marcus and his security men. I remembered the shudder in her voice when she'd said, *You don't even want to know the things he's made me do. Him and his . . . friends.*

I didn't want to know. But I could imagine. I could imagine all too well, and it made me feel sick.

But did that really justify murder? If it did, it certainly didn't excuse what Pieter had done – and I was damned if I'd take the rap for him as well as Carrie.

'Why did *he* do it, Carrie?' I said at last. 'I understand your part — I mean, he was blackmailing you, effectively. You were his prisoner. But why Pieter? What had his father ever done to him?'

'He killed his mother,' Carrie said very simply. She gave a shrug, a kind of helpless shrug. 'At least, that's how Pieter saw it. His mother was told never to have any more children, and Marcus . . . well, Marcus is Marcus. He can be very persuasive, and when he can't persuade you, he takes what he wants anyway.'

Maybe it was the flatness of her tone or maybe it was the hopelessness of her expression, but something in her words chilled me.

'The irony is, he never did have any more children,' Carrie added with a little bitter laugh. 'Though not for want of trying, believe me. It seems like Pieter was a medical miracle, let alone that second baby, the one that killed poor Elke. But it must be pretty fucking rich to know that you were never enough. That your father was prepared to let your mother die rather than live with you as an only child. That knowledge . . . that would change a person, you know?'

I didn't say anything, but I nodded. That would change a person.

'I've known him a long time,' Carrie said now, her voice softening. 'Almost ten years. And he was young when I first met Marcus, barely out of university. You get to know people in that time. He's a good man, Pieter. And he loved Marcus — or I think he did when I first met him. But he watched what Marcus did to me for ten years and I suppose . . . ' She stopped, swallowed. 'I suppose it made him think back to other things, see them in a different light. And when he stood up to his father, well, Marcus didn't like that. He didn't like people who were prepared to tell him he was out of line. He began to threaten Pieter too — threaten him with disinheritance. And I think for Pieter, that was the last straw.'

There was another long silence. Then I cleared my throat.

'Marcus was going to try to blackmail me, you know. At least I think so. He had photos of me on his phone. Of me and . . . ' I swallowed, the shame still bitter in the back of my throat. 'Of Cole Lederer. Kissing.'

Carrie shook her head. There were tears in the corners of her eyes.

'I'm sorry, Lo. I should have told you. It was one of his things, one of the reasons he was so keen on Pieter's high-end hotel idea. He liked recording people; he liked watching them, especially when they didn't know. And the more important the person, the better. It's all leverage at the end of the day. And leverage is power. And power – power's everything to Marcus. Was everything, I mean. More important than sex, money, family. More important than anything else in the world. I think . . . ' She stopped, and I saw the muscles in her slim throat working. 'I think in the end, maybe that was why he wanted me so much. He could have had women just as beautiful – more beautiful, let's be honest. But he had absolute power over me. Absolute. And the more I hated what he made me do, the more he felt that power. It's why I *knew* he'd come after me rather than setting the police on me or alerting the authorities. He could have had me arrested any time he liked – but he didn't want to, because that would have been handing his power over me to someone else. No, I knew that he would want to catch me himself, make me his own prisoner for as long as he desired. Maybe until I died – or he killed me.'

There was a long silence. I had no idea what to say – no idea what the right thing was here. For Carrie to go to prison for freeing herself from a man like Marcus – well, that didn't seem like justice. But if the police kept their sights trained on me, I could end up in jail myself. I could end up stuck in a British prison for years, far from my kids, while I exhausted appeal after appeal, and she and Pieter got away – literally – with murder.

'You have to turn yourself in,' I said at last. 'Carrie, you know that, right? You *have* to turn yourself in. If you go to the police and tell them everything that happened, how Marcus was abusing you, how he was keeping you trapped – if you give them everything you have on Pieter, they'll agree to some kind of plea bargain, I know they will.'

I heard the desperation in my own voice as I said the words – and I could only hope they were true. But they had to be, didn't they? What Carrie had done paled in comparison to the crime Pieter had committed, killing his own father, and for what? As persuasive as Carrie's account of Elke's death had been, I didn't buy it, or not completely. It was too convenient, too tied in with the suggestion Marcus had made about passing over his son. Looking at it cold-bloodedly, Pieter had put up with his father as long as he stood to inherit the Leidmann Group crown. It was highly coincidental that he had developed a conscience the same week his father had started to raise questions about the succession of the company.

'You're right.' Carrie's face was pale, but she looked like she had made up her mind. 'I know you are. And in a way it'll be a relief when it's all over. I've been running for so long, and I'm so tired of looking over my shoulder all the time. Just . . . ' She shut her eyes, pressing her fingers into her eye sockets. 'Just don't turn me in to that fucker Dickers. I can't stand him.'

'Who, then?' I asked. 'Do you want me to call 999?' Though even as I said the words, I had no idea what I was going to say. *Hello, operator, I have a two-times-wanted murderer here with information on a co-conspirator.*

'I don't know,' Carrie said wearily. 'What about that other guy, the one from Interpol? I think they might be more lenient on me. I have a lot of dirt on the Leidmann Group – it's one of the reasons I knew Marcus would never let me go. There's tax stuff they've been looking into for years. It's probably way more valuable to Switzerland than the UK. I don't suppose it really matters who arrests me – the important thing is that I give them all the stuff I've got on Pieter and Marcus and argue my way to the best plea deal.'

'Inspector Capaldi?' I said. I was a little surprised, I don't know why, but on reflection, going to Interpol was a good idea. 'I guess that could work. And actually, he asked me to keep in touch. I have his mobile number somewhere.' I tried to remember what I'd done with his number. I'd put it in the pocket of my jeans, I was fairly sure of that. But it wasn't the pair I was wearing today. Which meant it must be in the car. 'I think I left the number in my bag. You want me to go and get it?'

'Sure,' Carrie said. She stood up, the couch springs protesting. In the slightly grey light filtering through the net curtains, she looked washed out and both very young and every inch her age. 'Let's get this over with.'

'Listen, Carrie—' I stopped, unsure what I was going to say, and when she turned to me, her face resigned and exhausted, I felt my heart clench in my chest.

'What?'

'I just – I wanted to say . . . thank you. What you're doing . . . I can't imagine the courage it takes to turn yourself in. And it means a lot that you're doing it for me.'

Carrie's face softened. She put her hand on my right arm, turning it towards her, and I watched as her fingers traced the thin white scar that curved down my forearm. It was a scar that she had given me long ago, in a different life, and her gentleness as she traced the pale jagged line, almost invisible in the grey light, made me shiver. I knew what she was thinking as her fingers followed the line down my forearm because I was thinking it too: she was remembering how we had found ourselves once before on opposite sides of a terrible divide and how we had saved ourselves, and each other.

'I *will* save you,' I said now. 'Carrie, I swear it. I'll give character evidence, I'll talk about how Marcus was treating you, anything. I will make this okay. But you have to save me too. I can't go to prison for something I didn't do.'

'I know,' Carrie said. 'I know. And I'm sorry, Lo, for everything.

I've made a lot of mistakes in my life, done a lot of things I regret—' She swallowed, and I saw there were tears in her dark eyes. 'But helping you was not one of them. I've never regretted that. And I want you to be able to say the same thing. I—' She gave a shaky laugh. 'Is it dumb to say I love you?'

I shook my head. There was a lump in my own throat.

'No, it's not dumb. I love you too.'

Carrie smiled at that, a brittle, glittering smile that sent the tears cascading over her high cheekbones. Then she blinked them away and took a deep breath.

'Right. Let's do this thing. Let's commence Operation Shop a Motherfucker.'

33

The next hour was one of the longest and strangest of my life. All four of us – Carrie, her grandmother, Judah and me – sat in the cramped little living room, Judah's knees practically jammed against the coffee table. He made tense, polite conversation with Carrie as her gran offered him drink after drink and snack after snack, apparently entranced by this tall, handsome American.

Inspector Capaldi had been brief but to the point. I had told him the bare minimum, but it was pretty much everything he needed to know: that I had found Carrie, that she had admitted to helping Pieter kill his father, and that she was hoping for some kind of immunity or plea deal in return for giving evidence against him and information on the Leidmann Group as a whole.

I had given him the address and my promise that none of us were going anywhere.

'I will be there in one hour,' Capaldi had said tersely. 'Arrivederci.'

And then he hung up.

Now it was exactly one hour and seven minutes since I had called, according to the surreptitious peeks I took at my mobile, and he was still not here. Carrie was looking more tense and strained by the moment. Judah kept shooting me glances that I knew meant

Where the fuck are the cops? Carrie's grandmother, meanwhile, had brought out the Quality Street and was trying to force Judah to eat just one more toffee penny.

When the doorbell rang, I practically leaped out of my seat, as Carrie's gran began struggling with her cane.

'Please don't worry,' I said. 'I'll get it.'

'It's like Piccadilly Circus around here,' she grumbled as she sank back down into the cushions. 'I've no idea what the neighbours will be thinking.'

It was a good question.

Through the rippled glass of the window in the front door I could see a man's form. This had to be him. I took a deep breath and opened the door.

I don't know what I had expected – perhaps a phalanx of police cars, blue lights flashing. Maybe some officers in uniform just to titillate Carrie's gran's neighbours.

Instead, it was just Inspector Capaldi, wearing a suit and looking even more handsome than he had before, a sleek black car parked at the curb behind him.

'Ciao, Laura. It is good to see you again. May I come in?'

'Of course,' I said, trying not to sound taken aback. 'Look, I don't mean to be rude, but . . . I thought there would be more of you.'

Inspector Capaldi nodded.

'I should have said. Interpol are a comparatively small force in the UK, and as it's a Sunday, I didn't want to waste time by calling out colleagues. And given your friend's wish for a plea bargain, I thought it best for everyone not to involve the British police until we have ironed out some of the . . . ' He paused, searching for the word. 'Creases.'

'Wrinkles,' I said automatically. His reasoning made sense. I could imagine that once Dickers and Wright had their hands on Carrie, any international plea deal was going to go out the window. They were unlikely to care about the intricacies of Swiss and Belgian tax law; all they would be interested in would be getting a case off their desks and putting someone in jail. And with Pieter Leidmann's lawyers involved, there was a very real risk that that someone might end up being Carrie alone. 'I understand.'

'Hi.' The voice came from over my shoulder, and I turned to see Carrie, pale but resolute, standing in the doorway to the living room. 'Are you the guy from Interpol?'

'I am Inspector Filippo Capaldi, yes.' Inspector Capaldi held out his hand, and Carrie took it and shook it with a smile that didn't reach her eyes. She looked tense, and I didn't blame her. 'You must be Carrie, yes? Are you ready?'

'I think so. Can I – is it okay for me to bring some clothes?'

'No problem,' Inspector Capaldi said with a very Italian little shrug, and before I could protest, Carrie had disappeared upstairs. From the living room I heard the creak of springs as Judah got hastily to his feet and came to stand beside me, and I knew from the tense way he was holding himself, poised as if to run up the stairs, that he'd just had the same thought as me – what would we do if Carrie changed her mind and bolted out of the bedroom window?

But apparently, she hadn't, for just a few minutes later, she reappeared at the top of the stairs, carrying two bags – a bag for life with a Tesco's logo on the side, filled with what looked like clothes and a jewellery case, and my suitcase, which she handed over to me with a slightly shamefaced smile.

'Sorry about the case, Lo. Poetic justice, huh.'

I smiled at that, and for a moment Carrie smiled back. Then her face crumpled a little, as if the reality of what was about to happen was suddenly striking home.

'It's going to be okay, yeah?' she said to me, her voice pleading, and I nodded with an assurance I didn't really feel.

'Of course it will. Inspector Capaldi has said he'll do everything in his power to get you a plea deal.'

'I cannot promise anything, you understand,' Inspector Capaldi said seriously, 'but there are a number of issues with the Leidmann Group that we have been actively pursuing for several years now, and I think I can say with confidence that any information you can give will go a long way to helping your situation.'

'I am prepared to sing like a fucking canary,' Carrie said frankly. Then, as a disapproving tut came from the living room, 'Sorry, Gran, I didn't mean to swear.'

She set the case down, moved back into the living room, and bent over to hug her grandmother.

'Look, Gran, I have to go away for a bit. But you'll be okay, yeah? You'll look after yourself?'

'Of course I'll be all right.' I couldn't see her expression, but the old lady's voice was offended. 'I've been all right without you for the last ten years, haven't I? Now you come waltzing in here pretending I can't be left on me own. I'll be perfectly fine. I don't even have carers, you know. Or a stair lift. I'm ninety-two but that doesn't mean I'm gaga.'

'I know,' Carrie said. Her voice was soft, and I heard the crack in it as she said, 'I'll come and visit you as soon as I can, Gran. I love you so much.'

'I love you too,' her grandmother said, her tone a little austere. 'Now, you'd better not keep your friend waiting.'

Your friend. Did she have any idea what was going on here? I had a strong suspicion not, and there was something more than a little heartbreaking in that thought — in the idea that Carrie might be behind bars before her grandmother knew what this goodbye really meant.

Carrie came back into the hallway wiping her eyes, then lifted her chin with an obvious effort and turned to me.

'So I guess this is it.'

'I guess it is.'

We stood staring at each other, and I wondered if she was remembering, as I was, the last time we had said goodbye, ten years ago, unsure if we would ever see each other again. What was it she'd said? *Don't thank me. Just pull this off – for both of us. And don't look back.*

I had pulled it off. And so had she. We had both fought our way into new lives, new identities – but I *had* spent my life looking back, wondering if she was okay, what price she had paid for everything she'd done.

Now I knew.

'It's going to be okay, Carrie,' I whispered, and she closed her eyes briefly and nodded, hard.

'I know. And it'll be okay for you too, I swear it. I'll make sure of that. Be well, Lo. Give those boys a kiss from me. And you—' She turned to Judah, standing uneasily behind me. 'You take care of her, okay? You've got a fucking queen here. Don't forget it.'

'I know,' he said. There was a lot else he could have said, and I knew it. *Don't fuck with my family again* being the main one. But Judah was nothing if not generous – and he knew that he had won, and Carrie, in so many ways, had lost. She was giving everything up for me. 'I won't forget it.'

Inspector Capaldi pulled out a pair of cuffs and Carrie looked down at them, then up at him, her brows knitted in a way that made her look suddenly young and very scared.

'Could we – could we do all this outside?' She nodded at her grandmother, still sitting in the living room, oblivious to how all this was playing out, and lowered her voice, pleadingly. 'I don't want her to . . . you know. Worry.'

For a moment Inspector Capaldi hesitated, then he nodded.

'Of course.' He took her arm and led her out to the waiting car. There, where they couldn't be seen from the living-room window, he put the cuffs carefully around her wrists, and said something, presumably reading her her rights. Then he opened the rear door and stood, patiently, as she climbed awkwardly into the passenger seat.

'I'll be in touch, Laura,' he called back to me, as he climbed into the driver's seat.

My throat was too tight to speak. Judah and I watched as the engine started up, and the long black sedan pulled away from the curb. We watched as it turned the corner and disappeared. And then we turned back to the house.

'Time to go?' Judah whispered. I nodded, then raised my voice to Carrie's gran, still sitting hunched in the lounge. She heaved herself to her feet as we entered, looking up at us quizzically.

'Goodbye, Mrs . . .' I stopped. I didn't even know her name, I realized. 'I'm afraid . . . I'm afraid we have to go now too.'

'Goodbye, dear.'

As the car pulled away, I didn't look back at her small figure, standing alone in the doorway of her house, her shape growing smaller and smaller in the distance. I thought if I did, my heart might break.

34

'Mum, for the last time, *please* get off that bloody ankle.' I had been home for less than twenty-four hours, and I was already starting to lose my rag with my mother.

'The doctor said I had to stay mobile,' my mum said placidly from where she was washing up at the kitchen sink.

'He also said that you should be careful about weight-bearing for longer than necessary. For goodness' sake, please sit down and let me do the washing up. Or load the bloody dishwasher. I don't know why you have one if you never use it.'

'I do use it! At Christmas, anyway.'

'Pam.' Judah's deep, calm voice cut through our bickering. 'Pam, why don't you come out to the yard and show me what you want me to do to the holly tree. Lo can finish up here.'

Thank you, I mouthed over the top of my mother's head as she put down the dishcloth, and Judah grinned. He had always been able to wind my mum around his little finger. In fact, he had the same effect on her as he'd had on Carrie's gran, turning them both into fluttery, twinkly old ladies.

My mother grabbed hold of her walker – she was looking shockingly old, and the sight caught at my heart – and stumped after Judah into the back garden of her little house. I let out a sigh of relief, and was about to turn back to the dishes when my mobile began to ring. A glance at the screen showed Judah's mother's number, and my heart leaped.

'Hello?'

'Lo!' Gail's warm voice came over the phone speaker. 'How are you, honey? Judah said your mom's out of the hospital and the stupid misunderstanding at the police station is on its way to getting sorted out?'

'Yes,' I said. I could hear the smile in my own voice, the relief that one single word was bringing me. 'Yes, I don't know if we're home and dry yet but . . . it's all looking good. In fact, I thought you might be my lawyer. I've been half expecting him to call.'

I'd left a very brief message yesterday on the drive up from Woodingdean explaining that Interpol had made an arrest and asking him to call me when he was back in the office on Monday to talk through the implications. What I really wanted to know, what I hadn't felt able to ask in front of Carrie, was whether *I* was likely to face any charges myself for obstruction of justice, but it had seemed a little selfish to ask in front of someone facing a potential life sentence for murder. Still, the question had started to weigh more and more heavily on my mind as I made my way back to St Albans in the car and overnight. What *was* the consequence for lending Carrie my passport? Could I gloss over that part? Of course, it was a hell of a lot better than murder, so I would take whatever was coming. I just wanted to *know*.

Dan must have got the message by now, but he hadn't called back. Still, it was only just gone noon. Maybe he was in a meeting.

'Well, we're having a *fantastic* time here.' Gail's tone was performatively enthusiastic enough that I knew the boys must be in the room. 'Aren't we, boys?'

'Yes!' I heard from Eli, good little cheerleader that he was, and a slightly less enthusiastic 'I wanted to play on the iPad' from Teddy. I suppressed a laugh. Poor Gail was no doubt dealing with the sharp end of screen-time limits and Teddy's burgeoning addiction to Angry Birds.

'Well, we're not going to play on the iPad now,' Gail said encouragingly, 'because we're going to talk to Mummy. Would you like that?'

'Yay!' I heard from both boys, then Gail's voice came back on.

'Shall I put you on FaceTime?'

'Oh, please.'

There was a moment's pause as the call cut out and then reconnected with Gail's smiling, sun-weathered face filling the screen, Teddy on her lap, and Eli bobbing up and down beside her.

'Mummy!' Eli yelled, and Teddy, predictably, burst into tears.

'Oh, my loves!' I felt my own throat tighten in response, took a deep breath, and plastered a cheerful smile on my face. 'Teddy, honeybun, don't cry. Eli, are you having a lovely time?'

'Yes!' Eli said. 'Granny took us to the movies. We saw *ET*. Teddy cried.'

'They were doing some kind of anniversary screening at the Regal,' Gail explained. 'I hope you don't mind, I had it in the back of my head that it was rated G, but it turned out to be a PG and I think Teddy found some of the scenes where ET was in the hospital a bit scary.'

'I didn't!' Teddy said at once, sniffling manfully. 'It wasn't scary. I knew ET was going to be okay.' He wiped his face and sat up self-importantly. 'He was in the garbage—'

'Bins,' I said automatically, but Teddy took no notice.

'And they thought he was a cat but it wasn't, it was him, and then he watched a lot of screen time, and the little boy was his friend but then he got sick—'

'He didn't get sick,' Eli interrupted. 'They *made* him sick. The bad men came and took him away. And he was called Elliott, a bit like me. Only he had a little sister, not a little brother.'

'And he had a bicycle, right?' I said, smiling into the little screen. 'ET rode Elliott's bicycle?'

Both boys stared at me like I was insane, and then, just as I was beginning to wonder if Gail had taken them home halfway through the film and they'd missed the pivotal scene, Teddy said with withering scorn, 'Mummy, ET couldn't ride a bike. Elliott had the bike.'

'Oh.' I tried to remember. On reflection, I thought they were correct. 'Sorry, you're right. ET sat in the basket, didn't he?'

'Yes,' Eli said, laughing with the slightly patronizing air only a small child correcting a parent can muster. '*Obviously* ET couldn't ride a bike, Mummy. His legs are way too short!'

'Obviously,' I said dryly. 'I mean, that would be ridiculous.'

'Yes, *obviously*,' Teddy said, giggling enthusiastically at my stupidity. 'That would be rict—' He stumbled over the unfamiliar word. 'Ricket-ulus, Mummy!'

'Yes, totally ricket-ulus,' I said, smiling into the screen at their laughing little faces, Teddy's glistening with his now forgotten tears and both still lightly garnished with the remains of whatever nutrition-free cereal Gail had let them have for breakfast. 'Now, my loves, what are you going to do today? Have you got anything fun planned?'

'Well,' Gail said, 'Eli tells me they're studying dinosaurs in kindergarten this month, so I thought perhaps we'd go to the Museum of Natural History and look at some of the bones. We might even buy something in the shop. Would that be fun, boys? Go look at some dinosaurs?'

Gail's voice on the tinny little phone speaker was immediately drowned out by Teddy's and Eli's enthusiastic assent, and I saw Gail shift the phone in her grip, bringing it closer to her ear.

'What do you think, Lo?'

'I think that sounds amazing,' I said sincerely. 'And thank you, Gail, I'm so grateful you're doing this.'

'Nonsense,' Gail said briskly. 'Thank *you* for letting me spend some quality time with my grandbabies, honey. Now, if you're all set, I think I'd better say goodbye and go make us all some sandwiches. I'm not paying ten dollars for a PB and J in the museum café.'

'I don't know if they even *do* PB and J,' I said doubtfully. 'From what I can remember, it's more hummus flatbreads and sun-dried tomato panini. But that might be just the café – I think the food court has more options.'

'Well, whatever it is, I'm not paying for it,' Gail said. 'I don't know if you've noticed, but New York is so expensive these days!'

'I had noticed, yes,' I said, trying to suppress my smile. 'Thanks again, Gail. And love you, boys!'

'Love you, Mummy!' Eli shouted from behind Gail's shoulder. Teddy had disappeared somewhere out of the shot but I heard him yell something about buying a dinosaur in the shop.

'Okay, well, goodbye, honey,' Gail said. 'Give my love to Jude.'

'I will. Lots of love to you too.'

Then the call ended.

For a moment I just sat there looking at the screen, feeling my heart well with a mixture of love and homesickness. Then, just as I was pulling the washing-up gloves on, the phone rang again, this time with a UK landline number I didn't recognize.

I picked it up. 'Hello?'

'Laura? It's Dan.'

'Oh!' I looked at the screen, a little puzzled. 'Your number is different.'

'I'm calling from the office – this is my desk phone.'

'Oh, no worries. That makes sense.' I felt my heart quicken. I was about to get answers to all my questions – I just prayed they'd be the ones I was hoping for. 'Well, I take it you got my message?'

'I did.' His voice was . . . well, it was less jubilant than I would have thought. If anything, it was puzzled. 'I'm not sure if I properly understood, though. You said *Interpol* have arrested someone?'

I swallowed.

'Yes. Someone they think was working with Pieter Leidmann.' I hadn't gone into detail on the message. The whole business of Carrie's past and my own involvement in her escape didn't feel like something that was sensible to commit to tape. But Dan was still talking.

'That's not possible,' he was saying, his voice puzzled. 'Interpol don't do that kind of thing; they don't have any powers of arrest. They don't even really investigate on the ground, as far as I know – they leave all that to the local forces.'

'What?' I felt the shock run through me like little prickles of ice, and the hand that was holding the phone grow cold. I let the washing-up gloves drop, walked across to the kitchen table, groped for a chair, and sat. 'But – wait, sorry, that's not possible. I was right there. I have the officer's name and everything. He interviewed me.'

'You said in your message that the guy was an Inspector . . .' Dan sounded like he was consulting a piece of paper. 'Filippo Capaldi, was that right?'

'Yes. And he's part of the investigation. He came to see me after Dickers and Wright did. He said he was working the case for Interpol because of the international angles.'

Was it possible he hadn't actually arrested Carrie? I had seen him put on the cuffs, but I hadn't actually heard him read her her rights, just assumed that was the exchange I'd seen outside the car.

'Did he show you any ID?' Dan was asking.

'Yes!' I said indignantly – then stopped. *Had* he actually shown me any ID? Now I thought about it, I couldn't remember. I remembered Dickers and Wright flashing their identification cards, but I couldn't for the life of me remember whether Capaldi had done the same. He had turned up so hard on their heels, representing himself as more or less part of the same team, that I had run the two encounters together in my head. I felt a kind of sickness starting deep in my stomach. 'Actually, I can't completely remember. But, listen, it's not possible that he's a fake. He knew everything about the investigation, stuff he could only have got from Dickers and Wright. And he knew about me. He'd clearly been speaking to the Leidmann Group – he knew that I'd been in Switzerland, that I'd talked to Marcus. How did he know all that if he wasn't who he said he was?'

But even as I said the words, the answer came into my head – and it felt like a cold hand around my heart. He could have known if someone else had told him.

Someone on the inside at the Leidmann Group.

Someone who wanted very badly to know what *exactly* had gone down between Marcus Leidmann and me and how much I knew.

I remembered Inspector Capaldi's words to me, but now they had a very different connotation: *It is much better to be frank about these things, I find. Honesty is always the best policy.* The words, in fact, of someone who wanted me to spill every piece of information I had so they knew exactly what they were up against.

'Are you saying . . . ' The sickness in my stomach was rising now, a kind of acid in my gullet, and I swallowed hard against the feeling. 'Are you saying he *wasn't* Interpol?'

'I have no idea. But that's why I took a beat to call you back, because I wanted to speak to the police in West Tyning and find out if there'd been some crossed wires – if it was maybe someone from their department. But they were very clear: they aren't working with Interpol, they haven't made any arrests, and they've never heard of an Inspector Capaldi. So all I can say is, if this guy surfaces again, please be very, very careful. And maybe consider calling the police – the real police, I mean. I don't think he is who he says he is.'

'Okay,' I managed. The sickness was almost too great for me to speak, and I had to force the words out. 'Thanks, Dan.'

And then I hung up, walked shakily to my mother's downstairs cloakroom, the one with the peach toilet and the rug in the shape of a leaping salmon, and I threw up.

35

'For the last time, I don't know what this means,' I said. Judah and I were closeted in the spare room upstairs, me sitting on the bed with my head in my hands, Judah pacing, pacing, pacing in a way that was starting to make me want to hit him. 'All I know is, Dickers and Wright have apparently never heard of him, and it's looking extremely like we might have just handed Carrie over to one of Pieter Leidmann's henchmen.'

Pieter Leidmann's henchmen. It sounded like something out of a James Bond movie – but I'd had time to think since Dan's call, and it was the only explanation I could come up with. If Capaldi wasn't a member of the investigation team, then someone had planted him there, someone desperate to find out how much I knew and what I was saying to the police. And who else benefited from Carrie's disappearance right before she was about to testify against him? Pieter must have been terrified when she disappeared and left him holding the baby – as terrified as I had been when I thought she'd done the same thing to me. And now I'd not only led him to her, I'd handed her over like a wrapped Christmas present.

'Fuck,' Judah said. He reached the end of the little bedroom, turned on his heel, and walked back the other way. 'Fuuuck.' The word came out like a groan. 'So are we back to square one?'

'If you mean am I still on the hook for Marcus Leidmann's murder, I would say the answer is yes. In fact, it's probably more likely than it was before. Everything that applied to Carrie applies to me. *I* could have made that call from my own bathroom to try to establish an alibi. *I* could have thrown the phone back in the tub when I came barrelling in. Hell, I could even have been having a relationship with Marcus Leidmann – it would certainly explain why he had compromising photos of me. She was the only person who could testify against Pieter – testify to the whole plan. And now she's gone.'

'I think you have to come clean, love.' Judah sat beside me, took my hands in his. 'You have to tell Dan what really happened – as much for Carrie's sake as yours. She's being trafficked, basically. I imagine the police will give you both the benefit of the doubt in light of that, but you have to tell them about Pieter so they can get Carrie back and get Pieter convicted.'

'I know.' I shut my eyes, feeling the fear and exhaustion wash over me. He was right, but that didn't mean I shared his confidence in the outcome. I had to tell the police the truth for Carrie's sake as well as my own safety, but I didn't imagine there was much they'd be able to do to help either of us. They might, if they were very lucky and a jury could make sense of this fantastical tale about cordless phones and key-card alibis, get a conviction on Pieter Leidmann, but I doubted it. The case was shaky enough and the evidence sufficiently circumstantial that someone like Pieter, with his high-priced lawyers, would be able to punch a hole straight through it. But Carrie, I was pretty sure, would be out of the country already – whisked off to somewhere as untraceable as possible where money talked. 'I know you're right. I just – God, I can't believe I was so stupid. How could I not have realized something was up?'

'Look, I'm a fucking international correspondent, and I had no idea Interpol couldn't arrest people,' Judah said frankly. 'If anyone's stupid here, it's me.'

'But it wasn't just that – I *knew* him. When he first turned up, I remember thinking I'd seen him before. I put it down to the fact that he must have been at the crime scene, but when I thought about it this morning, really thought, I realized I was wrong. I got Cole to text me over some pictures from the hotel. Look.'

I scrolled down to one of the photos from the mushroom-gathering trip we'd taken on the second day. There was Gottfried, holding a basket of chanterelles or whatever they'd turned out to be. There was Ben Howard. And there, standing a few feet behind Gottfried, in the shade of one of the pines, was the guy who had been our driver that day. His face was in shadow, but he looked an awful lot like Inspector Capaldi.

'I'd say that's him, isn't it?' I held out the phone for Judah to see, and Judah pulled down his glasses and stared at the little picture, zooming in to see the driver's face more clearly. After a minute or two, he shrugged.

'Honestly? I don't know. It could be. It might not be. It's too dark to say. Maybe Cole could increase the exposure . . . I don't know, Lo. But yeah, it could be the same guy.'

'It's the same guy,' I said with finality. I was not particularly good with faces – Carrie had pulled the wool over my eyes for long enough on board the *Aurora*, after all – which was maybe why it had taken me so long to make the connection with Inspector Capaldi, but now I *had* joined the dots, I was sure about this. 'He was even Italian – he just had a much stronger accent in Switzerland; that was probably why I didn't recognize his voice. But it's him. One of Marcus Leidmann's employees – and we just handed Carrie over to him.'

'So you call Dan,' Judah said, 'and you come clean, and you tell him everything. And you let the West Tyning police figure out how to get this guy. There must be a paper trail. He'll have entered the country, for one thing. And he'll have left it with Carrie.'

'Probably on *my* passport,' I said bitterly. 'That was another thing I realized this morning. She still has my UK passport.'

'Look, she's a smart cookie,' Judah said. He put his arm around me. 'She's survived worse. I have a feeling she'll be okay.'

'I hope you're right,' I said, but my voice, even to my own ears, was a little despairing. 'I really hope you're right.'

I didn't say what I was actually thinking, which was that if Pieter Leidmann was prepared to kill his father for disinheriting him, he would certainly be prepared to kill the woman who knew he had done it – and maybe me as well. There was every chance that Carrie was dead. And if I didn't play my cards very carefully, I could be next.

'SO LET ME get this straight,' Dan Winterbottom said slowly. He was rubbing his temples. 'You let this woman – Carrie – come to the UK on your UK passport because you believed she was being abused by her partner, Marcus Leidmann. Then you think she conspired with his son, Pieter Leidmann, to kill him. And then when she threatened to turn on the son, Pieter had this fake Interpol guy kidnap her, and now you have no idea where she is, but you think she could be in danger?'

'That's about the size of it,' I said reluctantly. Under the table I felt Judah squeeze my hand supportively. In the end, Judah and I had agreed that this conversation was one for a face-to-face meeting. Attorney-client privilege or whatever it was called outside US cop shows might stretch only so far in a case like this, and I wanted to see Dan's face as I made this confession – figure out the ramifications of what I had actually done and what I might be dealing with.

'More important, as far as I'm concerned,' Judah said, 'I think my wife could be in danger too. I'm sorry,' he added, turning to give me a look that said *I know you won't like this, but I want my say*, 'but I don't give a shit about Carrie. I mean, I hope she's okay, but she got herself into this mess, and she dragged you in too. I'm interested in making sure *you* aren't next in this Leidmann guy's firing line. It looks like he's already bumped off two people – he's not doing the same thing to my wife.'

'Okay,' I said, a little shortly. His words had made me a weird mix of touched and irritated. 'I mean, I don't want to be next for the chop either, that's a given, and I'm sure Dan knows that.' But I squeezed his hand back under the table.

'I'm just saying, that needs to be our priority. Finding Carrie – sure. But getting Pieter Leidmann locked up, far away from you, that's my number one. Listen, do you have any idea what Lo might be facing here in terms of sanctions?' he said, turning to Dan. 'I mean, is she likely to face any charges for this?'

Dan had moved on from rubbing his temples to massaging the bridge of his nose, and now he stood up, pushing his chair back.

'Look, I think I need to make a few calls, try to find out where we are with this. Do you mind waiting here? I won't be long.'

'No problem,' I said resignedly. Then, as he left the room and the door swung shut behind him, I sank back into the chair with a sigh.

'How d'you feel?' Judah asked, eyeing me from where he was sitting on the other side of Dan's desk. I shook my head.

'I have no idea. I guess . . . better? However it turns out, it's a relief to get this all off my chest.'

'I wonder who he's calling,' Judah said. 'I'd bet probably Dickers, in an *If, theoretically, my client had this information, what charges would you be prepared to drop?* kind of way.'

'I don't know if the UK system works like that. We don't really have plea bargaining here in the same way.'

'Sure, but there must be some back-and-forth, right?' Judah looked thoughtful. 'I mean, the police have discretion over what they put forward to the CPS. There's got to be room for some horse-trading in that area.'

'For the last time, I don't *know*,' I said, a little more snappily than I had intended. Judah's theorizing about the case was starting to get on my wick. Sure, I was his wife, and he didn't want me to go to prison, but *I* was the one facing jail time here, and Judah playing true-crime podcaster in the corner of the room was fraying my last nerve. Judah's hurt face told me I'd overstepped the mark. 'Sorry, I'm sorry. I didn't mean – I know you're just looking out for me. I just – I'd rather see what Dan says instead of second guessing. Is that okay? All this what-if-ing is stressing me out. It might not go the way I want it to. I have to prepare for that.'

'I'm sorry,' Judah said. He got up, walked over to me, and wrapped his arms around my shoulders, and I stood up and hugged him back, burying my face in his chest, inhaling the familiar scent of his soap, deodorant, our shared laundry liquid. 'I know. I know this is your real life and not some true-crime podcast.'

It was so close to what I'd been thinking myself that I let out a weak laugh, then pressed my forehead into his shoulder.

'God, I want to go home. I miss the boys so much. What if they never let me go? What if I end up having to stay here while Pieter Leidmann and his lawyers run rings around the court?'

'It won't happen,' Judah said urgently. He put his hands either side of my face, lifting my eyes to his. 'You hear me? And if it does, then I'll move back here with the boys while you sort it out. You're British. They're British. I'm sure I can get a work visa. We'll figure it out, hon. One way or another, it'll be okay.'

I nodded. I wanted to believe him. I wanted to believe him so much. But being stuck here facing charges for something I hadn't even done was a very real nightmare, no matter how I spun it. We were still standing there, arms around each other, when the doorknob turned and Dan came back into the room, his face more puzzled than when he'd left. Judah and I broke apart and stood looking at him, trying to analyze what his expression meant. He didn't keep us waiting, just shut the door and slid into his seat.

'Okay, I've left this with Dickers. He's looking into it. I must admit, I had a job explaining it all to him.'

'Did they say anything about whether they're interested in pursuing Lo over the passport stuff?' Judah asked. Dan shook his head.

'Nothing definitive, but I get the impression it's certainly not very high on their radar.'

'And Carrie, are they looking for Carrie?' I asked urgently. Dan shook his head, not in negation, more in an *I don't know*.

'All they told me was that they'd look into it as a matter of priority. Are you staying at your mother's tonight?'

I nodded and Dan said, 'Okay, well, listen, the police are certainly going to want you to come in for another interview, but don't talk to them without me being present, okay?'

I nodded again, and Dan stood up with the air of someone bringing things to a close.

'Okay, well, leave this with me, Lo. And Judah, nice to meet you. We're going to do our very best for your wife, okay?'

'Okay,' Judah said. He stuck out his hand and shook Dan's, and we turned and left his office to begin the drive back from south London to St Albans.

THE JOURNEY BACK to my mother's house was longer than either of us had expected – the M25 was even more congested than normal and full of stop-start traffic and bad-tempered lorry drivers that had Judah glaring in his rear-view mirror. It was dark when we finally parked and got out, but when we opened my mum's front door, we found her sitting on the bench in her hallway putting on her coat.

'Mum?' I was taken aback. 'What on earth are you doing?'

'I'm going to go to the shops. We're all out of milk, and I need some bits for supper.'

'Mum—' I felt exasperation rise inside me. 'Mum, this is ridiculous. You're not supposed to be standing on that ankle, let alone walking to the shops in the dark. I'll go.'

'The doctor said to keep mobile,' my mother said stubbornly. 'And I'm going stir-crazy looking at four walls, Laura. The only people I've talked to all day are cold callers.'

'Pam, why don't you let me drive you,' Judah said.

'She shouldn't be walking around a fucking supermarket!' I snapped.

'Lo,' Judah said, giving me a look, at the same time my mother said, 'Laura Blacklock, don't you swear at me!'

'I'm sorry, Mum.' I put my fingers to my temples where a pounding headache was starting to build. 'I didn't – I wasn't swearing *at* you. I'm just – I'm really stressed. And my head is killing me.'

'Look,' Judah said. He put his arm around me. 'Why don't I take Pam to that big green supermarket on the road to Hatfield, the one with the café – what's it called? Michaelsons?'

'Morrisons,' I said wearily. Sometimes it was hard to remember that Judah had lived in the UK for four years, but we'd lived in London – they didn't have many Morrisons when we were there, so perhaps it wasn't surprising he didn't remember the name.

'That's it. Then, Pam, you can sit in the café if your ankle starts to hurt, and I can be your errand boy.'

'That sounds fine, Judah, love,' my mum said, her voice so consciously soothing that I had to grit my teeth. 'I do enjoy a trip to Morrisons.'

'And you—' Judah put one hand on my waist and smoothed my hair off my face with the other, '*you* should go take a bath and some Tylenol. You need to relax.'

'It's called paracetamol here,' I muttered sulkily, but I knew he was right – even though there is almost nothing more annoying than being told you're stressed. 'Okay. Okay, fine. Let me make a cup of tea first.'

'*Go,*' Judah said. 'Go on upstairs. I'll bring you up a cup of tea.'

'I can get in the bath without being told to, Judah, I'm not a kid,' I said, but my throat was tight – partly at how nice he was being, when I knew I was being a complete bitch, and partly because the whole exchange had reminded me so painfully of what I would have been doing around this time back home – chasing Teddy and Eli into baths with a mixture of nagging and bribery, only to have to bribe them out again an hour later after they'd drenched each other and the floor with their Octonauts bath toys. When was I going to get to see them again?

'Anything you want from the shops, love?' my mum asked, and I shook my head and then turned and walked slowly up the stairs to the bathroom.

WHEN I HEARD the front door close behind them, I felt a tension that I hadn't known I was holding leave my body. My mum's house in St Albans wasn't my childhood home – that had been sold when my parents split up, when I was fifteen – but there was still something about being back here that turned me into a petulant teenager even on a normal visit. Now, riven with a mixture of worry for my mum, longing for my kids, and stress about everything that was happening, I was close to losing it completely, and as I sank beneath the water, letting the bubbles cover my head, I felt a wash of gratitude to Judah for recognizing that fact and getting Mum out of my firing line.

I had finished the cup of tea Judah had brought up, scrolled my phone, done the *New York Times* sudoku (easy, medium and hard), and was shampooing my hair when I heard, faintly through the bathroom door and the noise of the extractor fan, the unmistakable sound of the front doorbell, and let out a groan. For a minute I lay there, wondering what to do. Should I get out? I was only halfway through washing my hair, and it would likely take me longer to rinse out the suds than it would take them to give up and go away.

It couldn't be anything *that* important. Judah and my mum both had keys, so it couldn't be them unless they were wanting a hand with the supermarket bags, which was unlikely. The most probable scenario was either a parcel – in which case they would probably dump it on the step – or one of my mum's friends come round with a casserole or something, in which case I would be stuck, dripping and towel-clad, making small talk with someone I barely knew while her husband revved the engine at the curb.

In the end I did nothing, just lay there and waited to see if they rang again, but they didn't, and I let myself sink beneath the foam and close my eyes, swishing my fingers through my hair and feeling the suds escape to the surface of the bath. I was almost, *almost*, relaxed when another sound brought me sitting up, listening intently, this time more puzzled than annoyed. It was the sound of a mobile phone, and it was coming from somewhere inside the house.

The strange thing was, it wasn't *my* mobile. Or Judah's. Or even my mum's. I knew the ringtones for all three well enough – and this was a weird jingle I hadn't heard before that sounded a lot like a default ringtone. I certainly couldn't imagine anyone choosing it deliberately. Had someone left their mobile here? Was that why they'd been knocking at the door?

My hair was soap-free now and I was just about to haul myself up and out of the bath when the phone stopped, and I let out a sigh of relief and sank back into the water. Almost immediately, though, it started up again and this time I stood up, grabbed for a towelling robe, and opened the bathroom door.

Away from the small, steamy bathroom, the upstairs of my mother's house was almost unbearably chilly, and I was shivering by the time I was halfway to the source of the sound – which seemed to be coming from the spare bedroom. *My* bedroom, in fact, the one Judah and I were currently sharing. Had my mother had a guest who'd forgotten their phone? It seemed unlikely, particularly given she'd been in hospital for the past three days, but I couldn't think of any other explanation.

The phone was still ringing as I reached the bedroom, and I stood still, trying not to let my teeth chatter, as I triangulated the direction of the sound. It was coming from the wardrobe, where my clothes were hanging, and when I opened it, I didn't need to search any further. I could *see* it, see the light of the screen shining out of the pocket of a coat. *My* coat. Not the rain mac I'd worn today but the denim jacket I'd packed for nicer weather.

Shivering, I reached into the pocket and pulled it out – a cheap burner phone of a make I didn't know and yet seemed, strangely, to half recognize – though I couldn't place it. I pressed the green Answer button and raised it to my ear.

'H-hello?' I was cold enough that the word came out like a stammer. There was a long silence on the other end.

Then I heard 'Hello?'

The voice was coming from two directions – from the phone pressed to my left ear, and from the doorway to my right.

I looked up. There was a man standing there. He was wearing a mask and holding a mobile phone.

'Hello?' he said again.

And that's when I screamed.

36

I didn't think. I didn't have time to think. I simply ran, bolting past the man like a rabbit into the darkness of the unlit staircase. He tried to grab me as I went, but his fingers, slick in black plastic catering gloves, slipped on my wet flesh, and I wrenched out of his grip with nothing more than a bruise and stumbled down the stairs, gasping with shock.

As I rounded the corner of the landing I had the presence of mind, somehow, to hang up the phone and dial 999.

'Police,' I gasped as I reached the front door. 'Home invasion – please come quickly.'

I could hear the operator talking, but I couldn't make out what she was saying – I had the phone clamped to my ear with my shoulder and was babbling my mother's address while at the same time trying to undo the stiff latch of the front door. At last I got the top lock free – but the door still wouldn't open, and that's when I realized: it was double-locked. I'd forgotten the fact that the front door in my mum's house could be dead-locked from the outside. It couldn't be opened from the inside without a key. And the key was in my handbag in the kitchen.

However the intruder had got in, it wasn't this way. And I certainly couldn't get out.

I was running down the corridor to the kitchen where the back door was when the intruder caught up with me and felled me with a rugby tackle that banged my head on the door frame. I screamed again and heard the operator's voice rising with alarm from the borrowed mobile phone buried beneath me. I couldn't hear what her words were, still less reply. I was too busy trying to protect myself from the man lying on top of me, grappling at me with hands that were frighteningly strong. He had one of my arms twisted up behind me, forced into a position that made me sob with pain, and I could hear his voice in my ear, panting and hoarse:

'Where is the fucking phone?'

'You're breaking my arm!' The words were an incoherent wail of agony; I'm not sure he even understood them, but I felt his other hand thrusting underneath me, groping for the phone. In that moment I would have given it to him – I would have given anything for the pain in my arm to stop – but it had got tangled with the folds of the robe, and in the darkness and the confusion he couldn't find it. He let go of my arm and flipped me over, and I took the chance – more by instinct than calculation – to knee him in the crotch.

He reared back, roaring with pain, and I pulled myself to my feet and ran. I was heading for the back door, which was open – clearly how he had got in. Behind me I could hear the man snarling in pain, pulling himself to his feet, but I was out, I was almost out – and that's when I saw the glass, shards of it, covering the floor, glinting in the moonlight coming through the empty frame. He must have smashed the window and reached through to the lock, perhaps when I was underwater rinsing the suds out of my hair, or maybe the sound just hadn't been audible over the roar of the bathroom fan. Either way, the realization had come too late to save me – my momentum was too great. I staggered to a halt but I had already trodden hard on the glass, and I felt a sharp splinter of it pierce my foot.

The strange thing was, it wasn't actually that painful. Perhaps it was the adrenaline, or maybe the cleanness of the cut, but it didn't exactly hurt; there was just a sense of deep, sickening *wrongness*. But then I made the mistake of looking down at the shard of glass sticking up through my foot and the blood beginning to pool beneath, and I knew I was going to faint.

I also knew I couldn't afford to.

For what felt like a tiny eternity, I simply stood there, steadying myself on the countertop and trying not to let my knees give way beneath me. The man was watching me, and perhaps it was my imagination, but in the darkness I thought I could see the outline of a grim smile beneath the mask.

'Give it up, Laura,' he said, and now that his voice wasn't distorted with the effort of holding me down, I knew it. I knew his voice, and I knew where I'd heard it before. And I knew, suddenly and without a shadow of a doubt, where I had seen this phone before too.

'Pieter?' I said. There was a long, long silence. And then Pieter Leidmann pulled off the mask and stood in front of me, his face pale in the moonlight. His chest was rising and falling, and his expression was still twisted with the aftermath of the pain I'd caused him.

'Yes,' he said at last. 'Though it would have been better for you if you had pretended not to recognize me.'

I felt my stomach twist as I realized the truth of what he'd just said. Stupid Lo. Stupid fucking Lo, always rushing headlong into the need to be proved right.

'And you're here for Carrie's phone.' I held it up, and he nodded.

'You weren't supposed to be here. I was watching the house – I saw you leave. All the lights were off.'

I shut my eyes. Of course. That had been Pieter ringing the bell, making sure the house was empty. Only it wasn't.

'I never wanted to hurt you, Lo.' He said it softly, as if he meant it, but he was moving forward, step after step, his shoes crunching on the glass. 'I just need that phone.'

'What does it have on it?' I took a step back, wincing as the glass pressed against the inside of my foot, glass scraping against bone and flesh and tendon. I felt the blood seep hot beneath the sole of my foot. 'Your messages to Carrie? Recordings of the two of you agreeing on the plot to kill your father? It must be something pretty bad – something concrete enough to convict you – or you wouldn't have taken the risk of coming here yourself.'

'It doesn't matter.' His voice was soothing, almost as if he were trying not to frighten an animal. He held out his hand towards me coaxingly. 'It doesn't matter now. Just give me the phone, and no one has to get hurt.'

But I knew that wasn't true. He had made that clear himself with that unguarded remark when I had said his name. And now I had seen his face. There was no going back – not for either of us. My only hope was to keep him talking long enough for the police to arrive. I let my eyes flick to the corridor behind him, looking for the flash of blue lights in the window of the front door, but there was nothing, and I could hear no friendly wail of sirens either – only the swish of a passing car.

'How did you find it?' I said. My voice was shaking, a mix of cold and, I suspected, shock. *Please don't faint, Lo.* 'The phone, I mean. How did you find it when you realized Carrie had left it behind?'

Pieter shook his head. There was a faint smile on his lips.

'Oh, Laura, if you have enough money, anything is possible. Tracking a phone, it's nothing. For a fee, there are people who will triangulate which cell phone tower it is pinging, which Wi-Fi it has connected to. It wasn't difficult. I had an address within hours. The problem was, your mother was home. She's very talkative, you know.'

My mum's voice came back to me. *The only people I've talked to all day are cold callers.* He must have been outside for hours, waiting for her to leave, ringing the doorbell and pretending to be – what? Some double-glazing salesman? The thought of it – the thought of my dear, frail mum, answering the door to Pieter fucking Leidmann... the thought made my blood boil and gave me the courage to speak.

'Look, Pieter, I know I'm not getting out of here alive. But neither are you. You know that, don't you? I called 999 off that phone. They heard everything.' The phone had gone silent somewhere in the struggle on the floor, but Pieter didn't need to know that. For all he knew, the operator was still on the line, had heard me say his name. I saw his face pale at that and then twist into a kind of ghastly grin, a show of bravado.

'You think that matters? When you have connections like mine... I'll be out of the country in five hours, Laura. I have my private jet waiting.'

'Is that really what you want?' The puddle of blood had spread very far now, and I was having to hold myself upright on the counter because my knees were ready to give way. My hands were cold and looked blue-white in the moonlit shadows of the kitchen, but I was no longer shivering. I was pretty sure that, Pieter Leidmann or not, this was it. If the police didn't come in the next few minutes, Pieter Leidmann wouldn't need to do anything, because I was bleeding out here, on my mother's kitchen floor. But I had to keep him talking. If I was going down, I was taking Pieter Leidmann with me – for my sake, and for Carrie's. And that meant keeping him here for as long as humanly possible. 'That's the life *she* led, Pieter, for ten years. Carrie. On the run, trusting nobody, never able to say who she really was, in the power of anyone who found out her secret. Is that the life you want for yourself? Could you really go from all this—' I waved my arm, my gesture encompassing not my mother's little kitchen and the dark outside but Pieter, his life, his wealth, the enormous luxury of everything his father and grandfather had achieved. 'From all this to a life in hiding? Could you really do that?'

'I have no choice,' Pieter said, and there was a steel in his voice that I hadn't heard before. He took another step forward, the glass under his feet scritching against the kitchen tiles. He was standing in my blood now, his shoes wet with it. 'Give me the phone, Laura.'

'You don't want this,' I whispered.

And then two things happened. From the front door came the sound of a key scratching in the latch. And I heard, faint and far off, the noise of sirens. Pieter Leidmann heard it too, and he swung around – and I saw that he was reaching for something in his jacket pocket.

'Lo, honey?' The door swung open, and I saw Judah there, silhouetted against the light from the street, groping for the switch. 'We're back.'

'Judah, he's got a gun!' I screamed.

And then Pieter Leidmann raised the gun in his right hand and fired.

37

I had never seen a gun fired before. Never heard it either. The noise, in the small space, was astonishing, like someone had smacked me on the head with a club.

And the flash of the muzzle, and the smell of burning – it was like nothing I had ever experienced. I saw Judah stagger backwards, heard my mother's distant shocked scream. I realized that something had hit me – droplets of something sticky and warm.

And then I saw Pieter Leidmann collapse, the gun still clutched in his hand. He fell backwards onto the soft ruined mass at the back of his head, but his face – his face was almost untouched, apart from the dark oozing hole beneath his jaw. He had put the muzzle beneath his chin and fired, blowing his brains through the back of his head.

Slowly, slowly, I let myself sink to the ground. There were soft, gritty spatters across my face and chest, and I realized with a sort of sick detachment that they must be pieces of Pieter Leidmann's brains and skull.

'Lo,' I heard as if from very far away. 'Lo, honey, stay with me. Fuck, stay with me, you hear me?' Then, 'Pam? Pam, where are you? Call 911! Shit, I mean 999. You know what I mean. Get the police, get an ambulance, Lo's hurt.'

I could hear my mother crying a long way off, saying something I couldn't make out.

I could hear the sound of sirens coming closer.

I could hear Judah begging me to stay conscious, stay with him, feel his hand in mine. I could hear him asking me where I was hurt, where all this blood had come from, what had happened.

Then everything slipped away.

THE NEXT FEW hours were a confused jumble of memories – the shouts of the police as they entered my mother's little house, yelling at Judah to stay back, drop his weapon, Judah bellowing that he didn't have one and his wife was hurt. Then the ambulance, the paramedics binding up my foot, stabilizing the huge shard of glass, wheeling me out on a gurney.

Someone must have taken Pieter Leidmann's body, I don't remember that part. But I do remember trying to hold on to the phone as they lifted me, pressing it into Judah's hands in the ambulance, begging him to get it to Dan with words that slurred and stumbled over each other.

'I don't give a shit about a phone, Lo,' Judah said. He was crying – I couldn't remember the last time I had seen him cry. 'You're the only thing that matters.' But somehow, I managed to hold on to my thoughts long enough to make him understand – this wasn't just a phone, this was my freedom, this was what this whole thing had been about. At last he took it and told me I wasn't to worry anymore, and I lay back and let the tears of pain and exhaustion and relief leak out of the sides of my eyes and soak into the synthetic pillow they put under my head in the ambulance.

Next was the disorienting nightmare of Accident and Emergency: children crying, an elderly woman heaving into a bowl, a resigned-looking teen with his arm in a sling. I was wheeled into a side room, where I was checked over, floating in and out of consciousness while a doctor asked me questions I didn't know the answer to, questions I suspected were mostly just trying to keep me conscious and make sure I wasn't slipping away to the beckoning darkness.

After that, they pumped me full of IV fluids and what I had to assume were extremely good drugs, judging by the way the throbbing agony in my foot suddenly became distant and unreal, and then somehow, someone removed the glass. I didn't see it happen, but I remember holding Judah's hand so tight I felt his knuckles crack and gritting my teeth as I endured the strange sensation of glass grinding against flesh and bone.

'She's very lucky,' I heard one of the medics tell Judah. 'It could have severed a tendon, but it's very clean.'

And then, at last, sleep – not at home, but in a ward, floating on a cushion of morphine that wore off slowly through the night, leaving me fractious and snappy at the nurse who came to check my blood pressure. And in between, the strangest dreams – dark, hallucinogenic dreams of the kind I hadn't had since I was pregnant. I don't remember them all – just the strange vividness of the images and the disorientation when I awoke each time, unsure where I was or what was happening. There was one where I was helping Pieter Leidmann put his brain back in his head piece by piece, sifting through the broken glass with bloodstained fingers for chunks of his cerebellum, helping him stuff the pale, soft mush back inside his skull.

And then, later, another Pieter Leidmann was lying at my feet, dead, and somehow in the dream I was the one who had killed him, but I didn't care about that – all I cared about was running after a woman who looked like Carrie but wasn't. I chased her down dark, twisting corridors that moved around us both like a living organism, and when I finally caught her and she turned to face me, I saw that she was myself – that her face had morphed into mine and we were the same person. I had been chasing myself.

In the last dream, it wasn't Pieter Leidmann's brain but Carrie's phone I was trying to put back together – a soft, gel-like phone that was falling apart in my hands, melting as I tried to keep it in one piece. The soft fragments were slipping through my fingers as fast as I could scoop them up, and I found I was crying, begging Judah to help me – but he wasn't listening. He was walking away, towards a woman who looked like me but wasn't. In the dream I called for him until my throat was raw – but he was gone, and the phone in my hands was nothing but a puddle of melted goo.

When I woke from that one I was sweating, and I looked around first for Judah and then, when I remembered that I was in the hospital, for my own phone – but it was nowhere to be seen. All I wanted was to text Judah, make sure he understood the importance of what I had given him before they took me away. Did he get the implications of what must be on that phone? Did he realize that whatever was on it, it was damning enough that Pieter Leidmann had broken into a house with a gun to try to retrieve it?

I lay there stewing silently in my own dread until at last some invisible line was crossed. The sky outside was as dark and leaden as it had been ten minutes ago, but the lights went on, and the ward began to come to life, with orderlies bringing around breakfast and starting ward rounds. Taking this as permission, I levered myself to standing, then hobbled my way across to the nursing station and begged them to contact Judah.

'I have to see my husband. It's life or death.'

'The only thing you *have* to do is keep your weight off that foot,' the nurse said, a little austerely. 'Your husband was sent home last night, but he'll be here as soon as visiting hours start.' She had the air of someone who'd heard it all, and I supposed I couldn't blame her. In her line of work, it literally *was* life and death, so it must be hard to take the assertion seriously from a woman moaning about calling her husband.

'And what time is that?'

'Ten a.m.'

It was only just gone seven. Ten o'clock felt like a lifetime away, but there was nothing to do but wait.

WHEN JUDAH FINALLY did arrive, I surprised myself by bursting into tears. Again. Maybe it was the drugs, but this was becoming a habit, and one I didn't particularly like. At first, he couldn't understand what I was asking him through the sniffles, but eventually I made myself understood — had he taken the phone to Dan?

At that, he nodded.

'Yes, well, I mean, not exactly, but he knows about it and so do Dickers and Wright. I'm handing it over this afternoon. Do you know what's on it?'

I shook my head. 'No, but I know it must be bad for Pieter Leidmann. It was the phone that Carrie was using when they did the murder, so I'd guess maybe photos, maybe recordings of them discussing their plans. She wasn't stupid, Carrie. Isn't, I mean.' Talking about her in the past tense had made my stomach shift, though I was by no means sure the present tense was correct either. If Pieter Leidmann had been prepared to break into the house of an elderly woman to protect himself, I had no illusions about what he would have done to Carrie. 'She'd been collecting information on Marcus for years. I'm sure she would have done the same to Pieter. It was her only means of protecting herself.'

'And it might just have gotten her killed.' Judah's face was sober. I shook my head, but not because he was wrong — more because I couldn't bear for it to be true. Because if it was, *I* had done this. I had handed Carrie over to Pieter Leidmann's charming, handsome henchman and watched as she was driven away, probably to her death. How stupid of me not to have suspected that someone as clever and driven as Pieter would want to know exactly what I was telling the police. I thought again of Inspector Capaldi's words the first time I had met him, words that had stayed with me over the days since. *It is much better to be frank about these things, I find. Honesty is always the best policy.* It made such sense – to plant someone in the investigation to find out exactly what I knew, who I suspected, how far I was prepared to go to protect Carrie.

How afraid Pieter must have been when Carrie bolted from the hotel. Whatever their original exit plan had been – and I still wasn't sure whether Pieter had believed they'd be running off into the sunset together or whether their pact had been more pragmatic – I doubted their agreed endgame would have included a midnight flit where Carrie disappeared without a word just as the police were putting two and two together and preparing to break his alibi. He must have been frantic about where she was going, wondering whether she was planning to turn him in. And how he must have laughed when, just a couple of days later, I proved his worst fears right and solved them in the same phone call. I rang Capaldi up and offered Carrie there, on a plate, sending her right into his clutches.

The only problem? She had left her phone behind – the phone with a record of all their calls and plots and messages. Maybe she even told him, taunted him: *You can kill me, but the evidence is out there, I've left it with someone I trust.*

Little did she know that, to someone with money like his, nothing is untraceable.

'Lo, honey, it's over.' Judah was touching my face, trying to bring me back to the present. He knew me well enough to recognize the signs that I was spiralling into my own black void of anxious despair. He had seen it too often to let it slide. 'Listen to me, it's over. And whatever happened to Carrie – it's not your fault. She lived a dangerous life, and she dragged you into it. But you fuck around long enough, you'll find out, and unfortunately, she did. That's not on you, hon. You did everything you could to save her.'

'I know,' I whispered. I shut my eyes and let the last of the tears I'd shed earlier slide down my cheeks into Judah's shirt. 'I know.' I had done everything I could – just like she had done her best to save me, once upon a time. The difference was that she had succeeded, and I had failed.

38

Stepping awkwardly off the plane at JFK, Judah beside me, my US passport in my hand, I had a strange thought. And that thought was *I'm home.*

Home. In a way, that wasn't surprising. For a long time, years now, home had been where Judah and the boys were, no matter where that was – and as I waited patiently at the e-passport gates, I felt a thrill of excitement that in just a few short minutes I was going to see them, hug them, hold them in my arms. Gail had offered to bring them to JFK to meet us at the gate, and of course I had told her that she didn't have to – picking someone up from JFK was a nightmare at the best of times, let alone with two excitable preschoolers in the car – but like the amazing mother-in-law she was, she had waved a hand and said don't be silly, they would enjoy the adventure, all three of them.

No, that part wasn't surprising. The surprise was that I hadn't entirely been thinking of the boys when the word *home* came to me. I had been thinking of . . . here. America. A place I had only come to because of Judah and where for a long time I'd felt anything *but* at home. Home to me had always been Britain, and I'd told the boys so again and again – making sure they knew the taste of baked beans on toast and Marmite and Monster Munch just as much as they knew

Kraft mac and cheese and Skippy peanut butter and Cheez-Its. And in a way, that was still true. But as I stood there in the queue, listening to the babble of different American accents around me, feeling the indefinable hum of energy that was New York, I knew that home was here too – independent of where my family was. I had been American on paper for a while; the passport I was holding out to the immigration official proved that. But now, for the first time, when the agent looked down at the photo in my passport and up at me and said, 'Welcome home, ma'am,' I felt the words to be true in my heart as well.

I *was* home. And although eventually I would have to report my old, familiar UK passport as lost or stolen and get it reissued, for the moment I couldn't quite face that. For the moment I was content to be . . . simply American.

IT TOOK ALMOST longer than I could bear to get out of immigration, pick up our luggage, and fight our way through the crowds at customs – particularly because I was still on crutches and couldn't move as fast as I wanted – but at last, Judah and I were approaching the big glass doors that separated landside and airside at JFK arrivals, and I could feel my heart thumping in my chest. It was almost two weeks since I had seen the boys – more than twice as long as I had intended to be away, and more than ten times longer than we had ever been separated before. As I limped my way to the barrier that kept back the waiting crowd, I found myself looking downwards, scanning the faces of the kids who could barely peep over the bar, and I felt my heart sink – where were they?

Beside me, Judah had halted, and I could see him looking too, up and down, up and down the dense crowd. For a moment I hated every single one of them. That beaming woman standing there with a bunch of flowers almost bigger than herself, obscuring half the people behind her. That man in a suit with a huge whiteboard saying ALLINGHAM. Why on earth did he need such a big sign? Why was he selfishly crowding right next to the barrier when he was tall enough to see over the heads of the people in front? What if there was some little kid desperate to spot their mum and dad stuck behind, unable to see anything but the back of his suit?

And then I heard it. A high-pitched 'Mummeeee!'

And I turned and saw Teddy and Eli running towards us, weaving through the passengers like tiny quarterbacks. And my heart exploded.

'Teddy!' I gasped, scooping him up as Judah remonstrated with him about my foot and not jumping all over me. Then Eli caught up, and I let Teddy slide down and crouched to the floor so I could hug them both, pressing my face into their hair, inhaling their sweet little-kid scent. I could hear the tuts of the passengers surging around us, knew that I was blocking the way, but I didn't care. It was my turn to be selfish – and I loved every single one of them, even the ones who banged me with their cases as they barged past. I wanted to hug every single passenger in the concourse – even the man with the big sign.

'Oh, I've missed you,' I was saying over and over. 'I missed you both so much.'

'We saw the dinosaurs!' Teddy was shouting.

'We missed you too,' Eli said. He had one hand in mine and one in Judah's and looked like he didn't know whether to beam or cry. I felt something similar myself.

'Hi there, honey. Hi, Judah, sweetie.' I looked up to see Gail standing in front of us, beaming. 'Did you have a good flight? Oh my gosh, your poor foot, Lo. Is it still bad?'

'Honestly, it's fine. And, Gail, thank you so much for everything.' I stood up, Teddy still holding on to my arm. 'I don't know how we can repay you.'

'Psh.' Gail waved a hand. 'It was nothing. A chance to spend time with my grandbabies, what could be nicer? Now, come on, my sweets.' She patted Eli on the head, but I had the feeling she was addressing all four of us. 'Let's go home, and you can tell me all about it.'

IT WAS... GOD, I had no idea what time it was. But late – maybe half past nine by East Coast time and much, much later for my body clock.

The boys were in bed, finally, after much excitement and silliness and tearful demands for extra stories and cuddles. In the end I had lain down on a floor cushion between their beds, Teddy nuzzling my hair from one side, and Eli holding my hand on the other until they both fell asleep, and Judah came tiptoeing in to prod me before I fell asleep myself.

Gail had gone home a few hours ago, waving aside our offers of a bed for the night and telling us she needed to get back to Judah's dad before he started any more home-improvement projects.

And now Judah and I were alone, on our own sofa, in our own home, with a plate of Gail's famous spaghetti and meatballs fresh from the microwave in front of us. And in spite of the fact that I'd been dining off Michelin-starred food prepared by the finest chefs in Europe for the best part of a fortnight, I honestly thought that nothing had ever tasted so amazing.

'Good to be home?' Judah said, and I gave a shaky laugh and nodded.

'God, yes. There's nothing like being threatened with a life sentence in jail to make you value your own bed.'

'Still no news on Carrie or Capaldi? Or whatever his real name was.'

I shook my head. 'Nothing. I checked my email as soon as we landed, but it all seems to have gone completely cold. I don't know if Dickers would say anything, but I feel like he'd tell Dan, don't you? I mean, it's kind of a personal-safety issue for me if Capaldi resurfaces.'

'Do you think . . . ' Judah asked, then stopped and shook his head. He put a meatball in his mouth and said around it, 'Never mind.'

'No, go on. What were you going to ask?'

'Well . . . ' He looked sideways at me as if gauging my reaction. 'Actually, what I was going to ask was . . . do you think she's dead?'

For a minute I didn't say anything, just swirled the spaghetti thoughtfully around my fork. It was a good question and one that had occupied more of my sleepless hours over the past few days than I cared to admit.

I knew why Judah had been reluctant to say it out loud – because if Carrie was dead, it meant that I, almost as much as Capaldi, had killed her. I had been the one to make that phone call, after all. I had stood there as he drove her away – had practically handed her over to him.

But it was also a question that I had not been able to answer – and I still wasn't sure.

Because, try as I might, there were things about what had happened that still didn't make sense to me. The version of events I had given to Dickers and Wright – Carrie running away with my suitcase and passport, me following, Capaldi's 'arrest', and Carrie accidentally leaving her phone behind – all of that apparently made sense to them. But I wasn't sure it was true.

The problem was, the more I thought about it, the more I was certain that Carrie *hadn't* left her phone behind accidentally. She had used the moment when she'd gone back for her clothes to slip her phone quite deliberately into the pocket of my denim jacket, trusting that I wouldn't find it until later – which in the end turned out to be much later.

Which meant . . . well, I wasn't sure what it meant. It could have meant several things. It could have meant that she knew, or suspected, that Filippo Capaldi was not who he said he was. That she was leaving her phone behind with me for insurance, so that if anything happened to her, there would be a trail leading to Pieter Leidmann.

But if she truly suspected that Inspector Capaldi was in league with Pieter, why would she have gone away with him? Why not demand I call 999 and wait for a fleet of undeniable police cars?

No, if that was the case, then there was only one reason she would have gone with Filippo: because she wanted to. Either because she knew his real identity, and was fairly sure she could overpower him or get round him, or – and here was the part I wasn't sure I wanted to say out loud, even to Judah – or because Filippo Capaldi hadn't been sent by Pieter at all. Because he had come to collect Carrie and take her away before the shit hit the fan.

If Filippo and Carrie were in league together, then the mobile phone was not insurance for her at all. It was insurance for *me*. To make sure that I, the person staying behind coping with the fallout, didn't get convicted of murder.

Because the more I thought about it, about Filippo Capaldi's handsome, laughing face, his kind eyes, his seductive accent, the more I found myself comparing him to Pieter Leidmann and wondering if I were Carrie, who would *I* want to spend the rest of my life with? The weak, traitorous son of a man who had more or less blackmailed and trafficked me or the kind, handsome Italian chauffeur I had befriended over the weeks and months and years of my captivity?

And I thought I knew the answer.

Marcus Leidmann had known the truth about Carrie – and that had made her his prisoner. But from what Carrie had said, Pieter Leidmann knew that truth too, and I couldn't imagine Carrie accepting a solution that had her stepping from one cage into another.

But there was another problem too – another piece of evidence I had not been able to reconcile with the rest of the pattern – and that was around not Carrie's actions but Pieter's. Because if Pieter had been the kind of person to delegate his dirty work, he could have hired someone to kill his father, staying far away from the hotel and even the UK. And when he realized that Carrie had slipped through his fingers, he could have hired someone to break into my house and retrieve her mobile phone. He hadn't. He had done those things himself – at great risk to his personal safety, but it was a risk he was prepared to take to avoid the same fate as Carrie, beholden to anyone who knew her secret.

It was an argument that applied almost as much to Carrie herself – though at least she had as much to lose as he did. But Filippo Capaldi . . . what did he have to lose? Why would Pieter, after risking everything to keep the murder between himself and Carrie, jeopardize that by bringing his chauffeur into the plot?

I had thought that Pieter Leidmann was the obvious person to have sent Capaldi because he was the one person who urgently needed to know how much I knew, how far I was prepared to go to protect my friend. But I was wrong. He was not the only person. Carrie would have needed to know that too.

What if *she* had sent her lover to 'interview' me, to figure out my suspicions and gain my trust? And then, as she realized I was preparing to give her up to save my own skin, what if she had repurposed him as a way out?

If I was right, then Carrie had played us all from the start, almost every step of the way – right up until her final bid for freedom. But the reason I didn't want to say the words to Judah wasn't because I feared they might be true. It was because a part of me – a big part of me – hoped they were.

WHEN I FOUND the Instagram message, I was standing in the playground after school, watching the snow fall and waiting for Teddy and Eli to get off the climbing frame. It had landed in my requests folder, which I checked only occasionally, and the sent date read *4w* – four weeks ago.

Getting an unsolicited message in itself wasn't that strange – ever since my piece in the *FT* about the collapse of the Leidmann Group in early December, I had been getting regular requests from business outlets for my insider scoop, and a surprising number of them had come via social media. But the profile picture was a cartoon flower, which didn't exactly scream *high finance*, and I wasn't sure what to expect when I clicked through.

When the message opened, I was not much the wiser. There was just a grey box with text reading *Images sent in message requests are covered. Tap to see blurred image.*

The blurred version of the picture looked suspiciously like a couple on a beach and I had a slight sinking feeling that I was about to be confronted with some unwanted porn, but I was committed now, so I tapped again; the picture shifted into view – and I caught my breath.

It *was* a couple on a beach, hand in hand. She was wearing a bikini and standing on tiptoe in the sand, one foot kicked out behind, kissing the man's cheek. He was wearing Bermuda shorts and grinning into the lens, holding the camera at arm's length, selfie-style. They looked young, tanned, and almost unbearably beautiful. They looked like they were in love.

The couple was Carrie and Filippo.

I stood there for a long time just staring down at the image, wondering what to do. Should I send it to the police? Email Dan? This was evidence. Evidence that Carrie had survived – and, after all, she *was* still wanted by the police.

In the end, I did neither. I just stood there, my finger hovering over the Reply button. Then I typed, *Dear Tigger, glad you bounced x*

Then I shut the phone down, shoved it back in my pocket, and went to take my kids home for supper.

ACKNOWLEDGMENTS

Every book is a process of learning how to write a novel all over again – but you would think after nine standalones that feeling might have faded a little. Instead, writing *The Woman in Suite 11* felt even more baffling than usual, because of course it's the first whodunnit I've written where I was returning to old characters. Coming back to old familiar friends was a joy – but also a challenge I'd never faced before. How to write a book that would appeal to new readers, while living up to its predecessor?

That predecessor, *The Woman in Cabin 10*, was in many ways the book that made me the writer I am today – and my memories of writing and editing it were in the forefront of my mind as I began this follow-up. For that reason it feels right to begin these acknowledgements by saying a huge thank you to the team who helped make Lo and Carrie's original adventures such a success. To my then-publicists, Meagan and Bethan, I am so grateful for everything you did to help get Lo and Carrie out into the world. To Jane and Penny and Monique, who sold it around the world. To all the marketeers and sales people who worked tirelessly to get the book into shops and into the hands of readers. I am so thankful to each and every one of you. Of course to my amazing agent Eve White, who has stuck by me for a decade and a half (and counting). But there wouldn't have been a book at all without two brilliant editors, Alison Callaghan and Alison Hennessey, both of whom shaped and inspired *Cabin 10* in too many ways to count. I owe you both more than I can say, and I'm so grateful you took a chance on me and my weird, fucked-up characters.

Suite 11 however, is a whole new book, and requires a whole new litany of heartfelt thank yous – to the powerhouse teams at Simon & Schuster in the UK, US, Canada and Australia and at my publishers in other languages and abroad. To my editors, Alison, Jen, Suzanne and Katherine – I am so grateful for the care and brilliance you've poured into this book and all the others you've worked on. To Ian, Jessica, Sydney, Sabah, Taylor, Nicole, Mackenzie, Gill, Dom, Nicholas, Hayley, Sarah, Harriett, Matt, Francesca, Richard, Genevieve, Louise, Jennifer, Aimee, Sally, Abby, Anabel, Caroline, Jaime, John Paul, Brigid, Tracey, Rita, Mary, Ludo, Emmanuel, Steven and Lisa – I feel like the luckiest author in the world to have your support. And to Rich and everyone at Gotham – we did it!

As always, friends and consultants saved me from a variety of procedural and factual errors, and provided much needed sanity checks and encouragement – I owe huge thanks to Graham Bartlett, Susi Holliday, Micheal Forrestal, Neil Lancaster, Tony Kent, Helen Fields, Liz Kessler, Nadine Matheson and Colin Scott. Any errors are most definitely my own, and possibly deliberate, or at least I'll pretend they were.

To my dear family and friends, I love you all, and I could definitely have written this book without you but it wouldn't have been nearly as much fun.

But final and biggest thanks must go to my amazing readers. For years I've been asked if I would write a sequel to any of my books, and I always said no – partly because I felt like I'd put my poor characters through such a wringer that the least I could do was leave them alone at the end of it. But the letters and emails and questions I got about Lo

Lo and Carrie kept me thinking and wondering and pondering. And finally that pondering turned into plotting. And that plotting turned into writing. And that writing turned into *The Woman in Suite 11*.

The Woman in Cabin 10 would not have existed without my editors. But *The Woman in Suite 11* would not have existed without my readers. And so, in a very real way, this book is my love letter to every single person who begged for a sequel, who asked me how I thought Lo was doing, or whether Carrie escaped – to everyone who wished there was more. It's for everyone who reviewed, or recommended, or loved one of my books. If that was you, well, I only get to do this crazy, amazing job because of you – and I will never stop being grateful for that. So thank you. For everything. I dedicated this book to you, and I meant it.

Join Ruth Ware's Book Club

© Gemma Day

For event news, exclusive content and a free short story, sign up to Ruth Ware's Book Club at **ruthware.com**